MEDICINE FOR THE BLUES
a trilogy of novels

D0172013

Based on extensive period research, *Medicine for the Blues* explores the complexities of gender and sexuality through the historical lens of the early 1920s.

Book 1 *Acquaintance*

As a young surgeon, Carl Holman has experienced the horrors of World War I and the death of his lover, a fellow officer. Back home after the war, he befriends a young jazz musician who he hopes will become a companion he can share his life with. But this is Oregon: the Ku Klux Klan is gaining influence, homosexual acts are illegal, and such a relationship will jeopardize Carl's promising medical career. Musician Jimmy Harper has his own dreams for the future and his own obstacles to overcome before he will allow himself to accept Carl's love.

Book 2 *Chicago Blues*

Jimmy Harper arrives in Chicago with the Diggs Monroe Jazz Orchestra, seeking fame and fortune. Instead he descends into the jazz underworld where he becomes entangled in dark dealings with a sinister mob boss and in an erotic affair with a black drag performer. In this unfamiliar world, Jimmy begins to question whether he can trust anyone, even his old band members.

Book 3 *Dangerous Medicine*

The story returns to Portland where Carl Holman struggles to navigate his medical career in the face of social and personal obstacles from the KKK, society, and other dangers.

DANGEROUS MEDICINE

Book 3:
MEDICINE FOR THE BLUES
trilogy

by
Jeff Stookey

Jeff Stookey (signature)

PictoGraph Publishing
Portland, Oregon 2018

Medicine for the Blues trilogy
Book 3: *Dangerous Medicine*

PictoGraph Publishing
©2018 by Jeff Stookey

Book and Cover Design
Amy Livingstone, Sacred Art Studio
sacredartstudio.net

ISBN: 978-1-7326036-2-2

Library of Congress Control Number:
2018908705

PERMISSIONS PAGE

Cover Photos:

Two men on a porch, two women on a porch, courtesy of Ken Barker, private collection.

Klan photo:
Unknown photographer, courtesy of Oregon Historical Society, image number OrHi 38897.

Dedication:

"For the young who want to," 1982 by Marge Piercy; from CIRCLES ON THE WATER by Marge Piercy. Used by permission of Alfred A. Knopf, an imprint of the Knopf Doubleday Publishing Group, a division of Penguin Random House LLC. All rights reserved. Any third-party use of this material, outside of this publication, is prohibited. Interested parties must apply directly to Penguin Random House LLC for permission.

Excerpt from Jean-Jacques Rousseau's *Confessions*, translation by Jill Kelly, PhD; courtesy of Jill Kelly, PhD.

Excerpt from THE DUINO ELEGIES AND THE SONNETS TO ORPHEUS by Rainer Maria Rilke, translated by A. Poulin, Jr. © 1975, 1976, 1977 by A. Poulin, Jr. Reprinted by permission of Houghton Mifflin Harcourt Publishing Company. All rights reserved.

DEDICATION

from "For the young who want to,"

Talent is what they say
you have after the novel
is published and favorably
reviewed. Beforehand what
you have is a tedious
delusion, a hobby like knitting.

—Marge Piercy

For Ken:
When you first began learning to knit, you unraveled
the yarn of that sweater over and over, only to start again.
Where would I be without your fine example?
If the sweater fits, wear it.

After his death in 1983, Dr. Carl Holman's memoirs were found in a desk drawer. The estate sale manager donated the document to the local historical society. This quotation was paperclipped to the front of the manuscript:

"I've held nothing back of the bad, added nothing extra of the good, and if it happens that I've used some small embellishment, it's only because of the gap in my memory; I may have supposed something to be true that could well have been so but never something that I knew to be false."

—Jean-Jacques Rousseau, *Confessions*

Facsimile of the title page from Carl Holman's manuscript.

Memories of Jimmy

by Carl Travis Holman, MD

completed 1981

"Oh, let me, true in love, but truly write."
-William Shakespeare, Sonnet 21

We are the violent, we can last longer.
But when, in which of all possible lives,
are we at last open and receivers?

—Rainer Maria Rilke, *Sonnets to Orpheus*
Sonnet #5, Second Series

ONE

October 1923

The autumn rains began in Portland as soon as Jimmy went away to Chicago with the jazz band. The weather mirrored my melancholy mood. Every time I remembered him waving goodbye from the front porch as I drove off to work, I felt an ache deep inside.

But life went on. A few days a week Joe Locke continued to cook and clean for me and deal with my dirty linens at his family's laundry. Soon after Jimmy's departure, Charlene Devereaux telephoned and said in that lilting voice she used as a telephone operator, "Carl, it's Charlie. Come on over for dinner with Gwen and me. She has a pot roast on." Her cheerful invitation was a welcome diversion from my quiet and lonely house. That evening in their comfortable apartment, I enjoyed the company of these old friends with their easygoing conversation.

At work I was surprised to discover that once Jimmy was out of the picture—heartbreaking as that reality was—I felt more at ease around the clinic. The pressure to hide my relationship with him was gone. There was no more fear of being exposed by my neighbor Minnie Mitchell or the Ku Klux Klan, or of being blackmailed by someone who might discover my secret. My bogus "engagement" to Gwen Cook was a known fact, and I felt comfortable that I could call on it to support the illusion of convention for public consumption.

I began to feel that working with Drs. Gowan and Bleeker was not so bad after all, even though I knew they belonged to the Klan and wanted me to become a member. Bleeker took me aside one day and rather than pressure me to join up, told me that he had always agreed with my insistence on keeping careful medical histories. Although Gowan resisted the policy, Bleeker said he had encouraged him to adopt the practice, and Gowan was beginning to see how important it could be. Another day, before any patients arrived, Gowan gathered Bleeker and me with Vivian at her reception desk to announce that our business was doing very well financially according to the bookkeeping firm that handled our accounts, and we were all to receive a substantial bonus. What was more, at his direction, the clinic would be giving a generous donation to a local orphanage and he encouraged each of us to put in a bit for the cause. I later found out that the orphanage was a project of the Klan. Meanwhile, Gowan continued to support the new Lutheran hospital that his friend Jack Iverson was helping to finance. With its promise of modern equipment and amenities this new venture was cause for public admiration that reflected on our clinic. I began to feel that, although I held on to my reservations about him, Gowan was a tolerable sort.

I was employed in an established business with a high-class clientele. I had to admit that for all my disposition toward humility, I was proud to be associated with such a prestigious practice. Gowan was, at the end of the day, a shrewd businessman, and I was grateful to be relieved of the responsibility of running a small medical office all by myself, since I had grave doubts about my own business acumen and management abilities.

What's more, I loved my medical work, and at Gowan's clinic I could concentrate on just that. Each patient presented a new challenge, and I was always learning.

The routine at the clinic continued. I threw myself into my

work, and there was plenty to keep me occupied. And the more I worked, the less time I had to think about missing Jimmy.

When Jimmy had been gone about a week, I got a call from St. Mary's Catholic Hospital. Dr. Osborne wanted help removing a bullet from a man's leg. The patient was a bootlegger who had been shot by a rival outfit while making a delivery to a local speakeasy. Osborne knew I'd served in the medical corps during the War and had experience with gunshot cases.

After I removed the bullet and changed back into my street clothes, I was talking with one of the nuns at the nursing station when a tall man in a suit approached us. He introduced himself as Steve Bateson, a vice officer with the local police. After a run-in with MPs in the service, I'd never felt comfortable around policemen, but now I remembered hearing Bateson's name before—he was said to be a member of the KKK.

"I need to talk to the doc who removed the bullet," he said.

"That would be me," I said.

"Your name?"

"Carl Holman."

He fixed his cold green eyes on me. "Ah, yes. You work with Gowan and Bleeker."

I nodded.

He looked to be sizing me up for a police crime report. I imagined his description: Caucasian male around 30, dark hair, hazel eyes, medium build, slightly above average height.

"I would have thought you'd do the surgery at Lutheran," he said.

So that's where I knew the name from. I'd overheard a conversation between him and Dr. Ferguson at the Lutheran Hospital a month or so earlier when he was investigating another shooting. Bateson had asked Ferguson about me and when Ferguson praised my work, Bateson wanted to know if I was connected with "the Catholic hospital." His tone implied a disdain for Catholics. But when Ferguson mentioned that I worked with Gowan, Bateson sounded like he was on familiar terms with Gowan and Bleeker. I had taken that to mean they all knew each other through the Klan.

"The patient was brought here to St. Mary's straight from the speak, and Dr. Osborne called me in to help," I replied.

Bateson stared at me just long enough to make me uneasy. "I'll need the bullet for evidence."

"Sure, Sister Gertrude can show you to Dr. Osborne's office."

Bateson gave the nun a derisive glance. "I'd rather you did."

I smiled and nodded at Sister Gertrude. "Follow me," I said and led him down the hall in silence. I tried to think of something to say, but being alone with him made me increasingly uneasy. After I left him with Dr. Osborne, it occurred to me that I could have opened a conversation by telling Bateson about the operation.

As I was preparing to leave the hospital, a familiar face greeted me. Tom Harris, my neighbor across the street, was at the nursing station. He smiled at me as he ran his hand through his wiry hair in a futile effort to subdue it.

"Just the man I wanted to see," he said. "The paper told me to get out here pronto." He adjusted his thick horn-rimmed glasses. "I need to find out about this bootlegger who got shot. We want the story for the evening edition."

He took out a small notebook and made notes as I summarized what little I knew, including a description of the bullet involved. "Sister Gertrude can give you more information," I said. "I went right into surgery when I got here. Dr. Osborne didn't even give me the man's name."

After Tom spoke with the nun and made some more notes, I asked if he would walk with me to the parking lot.

"First I need to talk with Osborne," he said.

"I believe he's with Vice Officer Bateson right now."

Tom raised his eyebrows.

I nodded. "Come have a chat with me before I leave. I have to get back to the clinic."

He seemed to understand that I wanted to talk privately, so we went outside to the portico at the front entrance. It was raining hard and the cool air felt refreshing. The stairs down to the sidewalk glistened with rain and across the street the leaves on the trees were showing their fall colors as they swayed in the wind.

"You mentioned Bateson to me a while back, remember? What more can you tell me about him?"

"Well, as I said, he's with the Klan. He seems to have it in for sexual deviants. He's pretty much the one responsible for shutting down Dixon Calder's saloons."

"I wonder if he's on to me." Besides being my neighbor, Tom was an old friend and he knew about my relationship with Jimmy. "When I spoke to Bateson just now, I got a bad feeling. A while back I got the impression that he figured I was okay when he heard I worked with Gowan."

"Could be, since they're both Klan members. Hard to say. But I can tell you this—since you announced your engagement—phony as it is—the neighborhood gossip seems to have died down."

"You were right about all that. Gowan seems pleased with my engagement too." I looked out at the rainy street and thought of Jimmy. "The rumors about Jimmy and me haven't come up, now that he isn't around."

"He's in Chicago now?"

"Well on his way anyhow."

"I've been hearing about the gang wars back there. Sounds brutal."

"Hmm." I glanced at Tom. "That's troubling. Anything else I should know?"

"Since you never read the papers, I should tell you about an incident down in the Willamette Valley. Some Klansmen abducted a couple of Japanese farmers. They roughed them up and put on a mock hanging, just to scare them. Then chased them out of town."

I was reminded of the time last spring when I went to a rural dance that Jimmy and the band played at the Bisby Grange outside of Portland. The Klan had prevented him from singing because they thought the lyrics were indecent. Later on my way home I'd driven past a group of Klansmen in their white hoods harassing a young couple they'd found spooning in a car.

"Since that Alien Land Law was signed in February," Tom went on, "there's been a lot of bad feeling directed against the Mongolian races, especially among the white farmers."

"Good grief. Is my Chinese houseboy in for trouble?"

"Hard to say. You know the Chinese aren't exactly well liked. There seem to be factions within the Klan. Most don't seem to condone violence, but some groups have been thrown off the rolls for vigilante actions."

Just then, Bateson emerged from the building. He spotted us at the end of the portico. I felt a chill, but I smiled and tipped my hat. Bateson paused and stared at us as he took out a cigarette and lit up before proceeding down the stairs to the street.

"He gets around," Tom said.

Since I knew Tom reported on crime, I gathered that they often covered the same incidents.

I showed Tom to Osborne's office before driving back to the clinic.

TWO

The very next day a disturbing case came in. A woman named Betty Haskell brought her young son into the clinic. The Haskells had been seeing Dr. Gowan, but he was away at the time and the boy was referred to me. Henry, age 12, presented with severe pain in his right lower abdomen, which was rigid to palpation. Mrs. Haskell said that the boy had been sick since before the weekend. I diagnosed acute appendicitis and sent him off to St. Mary's, the nearest facility to my office.

When we got the boy on the operating table and opened up his abdomen, a foul odor filled the air. The boy's appendix had burst.

Worse still, Henry had developed peritonitis, an inflammation of the membranous sac lining the abdominal cavity. Such an infection requires time to develop, so I knew that the boy had had this condition for a while before he was brought in. He should have been seen sooner.

In the process of examining him, I saw that he had a significant growth of venereal warts around his anus. This raised suspicions. Of course the boy could have been experimenting sexually with school-age friends, but this kind of growth was not common in youngsters. The warts and the delay in bringing the boy in for medical attention gave me a bad feeling that something was going on here, something far less innocent than schoolboys fooling around.

I showered and changed and headed toward the surgery waiting

room. Checking my pocket watch, I saw that it was after 6. We'd
been in surgery for over two hours.

Gwen Cook, "my fiancée," was working the surgery desk. After
the ordeal of the surgery she was a welcome presence in her crisp
white nursing uniform. She noted my somber mood.

"Things haven't gone well?"

I shook my head.

She told me the boy's mother was still waiting. "She told me
how worried she is. I tried to reassure her. The boy is her only
child."

"Poor woman," I said as she handed me a sheaf of hospital
paperwork.

"Her husband has just joined her. His name is Lloyd."

I thanked her. The name sounded familiar. Lloyd Haskell. As
I glanced through the papers, I remembered where I'd heard it.
Dr. Gowan had been seeing the family, and he had mentioned a
pharmacist named Haskell. Tom Harris had also mentioned the
name in connection with the Klan. And that was the name of the
druggist Jimmy's friend in the band had bought liquor from.

I recognized the mother sitting down the hall in the nearly
empty waiting area and assumed that the man pacing beside her
was her husband. He was on the short side, a trim wiry man with
smooth, clear skin and regular features.

I cannot explain how, but as soon as I laid eyes on him, I
knew in my gut that Lloyd Haskell was attracted to men. The
impression did not arise from anything in his manner or behavior.
There was nothing unmanly about him. But walking toward him,
I was convinced beyond a doubt that my intuition was true—even
before he looked around and saw me.

For some reason I took particular notice of the man's shoes.
They were brand new, brown-and-white Oxfords with that fancy
stitchery around the edges. Spectators, I'd heard them called. I
remember wondering what kind of a man would wear shoes like
that. Such footwear might have been fashionable in Palm Beach,
Florida, but Portland, Oregon, was not a fashion haven. Only a

man who held a particular impression of himself would adopt such a detail of dress here.

Betty Haskell had been sitting quietly while her husband paced. She rose to her feet as I greeted her. Her eyes were red and her face was puffy.

Mr. Haskell took charge. "You sit down," he said to his wife. "I'll handle this." He turned to me. "How is he?"

"We won't know for some time. We're doing all that we can at the moment. I'm Dr. Holman." I extended my hand, "You must be Mr. Haskell."

He ignored the gesture.

Although I was caught off balance by such a breach of decorum, I gave him the benefit of the doubt. These were, after all, unfortunate circumstances.

Betty Haskell looked up at me, her brow furrowed. I smiled hoping to calm her distress.

"Dr. Holman, I need to have a word with you privately," Haskell said. He walked off down the hall. I followed, anticipating the worst, so I decided to take the initiative.

"Tell me, Mr. Haskell, when did the boy's symptoms first appear?"

Our footsteps echoed in the hallway.

"Well, let me recall." Haskell thought a moment.

I was relieved to have sidetracked his original train of thought, which I suspected was building up to an angry outburst.

"It seems to me, he first started complaining about a pain in his stomach late Sunday evening. He said the pain was here, on the right side."

"And how was the boy's appetite before he complained of the pain?"

"Oh, his appetite was just fine. He ate like a horse. He's always had a good appetite."

I nodded. "I understand that you are a pharmacist. Did you give the boy anything for his condition?"

"He was in such pain, and I figured it was just stomach cramps, so I gave him some laudanum."

Haskell had confirmed my suspicions. Not only had his story contradicted his wife's version of the boy's symptoms, but his description was not consistent with the normal course of appendicitis. According to common wisdom and my own experience, appetite was suppressed in the early stages, and the abdominal pain was felt first in the center of the belly. Plus it was rare for the appendix to burst in the first 48 hours. I suspected that Henry Haskell had been ill for at least four days. The laudanum might have suppressed the boy's peristalsis, besides relieving the pain. But I sensed that Haskell had something he was trying to hide, something that had caused him to delay allowing the boy to be brought in for medical examination. All this, combined with the physical evidence of the boy's anal warts, made it impossible to ignore my suspicions that Haskell was sexually assaulting his son. But there was no way that I could confront him on the issue. All I could do was give him an honest opinion of the boy's chances of survival.

"I'm afraid that things do not look good for your son, Mr. Haskell. The appendix had burst by the time we got him to the operating room, and peritonitis had already set in." I studied his expression to see if he understood. "I'm afraid we've done all we can do. Now we must wait to see if Henry will recover on his own."

He became agitated and his eyes began shifting around. His short, compact frame tensed. Anger distorted his face. His temper, wound tight as a clock spring, seemed pushed to the breaking point. "What kind of a doctor are you?" His voice echoed down the empty hallway. "If Dr. Gowan was here, this wouldn't have happened."

At Haskell's outburst, the few people in the waiting area turned toward us. Betty Haskell's face darkened with fear. I placed my hand on the back of his shoulder to direct him down the hall, so we could have more privacy. At the touch of my hand, he jerked away. In that instant, I sensed an animosity toward me that went well beyond the moment. I wondered what he might know about me.

Had Dr. Gowan said something? Or had Haskell unconsciously recognized my homosexuality, by instinct, as I had about him? Perhaps a similar intuition had stirred up an irrational anger that even he could not explain.

"Very well, Mr. Haskell. I'll contact Dr. Gowan as soon as I can. He should be back in the morning." I realized there was nothing more I could say, and I walked off down the hall. As I turned the corner and passed through a swinging door to the operating suite, I heard footsteps behind me and realized that he was following. When I turned, Haskell was on me. He swung me around by the arm. Grabbing the front of my white coat, he backed me into the wall. His body was full against mine as he held me pinned. I felt an unsettling sexual tension in the encounter. In different circumstances I would have sworn that he was about to kiss me.

Instead, he raised his index finger, jabbing it against my chest. "I want Bleeker to take over until Gowan gets back. And I want that boy moved to Dr. Adrian's hospital immediately."

"Mr. Haskell," I said, struggling to remain calm. "The boy is in no shape to be moved anywhere."

Haskell's face reddened with fury, but his voice became a concentrated whisper. "You call Bleeker this minute, or I'll call him myself. So help me God, there's gonna be hell to pay." He hesitated for a moment, and again I had the disturbing feeling he was about to kiss me. Then without warning he spit in my face.

The erotic aspect of the encounter was unmistakable. Carnal energy seemed to lie behind his hostility and anger. Maybe this violence was the only way his sexual feelings were able to express themselves.

He snorted and with a little shove Lloyd Haskell relaxed his grip.

There was nothing I could say to him. His anger was beyond all reason.

"I'll telephone Dr. Bleeker directly," I said and walked down the hall taking out my handkerchief to wipe my face.

I will never know for sure about Lloyd Haskell. He did not know his own heart or I'm sure he would never have gotten into the trouble that he made for himself. Much later I learned the nature of his relationship with his wife, but observing them together that day, I saw it wasn't a warm and loving one.

Perhaps Haskell was attracted to both men and women and the unacceptable attraction to men called into doubt the whole of his masculinity, confusing and destabilizing his attraction to women. I sometimes wonder if those in the middle of the continuum between homosexuality and heterosexuality do not fight the fiercest battles with their desires when they cannot accept them. Or perhaps he was attracted solely to men and was not able to deal with that reality. The exclusively homosexual male, who cannot accept his desires, must repress them. That leaves him with no choice but to live out a pretense with women or remain celibate. Or maybe, for Haskell, his sex drive was some twisted and obscure will to power that manifested itself in taking advantage of the weak and innocent.

There is no telling.

Whatever the case, I believe that with men like Lloyd Haskell some sexual variation of Boyle's Law comes into play and the pressurized gas of erotic desire seeks an outlet. As internalized societal repression constricts the volume of the chamber holding the gases in containment, the fires of lust cause the gases to expand. When the pressure increases beyond the breaking point, the desire inevitably explodes, rupturing its container and bursting out in a violent display that knows no control and must discharge in any direction that presents itself.

When I reached Dr. Bleeker, I summarized the medical case. "The boy's father, Loyd Haskell, is in a rage—acting completely unreasonable under the circumstances," I said. "What's more, I suspect from the looks of things that his boy has been sick for several days. If he had been brought in sooner, we could have saved him."

There was no way I could raise the subject of the venereal warts and their implications. The issue of homosexuality combined with incest was too sensitive. On top of that, I didn't want to give any hint that I had personal knowledge of acts considered criminal. My reputation had already been called into question. Bleeker would be doing his own examination anyway.

"Yes," Bleeker said, "Haskell's a hothead. I've seen him show his stuff at some of the meetings. I'll be right over. You can go on home. Bob's due back tomorrow morning. I'll keep him apprised."

As I hung up the phone, I felt sick. "The meetings" Bleeker referred to had to be Klan meetings. Although he could have referred to some medical association meeting or a fraternal organization, something in his tone made me certain that Bleeker meant the Klan.

No doubt Lloyd Haskell was offended that I had brought his son to a Catholic hospital. He had made it clear that Adrian's private hospital was his first choice, but I already had my own misgivings about Adrian's establishment.

The possibility of Haskell's connection to the Klan brought some clarity to the situation for me. Perhaps Minnie Mitchell's rumors about Jimmy and me had reached Haskell through his Klan affiliation. Still I had an unsettling feeling that something more was involved.

After a poor night's sleep, I returned to the clinic and tried to attend to my patients and the work at hand. But my mind kept wandering back to the gravely ill Haskell boy. His father's outburst and my suspicion that the boy might be a victim of his abuse added to my uneasiness that the father belonged to the Klan.

Before I left work, I telephoned the hospital to see how Henry Haskell was doing. When I got hold of Bleeker, he sounded discouraged. The boy was deteriorating. I told him to contact me at home if there was any way I could help.

The next morning at the clinic, I received a call from Gwen that the Haskell boy had died in the night. I had lost plenty of patients before—hundreds of young soldiers during the war and, later, stillbirths, pregnancy complications, and elderly patients—but never a 12-year-old boy. Boys are supposed to break their arms falling out of trees, or get unexplained stomach aches from surreptitiously eating stolen green apples or smoking cigars behind the garage. Twelve-year-old boys were supposed to grow up and die much later—as grandfathers or maybe as soldiers. I was shaken by the sudden loss of all that unfulfilled potential.

I tried to comfort myself with the knowledge that I had done all that a doctor could do. Although the lay public puts its faith in the medical profession, I knew how puny and primitive our efforts were. Death is a fact of life.

Mixed in with my personal feelings and professional misgivings, I had to wonder about the possibility of retaliation from Lloyd Haskell. Bleeker had described him as a hothead. The Klan presented an even larger problem.

I didn't regret declining Gowan's earlier invitation to join the Klan. However, the social and political power of that growing organization now took on a disturbing reality for me. Until this Haskell case, the Klan had been a vague and peripheral nuisance. Now I began to feel that it could become a very real and a very personal threat.

Late in the afternoon, the day Henry Haskell died, Bob Gowan told me he wanted to see me in his office. I expected a lecture from him, so I was prepared for the worst. Once the door was closed and he had settled his bulk behind his desk, he said he was sorry to hear about the Haskell case.

"It's a sad day when you lose a youngster in your care," he continued. "As a father, I know better than anyone." He adjusted his gold-framed spectacles and looked at me sympathetically. "I know you did all that you could."

"I appreciate your understanding."

"And don't worry about Haskell. I believe we can deal with him." He ran a hand over his bald head. "Just try to stay out of the way, and I'll handle it."

I thanked him.

"Something else I've been wanting to say. Don't you think you've been working too hard lately? Why don't you slow down a little? Schedule more time between your appointments and your surgeries. You'll work yourself into an early grave. Spend more time with your fiancée."

I had the feeling he was probing me. Although I resented his advice, he was right. "I'll take that into consideration."

"I just returned from something of a vacation myself. Besides that medical conference in San Francisco, I took my oldest boy down to see the Stanford campus. He's hoping to enroll there in the fall." He watched me for a moment. "You'll want your kids to attend college someday."

I laughed off his comment. "That's a long ways off, I think."

"Miss Cook must be deeply devoted to her nursing career."

That seemed an odd phrase to hear from Gowan. I sensed something was behind his remark.

I laughed again. "Yes, she's quite a girl."

After a pause, he said that was all he wanted to say. I was a little surprised that he didn't press me again to join the Klan. I went to the door, but just before my hand touched the doorknob, he said, "Say, Carl, is that boarder still living with you?"

I turned, puzzled that he should bring up the subject at that moment. "No. He's gone to Chicago."

"I see." He paused. "That must have helped you keep up with the mortgage."

His remarks were not accidental. I believed that he was trying to catch me off guard and sound me out about my relationship with Jimmy. I didn't know how to respond so I simply looked at him.

"Say, have you set a date for your wedding yet?"

"Miss Cook and I are both quite busy professionally right now so we're putting off announcing a specific date. We're not in any hurry."

"Of course," Gowan replied. "Well, Carl, I think matrimony will do you good. You need to have some kids. Why, look at these four healthy young lads." He indicated the family photograph on his desk. "Best thing that ever happened to me."

I smiled and nodded. There was so much he was not saying.

"Maybe after the wedding is over, you'll reconsider my invitation to join the Invisible Empire."

So he had finally gotten around to the Klan. I assured him I was keeping that in mind and made an excuse to get back to my work.

My sense of unease grew as I turned our conversation over in my mind throughout the day, but I resolved that I wouldn't let it bother me. I had to carry on the best I could.

THREE

Gwen called me that evening.

"You must be devastated by the death of that Haskell boy. I'm so sorry."

"There was little we could do."

"Still, it's a tragedy. Look, will you come join Charlie and me for dinner tomorrow night?"

I told her I would be delighted.

"And she said to ask you to bring the Halma game."

The Halma game. I hadn't taken out that beautiful inlaid wooden game board with its pawn-like playing pieces since Jimmy left. The game was part of our courtship and it had become a ritual in my relationship with him. We had spent many hours competing to be first to get all our playing pieces home across the board— from here to there. I made a wish that Jimmy would someday make it home from there to here.

Later we had taught Gwen and Charlie how to play and it had become part of our friendship with them. I was so touched by Charlie's request that I didn't know whether to smile or cry.

The rains didn't let up. I had to use my umbrella just to walk the short distance from my Ford to the front door of the building where Gwen and Charlie had their second-floor apartment.

Charlie greeted me as I stood in the hallway shaking the rain off my umbrella. Her short blond hair framed her lovely face, which could have easily graced the cover of a magazine.

"Oh, you did bring the Halma game. What fun!" She kissed my cheek. "Let me take your things."

Charlie looked smashing in a pale green frock. Her sylphlike figure was suited for the fashions of the day. She moved with characteristic grace as she hung up my coat and stowed the wet umbrella.

"Come into the kitchen. My sweet Gwen has made our favorite soup."

As I entered, the aroma of split peas and ham filled the air. Gwen had her back to me searching through a tall cupboard. The highlights in her auburn hair, done up as usual on top of her head, caught the kitchen light as she hunted through the spice jars. When she heard me, she turned and a welcoming smile lit up her broad face. She gave me a warm, full-figured hug.   "Hello," she said as she held me at arms' length and examined my face. "It's so sad about the Haskell boy."

"There's no changing the outcome." I appreciated her sympathy. Concerns still haunted me about why Henry's treatment was delayed and my suspicions about Haskell's sexual behavior. But it was not something I wanted to discuss, even with Gwen.

"Of course," she said. "You can't heal everyone."

"Well, let's not dwell on it. It's a treat to see you both."

"Have a seat while I finish putting these rolls in the oven," Gwen said.

I sat down at the table. "Besides, I've had other cases that have been quite successful. I recently diagnosed a patient with a benign tumor of the large bowel next to the liver and I was able to resect it. Those kinds of cases are very satisfying."

"I know you love your work," Gwen said. "But I do worry that you work too hard."

"Dr. Gowan told me the same thing today."

"I'm surprised he even notices," Gwen said.

"He told me I should spend more time with my fiancée."

"He didn't!" she said.

"That rascal." Charlie laughed. "He's intent on having you steal my darling."

"I finally met him and Dr. Bleeker at St. Mary's," Gwen said, "the day before Henry Haskell died."

"That's a surprise," I said thinking back on my latest conversation with Gowan. "So that's what he was getting at. He's been pressuring me about a wedding date."

"That pushy old scamp," Gwen said, "It's none of his business. Still and all, I think announcing our engagement was the right thing—pretend as it may be."

"It sure seems to have quashed those rumors about Jimmy and me. At least that's what Tom Harris said."

"I suspect having Jimmy off in Chicago helps, too," Charlie said.

"We dodged a bullet there," Gwen said, "hushing up that Mitchell woman. My mother hasn't brought up those rumors since she first told me what she'd heard at her meetings. I guess those Ladies of the Invisible Empire have moved on to other concerns. But it is surprising that rumors would spread all the way to Astoria. Mother said that now our engagement is on everybody's tongue."

"Boy," I said, "that Invisible Empire is quite a network." Having tired of talking about us, I changed the subject. "Any more news about the Compulsory Education Act? Are they actually going to shut down all the Catholic schools and make everyone attend public ones?"

"Sister Gertrude tells me that the law doesn't take effect for a few years, so the Society of Sisters is going to challenge it in court as soon as they can. There's been a call for contributions from Catholics in other states to fight it. I hear they've collected a substantial war chest."

"I went to Catholic girls' schools, and it didn't do me any harm," Charlie said.

"I agree," I said, "it doesn't make any sense. I just hope the Klan hasn't infiltrated the court system the way they have other parts of the government. We know the governor has supported them—he even signed this ridiculous school law. Gowan says that there are pillars of the community that belong to the Klan—even members in the police force."

"Are you sure you aren't being a little overly suspicious?" Gwen asked.

"Tom Harris confirmed that a lot of policemen are members. I admit I've always been a little nervous around cops. I had some bad experiences with the military police during the War. And ever since that Human Sterilization Bill was signed into law here, I've got to say I feel a bit uneasy. If I were caught in a compromising position and convicted, I could find myself facing an unpleasant operation."

"I remember that eugenics lecture we went to last spring," Gwen said. "I was praying that legislation wouldn't pass. But it did."

"And I'm one of the quote moral degenerates they targeted. Now I've got to worry about police Klansmen. At St. Mary's a few days ago I had a run-in with a Vice Officer Bateson. The man gives me the willies. Tom believes he's in the Klan. He says the fellow has it in for sexual deviants."

"That sounds like a recipe for trouble," Gwen said. "Has Gowan leaned on you any more about joining the Klan?"

"Indirectly. But I worry there will come a time when things come to a head with him."

"You know, Carl, you could always hang out your own shingle," Gwen said.

"I suppose. The thought has crossed my mind." I didn't dare mention going to Chicago to practice so I could be near Jimmy—another thought that had crossed my mind. "But Gowan's clinic offers me so many advantages. They take care of all the billing so I can focus on treatment, which is what I love most. I'm afraid I wouldn't make a very good businessman."

"Nonsense," Charlie said. "You're an intelligent person. You'd figure it out. Besides you can always hire people to help with bookkeeping."

"But there's another thing," I said. "I've gotten the impression that as long as I work with Gowan and Bleeker, I'm somewhat insulated from the Klan—since they both belong."

"How long can that arrangement last?" Charlie asked.

That silenced us all. Gwen moved to the stove and stirred the soup.

"I've been wanting to ask you," Charlie said, "if you can help a friend of mine from the phone exchange. She wants to find out about Margaret Sanger's birth control methods."

"I could counsel her, I suppose. Is she married?

"Engaged."

"Hmm. Sort of the reverse of eugenics," I joked. "If we can keep it very quiet, I'll talk with her."

"I'm sure she'll be grateful."

A timer rang and Gwen took the rolls out of the oven. "I think we can sit down to dinner now."

After dinner Gwen and I talked while Charlie stacked the dishes and took them to the kitchen.

"Any word from Jimmy?" Gwen asked.

"Nothing yet, speaking of the past," I said.

"No, speaking of the future," Gwen said. "I'm sure we'll see him again."

"Oh, God, how I hope so." I sighed.

"You worry too much. I know he loves you."

"But there are so many hazards. That jazz band is terrific. There is every reason they will be successful. And who knows what kinds of temptations he might encounter in Chicago. I'm just a provincial doctor. What glamour is there in that?"

"Carl! Now you're going too far."

"And you know that young woman that used to be his girlfriend here—Mary Hall—she's gone back to live with her parents in Chicago. I even encouraged him to contact her—so they could say a proper goodbye and settle the hard feelings from when they broke up. So he wouldn't feel bad about it all. What if they rekindle their relationship?"

"Listen," she said. "I remember how lost you were when you got home from Germany."

I had to glance away. Gerald. That morgue in Berlin. The fathomless sense of loss.

"You couldn't see anything but the negatives back then."

I couldn't look at her.

"Jimmy isn't dead like Gerald. Be hopeful. I truly believe he'll come back. Have faith."

"Faith. That's always been easy for you."

"Then believe in love."

I had to give her credit for that. That was something we both believed in.

After Charlie finished rinsing and stacking the dishes, we sat down to a game of Halma. As we set up the playing pieces on the ornate wooden game board, I remembered the day I bought it. The beginning of my relationship with Jimmy. So many memories.

"I sure wish Jimmy could be here to play with us tonight," I said. From there to here, I thought again.

"We both miss him, too," Charlie said. "That's why I asked you to bring the game."

FOUR

It was sometime during the next week that a young man came into my office claiming to be an old friend of Jimmy's. He was a slight fellow with dark hair slicked back, just the way Jimmy wore his, though Jimmy's hair was light brown. His name was Vance and he claimed he sometimes played piano at Bagwell's speakeasy downtown. I'd taken Gwen and Charlie to hear Jimmy's band when they played at that speak last summer. Vance kept running his hand through his hair and bouncing one leg up and down, but he had a friendly manner, and I was glad to have some connection to Jimmy, however remote. He told me his aunt was suffering something awful from kidney stones and he was hoping I could give him something to ease her pain—until the stones passed. I became suspicious. I knew this was a common ploy of addicts to get morphine, but I'd never been solicited like this. I asked why he hadn't brought his aunt in to see me.

"She's in so much pain—it's something awful to hear her screams—I couldn't think of moving her." His eyes darted around the room and he squirmed in his chair. "I thought that…that since you were a friend of Jimmy's you'd help me out."

"Help *you* out," I said.

His mouth twitched. He looked away as his knee bobbed up and down. "Doc, you've gotta help her. She's an old woman. She doesn't deserve to suffer so."

"Roll up your sleeves."

"Why? I'm here for my aunt, not me." His face flushed.

"I can't give you prescription drugs without an exam."

He rolled his eyes. "I told you, I can't bring my aunt in." His voice was becoming agitated and he leaned toward me, his face contorted with exasperation. "She's in hellish pain."

"Let me see your arms. I'll keep this confidential."

He glared at me for a second before standing up. "If you aren't going to help me, I'll find someone else who will." He headed for the door.

"Now wait. You need help. I can refer you to a clinic…"

But he was already out the door. I followed him to the reception area and watched him leave. I'd seen some soldiers addicted to morphine during the war. It was not a pretty sight. I didn't want to contribute to the same problem here at home. As I turned to go back to work, I caught Vivian at the reception desk looking at me with a puzzled expression. I shrugged and returned to my office.

FIVE

Ever since the Henry Haskell case, I felt that Gowan was treating me with kid gloves. A week or so after the boy's death, he told me there was a medical meeting on Thursday night that he wanted me to attend. He insisted that I keep my calendar open. I said I would and asked him what sort of meeting it was. He was rather coy at first, suggesting that it would be social, including dinner, but there would be medical professionals discussing "problems of the day." This struck me as odd, but he added that my experience with the American College of Surgeons would benefit the gathering. This, too, was unusual because I was well aware that my association with the College had not endeared me to Gowan. But if I could use the occasion to help spread the philosophy of using evidence-based medicine and clinical notes, I was interested. I told Gowan as much and he said, "This will be a contingent of the best up-and-coming young medical men in the city. I think you'll find it most stimulating."

After work on Thursday, Gowan and Bleeker insisted I ride with them. Along the way we picked up a young dentist that Bleeker knew, a tidy-looking blond fellow with a glum face. The assembly was to gather not far from downtown at a small church meeting hall. Located in a nice neighborhood, the building appeared brand-new. As we entered, the murmur of many conversations filled the well-appointed room, which was set up for a fancy banquet. The crowd appeared to be well dressed professional men, maybe 50 in all. They milled about, talking, and Gowan and Bleeker seemed to know many of them. I had been apprehensive that we might run into Dr. Adrian, but I didn't see him. I was introduced to a couple of young physicians, a chiropractor, and a gynecologist.

After some small talk, Gowan waved and beckoned to someone through the crowd. I recognized that wiry frame. Lloyd Haskell came toward us. I had not seen him since our difficult encounter at St. Mary's and my guard was up. He was looking very smart in a colored shirt and the spectator shoes that had caught my attention at the hospital. Not the attire I expected for a mourning father. He seemed to freeze when he recognized me. But Dr Gowan was his jovial self, welcoming Haskell over. As he began to introduce me, Haskell interrupted and said, "We've met." His voice was cold.

Gowan continued, but with a more serious tone. "Of course. And under the most unfortunate circumstances. As a father myself, I share your heartbreak."

Bleeker spoke up, as if this had been prearranged. "Mr. Haskell, we all want to express our profound condolences at this tragic passing."

Gowan went on. "A surgeon's role is a vital one, but our heavenly father makes the final call, isn't that right, Dr. Holman?"

This sounded like a setup, but one that I felt all right joining in with. It had been just two weeks since his son's death, and regardless of my discomfort with Haskell's behavior and my suspicions about him, I felt sincerely grieved by his misfortune. I regretted that there wasn't more I could have done to save his son's life.

"There are no words," I said "to express my sympathy for your loss." I extended my hand. "I can only imagine a father's grief."

He hesitated and eyed me warily before he turned to Gowan. I kept my hand out.

"All of us in the medical profession understand the gravity of our responsibilities," Gowan said, staring at Haskell as if to drive home a message.

Something in Haskell seemed to give in. He stiffened and gave me a look that seethed with anger, but he finally shook my hand in a concession to social formalities. His grip was feeble, as if he was loath to touch me. I tried to make my expression convey as much sympathy as possible. He looked away and told Gowan he had to find his colleagues.

The sound of silverware tinkling on a water glass got our attention and a tall thin man at the head of the hall invited us to find our places so the program could get underway. "We've seated you with your associates, so please look for your name on the place cards."

Half a dozen tables were spaced out across the room and there was a hubbub as the men searched out their names and, with the scraping of chairs, got settled.

I was seated between Bleeker and the young dentist who had come with us. Gowan sat across the table. The tall man at the front of the room called the meeting to order. The proceedings began with a brief welcome, followed by the pledge of allegiance to the flag, and singing of "The Star-Spangled Banner." This was all routine, but the patriotic fervor in the room made me uncomfortable.

As the banquet meal was served by a bevy of women from the kitchen, a male quartet sang a few popular songs. The smell of roast beef and over-cooked vegetables filled the air.

After a while, the keynote speaker was introduced and after robust applause, the ruddy-faced fellow began.

"I want to invite you tonight, to step out of yourselves—and broaden your vision to take in all our great civilization and society. There have been many triumphs in our history—our magnificent Constitution, our proud founding fathers, advances in science and industry. And there have been many grave trials—our bloody Civil War, the War in Europe that claimed so many young men's lives."

I agreed with him on the last point. While he was a bit patriotic for my taste, I was willing to hear him out.

"But today there is a serious crisis. We are faced with a variety of medical problems—tuberculosis, Spanish flu, diphtheria, venereal disease, malnutrition. And much of this is the upshot of moral decay in our society. Unclean living conditions, poverty, ignorance, laziness, drunkenness, and vice—all these foster the illnesses that our practice is forced to deal with."

This was beginning to sound a bit like a tent revival.

"So we have gathered together many of the bright young medical men of this community to discuss these problems and talk among ourselves to come up with solutions."

Well, I thought, maybe in view of my experience with the College of Surgeons, I could make a contribution.

"At each table we have assigned a senior member of the medical community to lead a discussion. As you talk among yourselves, please search your hearts and your brains to generate ideas. We need your ingenuity and innovative thoughts to make this a better city and a better world."

A buzz of conversation arose as attention shifted from the speaker to those seated around the tables. Gowan stood up and introduced himself as a member of the Gowan Clinic. "Let's start by going around the table and introducing ourselves. Take a moment to tell us one or two issues that are of concern to you."

I was hoping to fade into the background, but now I was going to be forced to speak for myself somehow. Well, I would try to come up with something vague and neutral.

Starting at Gowan's right, a stocky young fellow with dark curly hair introduced himself as Dr. Rosenfeld, a gynecologist just starting a practice in Portland. He expressed concerns about improving medical education along the lines suggested by the Flexner Report. I could go along with that.

The next fellow was a large man with such a sallow complexion that I wondered if he might have cirrhosis of the liver. He was worried about "race suicide" and wanted to protect "our" women and motherhood. "We've got to put an end to this birth control business. There aren't enough native-born Protestant women having babies these days. Those damn Catholics breed like rabbits and they'll soon outnumber us." There was a scattered murmur of assent around the table.

Bleeker had taken out a small notebook and was jotting things down after each speaker.

Moving on, others voiced concerns about ensuring adequate garbage disposal, pro bono work for the indigent, and more asylums for the mentally deficient. A small, thin man with a sour expression argued for cleaning up vice. I listened but only with half my attention.

I caught a familiar voice at the table behind ours talking about the scourge of bootlegging. It was Lloyd Haskell. "From a medical perspective, alcohol is one of our most destructive afflictions." After hearing Jimmy's friend talk about buying liquor from Haskell's pharmacy, I was struck by the blatant hypocrisy—or was he railing against bootleggers because they competed with his sales?

At our table Bleeker was recommending a requirement to pasteurize the milk supply. He was reasonable, as usual.

My turn came next and I mentioned my support for keeping accurate records of patient histories and following the latest scientific techniques.

The glum dentist beside me spoke out against the Catholic hospitals who he said were denying patients treatment unless they converted. His voice grew louder as he became quite steamed up. "Why, imagine lying in bed wracked with pain and you've got to swear allegiance to the Pope before they will help you." A number of voices around the table agreed vigorously.

I knew this to be the sort of propaganda the Klan was putting out and to hear so much approval in this group made me suspect considerable Klan sympathy. Having spent so much time at St. Mary's, I could attest to the inaccuracy of such claptrap. Some of the nuns might appear stern, however I knew their hearts were in the right place, and this kind of malicious falsehood raised my indignation. I wanted to protest, but this fellow had come to the meeting with us, plainly a friend of Gowan's, and in this atmosphere of Klan partiality I knew any dissent would not be tolerated. I held my tongue.

Again Gowan stood, saying he wanted to open up the discussion to solutions addressing some of the problems that had been raised.

Bleeker spoke up and offered his ideas for legislation regarding pasteurization of milk. Another fellow suggested hiring more public health workers.

The sour-faced advocate for cleaning up vice rose to speak out against Hebrew libertines who, he said, lured young Protestant women into working at movie houses, dance halls, and other cheap entertainment establishments.

I glanced over at Rosenfeld, wondering if he was Jewish, but he kept his attention on his dinner plate.

The anti-vice speaker went on. "These places like Goldstein's arcade are just fronts for white slavers. The poor girls who fall into such traps end up in a life of prostitution. If you want to curb venereal disease, this is the place to start. An ounce of prevention is worth a pound of cure."

"That's right," said the dentist beside me.

Here, again, I recognized standard Klan propaganda. I could not understand how educated men could accept such obvious falsehoods.

The sallow opponent of birth control spoke up. "Our country is being flooded with foreigners of the most unwholesome type. That's where you'll find the source of so much of the disease in our society. Look at drunkenness. All the illegal alcohol being sold in our city is because of the Catholics, those drunken Irishmen that are supporting it. And those ignorant niggers who sell their moonshine at those cheap blind tigers up in the north end. And if you want to better manage infectious diseases, we need to burn down those lousy tenements on Wilshire Street where these filthy foreigners live. Those Greeks and Sicilians don't know anything about hygiene. Why the other day a woman living down there brought in her child to see me and the poor little girl was covered with lice. Talk about lazy and ignorant. If those people had any drive, they wouldn't be living in such poverty."

As more men at the table voiced agreement, I felt more and more isolated.

I was glad to hear Rosenfeld speak up. He suggested forming a good governance club to combat corruption in electoral politics and shady dealings in public offices. There was an idea I could support. But overall this meeting was giving me a bad feeling.

Again the clank of silverware against a glass brought everyone's attention back to the head of the room. The tall thin man thanked us for the lively discussion. He had been roaming the room during our exchange of views and he now summarized some of the topics he had heard expressed. His review aligned with many of the topics brought up at our table—disturbingly so in regard to some of the more extreme views that came from those I thought might be Klan supporters. He concluded by urging everyone to sign up for future contact at the table by the door.

"We've made a good start this evening in identifying various paths forward and methods of attack. Together we can make progress toward a more perfect union. And now before I close, I want to bring your attention to the envelopes at the center of each table. As you know our city is anticipating the creation of a brand-new Lutheran Hospital with all the latest in medical advances. While our friend Mr. Iverson has donated real estate for the project, we cannot make this dream a reality without your help. I encourage you each to make a generous contribution in support of such an admirable addition to our city. Thank you all for coming tonight."

Now this all made sense. Gowan and Bleeker had maneuvered me into attending a disguised recruiting meeting for the Klan. And a fundraiser for Gowan's new hospital project to top it off. The ploy was a shrewd piece of engineering.

I was determined not to let the evening become an unmitigated disaster. Amid the commotion of getting up and preparing to leave, I made my way around the table to approach Rosenfeld. I extended my hand and restated my name. "Thank you for your suggestions tonight. I am in complete agreement with you."

He smiled and shook my hand. "These things seem to need no

defending," he said. His self-possession and seriousness won my respect.

Amidst the tumult of conversation surrounding us, I felt my remarks would not be noticed and I took a risk. "I hope that reference to Hebrew libertines didn't offend you." I watched for his reaction.

He seemed unflustered. "You're observant. I'm not offended. I've gotten used to the ignorance of others."

"Here, let me give you my card," I said. "We might be of help to each other at some point."

"I appreciate the gesture." He handed me one of his. "I'm new in town and I'm just setting up my practice."

"I've done some work with St. Mary's. A good friend—my fiancée—works with newborns there. I should introduce you sometime."

"I would like that. Thank you. Now I'd best be on my way." He made a path through the crowd to the exit without stopping to sign up at the table by the door.

I joined Gowan, who was hailing Bleeker and the dentist in preparation to leave. They all seemed to be in good spirits as we drove back. I was careful to keep my mouth shut.

SIX

That community medical meeting kept roiling through my mind all through Friday and Saturday appointments. I dreaded having to discuss the gathering with Gowan, but when we encountered each other in the reception area, he didn't mention it. I was relieved to go home early on Saturday, since I had no afternoon patients. I wanted to do some work in my garden.

That evening, Jimmy telephoned from Chicago. I hadn't gotten any news since he left, so I was elated to hear from him.

"I'm so glad you called," I said. "It's great to hear your voice. How are things going?"

He told me how excited he was to be in Chicago, and his voice became even more animated when he described the sorority dance at a fancy downtown hotel.

We didn't talk long. I told him that Gwen and Charlie sent their greetings and Jimmy said to tell them hello. I asked if he had talked to Mary and he said he hadn't had time yet, but he planned to.

Since he was calling from a pay phone, I didn't want to keep him with gossip about Gowan and the Klan and all—besides I figured it would worry him. I encouraged him to call me collect next time. I wanted to keep our conversation upbeat.

He told me he was glad he got to talk to me.

I said I missed him, and he said he felt the same.

There was a pause.

"Well…good night," he said.

I didn't want to hang up. At last I said good night. Then I blurted out, "I love you, Jimmy." But he had already hung up.

I sat and savored our conversation for a long time until the quiet of my empty house began to depress me. The clock on the wall ticked slowly. In an attempt to lighten my mood I built a fire in the fireplace—the fireplace with the decorative tiles that Jimmy had admired when I first brought him to my house to play Halma. I put some Mozart on the Victrola and stared at the picture hanging above it—the colorful print of the Tuke painting Jimmy had given me back in the summer, "Gold, Ruby, and Malachite." The young men swimming in the nude. So many memories. I stood there looking at it, feeling wistful.

When would we see each other again?

SEVEN

Monday morning, Gwen phoned and insisted we get together for lunch. She said she had some news that we couldn't discuss over the phone. We met at a small café near St. Mary's.

Gwen's face was glowing with excitement. "Carl, I've been asked to take on the position of head nurse in the maternity ward."

I congratulated her. "They couldn't find a better person for the position."

"Yes, I'm thrilled." She beamed at me for a moment. "I've already accepted. And there is more good news." She paused as a busboy clattered together dishes from the next table. "It's rumored that Dr. Osborne wants you for head surgeon at St. Mary's."

My face must have been a kaleidoscope of emotions. I was surprised, of course, since this was the first I'd heard of it. And I was happy—glad to know that Osborne thought that highly of me. I considered the responsibility—and the prestige. But when I thought of what Dr. Gowan would have to say about it, my thoughts turned dark. There was no way I could take on a position like this and still work with the clinic. And if I gave up my association with Gowan and Bleeker while accepting a key position with the Catholics, I would be placing myself in opposition to the Klan and all their influence.

I thought of the inspiring possibilities connected with all the latest equipment and modern surgical facilities of the new

Lutheran hospital. Since Gowan was instrumental in developing the new facility, there would be no possibility that I could do surgeries there without maintaining my affiliation with him. As an associate of the Catholic hospital, I would be announcing myself as an adversary.

Gwen must have seen all these thoughts and feelings play out in my expression. I couldn't speak.

Finally she said, "I'm sorry, Carl. I was so excited at first, but I see this isn't going to be an easy decision for you, is it?"

I shook my head and stared into space, considering all the ramifications. "It's going to require some serious thought."

"Of course." She paused as the waiter filled our coffee cups. "I thought the position would be an ideal situation for you, but I guess it's quite complicated."

I put on a brave smile. "Until, I get an official invitation, I'll continue to weigh my decision. But with things going the way they are with Gowan and the Klan and all, I don't see this as an advantage for my career."

"I see this puts you in a difficult spot. Only you can decide what's best."

The bell on the door clanged as a couple of nurses left the café.

Gwen added, "Speaking of the Invisible Empire, there is other news I have to share with you."

"I hope it's good news."

"I wish it were. I heard a story the other day that the LOTIEs have been distributing Protestant Bibles to children in the public schools."

"The Ladies of the Invisible Empire?"

"Yes, they aren't even trying to hide their identity. They're wearing their full regalia, except for the masks, when they pass out the books—along with little American flags. Why, even the Catholics wouldn't go that far. Separation of church and state and all."

"Holy cow," I said.

The waiter asked if I was done and took my plate away.

"And there's something more."

I wasn't sure I wanted to hear anything more.

"Mother has been pressuring me to join." Gwen tapped her fingernails against the side of her coffee cup. "She thinks that since we will be married soon, we should both join up. I told you her friends are all atwitter about our engagement. She goes on about all the fine activities that the LOTIEs are supporting. And those friends of your neighbor Minnie Mitchell are recruiting women from all over town. They make it sound like a social club with tea parties and card parties. They're appealing to community ties and church groups saying that only the better people are becoming members."

"I would have guessed that, because you work with the Catholics, you aren't considered one of those better people," I said.

"Yes," she sighed, "even Mother disapproves of my work with the nuns." She looked down at her sandwich. "I think I've lost my appetite."

"Let me give you some good news to think about. Jimmy telephoned last night. It sounds like he's having a great time of it in Chicago. The band played for a fancy sorority party the other night. Sounds like they were well received."

"I hope they aren't too successful," Gwen said. "I miss him."

"He said to say hello for him. He misses you and Charlie."

We both smiled, but they were wary smiles. The future seemed so uncertain.

All the way back to my office, I had the feeling I was returning to enemy territory.

EIGHT

A few days later, as Vivian was handing me my list of appointments for the day, Gowan came up to me. "Dr. Holman. A word."

I looked at him and nodded. Ever since I told Gowan that Jimmy was in far-off Chicago I felt a sense of security that Jimmy would not be the topic of conversation. But I never knew what Gowan would come up with in the current state of my world. I was still troubled by that medical recruitment meeting.

When we were settled in his office behind the closed door, he began. "Let me be candid. You're no doubt aware that our gathering the other night was to identify new candidates for possible naturalization. And Bleeker and I wanted to take the opportunity to smooth any ruffled feathers after the Haskell case. We need to keep peace in the ranks."

My defenses were up and I kept my face neutral as I made a slight nod. "I tried my best," I said. "Now it's up to Haskell to forgive and forget."

He nodded, unhurried. "He'll come around."

Remembering Haskell's fury in the hospital corridor, I had my doubts.

"We did you that little favor there. Now you can return the favor by joining up. We want you to be part of this."

I didn't move. He regarded me.

"This is important for our clinic—and your career."

A chill went through me. I scrambled for a response. "My wedding plans are a pressing concern right now. I'd like to wait till after that to commit myself. Besides, my fiancée, Miss Cook, should be in on my decision."

"The man of the house should make the decisions, Carl." His voice was adamant and he faced me squarely. "But that gets me to my next point. I understand that she is a nurse at St. Mary's." He paused. "Bleeker and I met her there while we were attending to the Haskell boy. You told me she was a nurse but I didn't know that she worked at a Catholic hospital."

"So your point...?" I knew just what he was driving at.

"My point is that it doesn't look good for our clinic, our standing in the community, to have one of our doctors engaged to a woman who works at a Catholic institution." His eyes focused on me like spotlights.

I remained still and took a deep breath. "But Miss Cook is a Protestant. She was raised Methodist."

"And she works with the Catholics," he said.

I returned his gaze and said nothing.

"And you are still doing surgeries there."

I looked away toward the bookshelf. To deflect the attention from my connection with St. Mary's I said, "Miss Cook loves her work."

"With newborns, I hear." He paused. "I've heard that she will be given a position as head nurse in the maternity ward." He had been more thorough in investigating her employment than I would have guessed. And what had he heard about me?

"She's been doing important work there. They are learning more and more about neonatal care—especially in difficult cases."

"You know, the Lutheran Hospital would like to start such a program. And our new hospital project has plans for a whole maternity wing. Iverson said he would make a substantial donation to support it." He paused to let the information settle in.

This was the first I'd heard of the plan. I didn't know how to respond.

Gowan went on. "I could use my influence to get her a position with the Lutherans. And when the new hospital is up and running, she would be in a good place to help organize the new maternity wing. Why, in advance of that we might even get her advice about the architecture and so forth."

I could hardly believe my ears. "I don't believe Miss Cook is interested in changing her situation."

"And again there is the problem of your work at St. Mary's. You shouldn't have had the Haskell boy taken there."

I shifted my weight in the chair. "I had no way of knowing that the Haskells would be put off by admitting him to St. Mary's. That was the closest hospital and it was an emergency."

"Over the past few weeks, we have lost a number of patients who take issue with your Catholic associations." He sat forward in his chair. "First there were the Hamlins—the grocers. Mrs. Hamlin had a gall bladder attack and when Dr. Ferguson at the Lutheran Hospital recommended you for the surgery, Mr. Hamlin pitched a fit. He insisted on another doctor—any doctor—to perform the operation."

This was all news to me, but after Mr. Hamlin threw me out of his grocery store and told me not to come back, I was not surprised. Hamlin didn't like my Chinese houseboy coming in his 100% American shop—and he didn't think my character was up to snuff either.

"Now I'm hearing rumors that you've been tapped to become head surgeon at St. Mary's. This can't continue."

Where had he been getting all this information about me?

"You can easily get privileges at the Lutheran Hospital. I would be glad to recommend you. Besides, you've already helped out over there on occasion. They would be glad to have you. Of course, you can always use Adrian's hospital. He doesn't require any of that fancy paperwork." Again he watched me as he paused for effect. "But you must cut your ties with St. Mary's."

I felt the ground shifting under me. This would cause a major disruption in my practice. I was familiar with the procedures and the staff at St. Mary's. I already had a couple of surgeries scheduled there. Moving all my surgeries to the Lutheran Hospital would upset my whole routine. I told him as much.

"The time has come for you to make a number of changes, Holman. As I said, your career depends on it. We must maintain the reputation of this clinic."

Would he actually go so far as to kick me out? My heart was pounding and I could feel the sweat making my shirt stick to my back. The truth was he was in a position to concoct any kind of an excuse to ruin my career and get rid of me.

He went on. "And if Miss Cook insists on staying on with the Catholics, I think there is an easy solution for that."

I returned his stare with curiosity.

"Being a housewife is one possibility. The hearth is central to all that is of value in American life. And as I said, the man should make the decisions." He waited for me to take that in. "On the other hand..." he paused for effect, "if your wife were to become pregnant..." He paused again. "Babies seem to be her specialty."

I thought of Charlie. What an upheaval a pregnancy would be. "Miss Cook is not keen on starting a family right away."

"Carl," he tapped his fingertips together, "we need a family man in this clinic." He was deadly serious. "I was happy when I heard that you were engaged—a man can't remain a bachelor. But marriage is just the first step. The embodiment of the white woman's virtue is motherhood."

I stared back at him in stunned silence. Not only was this pure Klan propaganda, but Gowan was demanding that Gwen and I follow through with our wedding engagement, which we never intended to do, and to top it off, that we start having children. And soon. I resented his presumption to interfere with such a personal decision. And I was indignant at the audacity of him making this a condition for continuing my association with his clinic.

"Let me put it to you this way..." Gowan leaned back in his chair, "as a proposition. Later in November, the Klan is planning a mass wedding—all the young men who have been naturalized and plan to marry will be wed in one grand ceremony, welcoming their wives into the fold. We have already performed a number of Klan baptisms led by good Protestant ministers, dedicating these new little lives to God and country and the Invisible Empire." He raised his arms in an expansive gesture. "We even have clubs with activities for youngsters. And just the other day I went to a Klan funeral service." He smiled. "Become a part of this glorious organization. Including your fiancée. And your future children."

I was filled with horror. The size and scope of this organizational plan made my head spin. Was there any way out of this? Could I conceivably give in and join but remain a silent member, staying neutral, doing nothing to promote their causes—a kind of ghost member?

"But there must be a lot of men in Portland who are not members of the Klan," I said.

"They are not brothers. Only the best people join the Invisible Empire. Everyone who is not a member is an alien." Gowan leaned forward and looked me in the eye. "I will give you until the end of the year to make some changes. We must present a unified front here at this clinic. Protecting this nation and its heritage is our sacred duty."

This had gone too far. I had to put Gowan off somehow and get out of his office.

I composed myself. "Dr. Gowan, you make a powerful case. I see what you envision and I understand your passion for this… grand plan." I took a breath. "I will carefully think this through. But my marriage is a partnership and I must discuss all this with my fiancée." We stared each other down for a moment before I added, "I can't rush into this sort of thing. I'll need some time before I can promise any specific steps."

"You can't delay this forever," Gowan said. We looked at each other for a moment longer. We both knew how much was at stake.

He stood and said, "Well, I won't keep you any longer."

NINE

I stewed over my situation all through the day. That afternoon I left work as soon as my last appointment was over and went to Bagwell's speak. I thought a drink would help me relax. After giving the password at the alleyway entrance, the brawny doorman let me in and I went downstairs to the bar. As I sipped my gin, I mulled over Gowan's words. He was speaking a foreign language. Not just all the strange K words, but the tongue of another world that divided the human race into the 100% American white Protestant Klan and everyone else—the aliens. There was no No Man's Land. You belonged to either one camp or the other. Things were looking more and more like I could not continue to practice medicine as I had been if I did not toe the line.

I ordered another drink. It was late afternoon and the dim basement room was almost empty. I was sitting by myself in a corner near the upright piano on the empty band platform. A scant few people sat drinking at that time of day, one young man at the bar—maybe a store clerk, two others alone at tables in different quarters of the small room. One lone couple, a man and a woman with gray hair, sat without speaking. Is that how Gwen and I would end up if we married? Even the bartender seemed removed, reading a newspaper. A sadness began to creep over me. Here I was, alone again. Jimmy had disappeared, just like Gerald in Berlin, and I didn't know if I would ever see him again. I felt like

Gwen and Charlie were my only friends.

Gowan had made the Klan sound almost like a church community, ministering to babies who needed christening, children and youngsters who needed clubs and activities, women who were looking for social outlets. All like-minded white Protestants were welcomed with open arms into a warm fraternal embrace. Even the dead were honored with funeral rites, clasped to the bosom of the Earth in a final caress.

I ordered a third drink.

Well, Gwen and I had said we would marry. She had been a friend for so long, through college and medical school, through the War—and later…

I took a long drink from my glass. She had been there to soothe my desolation after Gerald was ripped from my life and I returned to Portland. And I loved her family. I always enjoyed driving her out to visit those good folks at the family farm.

I had spent my whole life pretending to be different from what I was. Like a spy. Hiding my true feelings from the outside world. Maybe life would be easier if I…

I could make a pretense. I was used to creating excuses and putting on appearances. I had gotten good at making up half-truths to disguise who I was.

Maybe I could make it work. Maybe I could put on the mask.

I had another drink and decided to go visit Gwen.

"This is a surprise." My fiancée was drying her hands on a kitchen towel. "Come in." She gave me a hug in the small entryway and stood back. "You've been drinking."

I couldn't deny it.

"Come have a seat."

She led me into the cheerful living room with its rose-colored upholstery. We settled on her couch. The warm lamplight brightened the white drapes that covered the picture window, keeping out the cold darkness in the street below.

"You seem troubled, dear. Tell me what's up." She folded the towel on her lap and took my hand.

"Is Charlie here?" I wanted this to be a private conversation.

"Why, no. She's out shopping. Did you need to talk with her?"

"I wanted to talk with you—alone."

She looked concerned.

"Gwen, I think we should get married."

She laughed, then paused to see if I was serious. "We've all discussed this and we've agreed. You and I have announced our engagement. I have a ring to prove it. Even if it is all a pretense."

"But I don't mean that. I mean a real wedding. And soon. And there's another matter…"

Gwen was silent, watching me as I gathered my thoughts—and my courage.

"I'm thinking of joining the Klan."

"Carl!" Her surprise showed on her face. "You have been drinking. Surely you're not serious."

"Well, yes and no. You see…"

"This is a yes or no matter. You are either in the Klan or out of it."

"I know. That's the point. If I'm going to continue practicing with Gowan and Bleeker, I'll have to make some sacrifices. Put on the mask. Not just the white hooded mask. I can pretend. I've been pretending all my life. And we can have a Klan wedding just like Gowan suggested. We can put on a front. We'll fit in. We can hide what we are behind the facade. We'll be doing that anyway."

"Carl…" Her voice was stern with disapproval and she raised a hand as if to stop me.

But I went on. "And we can have babies. Gowan insisted that we have babies. He said it was important that I become a family man. It would be good for the clinic, he said. And I started thinking. And I realized that you are my oldest and best friend and if we had babies, it would make a lasting connection for me with another person."

Gwen sat listening to me babble until I ran out of steam. There was a long silence. At last Gwen spoke.

"Listen." She was quiet and direct, one of the things I loved about her. . "I understand. We are all under pressure. You know my parents are after me to join the Klan too. And a few days ago some women confronted me as I was leaving the hospital. They insisted I accept some of their literature—which I threw in the trash—and they harangued me to join up and abandon the Pope and his ways. You know I'm not Catholic, even though I work at St. Mary's. So I understand that part of it."

I turned to face her.

"And when it comes to babies, you know how much I love them—Lord knows, I work with them almost every day. I would be delighted to have children. I would be delighted to have your children. But, Carl, you're forgetting." She placed her other hand on mine and clasped it. "You're forgetting Charlie. I love Charlie. And I know you do too. But more importantly, you're forgetting Jimmy."

There was a long, deafening silence.

Gwen was right. She didn't have to mention Gerald. That memory hung in the air between us. She didn't have to remind me about talking me out of my support for eugenics and sterilization back in college. She didn't even have to remind me about Jimmy.

"I know you must be missing him." She was right again. "Loneliness can drive us to make foolish choices."

I remembered my wanderings in Pioneer Park after I returned from the War, seeking companionship to replace Gerald and finding only brief sexual encounters. I let out a long sigh, unable to speak. I was close to tears.

"But you know, I believe you will see Jimmy again. And I've got the feeling that you will win out over that band of his."

A clock struck 7 and brought me back to the present.

"You're right. You're always right, it seems. You are my north star."

Gwen patted my hand.

"But Gowan keeps pressing me for a wedding date. What can

I tell him? Anything just to put him off."

"I suppose we could put out a date. We could always change it if it's far enough out. But things get tricky. Other people will make plans."

"Maybe I could tell only Gowan. Just give him a date. We don't have to tell anyone else."

"I guess that's a possibility." Gwen squeezed my hand and let go.

"I would feel better if I could tell him something. How about next year sometime? Is that far enough out?"

"Possibly. But you must tell him that it's tentative. And that he can't tell anyone yet. Say that we're keeping it under our hats for now."

"If I just give him a date—maybe he will back off."

"I understand your concern." Gwen's fingers kept smoothing out the kitchen towel in her lap.

"What if I tell him some time in February? I'll just say we are thinking about mid-February."

"That's just vague enough. We could always say we changed our plans."

"Is it settled then? I'll say it's tentative," I said.

"All right."

We both stared at the carpet.

"If it will take some pressure off you," Gwen said

"It sure will."

"It's worth a try," Gwen said.

"Okay. I feel better already. You could—"

A noise at the front door interrupted me, and Charlie burst into the room like a fresh breeze.

"Look who's come to visit us," Gwen said.

Charlie greeted me and set down her shopping bags. I stood and she came to me and kissed my cheek. "What a nice surprise. It's good to see you. Won't you stay for dinner?"

"Yes," Gwen said. "You must join us for supper."

I didn't need any convincing about that.

TEN

A couple of days after Gowan's ultimatum, I came home to find a postcard from Jimmy in my mail box. The photo was a formal studio portrait of the Diggs Monroe Jazz Orchestra looking very sharp in their tuxedos. There was a brief note from Jimmy on the back, but his message didn't give me much to go on. Although he sounded upbeat, it seemed written in a hurry. If everything had been going well, he would have told me more and with his characteristic enthusiasm. Something about the postcard bothered me. I propped it up so I could study the photo while I sat at the dining table and ate the ham dinner that Joe Locke had left in the icebox. I imagined Jimmy sitting across from me like in the past.

But as I ate, Gowan's insistent call for changes in my medical behavior kept pulling my mind away. I was going to have to make some kind of concession to Gowan—or else I was going to have to upend my life and leave the clinic.

After dinner I tried to do some paperwork but couldn't keep my mind on it. I kept struggling with how I should deal with Gowan. I decided to bed down early. But I couldn't sleep.

I went to the living room for a book. Glancing along the row of titles, I was drawn by the volume at the end of the shelf, *Myths of the Ancient World*. The old stories of the Argonauts that I knew so well from childhood always made me think of Jimmy. At first I made the association because his jazz was such a musical adventure for him, but now it seemed even more appropriate since he was off on the journey of a lifetime. Yes, those old tales would be a worthy distraction. I read for a long time and finally dozed off.

The telephone woke me. I pulled myself together and went to answer. The operator announced a collect call from Chicago. That had to be Jimmy. After a pause his voice came through the line. I told him how glad I was to hear from him, that I'd just gotten his postcard that evening. That seemed to confuse him. He didn't remember the postcard.

He told me that he was in trouble and that he had been drinking. I could tell that from his voice. But what kind of trouble? He said he couldn't explain right then. He needed money for a train ticket to Oregon. He was broke. He sounded scared and lonely and desperate. It must have been after 2 in the morning there. I was scared too.

When I tried to get him to tell me where I could wire him some money, he seemed to be in a panic. He'd had a falling out with the band, he said. I could tell he was on the edge of tears. I was able to get out of him that he was at the Union Station so I told him to go to the Western Union counter and let them know I would be wiring funds. I tried to reassure him and finally said goodbye.

Now I was in a panic. I had to get to the nearest Western Union counter fast. As I dressed I kept imagining what kind of trouble Jimmy was in. Had he been robbed? Was he hurt? This couldn't have anything to do with the gang wars that Tom Harris had mentioned. But what had happened with Diggs and the band? I was selfishly relieved to hear there had been a rift. Did that mean I would no longer be competing with the band for Jimmy's attention?

By 3 in the morning I had sent money off to Jimmy and was driving home. Would I really be seeing him back here in Portland within days? How had things turned out so badly for him? How much trouble was he in? I was deeply concerned.

Then I began to factor Gowan into the equation. Having

Jimmy living at my house again would complicate matters. And how would Jimmy's presence impact the perception of my sham engagement? Would people begin to guess that Gwen and I never intended to go through with our marriage? As happy as I was to think about being with Jimmy again, it would not make my life any easier. By the time I got home, the strain of considering all this had worn me out. I went back to bed and slept till the alarm woke me at 6.

Later at the clinic, a telegram was delivered for me. Jimmy would be arriving by train Monday afternoon.

ELEVEN

That day at work was a struggle. I'd gotten so little sleep and my mind was full of concerns for Jimmy. But as always, I focused on my patients and that took my thoughts away from my worries.

Just before noon a young woman came in. She wore a pink dress that clashed with her red hair. Once we were alone in my office, she told me, without the least reticence, that she wanted to know about birth control. She worked at the telephone exchange and Charlie had sent her to see me. I asked if she was married and she told me that she was engaged to a very nice boy. They had to put off their wedding for a time because his mother was sick, but she confided in me that she had been sleeping with the fellow. She was very worried that she might become pregnant.

I had no qualms about prescribing birth control materials, but I suspected that Gowan objected to the practice. If I kept everything on the quiet, I figured no one would know.

I explained the various techniques in use, including the "natural" methods, but she wanted more certainty and elected the sponge. I told her she would have to come back for a later appointment while I acquired the device.

I escorted her back to the reception area to make the follow-up appointment. Gowan was talking with Vivian and he kept an eye on the young woman. I told Vivian that we needed an appointment the following week.

"Will you have it by then, Dr. Holman?" my patient asked.

I nodded, wishing she hadn't said anything in front of Gowan. I tried to avoid his eye.

My patient said goodbye and turned to leave. Gowan's gaze followed her out as her hips swayed with her graceful walk. He gave me an indecipherable look and turned back to Vivian.

I hadn't paid it much mind, but she was a rather pretty girl—with a sweet face, and that red hair was attractive. Maybe that was all that Gowan's look meant. But maybe he had intuited the reason for her visit.

TWELVE

It was raining when Jimmy arrived at the train station early Monday afternoon. I was able to get away from the clinic at noon to pick him up, but the train was late. By the time the arrival was announced, I'd been waiting for quite some time. He had entered through the doorway marked "Arrivals," hidden among a stream of passengers, and he shuffled along in the dispersing crowd, looking around the station, distracted.

There was my storm-tossed sailor, home from a turbulent and dangerous sea, wandering, dazed, like a ship-wrecked voyager washed ashore on some strange and deserted coastline.

He looked like hell. He wore a cheap, ill-fitting suit, rumpled from wear. His only luggage was a brown paper package tied with string, and this he held close to his chest. His face was pale, he hadn't shaved for a few days, and his sand-colored hair was oily and uncombed. I was overjoyed to see him.

When he noticed me, Jimmy put on a brave smile. I greeted him and gave him a hug. I could smell the alcohol. The odor was not just on his breath but seemed to exude from his pores. He'd clearly been drinking for days. He returned my embrace with one arm, holding his package close in the other. As he clung to me, he seemed desperate. I patted his back and shook him gently.

"Don't you have an overcoat?" I asked, stepping back and holding him at arm's length and looking him over.

He glanced around and shrugged.

"You remind me of the man who lost his coat," I said and laughed.

Jimmy looked at me, his eyes blank before they wandered off. He seemed to pass into a reverie and his expression became grave. Surely, he hadn't forgotten that, I thought. It was one of his favorite stories. He had changed. Something terrible had happened.

"Here, you wear my overcoat," I said slipping it off. "It's cold outside. Let me carry your package for you."

"No," Jimmy said. I caught a glimpse of the neck of a liquor bottle where it protruded from a tear in the paper wrapping. He clutched the package closer to his chest. "I can carry it."

I placed my coat around his shoulders. "Okay," I said, "let me take you home." I put an arm around him and guided him out of the station.

Jimmy wavered a bit as he walked. He was reluctant to talk, as if he were preoccupied. He would begin to say something and stop himself. He seemed to be uncomfortable looking me in the eye, and I sensed that he felt guilty. I gathered from his sniffling and coughing that he had a cold. His eyes were bloodshot, and his nose was red from blowing. He kept fishing a dirty handkerchief out of his pocket.

I drove Jimmy home and Joe Locke offered him something to eat. But he refused, saying that he was tired and just wanted to rest, so I showed him to his room upstairs. Everything was as he'd left it, with his books and sheet music neatly arranged on the bookshelf beneath the small bust of Mozart. His Victrola cabinet stood in the corner with his collection of phonograph records, his dresser and writing table in front of the dormer window. Joe had made sure everything was dusted and polished. But Jimmy didn't seem to recognize or take delight in the possessions he had so carefully moved into the room not so long before. Something was wrong. The light had gone out of his eyes. He insisted he just wanted to lie down for a while and he refused to undress.

As he stretched out on the bed, I sat beside him. I was worried.

Before I returned to work, I wanted to make some connection with him. Recalling our early courtship over the Halma game, I tapped my sternum and I said, "The shortest distance from here to there," I touched his chest, "is a straight line."

Jimmy looked puzzled.

"Like our Halma game. I'm glad you made it back home." I paused to see if he understood my reference.

He looked hurt and frowned. A tear appeared in his eye and he covered his face with his hands.

I leaned over and held him. "It's going to be okay." Letting go, I sat up and said, "You're home now."

He kept his face covered.

After squeezing his shoulder, I stood. "I'll see you after work. Get some rest." I left him lying there and went back to the clinic.

All was not well when I got to the clinic just before 3. Vivian was cross with me that I'd missed a 2 o'clock appointment and the patient had left in a temper. Now my 2:30 patient, an old woman with a sinus condition, was about to leave. I apologized profusely and was able to convince her to stay. We went into my office.

I telephoned late in the afternoon to tell Joe Locke that I had to drop by the hospital on the way home and wouldn't be there for dinner, that I'd heat something up when I got home. I asked him how Jimmy was and he told me that Jimmy hadn't come down from his room.

"Try to get him to eat some dinner," I said. "If he doesn't come down, fix him a dinner tray and take it up to his room."

When I got home around 8, I found Jimmy passed out on the living room sofa, fully clothed, with an empty liquor bottle on the floor beside him. I checked the cupboard. The empty bottle was my own.

I couldn't help laughing to myself as the words of that old sea shanty went through my head. "What do you do with a drunken sailor...?" I remembered Jimmy coming to visit me—drunk and upset—late one night last summer when we were first getting to know each other. Just like old times. But this time, I felt that I had a more serious problem on my hands—or, rather, that we had a serious problem.

I checked his room. His bed was rumpled, and I could see that it had been slept on, not in. The brown paper package, half torn open, lay against the wall at the foot of his bed. The liquor bottle I'd seen sticking out of it sat on the floor nearby—it was empty. Joe's dinner tray sat on the writing table. The plate was half-full, so I guessed Jimmy had eaten something. That was a relief. I carried the tray back to the kitchen and heated up my own dinner. For the time being, I would let sleeping dogs lie.

It was 10 at night before Jimmy showed signs of life. As I sat across from him reading, he groaned and started to raise his head, then fell back. When he raised his head again, realizing where he was and that I was there with him, he covered his eyes with one hand. I put down my medical book and moved the footstool over by the couch to sit beside him. I reached out and smoothed back his uncombed hair. He groaned again and moved his hand away from his face.

"We've got to talk," I said at last.

Jimmy said nothing. A coughing spell seized him and he moved his hand to cover his mouth. The cough subsided and he lay still.

"Talk to me, Jimmy. Tell me something—anything."

He didn't move.

I placed my hand on his shoulder and said, "Listen. I care about you."

Opening his eyes, he blinked and stared at the ceiling. His mouth twitched. "Oh…" He reached up and placed his hand on mine, gripping it. "They killed Eric." He closed his eyes, and his body shook as he fought back tears.

"It's all right." I placed my other hand on his. "You're safe here. I'll take care of you."

Jimmy turned on his side and brought his other hand up to hold on to mine. He lay there and wept, clasping my hands. When the tears subsided, he sat up. I handed him my handkerchief. He dried his face and blew his nose.

"Oh, God. I feel like I've been through hell." He paused to wipe his nose. "I've just lost so much. I don't know what to do."

I moved next to him on the couch and put an arm around his shoulder. "We'll get you back on your feet. It may take a while, but that's all right." I paused. "Rome wasn't built in a day." I was trying to appear positive, but I was concerned.

Jimmy sighed and stared straight ahead.

"How about some dinner?" I asked, giving him a squeeze.

"There's something I have to tell you," he said. He hesitated.

"What is it?"

"I had an affair in Chicago." He continued to stare straight ahead.

Even though I had expected this, I felt a flash of disappointment to hear Jimmy say it. A sense of panic gripped me. Had he gotten in touch with Mary as I had urged him? Had his affair been with her—or some other woman?

"Was it Mary?" I couldn't keep myself from asking. I felt that twinge of jealousy I'd felt back in the summer when I feared that Jimmy might still be interested in women.

A look of dismay came over him, then that far off gaze of reverie. Again tears came to his eyes. "No, it was Eric…" A sob shook him and he couldn't say any more.

I squeezed his shoulder again. "I expected when you left that you would sow some wild oats in Chicago." Did he still feel the same affection for me that he had before he went away? He had returned to me after all.

He became still again and wiped away the tears. "It's not just that. So much happened. I can't explain it all."

"That's okay." I moved my hand to his back and stroked it. "You don't have to tell me everything right now."

He sniffed, dried his tears, and handed back my handkerchief. I could feel his back expand under my hand as he took a deep breath.

"Come on," I said. "Why don't you go wash up and I'll feed you some dinner." I stood up and offered him my hand. When he was standing, I put my arms around him and pulled him close. He hesitated, then slowly returned my embrace.

I released him and stood back, holding his shoulders. "Everything's going to be all right." That was my hope anyway, although my fears persisted.

He finally looked me in the eye and nodded.

While Jimmy used the bathroom, I heated up soup and made toast. After setting out the meal in the breakfast nook I waited. Soon he joined me and began eating in silence.

After a time, I suggested that he drop in at the clinic in the morning, so I could give him a physical. "Just in case you picked up something in Chicago," I said. "We may end up getting intimate." I smiled at him.

He stopped eating and looked at me. A tear came into his eye.

"I still love you, Jimmy," I said.

He covered his face with his dinner napkin and wept. When his tears stopped, he took out that same awful handkerchief and blew his nose. "I don't know why I can't stop crying," he said.

"I understand." I leaned forward. "You've had a shock. "Tears are the body's way of excreting all that pain so that you can see clearly again." I watched his face. "When Gerald died in Germany, I never could have survived if I hadn't let myself cry it all away."

A look of revelation came over him. "You've been through this, haven't you?"

I nodded. "Something like it."

He shook his head. "How am I so lucky to have a buddy like you?"

After dinner I suggested that we walk around the block. I wanted Jimmy to move around some since I knew he hadn't been out of the house all day. I loaned him an overcoat and scarf, and we went out into the November night. It was cold and overcast, but there was no rain. We started off past Maude Williams' house next door.

"You remember Maude Williams?"

"I guess so."

"We took her some tomatoes last summer. Remember?"

"Yeah, the old woman. She was very nice to us—compared to that Mrs. Mitchell." His tone took on an edge.

I was encouraged to know that he remembered that.

"Well, Maude's daughter had another baby in early October—not long after you left. I helped with the delivery."

Jimmy shrugged.

We walked to the end of the block.

I asked him if he would like to see Gwen and Charlie. "They've been asking after you while you were gone."

He looked at me with surprise. "They have?"

"Sure. They're very fond of you."

He was quiet. A gust of wind whipped some fallen leaves across the sidewalk. "I guess I'd like to see them," he said at last.

We rounded the corner and passed the Mitchells' house. I told Jimmy that Clark had gone out for football and become a star linebacker on the high school team. When Jimmy didn't respond, I asked if he remembered Clark. Jimmy's attention came back to the present. "Sure, I remember him," he said. "The little punk who caused all that trouble during the summer—with those rumors about us." His recollection reassured me.

"I guess our plan worked. After all the brouhaha his mother stirred up with her gossip about us, Tom Harris tells me now all that the neighbor ladies are talking about is my engagement to Gwen." I laughed.

Jimmy was quiet.

As we walked back, I saw the lights go out at Tom's house across the street. "The Harris kids came down with measles recently. A lot of kids have been getting it. You remember Rachel and Will?"

He shrugged. "I guess so." He had enjoyed playing with the kids last summer when we visited Tom and Peggy, and this indifference disturbed me.

When we got home, Jimmy showered, and we got ready for

bed. He hesitated in the hallway and said, "Well, I guess I'll head on up to bed."

I took Jimmy's hand. "Come sleep with me," I said. "We won't have sex. But I think you need to be held. You shouldn't be alone."

He hugged me. "Thanks."

We undressed and crawled into bed. Jimmy curled up on his side, and I fitted my body against his back and hugged up to him.

Before we drifted off to sleep, I heard him singing under his breath:

"You need some lovin' when you feel sad...
you need some lovin' to make you real glad..."

In the middle of the night, I jolted awake as Jimmy's whole body jerked. He was calling out, "Water! Water!" As he thrashed about, he hit me in the forehead. I put my arms around him so he couldn't strike out. His breath heaved, and he made little whimpering noises in the back of his throat.

"It's okay. I'm here. You're all right. Everything's fine." I rocked him in my arms.

He became calmer. Maybe he remained in his dream world through the whole outburst or maybe he pretended to be asleep because he was embarrassed. I don't know. I held him for a long time. After a while, he began to make the little twitching movements of someone in slumber. An hour or so passed before I was able to get back to sleep as well.

THIRTEEN

In the morning before leaving for work, I sat on the bedside and woke him. He opened his eyes but wouldn't look at me.

"Good morning, honey boy," I said. "There's coffee ready in the kitchen. Remember, Joe Locke will be in today so have him fix you a good breakfast. I left you a note there on the dresser with the telephone number at the clinic and some pocket money. Give me a call after you get going this morning, and I'll work you into my schedule." When he didn't respond, I worried whether I was getting through to him or not. "Okay?"

Jimmy mumbled but didn't move.

I leaned over and kissed him. "I'll see you later."

All morning at the clinic I kept anticipating Jimmy's call, but he didn't phone. My anxieties deepened. But I had a full schedule and I focused on my patients to distract me. Between patients, I contacted the Lutheran Hospital and started off by saying that I worked with Gowan. I told them I had been assisting Dr. Ferguson on a few cases there and I wanted to apply for regular staff status with full admitting privileges. When they said they could send me the initial paperwork, I said I would drop by and pick up the forms.

At noon I called home. Joe Locke told me that Jimmy was still in my room sleeping. Well, he needs rest, I told myself, to put my mind at ease.

When I called later in the afternoon, Joe said Jimmy had gone out. Since I knew there was no more liquor at home, I suspected that he had gone to find a bottle. I began to anticipate finding Jimmy drunk when I got home. The thought aroused more fears. I knew that I couldn't ask Joe Locke to intervene. Keeping Jimmy out of the booze was beyond the realm of his household duties. I shouldn't even broach the subject with him. I was so troubled that I resolved to take action.

I telephoned Gwen at the hospital and left a message for her to contact me. When she called back, I said I needed her help. I told her about Jimmy.

"He never used to drink much." She sounded concerned.

"I know. That's why I need your help. You'll see."

I asked if she and Charlie could arrange to take different days off during the week so that one of us could stay with Jimmy each day. She said she'd find a way to trade her Sunday off with one of the other nurses. She'd call me back before I left work.

When the workday was over, Charlie had arranged time off on Thursday and Gwen on Friday. By rescheduling my Saturday appointments, I could stay with Jimmy and keep an eye on him during the weekend. That left the next day, Wednesday. I decided I could take Jimmy to the office with me in the morning for an exam and then hope that he could get through the rest of the day on his own. Wednesday evening Gwen and Charlie planned to come over and cook dinner for us all, since Joe Locke was off that day. Now we at least had a plan.

When I got home, Joe Locke said Jimmy was up in his room. "Should I prepare dinner?"

"No, we'll go out to eat. I'll give you a ride home as soon as I can get Jimmy going."

I found Jimmy sleeping on his bed, again fully clothed. I woke him. He tried to appear sober and said that he wasn't feeling well, but there was no hiding his drunken condition. He must have hidden his bottle. I knew that scolding and nagging would be useless, so I got him out of bed and insisted he come for a walk with me. His mobility was so impaired that I had to help him down the stairs, and I decided to drive him around a bit before going to the nearby park.

Joe helped me get Jimmy into the front seat of the car, then hopped in back. I drove him home first. The fresh air did Jimmy good, and by the time we got to the park, he was more coherent.

It had rained earlier and the park was wet, but it was not especially cold. Now that night had fallen, no one was around but us. We walked for a while following the paths, which were lit by ornate lamp poles. Many of the trees had lost their leaves, now strewn across the ground. As we passed the small pond, Jimmy picked up a handful of pebbles and began tossing them into the water, one by one, like he had done the night of the Bisby Grange incident with the Klan, when he was so upset.

"Remember when I met you at that country dance?" I asked. "That was the first time I saw Diggs and the band play."

Jimmy tossed a pebble. Then using more force, he threw another. With a burst of rage, he hurled one stone after another. "Yeah, I'd like to kill the bastards." He reared back and shouted, "Danny Felton too!" as he blasted his last stone at the pond. Ripples spread out from where it landed.

I put an arm around his shoulder, guiding him back along the path. "Tell me about it."

"It was that goddamned Larry. He kept accusing me of being a fairy. And Diggs and I didn't agree about the music. The whole thing wasn't working...so I walked out."

We followed the path in silence. A light breeze brought down a few dead leaves.

"Hell, I wonder if any of this would have happened if I hadn't gone to that cat house with the fellas," Jimmy continued. "I wanted to show them that I wasn't a pansy, so I asked if I could go with them. Oh, Christ, I don't know."

Jimmy took out a pack of cigarettes and lit one. He had a coughing fit and threw his cigarette aside. We went on around the pond.

After a time, I spoke up. "I want to give you some medical

advice. I don't want to nag. I'm telling you this because I love you. Understand? I want you to get well, and you can't get well as long as you keep drinking. You've got more to get over than just a bad cold."

He kept his eyes on the path in front of him.

"I've arranged with Gwen and Charlie to stay with you Thursday and Friday—to look after you."

Jimmy shot me a look.

"I don't think it's a good idea for you to be alone right now." I paused, but Jimmy didn't say anything. We kept walking. "If you get desperate for a drink, you can drink. I brought home a bottle. But try to be moderate, okay?"

Jimmy didn't speak and he kept his eyes straight ahead, but he took my hand in his. By the light of a nearby lamp, I saw tears glistening on his cheeks.

I stopped and pulled him to me. Jimmy returned my embrace and wept quietly on my shoulder. After a bit, I asked if he needed a handkerchief. He sniffed and coughed. "I've got one." He took out a clean one and blew his nose as we walked back toward the car.

"Do you feel like eating something? We could go to Hansen's where you used to work."

"I don't want to see anybody I used to work with."

So I drove us to another café nearby and enticed him to eat a bowl of soup. As we were finishing up, I suggested we take in the new Charlie Chaplin film at the Osiris downtown. Jimmy agreed to go, but without much enthusiasm.

As we entered the theater, I remembered going there with him when we were first getting acquainted. But Jimmy moved through the lobby like a sleepwalker. It struck me that we needed to get acquainted all over again.

As the movie started, he still seemed preoccupied. But after a while, he got caught up in the film, and at last he laughed out loud.

We went home to bed, and I held Jimmy in my arms until we fell asleep. In the middle of the night, Jimmy woke up weeping again.

FOURTEEN

I got Jimmy going early the next day and made coffee and breakfast while he was in the bathroom. When he came out, shaved, showered, and dressed, he told me he was feeling pretty shaky. I showed him where I had stashed the full bottle of gin in a kitchen cabinet. "I just need a little," he said, "to set myself up. That will be it." He poured himself a small glass and tossed it down before sitting down to breakfast.

I drove him to my office, hoping to examine him first thing, but Vivian had the whole morning booked with patients back to back.

Jimmy said he was feeling restless and wanted to walk around a bit. He had left a small amount of money in a downtown bank before he went to Chicago and he thought he'd stop by and draw out some cash.

I told him to do his errands and meet me back there at noon. I would give him an exam during my lunch break and then we'd grab a quick bite to eat. He agreed. As he headed for the door, I put an arm around his shoulder. "Take it easy, okay?"

He nodded and left.

When Jimmy returned around noon, I could tell that he'd had a few drinks, probably from a local speak. He was more talkative. No doubt the liquor had loosened his tongue.

I did a physical. Other than an upper respiratory infection, he was in good health, just tired. I drew blood for a Wassermann to see if he had syphilis and said we needed to repeat the test for the next few weeks.

After the exam we went to lunch at a café near my office.

"What are your plans for the afternoon," I asked as we ate.

"I might try to look up some of my old friends from the music business."

"Good plan," I said to encourage him. It would be good for him to get out and about, socialize a bit.

"You can ride back home with me after work—around 6—if you're downtown that late."

He hesitated. "I was planning to take the trolley back to the house. There are some things I need to attend to in my room."

"Remember that Gwen and Charlie were coming over around 8 to fix dinner for us."

Glancing aside he appeared to be making a mental calculation, then smiled and said, "It'll be good to see them."

All afternoon at the clinic, I kept thinking that Jimmy seemed to be doing better, and the thought cheered me.

Around 2, as I was finishing up with an older woman with arthritis, there was an insistent knock on my door. This was unusual. I was irritated to be interrupted while I was with a patient, but I excused myself to answer it.

When I opened the door, Jimmy stood there looking distressed. "You've got to help me. My friend is sick and needs to see you right away."

"Jimmy, I have another appointment lined up." I didn't try to hide my impatience.

"Please, this is important." He turned and gestured to a young man sitting across the reception room. I recognized Vance. He sat off by himself rocking back and forth, his knee bouncing up and down as he shuddered with chills. There was a patch of blood on the side of his face. He was sweating and kept mopping his brow with a handkerchief. His dark hair was wet with perspiration. Vivian and the waiting patients looked on with alarm and fascination.

"Go get him and bring him in," I said, making an effort to keep from sounding abrupt. I was not happy to be put in this situation. Since Vance had already been to see me, I wondered if he had coerced Jimmy to bring him to my office. Although I felt annoyed, Jimmy's anxiety was obvious and I wanted to ease his concern.

As Jimmy went to get Vance, I ushered my arthritic patient out and told her to come back in a week. Jimmy was helping Vance stand just as Gowan emerged from his office. All eyes were on Vance as Jimmy guided him past the reception desk. Vivian wrinkled up her nose as if assaulted by a bad smell. A woman in a fur coat got up and went to a seat at the far side of the room. I caught a glance from Gowan as I held my office door for them.

"It's going to be all right," Jimmy said as he ushered Vance in. A pungent odor hit me. Vance must have soiled himself. I closed my door, and Jimmy led him to one of the chairs.

Before they could sit, I said, "Let's take him straight into the examining room." I opened the side door and we walked him to the exam table. The smell was overpowering. He was shivering and his nose was running. He gave a prolonged sniff and mopped at his nostrils with his wadded handkerchief.

"You've gotta do something for him," Jimmy said. Although I thought he was naive about how bad Vance's condition was, Jimmy seemed frantic that Vance get help. While I was reluctant to get involved, I did feel sorry for the addict.

Vance shuddered as we got him onto the table. The smell of feces increased as he sat down. He rocked back and forth. I couldn't help noticing that he had an erection. I'd read that priapism was a symptom of withdrawal.

"Where did you find him?" I said.

"I went to Haskell's pharmacy—to buy a bottle. When Vance walked in, Mr. Haskell started yelling and threw him out. I couldn't just leave him on the sidewalk." Jimmy's alarm was palpable. "We used to take turns playing the piano at Bagwell's place." Vance's story unfolded in my imagination. So Haskell was not just pushing alcohol.

"He must have fallen. Is that where he got this scrape on his face?"

"Haskell pushed him out the door and he fell. He told Vance to come back when he had the money."

I turned to Vance. "How long has it been since you've had a shot?"

It took him a moment to answer and he spoke with difficulty. "Yes—yesterday—no the day before. M-maybe longer. I decided to quit...but it got so bad I couldn't take it. That—that's when I went to Haskell." He sniffled.

"Are you serious about quitting?" I said.

"I can't take it any more—with it or without it." His head twitched. "I just want to die."

"Okay, listen. If you're serious, I can refer you to a sanitarium in Seattle. Are you game?"

"Anything. I'll try anything." He wiped his nose with the handkerchief.

I went to a cabinet for some morphine and a syringe. "I'll give you a little, just to ease your discomfort, until we can get you to Seattle. But no one is to know about it. Tell them you just used your last dose this afternoon. You understand?"

"Anything." His body shuddered again and he groaned.

"Jimmy, roll up his sleeves." Jimmy helped Vance out of his jacket and struggled to unbutton Vance's cuffs.

I turned away and continued to prepare the injection.

"Jesus!" I heard Jimmy say. I turned back. He was staring at the discolored flesh of Vance's arms.

I tied a rubber tube around the upper part of Vance's right arm. I concluded that he was right-handed, since the left arm showed the worst bruising.

"Stand aside, Jimmy. Maybe you can support him from behind."

"I can't watch," Jimmy said and went to the other side of the table and held Vance's shoulders, his head bowed so he couldn't see the needle.

Finding a vein required all my skill, but I was able to give him an injection. I hoped the dosage was adequate, because I didn't want to have to locate another vein. If his tolerance was too high, this shot wouldn't provide any relief.

The amount of morphine must have been sufficient because Vance began to calm down, and after a while he lay back on the table and seemed to sleep.

Jimmy watched with horror. He kept looking from me to Vance and shaking his head.

After I had cleaned and bandaged the abrasion on his face, I said, "I think he'll be all right. Come into my office."

When the door was closed, I said, "Vance came to me a while back begging for drugs for his aunt."

Jimmy seemed to be sorting out all that was happening.

"He said she had kidney stones."

He looked puzzled.

"It's a common ploy to get morphine."

Jimmy sat there shaking his head in silence.

"We'll need to get him cleaned up. I have an extra change of clothes in my closet here. He can have my trousers. I want you to get a cab and take Vance to the rail station. Make sure he gets on the next train north, then call me with the arrival time. Once you get him out of here, I'll call the sanitarium director and have them send someone to pick him up. He should get there by evening, I think—before the drug wears off."

"He's been to see you before?" Jimmy said at last. He sounded bewildered.

"He seemed desperate then, too. But he wasn't sick."

Jimmy shook his head.

"I'll have to wire some money to the sanitarium. Sounds like Vance is broke. Does he have any family?"

"I don't know. We never talked about that."

"I can send a deposit to get him admitted. Maybe you can locate some family who will take charge."

"I've got some money in the bank. I'll help out."

"No, keep your money. It will be too expensive. Maybe we can find some charity funds if he doesn't have any family who can help."

I wasn't sure if I could trust Vance to go through with this plan, but it was the best I could do for him on the spur of the moment. If he was sincere about kicking the habit, this should get him started. Besides that, I wanted to get him out of the clinic. Gowan had not looked pleased.

"When I was at Haskell's," Jimmy said, "before Vance showed up—I mentioned that Larry from the band told me I could buy liquor there. Haskell said, 'Are you the little fairy that lives with Dr. Holman?' Then he said he wouldn't sell me any alcohol. I was flabbergasted. He seemed to know a lot about you."

"Yes, I've met Haskell. I'll tell you about it sometime. But now we've got to get Vance out of here."

Jimmy was somber. "Thank you. I…"

"What is it?"

"In Chicago I saw some things…" His attention slipped into some other place and he was silent for a moment.

"Go on." I was growing impatient.

"I…uh…saw a musician there who was in this kind of trouble. So I couldn't just leave Vance alone there—at Haskell's."

I looked at him with concern. Maybe Jimmy wasn't as naive about addiction as I thought. "You'll have to tell me about it sometime."

"Thanks for helping him out."

"He's got a tough road ahead of him. Now, you need to get moving. The medicine will only hold him for a few hours." I stood. "There is no time to waste. You'll need some money for a cab and train ticket." I handed him some bills.

"I've still got the cash I picked up at the bank."

"Use this. I don't want you spending your money on an addict."

I went to my office closet and got the trousers from my extra suit and a fresh change of underwear. "These may be a bit big for him but they're clean."

We went back to the exam room and got Vance upright. He seemed calmer, but he was slow to move.

"Can you walk?" Jimmy said.

"I think so."

We guided him to the sink and I got out some small towels. We helped him clean himself up and bundled up the soiled clothes. My pants were too long for him and Jimmy rolled up the cuffs. Once he was dressed, we walked Vance back to the reception area and I saw them out of the clinic. The other patients stared. As I turned back to my office, Gowan came up to me. "In my office," he said under his breath. He was gruff.

Once in private, he launched into a defense of the clinic. "It's unseemly to have that sort of degenerate on our premises. The fellow is clearly an addict. We can't have a lowlife like that disturbing our clientele. This is a respectable clinic. Did you see how the patients out there reacted?"

"I apologize if the other patients were upset, but that fellow needed help. As a physician I am obliged to help the afflicted." I might have been more conciliatory if I had not been so angry.

"There are some types that we cannot allow in this clinic. Holman, it's bad for business." He stared me down.

I looked back at him. What more could I say?

"So who was that fool who brought him in? You seemed to know him."

"He's my boarder." I refused to get pulled into an argument about Jimmy's character.

"I thought he was off to Chicago."

"He returned recently." I felt the need to give some explanation. "His business venture did not turn out as planned."

"Oh, an enterprising young fellow." I couldn't tell if he was saying this with sarcasm or approval. "He needs to learn to associate with a better class of people. I suggest you give him some advice."

"He was just trying to do a good turn. He is not medically sophisticated. You can't blame him for feeling some compassion."

Gowan looked at me for a moment. "Compassion?" he said. "That belongs in church, not in business." We stared at each other for a moment longer. I wasn't going to give any ground. "Don't you have some more patients to see?"

I nodded and left his office feeling sick at heart.

Later Jimmy phoned with Vance's arrival time. I made the call to Seattle and set the arrangements in motion. If I'd been a praying man, I would have sent a prayer in Vance's direction. He would need it.

FIFTEEN

When I got home after 6, Jimmy was not around, but as I passed through the living room I saw that the lid of the piano keyboard had been left open. In the kitchen there were dirty dishes in the sink but no Jimmy. I found him asleep on his bed upstairs, again fully dressed. I was afraid that he had passed out again from drinking. I stood in the doorway to his room, trying to decide what I should do next. Gwen and Charlie were due to arrive before long and I didn't want Jimmy in a drunken stupor. Then I saw the tuxedo.

The room was dark except for a wedge of light from the fixture at the top of the stairway spilling across the room. The closet door stood open and Jimmy's tux hung from the door knob on a wooden hanger. I stepped into the room. The brown wrapping paper of his package lay spread on the floor at the foot of his bed next to his black patent leather shoes. I switched on the table lamp next to his bed. A half-empty Mason jar sat there next to a key ring with two keys I didn't recognize. Why had Jimmy brought keys back from Chicago? I wondered what doors they might unlock. I picked up the jar and sniffed the pungent smell of moonshine whiskey. So he'd found a different bootlegger? He could have poisoned himself. I'd have to bring home some pharmacy alcohol that I knew was safe.

Jimmy was stretched out on his back with his arms folded

across his chest. He was clutching the tuxedo shirt and I saw that its white collar was stained with spots of blood.

I stood there watching him sleep a moment, before I sat down on the bed beside him. He stirred and murmured as he awoke. He jerked his head up, startled, before laying his head back onto the pillow. He blinked and asked what time it was. His speech was slurred with alcohol and sleep.

"Gwen and Charlie will be here soon," I said. "They are coming over to make dinner for us, remember?"

"Oh, yeah. I remember." Jimmy tried to rise up and appear alert, when he noticed that he was holding the tuxedo shirt and his head fell back again. He held up the shirt. "Oh," he said. A plaintive little utterance. His hands collapsed onto his chest holding the shirt close as he shut his eyes.

"It looks like you've gotten some stains on your shirt," I said, hoping to get him to talk about it.

Jimmy sat up. He dropped the garment in his lap and embraced me, burying his face in my shoulder. He didn't cry, but he held on for a bit before releasing me and looking down at the shirt.

"It's blood. It's Eric's blood. Danny Felton shot him while I was playing the piano." Jimmy's voice was emotionless. The liquor must have numbed him. He moved to the edge of the bed and swung his feet onto the floor. "The tux is ruined too."

I shook my head with a feeling of dismay, trying to imagine what he must have seen.

We sat next to each other in silence. This wasn't the time to press him for details. I put my arm around his shoulder and he leaned into me. "I'm here if you want to talk about it."

He sighed and shook his head. "I guess I'd better go wash my face." He moved to stand.

"Why don't I give these clothes to Joe Locke in the morning? Maybe they can get the stains out at the laundry."

Jimmy held up the shirt again, before handing it to me. "Maybe I'd better just get a whole new suit." He walked out of the room and down the stairs.

I turned on the overhead light to examine the tux. There was also blood splattered across the shoulder of the coat. I held the shirt up next to it and imagined the trajectory of the blood, the proximity of the gunshot. Jimmy had been dangerously near.

I examined the shirt. There, embedded in the fabric was blood that had flowed through the veins of what was once a person named Eric, blood that nourished the cells of his body and brought it life. Now, those cells were merely a stain on the collar of Jimmy's shirt. Who was Eric? What did Jimmy remember?

When Jimmy finished in the bathroom, I got him to walk around the block with me, hoping to sober him up.

We got back to the house a little before Gwen and Charlie showed up carrying grocery bags for the meal. They greeted Jimmy with hugs and kisses. As they took possession of the kitchen, the smells of frying chicken and the sound of conversation and laughter filled the house. The gaunt, desperate feeling that had settled on the place since Jimmy's return warmed into a festive atmosphere.

Gwen told a story about her father cooking a meal when her mother was sick, describing in detail the accumulation of disasters as his preparations devolved into chaos. Charlie made a salad while she chronicled some amusing telephone encounters at the switchboard. Jimmy and I got out the white linens and set a proper dinner table. We all sat down to an elegant feast of chicken and an array of side dishes.

A full house and family-like setting revived Jimmy's spirits. At moments he seemed almost his old self.

After dinner Jimmy built a fire, and Gwen suggested we play Halma. Charlie set up the card table in front of the fireplace, while I got out the game board. As we laid out the playing pieces, I watched Jimmy's face. When he gave me a knowing glance, I felt a wave of relief. Maybe Jimmy would be okay after all.

We took turns moving our pieces across the board. Jimmy lost himself in the game and even cracked a joke or two. Gwen was losing, with most of her pieces in the middle of the board and a few straggling back in their starting positions. She moved one player forward one space, and Jimmy seized the opportunity to bring the last of his stragglers up from behind and, after a series of jumps, moved that last man home. He raised his fists in triumph.

"Brilliant move," Charlie said.

Gwen groaned in defeat.

I reached over and gave Jimmy a congratulatory slap on the shoulder. We leaned back in our chairs.

"Let's play another round," Gwen said. "I have to redeem myself."

We began replacing the playing pieces for a new game. Jimmy got up to stoke the fire, absentmindedly humming a tune to himself. As he knelt on the hearth to put another log on, he began singing the lyrics under his breath.

"O, I went to see the doctor today…"

"Is that a new song you picked up in Chicago?" Gwen asked.

Jimmy stopped, realizing what he was singing. "No—" he paused. "No, that's an old tune." The fire popped and hissed. Jimmy stared into the flames. We looked from one to another.

Gwen broke the silence. "Can you play us something new? What's popular in Chicago now?"

"Oh, I don't know." Jimmy thought a moment. "There are different styles. I heard so many kinds of music there."

"Play something," Charlie encouraged him.

"Well," Jimmy said rising from the hearth. He stood deep in thought before moving toward the piano. He pulled out the piano bench and fussed with its position. Finally, he sat down. We waited. Jimmy raised his hands. I thought I noticed a slight shaking in his fingers. He seemed to be struggling with himself to touch the keyboard. After a long, torturous moment, his fingertips came to rest on the ivory. Another silence left us all suspended in time.

It seemed to take all his strength and concentration as he sounded a chord. The opening of a blues song began to unfold. Without warning Jimmy leapt up from the piano using such force that the bench fell over backwards. There was a loud bang.

Jimmy jumped at the noise and began trembling. The vibrations of the piano wires faded as the rest of us rose from our chairs. Jimmy ran out of the room.

In the kitchen, I found him pulling the gin from the cupboard. He uncapped it and drank straight from the bottle, holding it over his head, swallowing gulp after gulp. I reached out, pulling the bottle down and setting it on the counter. Jimmy didn't resist, but he swallowed and coughed. I put my arms around him and held him against me. His body was trembling. Slowly his hands reached around me, and as his grip took hold, he began to convulse with sobs.

"It's okay," I said. "Go ahead and cry."

SIXTEEN

Thursday morning Charlie came to the house early, before I had finished shaving. Jimmy was still sleeping in my bed downstairs, and Joe Locke had not arrived yet. After she removed her hat and coat, I showed Charlie where the gin bottle was and said that I'd told Jimmy he could have a drink if he got desperate, but he should be moderate.

"I don't understand why he is drinking so much," she said. "It's not like him."

"You saw how upset he got last night. Something's happened."

"Maybe I can get him to talk about it."

Charlie put coffee on while I finished getting ready for work. Then I went to Jimmy's room upstairs and folded the stained tuxedo and dress shirt and bundled them into a paper bag.

Downstairs Charlie was sitting on the living room sofa drinking coffee and doing one of the newfangled crossword puzzles in the newspaper.

"Joe Locke will be changing the linens today and taking them to the laundry. Tell him to give these clothes special attention. It's Jimmy's tux. It's gotten some stains on it." I handed her the package. "They're blood stains."

I saw the concern in her eyes.

"I have to get going," I said heading to the hall tree for my overcoat.

We heard footsteps and doors opening and closing in the back of the house. It was too early for Joe to arrive. It had to be Jimmy. The toilet flushed. There were footsteps in the hallway and into the kitchen. As Jimmy rattled around in there, Charlie went to the doorway. I followed with the overcoat on my arm and watched over her shoulder.

Jimmy stood facing the cupboard dressed in a bathrobe and slippers, his hair unruly from sleep. He leaned over and retrieved the gin bottle and poured some into his coffee.

"Good morning," she said.

Jimmy jumped, spilling some of the gin. Charlie was leaning against the doorjamb with her arms folded. I looked on from behind.

"My God, you scared me," he said.

Charlie laughed.

"Good morning," I said. "I was just leaving."

"I forgot Charlie was going to come by today. I thought I was alone."

"Obviously," she replied. "Is that what you call breakfast?"

"Well…what can I say?" He made a helpless shrug and laughed. "It's just a little bracer. Something to get me going."

"I'll make you a deal, Jimmy. I'll match you drink for drink today." Charlie regarded him with a good-natured smile.

"You're not serious," he said.

"Oh, I'm quite serious."

"You've made me self-conscious now. Besides, you've caught me at a disadvantage. I'm not even dressed."

"Good," she said and went to a cupboard and took down a glass. She held it out. "I'll have mine without coffee, thanks."

"Now you're making fun of me."

"Well, yes, I am. But I'm serious about my deal. Here. Drink for drink. Go ahead, pour me my share."

Jimmy poured a small amount.

"Is that as much as you put in yours?"

He added another dollop to Charlie's glass.

"Cheers," she said, holding it up. They touched their drinks together, and she downed her portion. Jimmy took a sip.

"Now how about some real breakfast?" she said.

"I think I'll wait till later," he said.

"Listen, Jimmy." She was firm but still gave her wry, good-natured smile. "Rule number one is that when you have a drink, I get a drink. Rule number two is that when you take a drink, you have to eat something."

Jimmy glanced away. "Okay." He shrugged and chuckled. "You're the boss."

"Good," Charlie said. "I think we'll have a splendid day together. How does bacon and eggs sound? Do you want to make toast?"

"I think I'd better go put on some proper clothes first."

"Goodbye, Jimmy," I said from the doorway. "I've got to get to work, but I see you're in competent hands. You two have a good day."

"Sure," Jimmy said. "So long. I'd better go dress." He shuffled off down the hall cradling his coffee cup.

Charlie followed me to the living room as I slipped into my overcoat. "Good luck today," I said.

"Don't worry. Jimmy and I will have a fine day. Gwen plans to come over after work, and we'll eat around 8. I found a magazine recipe for lemon sole. I'll have Joe Locke prepare it."

"Sounds like you have the day all mapped out."

She smiled.

"I'll call around noon to see how things are going."

Driving to the clinic, I thought back over Charlie's interchange with Jimmy and I felt optimistic.

I got tied up at the clinic and couldn't call home till after lunch. When Charlie answered, I asked how the morning went.

"I needed to go to the grocery store to get some things for our dinner. Jimmy tried to get out of going with me—I suspect he planned to have a few drinks while I was gone—but I told him I needed help carrying the groceries. At the grocery, Mrs. Hamlin was very nice to us. I believe she thought we were married."

"You didn't go *there*!" I sat forward in my chair.

"We did. But as we were leaving, Jimmy pointed out the 100% sign and told me you'd had some trouble with the Hamlins."

"That's an understatement. Yes, I've been going to Klaus Dietrich's grocery since then. Nice German fellow. Has Jimmy had anything to drink since this morning?"

"No. He gets restless, but I've been able to distract him. I asked him to build a fire and we looked at magazines together. Then we played Halma. He didn't even have a drink with Joe Locke's lunch."

"That's all good."

"Later we took a walk and gathered some fall leaves. I pressed them in one of your medical books. I hope you don't mind."

"No, that's fine." I glanced at my desk calendar to see what my afternoon looked like.

"A curious thing—while we were walking, he asked me if I believed in God. He said he isn't sure if there is a God. He keeps praying that the things he went through in Chicago were just a bad dream. Later I asked him to tell me about it. When he wouldn't, I said that he seems to have made a decision somewhere along the line to stay drunk all the time so that he won't have to face up to all of it. I told him that sooner or later he was going to have to talk about what happened."

"You have that right. He's got to open up."

"I think he wants to but he's afraid. It's too painful for him. Our friend Dr. Freud would say he's repressing things. He would benefit from seeing my psychotherapist."

"I agree, but I don't think he's willing to go along with that sort of thing."

Charlie sighed. "I told him about my father."

She had told me about his sexual advances to her as an adolescent. "Hmm. How did he react?"

"When I told him my father forced me and I didn't feel I had any choice but to give in, I could see a look in his eye—he knew what I was talking about."

"Jesus," I said under my breath. I knew about the blood and the gunshot. I did not suspect some kind of sexual trauma. This was going to require a delicate touch. "What's he up to now?"

"He's napping."

"Okay. I'll try to get home early this evening. Did you give Joe Locke the tuxedo?"

She told me she had.

"One more thing. Did you send another friend to see me— about birth control?"

She said she hadn't.

"I must be getting a reputation. This is the third young woman this week that has come to ask me for help."

After we said goodbye I sat at my desk and thought about how we could help Jimmy recover. Gwen would be there for dinner this evening and again tomorrow. She had a way with people who were suffering. I allowed myself to be reassured.

Late in the afternoon I called again to see how Jimmy was. He answered the phone this time.

"How are you?" I asked.

"I'm okay."

"Are you and Charlie getting along?"

"Of course we are. We've been playing the piano. Did you know she plays?"

"She told me she did, but I've still never heard her. Does she play jazz?"

"I haven't heard her do that, but she does a pretty good job with Beethoven. She played the 'Moonlight Sonata.'"

"I'd like to hear it sometime."

"And she taught me a French drinking song with the words

and everything. We worked it up and plan to play it for you after dinner."

"Sounds like you two are having fun."

"Yeah, after that we both had a drink, since it's a drinking song." He laughed. "Then Charlie insisted we have a French picnic with bread and cheese."

"I wish I could be there."

"Me too." Then he paused and, lowering his voice, added, "But I have to ask you something. Over lunch she got real serious." Jimmy's voice was somber. "Did you know about her father?"

"How do you mean?" I wanted him to tell me more, especially after what Charlie had said earlier.

His voice was almost a whisper. "She told me that...that he... forced her...you know?"

"She's told me something of her background. How did that strike you?"

"I was shocked. I'd never thought about—about that before." He paused.

"What do you mean, you'd never thought about it?"

"I guess I never thought that those things really happened."

"You didn't?"

"I don't know..." He sounded preoccupied.

I wanted to ask him what happened in Chicago, but I held back.

"But then she told me she'd had—" he lowered his voice again, "an abortion."

"Wait a minute. She told you that?" Now I was shocked.

"I couldn't believe her dad made her pregnant."

"She never told me that part." So that's why Gwen is so supportive of abortions, I thought.

Jimmy was quiet.

I heard a voice in the background. "Are you still there?" I said.

"Wait a minute. Joe Locke just brought in some green. He was out in the garden." He must have covered the mouthpiece to say something to Joe. His voice came back on. "He's working on dinner. Charlie wants me to help them. Look, I'll have to talk to you later. Gwen's going to be here for dinner, too."

"I know. I'll get home as early as I can."

I hung up the phone with more questions than I'd had before.

Gwen was the last to arrive. She came by taxi directly from the hospital, still in her white nursing uniform.

The dinner went well, although Jimmy became quiet from time to time as his attention drifted off somewhere else.

After we finished, Charlie and Jimmy wanted to play their song for us. Jimmy rekindled the fire while Gwen tried to help Joe clear the table until he shooed her away.

The two musicians sat down on the piano bench. The clatter of dishes sounded in the background.

"Come on, Gwen," Charlie called. "Leave the kitchen to Joe Locke."

Gwen came and stood at the entrance to the living room as Charlie and Jimmy began to sing.

"Chevaliers de la table ronde,
Goûtons voir si le vin est bon..."

As the song progressed, Gwen approached the piano. She watched them, smiling, her starched uniform catching the light from the fireplace. The music seemed to draw her in. When she was a few steps behind Jimmy, just off to the side where he could catch sight of her out of the corner of his eye, his playing faltered, then slowed before he stopped altogether. I stood up from my chair and stepped forward. Charlie broke off playing as well.

Jimmy was trembling, and beads of sweat gathered on his forehead. Without a word he bolted from the room. I followed him down the hall. Before I reached the bathroom, I heard the sound of retching. Jimmy was hunched over the toilet bowl and I smelled the acrid odor of vomit. He heaved again.

I dampened a cloth and held it against his forehead as he

convulsed. Gwen appeared at the door. After a few moments, Jimmy was still. He spit a few times before he stood, then took the cloth from my hand and wiped his face as he went to the sink.

"I'm okay," Jimmy said. "Just give me a minute."

"You're sure?" I said.

He nodded. "I'll be okay in a bit."

As Jimmy took a mouthful of water, I flushed the toilet and Gwen and I withdrew.

In the living room, Charlie was still at the piano and she turned as we entered. "Things went so well today," she said. "I don't know what brought this on."

I stood off to her side and a little behind, near where Gwen had been when Jimmy stopped playing. I imagined the trajectory of a bullet and the splatter of blood if Jimmy were at the piano bench. The stains on his tuxedo would have matched. Oh, Jimmy, my dear friend, how can I help you through this? I dared not try to explain any of my speculations to Charlie and Gwen.

A pall had fallen over our festive evening. We could hear Jimmy gargling down the hall. I felt helpless. None of us seemed to know what to say.

After a bit, Jimmy came to the doorway. "I'm sorry. I'm not feeling well. I'm going to bed." He turned and left.

Joe Locke was clanking pots and pans in the kitchen. Gwen said, "I guess we should be going. I want to get here early tomorrow. I'll call a cab." She looked concerned. "You go look after Jimmy. We'll share the taxi with Joe and make sure he gets home."

We all said good night and hugged. I went to the kitchen to tell Joe Locke he could ride with the girls but found Jimmy standing next to the cupboard drinking from the gin bottle. He lowered it to swallow but didn't put it down.

"I need something to help me sleep," he said.

I placed my hand on his shoulder. "I understand."

I told Joe to ride with the girls as Jimmy took another swig from the bottle and put it down. I capped it and put it away.

"Come on, let's put you to bed," I said.

I guided him to my bedroom and helped him out of his suit coat. He sat on the edge of the bed and began taking off his shoes.

I had to say something, even if my words were all wrong. "I studied the stains on your tux."

He turned the shoe over and examined the sole. "There are blood stains on my dress shoes too," he said as he sighed and let the shoe dropped. "Now every time I play the piano, I look to see if there is blood on the keyboard." He turned his palms up and studied his fingers.

I sat down beside him and put an arm around his shoulder. "Oh, Jimmy." I pulled him to me. "I'll do everything I can to help you through this."

SEVENTEEN

It was raining hard when Gwen arrived by taxi the next morning, just as I was preparing to leave for work. She carried in a couple of bags of groceries and said she was going to do some cooking. She planned to have Jimmy help. I showed her where the liquor bottle was and, after wishing her a good day, rushed off to the clinic.

When I called around noon, Gwen said she had made sure Jimmy ate a good breakfast. "I even squeezed him some fresh orange juice. He needs to get some vitamins in him."

"I knew I could count on you."

"After breakfast I put him to work helping me with an apple pie. While he was peeling the apples, he told me Charlie talked with him about her family situation."

"He mentioned that to me yesterday on the phone." I didn't want to bring up the pregnancy and abortion. I figured Gwen and I could discuss that another time. "I think it's a good sign. It might help him open up about what happened—in Chicago."

"Yes, Charlie hardly ever talks about her family. Except with her psychotherapist. I'm sure she was trying to get Jimmy to confide in her."

"What's he up to now?"

"Since the rain let up, I sent him to the grocery for a few things. He told me that you don't shop at Hamlin's any more. I hadn't heard that story so he told me all about it and how you started shopping at Klaus Dietrich's place."

"Best to shop where we're welcome. You know, Dietrich's accent reminded me of those two fellows I met in Koblenz—remember I told you about Detlef and Heinz. When I told him that I'd made some friends in Germany after the War, Dietrich became very genial. Quite a contrast from the Hamlins."

"When Jimmy said he would hike over to Dietrich's shop, I figured the fresh air and exercise would do him good."

"I agree," I said, and told Gwen I would try to be home before 6.

After lunch I got a call from Gwen, her voice breathless with alarm. "It's Maude Williams next door. She's had an accident and she needs medical attention right away."

"Can you have her taken to the Lutheran Hospital?"

"I've already called St. Mary's."

"I should have guessed. I'm trying to placate Gowan and I just thought… Never mind. I'll get over to St. Mary's as soon as I can."

I arrived at the hospital soon after the ambulance. Jimmy and Gwen were there to greet me. After examining Maude Williams, my provisional diagnosis was that she had suffered a concussion and a fracture of the distal fibula. She required a few stitches for the cut on the side of her head and we had to shave a patch of her long gray hair. The broken ankle was confirmed by x-ray. It didn't require surgery but had to be splinted until the swelling went down. Later her leg would be put in a plaster cast. Since she was still confused and in pain, I decided we should admit her to the hospital overnight. Maude's inability to answer questions about what happened was part of what had led me to diagnose a concussion.

Once we had Maude settled, Gwen and Jimmy sat down with me in one of the hospital offices. I wanted to know all the details of how they had found her and what condition she was in before they called the ambulance.

"Gwen sent me to the grocery," Jimmy said, "and as I passed by Maude's place, I noticed that her front door was open. That struck me as odd, since it was cold outside, but I guessed that maybe she was airing out her front room. When I came back—and that must have been three quarters of an hour later—it's a far piece to Dietrich's grocery—the door was still standing open. So I started up the stairs to her porch. You know how steep it is through that rockery she has in front. Well, first, I saw her cat pacing back and forth up there. Then I saw a broom lying in the shrubs next to the steps. Finally I saw the blood. There was a trail of it up to her front door. And there she was inside on the wood floor, lying in a pool of blood."

"Well, it wasn't a pool of blood," Gwen said.

"It was a lot. You know I can't stand the sight of blood. But I didn't get sick this time. I guess it was the panic and the feeling that I needed to help out. So I went and got Gwen."

"She was unconscious when I got there," Gwen said, "but she was breathing. And that poor cat was right beside her—a pretty black and white thing."

"That's true," Jimmy said. "It seemed like the cat knew something bad had happened."

"I kept talking to Maude and stroking her arm. Eventually I got her to come around. She said she was okay and that she was able to move. So we turned her over to look at her head wound. That's when she complained about her ankle. I could see it was swollen. I had Jimmy help me clean her up and put pressure on the side of her head to stop the bleeding. Then I called St. Mary's."

"She didn't say anything about how she fell?"

"She couldn't seem to recall anything." Gwen answered.

"Maybe after a night's rest she'll remember," I said.

"After I called for the ambulance, I thought of the apple pie I left in the oven. I stayed with Maude, while Jimmy went over to rescue the pie."

"It burned, so I left it out on the cutting board and opened a window," Jimmy said.

"You both did a good job."

"When Gwen went to call the hospital," Jimmy said, "Maude told me she remembered the tomatoes we took her last summer. So she remembers that, at least."

"That's a good sign," I said and smiled at Jimmy.

He smiled back. "I was sure glad I could help her out."

As the three of us were leaving the hospital, there was a commotion at the Admitting Desk. Maude's two oldest daughters had arrived and were having a noisy argument over visitation. I recognized the society daughter, the eldest, from my brief introduction to her at the fancy wedding reception where I met Jimmy. The other one I remembered from delivering her baby, which she now held in her arms. She had her two other children in tow.

The nun at the desk motioned me over and I explained to the daughters that Mrs. Williams was to have no visitors until at least the next day. Her concussion required bed rest and complete calm. This elicited vociferous opposition from the daughters. The baby began to yowl. This gaggle of offspring was not what the doctor ordered. I remained firm that there were to be no visitors.

When I suggested that Maude could return home the next day, the daughters resumed squabbling over who would take their mother home.

I was surprised when Jimmy stepped forward and offered to drive Maude home from the hospital the next day. Both daughters objected, but Jimmy insisted. Besides, he contended, neither of them would be able to move Maude by themselves. Jimmy suggested that he and I could get Maude from the car into her house. Since I had already arranged to stay home with Jimmy the next day, I agreed. Jimmy said he would stay with her while she got settled. He even offered to make sure she got some dinner. The daughters put up tepid objections, but in the end their relief to be excused from this duty was obvious. I suggested that one of them might attend to their mother on Sunday.

"But no children." I looked at the crying baby. "Your mother needs peace and quiet." The society daughter volunteered to visit on Sunday.

As I drove Gwen and Jimmy back to the house, Gwen wanted to know more about Maude's family. "I hear she has a passel of grown children."

"That's right," I said, "most of them live in other parts of the country, except for the two oldest daughters. When her husband died, her daughters talked her into selling the farm and buying the house next door. She's lived there by herself for a few years."

"I suspected she was a farm girl," Gwen said.

Back home a burnt smell lingered in the kitchen. While Jimmy made tea, Gwen cut away the blackened upper crust of the apple pie, the bottom, she said, looked fine. She served it in bowls like a cobbler. As we ate, Gwen told us the ambulance driver recognized Jimmy as the piano player for the Diggs Monroe Jazz Orchestra. "Jimmy told him that the band had gone to Chicago and he no longer played with them, didn't you, honey?"

"Something like that," Jimmy said. He seemed preoccupied while we ate. As soon as he was finished, he said he wanted to go back over to Maude's to finish cleaning up her floor. "Besides, someone should look after that cat." He excused himself and left.

When we were alone, I asked Gwen if Jimmy had taken any alcohol during the day.

"I smelled liquor on his breath after he went home to check on the pie."

"I thought I smelled it on him when I met you at the hospital."

"We can't keep an eye on him every moment," Gwen said. "Besides he's sure been helpful today."

"He's taken quite an interest in Maude, hasn't he?" I commended Gwen on her quick action in the emergency.

"I just did what any nurse would have done. I'm sorry I didn't think about the Lutheran Hospital and your situation with Gowan and the Klan."

"I haven't had the courage to spring our tentative wedding date on Gowan yet. Have you had any second thoughts?"

Gwen took a sip of tea. "It does give me pause. And Charlie's more than a little nervous about it. Our engagement was a big step." She sat back in her chair. "What concerns me is that we will have to go through with it sooner or later. Marriage would be quite a disruption. Are you prepared for that?"

"Whew." I pushed away my half-finished bowl of pie. "I don't know. I keep thinking that's way off in the future."

"February is not so far off."

"It's not. Can we just postpone it again when the time comes?"

"But how long will that work?"

"You're right." I turned my tea cup in its saucer. "Now I worry about what Gowan might do, with Jimmy living here. I did start the process of getting hospital privileges with the Lutherans. I'm hoping that will put Gowan off. I'm concerned about my career."

"I know, my friend. I am too. We'll just have to take things as they come. You're under a lot of pressure," Gwen said. "If it will take some strain off you…well…." She smiled. "I keep thinking about how happy my mother was when I told her we were engaged."

I took her hand. "You're an angel."

I had a few things I needed to finish up at the clinic so I headed back, stopping to pick up the staff application papers at the Lutheran Hospital. I assumed Gowan would hear about this latest admission at St. Mary's, and I wanted to let it be known that I was moving ahead with the Lutherans. Plus, I wanted to spring my new wedding date on him. That would be two pieces of good news for him.

I was all ready to approach Gowan before I left work for my weekend with Jimmy. When I told Vivian I needed to speak with him, she said he was away doing a hysterectomy that afternoon at Dr. Adrian's private hospital. "You can talk with him tomorrow—oh, yes, I see you're off tomorrow. We've rescheduled all your Saturday appointments. Maybe next week."

I returned to my office. Yes, maybe next week. I imagined Gowan doing a hysterectomy at Adrian's place. Sneering at the American College of Surgeons, Adrian had refused inspections, thus allowing himself the freedom to set his own standards—and I'd not heard good things about the conditions there. Adrian had converted an old mansion into operating rooms. One of my biggest concerns was how antiseptic he kept the place. I was relieved that I didn't have to work in such a facility.

That night Jimmy and I had a quiet dinner at home. He seemed less troubled. I asked him how Maude's cat was faring. "I think it's lonely. When I went back over there, it kept rubbing against my legs, and when I sat down on the couch to rest after I finished cleaning, it jumped right up in my lap—I've still got black hair on my pants. I put out a dish of milk before I left."

"You're a good neighbor to clean up over there."

"I wanted to be sure that Gwen locked the front door before we left in the ambulance. I made sure the back door was unlocked, in case we needed to get back in," he said. "Did you know Maude has a piano?"

"I've never been inside her home. We just stood on the front porch and talked when we took her those tomatoes this summer."

"It's got a very nice tone."

"You played it?"

"The house was so quiet over there. So I sat down and tried it out. I guess I was just curious to see how it sounded."

I was surprised. He'd had so much difficulty approaching his piano at our house. "What did you play?"

"Just a little Bach piece. I think I played it last at that wedding reception where we met. I admit I've gotten a little rusty. But, you know…it felt good to play."

Later, as we were getting ready for bed, Jimmy took off his shoes and again inspected the soles with intense interest. He drifted off into one of his reveries. I waited for him to say something.

At last he said, "When I first found Maude, all I could see was Eric's body lying there wearing that white dress and lying in a pool of blood." He paused. "I guess I never told you that Eric performed in drag." He set his shoes on the floor. "But it was just Maude, in her pink housecoat. Gwen was right. It wasn't a pool of blood, just a small puddle. I was able to clean it up without much fuss. Except from the cat." He gave a soft chuckle. "It wouldn't leave me alone."

"You did a good thing today, helping Maude. Gwen appreciated your help."

"I don't know why it is, but I felt so relieved that Maude was okay—and that I was able to lend a hand." He smiled.

I sensed that the dark cloud that had been hanging over him might be starting to lift.

Jimmy slept that whole night through without any bad dreams.

EIGHTEEN

Maude was doing better than I expected by Saturday afternoon. When Jimmy started to remind her what happened, she said it had all come back to her.

"When I opened the door, there were three of them. I think I recognized one—that Rena Storm. They said that Lloyd Haskell's mother sent them over to recruit me—that she knew I'd want to join up."

Lloyd Haskell. I didn't expect to hear that name. Jimmy and I exchanged glances.

"Well, I know Naomi Haskell," Maude went on. "We've been friends since we were girls and she knows just how I feel about the LOTIEs. The Invisible Empire! My word."

A nurse came by to check on the patient. "Oh, hello, Dr. Holman. I didn't know you were here." She adjusted the ice pack on Maude's ankle and withdrew.

Maude continued. "I was sweeping when they rang my bell. They started on their spiel and I let them know in no uncertain terms that I didn't want to have anything to do with them. Then they got bossy, and it so nettled me that I took to swatting at them with my broom. I chased them down the porch steps and when we got to the stairs through the rock garden, that Rena woman turned and shoved me. That's where my memory gets a bit fuzzy. I remember trying to get up but my ankle hurt so. Then I saw the blood and reckoned I'd better get to the telephone. So I crawled as best I could back to the porch. The next I recall, you and that young woman were at my side."

More Klan trouble. That's all I needed.

"You seem to be doing much better today, Mrs. Williams."

"Please, call me Maude. We're neighbors. Yes, I'm feeling loads better."

"All right, Maude. You can go home today, if you are feeling up to it."

"I'd like that. Everyone here's been so nice, but it sure ain't home. Besides, I miss my kitty-cat. Poor Blossom."

Jimmy said he had been taking care of the cat. I told her that we had agreed to drive her home and that her eldest daughter would come on Sunday to look after her. Maude frowned at the mention of her daughter and said, "I guess I'm going to need some help for a while, huh?"

"Yes, and you should get as much rest as you can—to heal from that concussion. Peace and quiet is what you need. That's why I didn't want your family visiting you yesterday."

"Thank you for that. Those girls of mine can get on my nerves."

Jimmy and I took Maude home. The hospital staff had given her a pair of crutches, but she wasn't ready for them yet and they would be no help at all getting her up all those stairs to her front door. "I always use the back door anyway," she said.

So we drove up the incline of her driveway and took her in the back door. With Jimmy and me for support, she hopped on one leg, one step at a time, and we got her settled in her bed.

I had her lie flat with her leg elevated on extra pillows. Jimmy prepared an ice pack for Maude's ankle while I reminded her she would have to apply ice three times a day. Jimmy said he would look in on her after a while and we left her to rest with the cat curled up on the bed at her side.

A while later Jimmy went back over to check on the patient. I got to work filling out the forms for the Lutheran Hospital. I wanted to show Gowan that I was making an effort.

About an hour later when Jimmy returned, he said he'd shown Maude how to use the crutches to get around. "I told her she had to keep her weight off that leg. She didn't want to have to go down the hall to the bathroom so she had me get out an old chamber pot from the closet and I set it up on a stool by her bed. While we were chatting I asked how she knew the Haskells. Seems they had a place not far from her farm in Bayfield."

If Maude knew Lloyd's mother, then she had heard I was involved in caring for Lloyd's boy. I hoped that Naomi Haskell did not blame me for her grandson's death.

That evening after dinner Jimmy prepared a tray of food and took it over to Maude.

Sunday morning Jimmy was anxious to look in on Maude again and I went with him. We found her sitting in her living room looking out the front window. Maude's foot was propped up on a stool with an ice pack on her ankle, the crutches beside her chair. The cat was curled up on the couch. The house was quiet.

"How are you doing?" Jimmy asked.

"Oh, I'm feeling cranky," she said. "I still have a headache."

"That's to be expected," I said. "It should get better in a few days. Let me know if it doesn't. Where's your daughter?"

"She said she'll be here after church. I don't know where that girl got religion. Sure doesn't come from me. I've never been a church-goer. I guess it's all about society for her. Ain't about God, I'll tell you that."

I was glad to hear that Maude and I had that in common.

"May we sit down a minute?" Jimmy said.

"Make yourselves comfortable."

Jimmy sat on the sofa, and the cat looked up.

"How's the ankle feeling?" I asked. "I see you've fixed yourself up with another ice pack."

"I can't feel a thing. The darn thing is numb from the ice. I guess I should take it off now."

"Here, let me remove it." I set the pack on the stool beside her splinted leg and took a seat at the end of the sofa.

The cat rose and approached Jimmy, sniffing. Jimmy reached out and petted the black fur on its back, then scratched the white under its chin. The cat settled in his lap.

"Oh, Blossom," Maude said. "Poor old cat."

"Nice kitty," he said as he stroked its back. "It looks like it's wearing a tuxedo. How old is it?"

"Oh, golly, she's over ten now. I brought her up from the farm with me. I'd have brought my dog, but I don't think people have any business keeping dogs in town. They need to be able to run free. So I left him on the farm—after my husband died."

"I'm sorry," Jimmy said.

"Oh, don't waste any pity on my husband. He was a miserable bastard. And anyway, I was tired of trying to keep that farm going. I couldn't run the place by myself. My oldest son came up from California and tried to run it for a while, but he just wasn't cut out for it."

Blossom began to purr loudly.

"I grew up on an orchard over by Hood River," Jimmy said. "I guess my brothers will keep the place going after my father gets too old. I'm not cut out for it either."

"What kind of work do you do?"

Jimmy paused. "Well…I'm a musician. I play the piano." Jimmy left off petting the cat and wiggled his fingers over an imaginary keyboard. "But I'm out of work right now." He paused. "So I'm glad to look in on you or help out around the place, if you'd like."

"Aren't you looking for work? There must be a lot of opportunities for a young fella like you."

"I haven't been well lately. I'm still recuperating from an illness. Maybe in a week or so, I'll be up to looking for work."

"You haven't got the consumption, do you?"

"Oh, no, nothing like that. I've had a cold. And I've been kind of run-down. But I'm a lot better, really."

Maude regarded Jimmy while he stroked the cat. "Well, Blossom seems to have taken to you."

"She's a real friendly cat."

Blossom was still purring to beat the band.

"You seem to be getting around with the crutches," I said

"They're a damned nuisance."

"You'll get the hang of it in no time," Jimmy said. "Here, let me show you." When he moved Blossom aside, she stood up and gave him a look of disdain before she settled back onto the sofa. Jimmy grabbed the crutches from their place next to Maude's chair and gave a demonstration.

"You're pretty good at that," Maude said.

"I broke my leg when I was in high school," he explained. "I was on crutches for six months." He swung back across the room and turned to her. "Come on. Give it a try."

"Not now. I'm okay" she grumbled. "I'll manage. Why don't you play me something on the piano?"

Jimmy hesitated, searching for an excuse. "Oh, not right now. Maybe some other time."

"Humph," she replied. "What kind of a musician are you?"

Jimmy looked surprised.

"My dad was a fiddle player," Maude said. "He played in his spare time. You didn't have to do any cajoling to talk him into picking up the bow." She fixed her gaze on Jimmy daring him to play. I sensed that if he did not rise to her challenge, she might write him off as a fraud. Jimmy looked a bit sheepish and gave in. I was glad to see that Maude's approval seemed important to him.

He laid the crutches beside her chair and went to the piano. After a hesitation, he sat down and lifted the lid. The cat raised her head and looked around. Jimmy took a deep breath and began a Bach piece. As he played, curiosity got the best of her, and Blossom went to the arm of the sofa and peered over at Jimmy's hands rippling over the keys. She settled into a sitting position, watching, her black tail twitching as if in time to the beat. Jimmy seemed to be lost in the music.

As the last notes faded into silence, Maude's applause brought Jimmy back to the present.

"Well, you are a musician," she exclaimed. "Even Blossom thinks so. Can you play something not so high brow, if you know what I mean?"

Jimmy launched into a lively rendition of the French song Charlie had just taught him, accompanying his playing by singing a chorus. When he finished, Maude asked what the piece was, and Jimmy told her how he'd learned it.

"How about something popular?"

Jimmy froze. "Well…" He seemed to be wavering. The cat settled on the back of the sofa. "Okay," Jimmy said, searching out chords on the keyboard and began a tune that I remembered he used to do with Diggs and the band. Maude got a kick out of that and encouraged Jimmy to play another. Blossom remained on the sofa back, eyeing every movement of Jimmy's fingers.

Jimmy's playing was interrupted by the arrival of the society daughter. After chatting a bit, I prepared to go. Jimmy seemed reluctant to leave Maude, but he too said goodbye and we left.

Walking back home, we heard a cawing overhead as a handful of crows were harrying a hawk. They swooped and dove, threatening their territorial rival. The hawk dodged, trying to evade them. After a time the crows escorted the hawk across the gray field of the November sky out of the neighborhood, disappearing into the distance.

NINETEEN

Early the following week two more women came to see me about birth control. One was married and said Charlie had referred her to me, but the other one was not married and said she had heard about me from a friend. I handled the cases as I had earlier ones and discreetly prescribed the requested devices.

Around the middle of the week, I had completed the paperwork for the Lutheran Hospital but still needed a letter of recommendation. Gowan was the logical choice—he had suggested he would write one. Although my apprehension made me hesitant to approach him, I decided I had to stop putting it off. We were both at Vivian's reception desk between appointments, so I invited him into my office to talk. The location was a strategic decision. This seemed to catch Gowan off guard and I was pleased.

"I have some good news for you," I said as I sat down behind my desk. "I'll get right to the point. My fiancée and I have decided to schedule our wedding in mid-February."

He didn't react with the enthusiasm I had anticipated. After a pause he said, "It's disappointing that you will not be joining our grand marriage ceremony later in the month."

"Of course. Well, Gwen—Miss Cook feels that there are too many arrangements to be made and we couldn't be ready by then. Family, you know. Both our parents live so far away."

"This is another missed opportunity for you, Holman."

I avoided his eyes. The conversation was not going the way I planned. I decided to change the subject.

"By the way, I've got my application here for hospital privileges with the Lutherans." I indicated the packet of papers on my desk. "It says I'll need a letter of recommendation. You suggested you would be happy to provide one."

Gowan neither smiled as I expected nor did he seem disapproving. He hesitated, expressionless, seeming to weigh some private options.

"That can be arranged…" He broke off. It sounded like he was dangling this favor as bait.

"You said they would be glad to have me on staff." I picked up a fountain pen and began toying with it. "I've worked with Dr. Ferguson."

"That would be a decided advantage for our clinic, as I've made clear. And if you want to work at Iverson's new hospital, you should establish a working relationship with the present Lutheran Hospital. But we don't want you sending any more patients to the Catholics."

"Is there anything standing in the way of a recommendation?"

"The problem is that you've been dispensing birth control devices."

I was left open-mouthed, but I scrambled to regain my composure. Before I could speak Gowan said, "I heard Vivian talking with one of the young women." He paused. "So I looked through your patient records. I'm beginning to appreciate your urging us to write things down."

All I could do was stare back at him. As I twisted the pen in my hands, I struggled to formulate a response. "It is the outcomes that are the most important aspect of medical records." This was a lame remark, but the best I could do in the moment.

"Let me recommend a different outcome. We need to produce more native white babies and these Margaret Sanger methods are diminishing our numbers. The Gowan clinic does not condone these techniques. Now if older women wish to prevent pregnancies, which is understandable, particularly if they already have large families, we should be sending them to Dr. Adrian for hysterectomies. It's a safe and legitimate operation. And I assure you that Dr. Adrian will make it worth your while."

We stared at each other for what seemed like an eon. Fee splitting is what the American College of Surgeons called it. I had taken an oath to renounce the practice. And aside from that there were my qualms about the conditions at Adrian's hospital.

Seeing no way out, I resolved to be conciliatory. I tossed the pen down on my desk.

"I can see your logic there," I said, though I didn't. "Under these circumstances I must agree with you about these Margaret Sanger methods, as you call them." I understood the circumstances, but I didn't agree. "I suppose my best move would be to tell my patients that we do not offer such services at this clinic." In my haste to avoid a discussion about the medical necessity of hysterectomies and fee splitting, and in the process save my career, I was willing to compromise.

Gowan smiled and nodded. "I thought you would see things our way," Gowan said as he stood. "I guess I can draft a letter for the Lutheran Hospital. I should let you get back to work now."

TWENTY

Jimmy had been spending his days looking after Maude. Over dinner that evening he told me that she was making good progress. It seemed that he was too.

Later that night the doorbell rang just as Jimmy and I were about to turn in. I sensed some uneasiness on his part.

"If it were Maude, she would have phoned," he said, putting down his toothbrush.

"I'll see to it," I said.

By the time I made my way down the hall to the beveled glass of the front door, there was no one standing under the porch light. At the curb a man got into the driver's side of a taxi and it pulled away down the street.

I swung open the door. At the top of the porch steps lay the body of a blond male.

"What the hell—" I sprang into action. Kneeling beside him, I placed my hand on his back. He was breathing. Turning him over as gently as possible, I recognized Jerry the Fairy. The smell of his violet perfume brought back the memory of our quick sexual encounter. Pioneer Park one night a few years before. His effeminate gestures. My ambivalent feelings of lust and revulsion.

Jerry's face was bruised and bloodied. His hair was bleached, as before, but there were deep gashes on his scalp and blood stained his white shirt and red tie. His suit was splotched with mud. The wounds were crusty where the blood had begun to dry, so it had been a while since the injuries. I guessed that the cabby helped Jerry to the porch and rang our doorbell. He must have been too scared to wait around.

Jimmy came to the door and froze as he took in the situation.

"Quick," I called to him through the open door. "Get me a wet towel."

He hesitated.

"Hurry," I said.

I felt Jerry's wrist and found his pulse strong and regular.

Jimmy returned and I applied the towel to Jerry's face and tried to clean away some of the blood. He began to moan but didn't regain consciousness. I heard a retching sound and turned to see Jimmy vomiting over the side of the porch.

"Are you all right?" I asked. I didn't need a second patient right then.

Jimmy spat and cleared his throat. "I'm okay. It's just the blood. I'll be all right."

"I need to get him to the hospital. He may have broken bones or internal injuries. Do you feel up to helping me? We have to get him into the car."

"I can help."

"Okay. Bring me a blanket from the hall closet."

While Jimmy went into the house, I backed the Ford out of the garage and down to the side of the porch. Jimmy brought the blanket and we laid it out next to Jerry's body. As we rocked him back and forth to work the blanket under him, Jimmy tried to avert his eyes from the bloody face.

"Now let's slide him down to the end of the porch," I said.

"Do you know this fellow?" Jimmy said as we tugged at the blanket.

"It's a long story, but yes I know him. I'll tell you about it later."

When we got to the end of the porch, Jerry began to groan. His eyes fluttered open.

"Jerry, it's Dr. Holman. We're going to take you to the hospital."

"Hey, Doc," he croaked and attempted a wry smile before letting out a small whimper.

"Can you stand long enough for us to get you into the car?"

"Maybe." He made an effort to raise his head. "Oof." He fell back. "I'll try."

"Take it easy. We'll lift you." We were able to help him stand, but he was heavier than I thought.

He groaned several times as we wrestled him down the porch steps and into the front of the Ford. When we lowered him into the seat, he let out a little cry and winced. I wrapped the blanket around him.

"Do you want to come with us?" I asked Jimmy as I opened the car door to get in.

"I'm still feeling kind of sick." He looked pale.

"Okay. Take care of yourself."

Jerry was quiet as I drove. He slumped against my shoulder. I wasn't sure if he was out cold or if he was just trying to get close to me. I tried to remember where I had seen Jerry since our fling in the bushes. There was Dixon Calder's private fairy party. And the haberdashery where Jerry was clerking. There Dr. Bleeker had addressed me as Dr. Holman and Jerry must have noticed. When he took Bleeker's check in payment for his purchase, Jerry would have known my colleague's name too. It wouldn't have taken much for him to learn where I practiced and where I lived. Now finding himself in trouble, he must have figured he was safer to have the taxi bring him to me than to a hospital. I was certain he had plenty of reasons not to contact the police.

I would have taken Jerry to the Lutheran Hospital, but I kept remembering Gowan's connections with them and my overhearing Bateson there talking with Dr. Ferguson. Between the Klan and the police, I reasoned that Jerry might be better off with the Catholics. At St. Mary's I put Jerry in the care of the doctor on night duty. I told him what little I knew and said I would come in the next day. I was anxious to get back to Jimmy.

Once home, I found him waiting up for me, holding a small

glass of gin. That he was neither drunk nor passed out, I counted as a sign of progress.

The next morning I went to St. Mary's to see Jerry.

If I had run into him on the street, I would have ignored him or tried to avoid him, but I was unassailable here, a physician in my own territory and a man supposedly engaged to be married. While my antipathy toward Jerry made me want to keep my distance, I was concerned for him, considering his present condition, which appeared serious. Besides I had to find out how he ended up on my front porch.

He must have seen me enter the ward and he stared at me as I approached his bed.

He wore a plaster cast on one arm and a bandage on his head that covered one eye. The unbandaged eye was made conspicuous by his tweezed eyebrow. The part of his head not covered with gauze displayed the bleached blond hair with dark roots beginning to show. Bruises discolored his face.

"I guess introductions aren't necessary," I said. "We already know each other."

"Yes, biblically," Jerry said. His speech was distorted by the injuries around his mouth. His lips were swollen.

There was no reply I could make to this. "Please, could we talk quietly?"

His lip curled. "Of course."

I pulled a chair up close to his bed.

"That same handsome mug. Just as I remembered." His tone lowered. "I remember some other things, too." He gave me a cheeky glance. His voice had a distinctive timbre that some would think of as effeminate and its cadence had a faint lilt to it.

"You look like you've been through the wringer. Was it an auto accident?"

"I got in a fight with my girlfriend."

"You're joking with me."

"No, I'm teasing you. You want the real story? Or the one the cops told?"

"Are you in trouble with the law?"

"Well, yes and no. Shall I tell you about it?"

"That's why I'm here."

"I was at this all-night diner, and these two gents come in. I think one of them is real cute and I can't keep my eyes off him. After a while I go in to use the washroom. I'm standing at the mirror combing my hair when the cutie walks in. I ogle him in the mirror and he looks me right back with those pretty green eyes. I think for a minute that maybe he's interested."

He paused as one of the sisters passed by.

"So while he's standing at the urinal pissing, he says to me, 'What is it with you? You some kind of sissy-girl cocksucker?' I look at him and say, 'Yeah, you big handsome brute, since you've got it out, I'll give it a lick. And you can return the favor by sucking my cock. Or would you rather kiss my ass?' Then I walk out. I pay my ticket at the cash register and leave the diner."

Jerry adjusted his body in the bed and groaned. He waited for the pain to subside and he went on.

"Well, the two gentlemen follow me out. Before I know what's up, they run over and grab me and start beating the shit out of me. I catch sight of a copper down the street and I start screaming, 'Help, police.' Well, the copper comes over and joins in with them, taking turns punching me while one of them holds me from behind. After a while they let me go and I fall to the ground. Then cutie-pie starts kicking me. That's when the copper says, 'Hold off, Bateson. You don't want a dead body on your hands.' And Bateson's buddy says, 'That's enough, Steve.'"

I felt myself recoil.

"So they back off and leave me lying there. 'What was he up to?' the copper asks him, and as they walk away, I hear Bateson say, 'Didn't you see that, Officer Franklin? The little cocksucker jumped me and tried to steal my wallet.' And the officer asks, 'Shall

I arrest him?' And Bateson's buddy says, 'Aw, leave him alone. I think we taught him a lesson.'" Jerry paused to catch his breath.

Good God, not Bateson. Something tightened inside me.

"Well, I lay there for a long time and must have passed out, because the next thing I know, there's some old codger bending over me. He asks if I need help and I tell him to get me a cab."

"So you had the taxi bring you to my house? I saw it pull away. How did you know my address?"

He gave me a coy look. "I looked you up—after you and your buddy, that other doctor, came into that men's shop. I put your address in my wallet. Just in case I ever needed a doctor. I guess it paid off." He coughed and his face twisted with pain. He lay back and closed his eyes until it passed. "Later on, the proprietor accused me of stealing and gave me the sack. It was just an excuse to get rid of me. I never took anything from that shop."

"Which doctor is attending you?" I asked.

"Dr. Richards. A bit of a fuddy duddy."

"He's a very good physician. Rest assured, you're in good hands. What has he told you about your injuries?"

"As you can see, I've got cuts and bruises to the face and head—and some stitches you can't see. I guess there's quite a shiner under this bandage. He says the eye will be okay. At least a couple of broken bones. It hurts when I breathe."

I reached for the chart at the end of the bed and leafed through it. "A fractured ulna—that explains the cast. And a rib fracture… hematuria, secondary to renal bruising. Brother, they really worked you over, didn't they?"

Jerry looked away. "Yeah, Doc. You might say that."

"Look, Jerry. I'm sorry. Is there anything that I can do to help?"

"Sure, Doc," Jerry turned back to me. "Maybe you can cure me of this unnatural disease. Maybe you can teach me to act like you do. Teach me to come on like a real he-man."

"Listen—" I wanted to tell him things were not so rosy for me, either. But he went on.

"Do you think it's easy for me, with this voice, with this face?

Walking the way I do, moving the way I do? I used to try to hide it, but I couldn't. It's just me. But you, you can pass. I can't. And now I've lost my job and can't pay my hospital bills. What am I supposed to do?"

I looked down at my hands. "There are people here at the hospital who can help you cover your hospital bills—they handle charity cases. And they have some social workers here who may be able to help you find a job."

"Oh, yes. The Catholic nuns?" He laughed, which caused him to wince.

"There are lay people you can talk to. If you are willing to try and work with them."

He turned his face away and was silent.

"Please, hear me out."

He didn't look at me.

"If you—or any of your friends—ever need a doctor, I'll be happy to see you. If you're broke, I'm willing to work for nothing." I took out a business card and held it out.

He didn't move.

"I'll be fair and honest with you. And discreet."

Jerry remained silent.

I stood. "I'll leave my card on the table next to your bed here."

As he adjusted the position of his broken arm, he heaved a sigh. I placed my hand on his shoulder.

At last he turned to face me. "Thank you, Doc."

All the way to the office, Jerry's story about Bateson gnawed at me. My feelings about Bateson intensified, a combination of dread and alarm, leaving me unnerved. Could I count on my association with Gowan to shield me from any possible encounter with such a man? When I saw Gowan in the reception area, I had to make an effort to imagine him as a good and decent person separate from Bateson and the Invisible Empire—even a safeguard against all that. It took a moment before I could smile and say hello. Afterwards I hoped he hadn't noticed my preoccupation.

Throughout the day I fretted about Jerry. I understood the way he felt and I couldn't blame him. But I didn't know how to say the right words to help heal the wounds life had dealt him, to help heal his self-loathing. We humans are so deeply flawed, except perhaps for a handful of saints. And I was not one of them. Gwen was right, I couldn't heal everyone.

TWENTY-ONE

That afternoon one of my birth control patients came in to pick up her pessary. She was a plain-looking woman whose boyfriend, she said, was very insistent. I had ordered a number of sponges and pessaries, so I was prepared to accommodate her. But the conversation I'd had with Gowan gave me pause.

When I told the woman that our clinic was revising its policy on providing birth control, she looked troubled.

"But I must have something today. I've made plans for the weekend and…" She broke off. Her fingers twisted the handkerchief in her lap.

"Of course. I have the pessary you requested plus the douching materials you'll need. What I mean is, in the future, I won't be able to help you."

"But what if the fit isn't right. I've heard that's important."

"I'll examine you today to make sure those concerns are addressed. And I'll give you complete instructions."

"And going forward? What if there are problems—or complications?"

"Mrs. Sanger's pamphlet explains everything clearly. She's quite adamant that women don't need medical assistance to use these techniques."

"But…but I don't feel competent on my own. I don't have any close girlfriends to help me." Her eyes darted about the room in a panic. "Charlie promised you could provide help and I thought you would be available for support. You must understand how difficult this is for me."

I wished she hadn't brought up Charlie's referral. Now I felt doubly obligated.

Tears welled in her eyes. "I can't go through this again with another doctor. You are the third physician I've seen—the others refused to help me. They all made me feel so ashamed—so dirty."

I couldn't help feeling for her, and it did not sit well with me to leave her on her own.

"I'll tell you what. Let me give you my home phone." I took one of my business cards and wrote my number on the back. "If you have any trouble, you can call me in the evenings." She took the card. "But you must not count on the Gowan clinic for these matters."

"Thank you. Oh, thank you, Dr. Holman."

I had been forced to decide on the spot that I still bore a responsibility in these matters. My spur-of-the-moment solution seemed reasonable, but straight away I had qualms about mixing my professional and home life.

"If you have any questions after you've looked through the pamphlet, don't hesitate to give me a call. But I think you'll find it very easy to follow."

We could hear a muttering of voices in the waiting room. I recognized Gowan's voice as he was seeing a patient out.

I lowered my voice. "You must keep this on the quiet, however. You see, the clinic has recently had some trouble—I'm sure you understand."

She nodded.

I saw that I would have to deal in a similar manner with the other women who had come to me for birth control. I didn't have the stomach for abandoning any of them. I needed a plan.

My meeting with this patient troubled me through the afternoon and continued to disturb me into the evening. I tried to keep Jimmy from noticing, but he seemed to know I had something on my mind.

As he was laying kindling in the fireplace after dinner, he said, "You're worried." He lit a match. "Is it the Klan?"

"Not exactly. I don't want to bother you with it."

"I've been a bother for you since I came back to town."

"No. You mustn't say that."

"Well, I wasn't much help last night with that fellow on the front porch. How is he doing?"

"You helped me get him into the car."

"I was glad to help—never mind that I got sick. Is he okay?"

"He'll be all right. They sure worked him over, though."

"Is that what you are worried about?"

There was plenty about Jerry's case to worry me—Bateson in particular—but I didn't want to go into all that with Jimmy. Not right then.

"It's another matter." I told him about Charlie's birth control referrals and Gowan's demands that I stop seeing them. "I have to come up with a way to deal with the situation. Today I gave one woman my home phone number. I guess you'll need to know about it. I suggested she call me here in the evenings if she has any problems. You may end up taking a call."

"I don't see any problem with that."

The fire popped as Jimmy put a small log on.

"It's a delicate matter. We have to be discreet. Not only do I need to keep word from getting around to the general public, but the ladies need to keep these matters private."

"What if you come up with some kind of code word? Like they do at some of the speakeasies."

"That's not a bad idea."

"Something like—I don't know—they want to buy some race records. You know, negro jazz."

"Brilliant."

"Besides, that fella came here to your place last night. No reason these women can't come here."

I frowned at the memory of Jerry's body on the porch. But

Jimmy's idea sounded workable.

"I suppose. But that wouldn't bother you—if I saw patients here in the evenings?"

"Not at all. I'll just go upstairs."

"We would need to limit the number of visitors, I suppose. Too much activity would attract attention." The plan was beginning to seem feasible.

"I could take phone messages for you if you aren't here. We could keep a calendar next to the telephone."

I felt gratitude for his suggestions and his willingness to help. "Yes, no more than two or three visits a week—after 9 when Joe Locke has gone home. I think this might work." The log on the fire crackled. "Thanks for helping me think this through."

"Yeah, Maude doesn't like to admit that she needs help, either." He pressed a friendly fist to my shoulder.

The next morning the idea of a home office kept circling around in my brain. As the plan took shape, I realized I would need an exam table. Dr. Rosenfeld, the gynecologist I'd met at Gowan's recruiting meeting, came to mind. If he was setting up a practice, he would know a good medical supplier. My crowded little office in one of the two downstairs bedrooms was not going to work for seeing patients. I had it in my mind that the best place to do examinations would be in the living room and I wondered if I could get my hands on some kind of a folding table so I could stow it away when I was not using the room for work.

When I got Rosenfeld on the phone, his voice sounded frazzled. I told him I was looking for a supplier of medical furniture and his tone brightened.

"You caught me at just the right time. I have an office full of furniture I need to sell off."

"What do you mean?"

"So you haven't heard."

"Heard what?"

"I'm leaving town. My wife and I are moving back East."

This was unexpected. "How can this be?"

"We were recently greeted by a welcoming committee. The Invisible Empire burned a cross in our front yard last week. I can't raise my little girl in such an environment."

A jittery feeling fluttered in my stomach. "Good Lord. I don't know what to say."

"I know there are good people in this town, even a great community of Jews, but my wife grew up in Russia and experienced pogroms as a child. She will not have our family live with this kind of threat."

"I am so sorry to hear this."

"We don't blame you, Dr. Holman. You showed me a kindness at that meeting where we met. But this isn't why you called. So let's talk business. You are setting up a clinic?"

"Not exactly." I told him what I was looking for and he seemed to know just what I needed.

"I used a folding exam table when I first got here, but I replaced it with a modern mechanical one. I will be happy to sell the new one to you. It has all the latest features. I can make you a good deal on it."

"No, I need something that I can fold up and put out of the way. I'll be using it in my home. Just for private charity cases. Is your folding table for sale?"

"Of course. All the furnishings must go."

I made an appointment to come by his office that afternoon and talk things over. When I drove home, I had Rosenfeld's folding exam table in the back of the Ford.

Saturday the clinic was busier than usual and at the end of the day, I was looking forward to spending a quiet Sunday with Jimmy. Before I left my office, I gathered up all the birth control materials I had ordered, including an assortment of condoms, and took them home.

During the week, Jimmy had spent much of his time with Maude. He seemed in better spirits than I'd seen since his return. An old sparkle had returned to his eyes. During our evening meals, he was even more talkative than when Gwen and Charlie were around.

That night as we got into bed, I took out a package of the condoms and handed it to him. "If you feel the urge, we can use these until we're sure there is no danger of infection."

He examined the package with a puzzled expression and laughed. That same sparkle appeared in his eye. "Golly, Dr. Holman, you'll have to instruct me in the proper use of these devices."

"Well, first off, let me examine your equipment," I said as I folded back the bed covers. That night Jimmy seemed more open to me, more relaxed and comfortable in his body than before he left for Chicago. As his fingers played over me, it felt as if he was learning to read on my skin the pleasures and desires he had come to terms with in Chicago.

TWENTY-TWO

Sunday morning, Jimmy and I woke up next to each other. I had been watching him sleep and he appeared to be dreaming, murmuring and twitching before he awoke with a start. He was quiet for a while before he smiled and said good morning.

"I'm glad to see you returning to your old self," I said.

Jimmy got a faraway look in his eye. "Return. Re-turn. I wonder if that is what she meant."

"What? What who meant?"

"Now I remember," he said.

"Remember what?"

"The dream," Jimmy said and his gaze wandered to some faraway place. "It was in that hotel room...after Danny Felton... that dream was so vivid. How could I forget it? If I could forget a dream that vivid, then maybe all these things I have trouble remembering from Chicago are just more stuff that I dreamed up."

"Can you tell me about it?" I said.

His brow furrowed with concentration "It was a twilight place. Or a dim underground cavern. I was kneeling, naked, beside a stream or a river. I was looking into the dark water and a plume of blood rose to the surface and flowed off down the stream like a ribbon of red. Then a white body floated to the surface of the water. It was a pregnant woman, there in the river. She was dead. Her belly floated just above the surface of the water. She had long blonde hair spread out around her head in that dark water, but I didn't recognize her face. The ribbon of blood on the water was flowing out from between her legs."

Closing his eyes he brought a hand up to his mouth as he focused his attention. "She began to float away. I reached into the water to keep her from drifting off. I took hold of her hand and held on tight. Just under the water, I could see that she had a wedding band on her finger. I knew that she was dead, but she looked up at me and she began to sing. They were the lyrics from that recording that Mary Hall gave me:

> *"It's right here for you*
> *If you don't get it,*
> *'Tain't no fault of mine."*

He shook his head from side to side although the movement was barely perceptible.

"But the current was too strong and it carried her away and her hand slipped from my fingers. I pulled back my hand and there was a ring now around the third finger of my left hand. When I looked closer, I saw that it was a severed foreskin…with a dark mole on it—like a black jewel in a signet ring. And then, I don't know why, but I started to cry."

He paused before he went on. "As the woman's body drifted away, she changed into an old hag. She called out to me, 'Re-member. Re-turn. Re-turn.' Then she turned away and disappeared into the dark current." He fell silent.

I stroked his shoulder. "Well," I said, "I'm not an interpreter of dreams like Dr. Freud, but I'm happy that you returned to me. I wasn't sure you would. I was prepared to follow you to Chicago if I had to. But you made it back from there to here. Back home to me."

Jimmy returned to the present and his eyes focused on mine. I smoothed back his hair. He buried his face in my shoulder and held me close.

After we showered together, I made breakfast for us. Later we got out the Halma set. As we played, I suggested that we take a Sunday drive up toward Mt. Hood. "We could go for a short hike. Alder Lake is a beautiful spot." Maybe I was thinking of our first fishing trip together, or maybe I was just needing a change of scene, but I thought it would do Jimmy good to get away from the city and out into the countryside.

Jimmy agreed and we both dressed in warm clothes. He seemed preoccupied as we got out gloves and coats. While we prepared a small picnic lunch, Jimmy seemed unaware that he was humming a tune under his breath.

It was mid-morning when I settled into the driver's seat and Jimmy hesitated as he was opening the passenger door. "Just a minute," he said and went back into the house, returning a minute later. "Sorry. I forgot something," he said.

The weather was cloudy and wet, but the higher we drove, the more it cleared off. By the time we got to the lake, it was clear and sunny but cold, with a stiff breeze. The mountain was covered in white, but we were far below the snow line. I drove off the road into a wild meadow and parked the car. The scene looked just like the picture postcards with the mountain reflecting in the lake's surface.

"Gwen first brought me here," I said, "back when we were both in training. Before the War."

We headed out toward the water's edge. "There used to be a good footpath around the lake," I said making my way through the tall grass. We soon stumbled upon the trail and began walking.

The trail led into a wooded area where we were surrounded by a stretch of naked alders. As we emerged from the trees onto a footbridge over the creek that flowed out of the lower end of the lake, a vista opened out toward the mountain, its image doubled in the surface of the lake surrounded by a brilliant blue sky.

"It's easy to see why the native Indian tribes considered the mountain sacred," I said.

Jimmy nodded.

As we stood admiring the view, Jimmy took off his glove and dug into a pocket. He took out the set of keys that I'd seen on his bedside table. Keys from Chicago. He held them in the palm of his hand for a few moments, looking down at them. Two projections fitted to two specific receptors. Two keys mated to two particular locks.

He reeled back and hurled the keys as far as he could toward the middle of the lake. A small splash gleamed in the distant water and a circular ripple radiated out.

He sensed my curiosity.

"Just cleansing myself of a bad memory," he said.

We walked on. The trail passed between the lake and a stretch of evergreens. Jimmy began to hum under his breath as we walked, and soon I heard him singing lyrics to himself.

"I went to see the doctor today
To see what he had to say.
Something must be wrong,
I'm worried all day long.
He said I had a love attack.
I must get my baby back.
He said to do it right away.
This is what he had to say:
'You need some lovin' when you feel sad.
You need some lovin' to make you real glad.
You need some lovin' when you feel blue..."

Jimmy caught himself and broke off. I was in the lead and I stopped and turned around. Jimmy glanced at me and looked away.

"I keep hearing you sing that song."

He stood looking out at the lake. "That's the song I was playing when Eric was killed."

"Go ahead and sing it for me."

He hesitated, glancing up at me and back out to the lake. "That was just about all of it."

"Sing another, then."

Jimmy thought for a moment. "Okay. Here's one I don't think you've heard. The band was just working this one up before we left."

I sat down on a large log next to the path to listen and he began to sing.

> *"Blues on my mind and blues all around my head.*
> *Blues on my mind and blues all around my head.*
> *I dreamed last night*
> > *that the man that I love was dead.*
>
> *I went to the graveyard, fell down on my knees.*
> *I went to the graveyard, fell down on my knees.*
> *And I asked the graveyard digger*
> > *to give me back my real good man, please."*

As Jimmy sang, the wind subsided, and the whispering evergreens nearby became silent, as if to better hear his song.

> *"The gravedigger looked me in the eye.*
> *The gravedigger looked me in the eye.*
> *Said, "I'm sorry, lady,*
> > *but your man has said his last good-bye."*

A chipmunk scampered up onto a rock and sat watching us.

> *"I wrung my hands, and I wanted to scream.*
> *I wrung my hands, and I wanted to scream.*
> *But when I woke up,*
> > *I found it was only a dream."*

Jimmy gave a little laugh. "I wish it *was* just a dream." He paused and laughed again. "That song got us a free ride in a taxi one night."

"Tell me about it," I said.

Jimmy sat down beside me and told the story of the taxi ride to the brothel. He gazed out over the water as he talked.

When he finished, I said, "What happened next?"

Jimmy hesitated so long I wasn't sure he would go on. "So much happened I can't tell you all of it." But he began by telling me that he met Danny Felton at the brothel. Felton offered him a job playing piano at a club. He told me about meeting Eric Halsey at a drag ball at the club and later his falling out with Diggs and the band. He talked about the turf war between the Irish and the Italian gangs and Felton's massacre of the Irish to keep control of Eric's club. "That's when I was playing that song on the piano— when Felton shot Eric. He thought Eric and his friends were a threat to him. I guess I can see why he thought that, but they just wanted to keep control of their club—and get a better deal on the booze. Felton could have killed me, too, but instead he told me to get out of town. So I came back to Oregon."

It was the barest summary but I could begin to piece together the story. It would be a long time before Jimmy filled in many of the details. Still I was grateful that he was beginning to get the story off his chest.

When he finished, we sat without speaking. The wind increased, raising ripples across the water.

"Do you think you are in any danger?" I asked.

Jimmy picked up some pebbles and began tossing them into the lake. "I'm banking on the fact that Chicago is a long way off."

"Would Felton come after you?"

He started to pitch another stone and paused to look at me. "Why would he do that?"

"It sounds like you were witness to a murder."

Jimmy's brow furrowed as an uneasy look came into his eyes. "I never thought of it like that before."

I hadn't intended to frighten him. "Well, you're right. Chicago is a world away. And I'm sure Felton has other fish to fry."

"I don't know." He tossed another pebble. "I hope so."

A distant screech drew our attention skyward. A large bird of prey, wings outstretched, hovered far above. We watched as it circled and glided off into the distance.

Jimmy threw his last few pebbles. "You know this might be a good place to come fishing sometime," he said.

I was glad he had changed the subject. "We should come back here again," I said. "Maybe in the summer—with Gwen and Charlie."

"We should. Come on," he said. "Let's walk before we freeze to death."

When we got home, Jimmy went over to check on Maude. Later he came back and built a fire on our hearth, and he didn't take a drink all that evening.

TWENTY-THREE

Monday, I left Jimmy home alone while I went to work. When I got home after work, he told me he'd spent most of the day at Maude's. I found no evidence that he'd had any alcohol, and my lingering concerns about his drinking began to subside.

I had scheduled my first home visit for that evening with a Mrs. Kemper. Over the telephone she sounded strong-minded. After dinner was over and Joe Locke had gone home, I closed the dining room doors. Jimmy helped me set up the new exam table before he disappeared upstairs.

Madeline Kemper showed up at 9 on the dot. She carried herself well and sat bolt upright as we talked in the living room. Her husband was a banker and they had three children who were proving to be a handful. She had a college education and had advocated for women's suffrage before the 19th Amendment passed. She was now an officer in a women's club and didn't want any more children making demands on her time. When I explained her options, she requested a pessary. She had done her research and knew what she wanted. I examined her and demonstrated the proper use of the device, which seemed unnecessary—Mrs. Kemper appeared quite knowledgeable and comfortable with her anatomy.

After she left, I folded up the table and stowed it away in a closet. So far, so good for my home office plan.

"Is this Dr. Holman?" the man's voice demanded.

Vivian had put the call through shortly before noon the next day, just as I was looking forward to my lunch break.

"Speaking," I said.

"This is Madeline Kemper's husband." He paused to let the name sink in. It didn't sound as if he was making a pleasant social call. "I found your card in my wife's purse. Have you been seeing her?"

"Yes, Mrs. Kemper had some medical matters she wanted my advice on."

"Medical?" This seemed to surprise him.

I waited.

"Excuse me for being plain-spoken. Are you having an affair with my wife?"

I couldn't help laughing, but I stifled it and tried to sound serious. "Nothing could be further from the truth. I'm a medical doctor. Mrs. Kemper came to see me for professional advice."

"Professional…" He paused. "What kind of advice?"

"It was a personal matter. I believe you should discuss this with her."

"Personal? I thought you just said it was professional."

"Perhaps I should say it was an intimate matter." I instantly regretted using the word "intimate."

"That sounds like a romantic affair to me."

"Not at all. My advice concerned a gynecological matter."

"She's not ill, is she?"

"No, it's nothing like that. But I think you should take this up with your wife."

"Did she come to you to discuss family limitation? I saw the pamphlet."

"I assumed she had discussed this with you."

"Then I'm right. This is about birth control methods."

I paused. "That's correct."

"Well, I'll be damned. You understand this is a marital matter."

"Of course. Perhaps you both should have come in to see me—together."

"What business do you have interfering with a man's conjugal rights?"

"Mrs. Kemper came to see me about her conjugal concerns."

"But—I'm the man of the house…"

"Mr. Kemper, may I suggest that in these modern times it is wise to consider marriage as a partnership. Your wife has some conjugal rights as well."

"Women may have won the right to vote, but family matters remain the man's prerogative."

"I urge you to consider that in matters of marriage hygiene, the woman's burden is great. Mrs. Kemper's concerns need to be taken into account."

"I am the one who brings home the bacon here."

"She told me that she feels three children are all she can handle."

"Why hasn't she told me that?" His voice was getting louder.

"That's what I keep suggesting, Mr. Kemper. You need to have this conversation with her."

"I have friends in high places who will put a stop to this kind of meddling. You've heard of the Invisible Empire." My stomach had been growling in anticipation of lunch, but now it tightened as his anger increased.

"I understand that you feel strongly about this."

"You bet I do." He was nearly shouting.

"I will be glad to take up the matter with your wife and insist that she consult with you before she proceeds."

"No, I will take up this matter with my wife. You stay out of it."

He hung up the phone with a loud click. The adrenaline was racing through my system. I took a deep breath. God help us, I thought.

I should have anticipated trouble from an irate husband. At

least the boyfriends of unmarried women, I presumed, would be eager to prevent unwanted pregnancies.

I was distressed. I had to do something to nip this in the bud.

I risked assuming that Mr. Kemper had telephoned me from the bank where he worked, and I called his wife at her home. When I gave her a polite version of my conversation with her husband, she was quiet for a moment.

"He seemed agitated," I said.

"He isn't usually like this. But he can put on the bluster when he gets annoyed." She paused again.

I heard a child bawling in the background. "Are you still there?" I said.

"I'm here, Dr. Holman. Leave this to me. I'll have a word with my husband directly."

"He made some threats. I just want to be sure you aren't...your safety is not at risk."

"Oh, don't worry about that. He's basically harmless. He'll change his mind."

She seemed confident as we ended the call.

My stomach was still in a knot at the prospect of the Klan becoming embroiled in what was already a contentious situation at the clinic. Rosenfeld's story cast a dark shadow. Was Mrs. Kemper in control of the situation or would her husband take the initiative and follow through with his threats? I did not need any further antagonism with Gowan.

Joe Locke brought back Jimmy's tuxedo and dress shirt in the middle of the week and left them in my closet. I found them there after work, as I was changing my clothes for dinner. There was a note on Locke Family Laundry stationery pinned to the front of the tuxedo jacket saying that they had done the best they could, but the stains would not come out. Traces of blood remained on both the shirt and coat.

After dinner I told Jimmy about it.

"Aw, the hell with it," Jimmy said. "You shouldn't have gone to the trouble. Let's just burn the damned thing. Where is it?"

I laughed and said, "You're not serious, are you?"

"You bet I am."

I brought the tuxedo and shirt from the bedroom. Jimmy had already started to build a fire. While the flames got going, he used scissors to cut the shirt and the tuxedo into pieces. Next he tore the pieces into strips and rolled them into small bundles that he laid on the fire, one by one, and watched them burn.

I thought of chemical reactions and the conservation of energy. What remained of Eric Halsey—those red blood cells caught up in the mesh of the fabric—was now consumed in the flames, transformed into heat and smoke and ash. So where in the universe was Eric Halsey now? I wondered.

The next morning I took a stack of old newspapers to the trash. When I lifted the lid of the garbage can, there in the bottom were Jimmy's patent leather shoes.

Ever since Mr. Kemper's angry phone call, I feared that Gowan would call me into his office. Knowing Rosenfeld's story, I began to worry that I could become a candidate for a burning cross at my house.

Mrs. Kemper phoned me at home one evening a couple of days later.

"You told me that my husband made some threats," she began.

"That's correct. He was rather angry."

"Did he bring up the 100% gang?"

"As a matter of fact, he did."

"I am calling to put your mind at ease, Doctor. You are providing a valuable service, and I believe you should be allowed to continue doing so."

"Thank you. The services seem to be in demand."

"I had an earnest conversation with my husband and I made it clear to him that I am resolute in my decision."

"Yes?" I said.

"Are you familiar with the play *Lysistrata*?"

"Where the Greek women refuse sexual favors to their husbands?

"You get the idea," she said. "If Mr. Kemper does not keep this information between the three of us, he understands there will be consequences. Trust me."

"I see."

"I know about the kind of mischief this Invisible Empire can make. I don't want you to become a target. If I have anything to say about things, this should be the last you hear about it."

I expressed my gratitude and we ended our conversation. Mrs. Kemper sounded determined and if her background was anything like she made it out to be, I had faith that she had taken full control of the matter. My anxiety diminished a notch.

TWENTY-FOUR

In the weeks that followed, Jimmy spent time with Maude every day. As her ankle mended and her head injury improved, so did Jimmy's outlook. He gave up drinking and began playing the piano regularly, more often than not at Maude's. He had also taken to helping Maude with household chores. Over dinner one night he told me that he had been dust-mopping the bedroom floor that afternoon.

"I was reaching the mop under the bed and it caught on something heavy. So I lay flat on the floor to see what it was. You'll never guess what I found. A double-barreled shotgun. I asked her about it later and she said she'd used it for bird hunting with her husband—back on the farm. Then she said something funny. She said that sometimes she wanted to turn the gun on him. Her husband! Can you imagine?"

"Well, when we first brought her home from the hospital, I believe she called him a 'miserable bastard.'"

"I remember. But she had all those kids."

"Maybe she would have used birth control methods if they had been available to her."

"Hmm."

Joe Locke brought in dessert and took away our dinner plates.

"Anyway, Maude said that when she moved to town, she decided to bring the shotgun with her, just in case she ever needed to defend herself." Jimmy laughed. "She's such a character."

Over time Jimmy told each of us—Gwen and Charlie and me—bits and pieces of what had happened in Chicago. As I expected and as I hoped, telling his story over and over helped Jimmy exorcise some of his demons. But more than anything else, it seemed that the opportunity to help Maude recover from her accident was the best thing that could have happened to Jimmy.

One evening I went with Jimmy to check on Maude's leg and her general health. Her concussion symptoms had cleared up and she was dealing well with the cast and the crutches. I suggested that we might be able to remove the cast by Christmas.

"That would be a blessing," she said.

Maude asked Jimmy to play an old church hymn she remembered from her childhood—back before she dropped away from religion. He didn't know the song but after she sang a bit of it, he was able to improvise.

When he finished, she said, "When are you going to find a job?"

Her question took me by surprise.

Jimmy turned back to the piano and played a chord. "I don't know. Soon enough."

"Jimmy, listen to me." Her voice took on a tone he couldn't ignore. He stopped playing and turned to look at her. "You have been taking care of me for all these weeks now. My ankle is practically healed. But I haven't heard you say one word about looking for work."

Jimmy began to speak but then shrugged and looked down at the carpet.

"You told me you had a job as a church organist before you went to Chicago."

"They hired someone to replace me when I left. The position isn't open."

"Where was that?"

"St. Michael's Episcopal Church."

"How many churches are there in this town? And how many of them have organs? And choirs?"

This was a conversation that I had been wanting to have with Jimmy, but I couldn't find the right time for it. Maude was ahead of me. Or maybe just more brazen.

"I catch your point, Maude. I just haven't felt..."

"Now don't tell me you're still sick. I've watched you over the weeks, and you're as healthy as an ox."

"No, I'm over that now. I just..."

"You're just procrastinating."

Jimmy met her gaze with a flash of hostility. But I sensed that he couldn't remain angry at her even if he wanted to.

After a moment he laughed and said, "Yup." He nodded and again let his eyes fall to the carpet. "You're right, Maude," he sighed. "I've been putting it off."

She regarded him with a smile and nodding.

Jimmy did not bring the subject up again, not with me anyway, and I doubt if he wanted to get into it with Maude any further. But within a week, he found a small Catholic parish on the East Side, not far from Sunny Grove that was looking for a backup organist and assistant choir director. He applied and Mr. Cassidy, the lead music director at St. Stephen's, gave him the job.

During these weeks, Jimmy continued to come into my office for his periodic Wassermanns, and I kept an eye out for penile and anal warts. When no evidence appeared and I determined that he was no longer in danger of carrying any infection, I told him we could forgo using the condoms.

Jimmy had let go of all the inhibitions that I remembered from before he went away, and he became more open and adventurous. Over time, we tried all of the things that Jimmy had discovered in Chicago, and some other things as well, but in due course we settled into our own particular habits of enjoying each other's bodies.

TWENTY-FIVE

Late one evening in early December while Jimmy and I were reading in the living room, we heard noises on the front porch. Cold gusty breezes were slapping rain against the house. Someone pounded on the front door.

Jimmy looked up from his magazine, and I closed my medical book and stood. A deep voice called, "Is Dr. Holman at home?" More loud knocking. As I went to the door, the voice shouted, "Open up in there."

Through the beveled glass I saw three Negro men standing on the wet porch under the light. My stomach tensed. The fellow knocking at the door wore a felt hat and had a nasty-looking scar on his cheek. Behind him a tall burly man in a tweed cap was supporting a shorter man who had blood on the shoulder of his suit.

I threw open the door to a burst of cold, damp air. "Quiet, you'll rouse the neighbors," I said. Rain was splattering on the walkways. "Come in here." I switched off the porch light.

The man in the tweed cap said, "Sarge, I think he's about to pass out." I hurried to the wounded man's side to help support him as we guided him in. He smelled of alcohol and cigars and his suit jacket was wet from the rain.

"Get the exam table out of the closet," I called to Jimmy as he stood in open-mouthed silence.

The one called Sarge slammed the door and peered out at the street.

"It's okay," I said to Jimmy. "We've got to lay him down."

He hesitated.

"Quick now."

He went to the closet.

The wounded man was wincing in pain and he let out a little cry.

"Let's sit him down here for now," I said, at once recognizing the signs of a bullet wound. "Help me take off his jacket." The burly fellow and I lowered his buddy onto a chair and we carefully removed his suit coat while he groaned.

"Is he drunk?" I asked.

"Not before he was shot. We gave him some hooch to kill the pain."

His white shirt was stained with blood. I directed the burly man to turn on the overhead light and pull a floor lamp closer.

"What happened?" I tore open the shirtsleeve and examined the shoulder.

Jimmy wrestled the exam table into the center of the room and set it up.

"Well…" the burly man began, then fell silent as he glanced over at Sarge guarding the door behind me.

"Jimmy, get me some towels and my medical bag—and put some water on to boil."

He looked a bit pale as he bolted from the room.

"Let's get him on the table," I said.

The man groaned as we tried to position him on his side. "Damn," he cried.

When I went to the other side of the table I saw that Sarge was pointing a pistol at me. I stopped in my tracks.

"RJ, go keep an eye on that other fella," Sarge called to the burly one. "See that he doesn't call the cops."

RJ followed Jimmy into the kitchen.

"Jimmy's okay," I said. "You can put the gun away." My military training took over and I turned my attention back to the patient. "I'm trying to help you." The wound was just below the deltoid. "How did this happen?"

Jimmy returned with my black bag, several towels, and a damp cloth. He froze when he saw the gun.

"Give him the stuff," Sarge barked.

Jimmy's hands were trembling as I took the things from him. He backed away, averting his eyes, and headed back toward the kitchen.

"Stay there," said the gunman. Jimmy stopped, his face turned away.

"It's okay, Jimmy. Just a little doctoring here and everything will be fine," I said as I cinched a tourniquet under the man's armpit and up over his shoulder. This brought back memories of the dressing station near the front line in France. Mortar shells and stray bullets fell all around us but we kept our focus on the wounded.

"Tell me what happened," I demanded. I took a bottle of rubbing alcohol from the bag and began swabbing the dark skin around the wound. The patient grimaced and let out a hissing gasp between clenched teeth. "Sweet Jesus, that hurts," he cried out.

Sarge hesitated.

"You wouldn't have come here if you didn't think you could trust me. I'm not going to turn you in."

"Okay," Sarge said. "We were making a delivery from the coast. Zeek was driving his car," he motioned toward the short fellow on the table, "and RJ and me were following in my Ford. Someone in a truck came up behind us. They sped past and started shooting. That's when Zeek's car went off the road into a field, and the truck raced off."

"How did you know to come to me?"

"A kid named Billy Butler told us."

Billy Butler! I paused cleaning the wound. I hadn't heard that name for over two years. Pioneer Park. Dark curly hair and that handsome face. I had been staggered when the kid tried to proposition me for money. Not my cup of tea. He couldn't have been more than thirteen, so he must be fifteen or so by now. I didn't trust him that night in Pioneer Park, and present circumstances didn't make me inclined to trust him now.

"Where in hell did you run into him?" I couldn't imagine how these people were connected.

"He was waiting at Haskell's pharmacy to take in the shipment."

Haskell? How had Billy Butler gotten mixed up with Haskell? I had a bad feeling about all this.

"We grabbed Zeek and the hooch and drove to the nearest telephone," Sarge went on. "When I called the pharmacy to tell Billy why we'd be late, he told us to come here. He said you weren't in with the vice squad and you weren't with the Klan fellas neither."

"He had that right. I said you could trust me."

I'd forgotten that I had given Billy my card and told him to contact me if he needed help. Now I worried that my address was getting around as a place to go for unorthodox medical procedures?

A loud squeal from the teakettle pierced the air. Jimmy's body jolted. Sarge flinched.

"Bring me a pan of hot water, Jimmy."

Sarge waved Jimmy on with the barrel of his gun.

I understood why these rum runners would be doing business with Haskell and wouldn't want the vice squad involved. But what did the Klan have to do with it? They were supposed to be teetotalers. Then again I knew Haskell was in with the Klan. Did Gowan know that Haskell's pharmacy was dispensing booze—not to mention illegal morphine?

The teakettle's whistling stopped and there was a clanking of cookware.

"I'll try to see if I can remove the bullet," I told Zeek. I prepared a shot of morphine and gave him an injection. "This should help with the pain."

Jimmy brought a pan of steaming water, keeping his eyes turned away from the blood. He retreated into the dining room doorway while I sterilized some forceps.

I gave Zeek a towel to bite on and had RJ hold him steady. A blast of wind buffeted the window with raindrops. Zeek let out a scream.

It didn't take long before I realized my efforts were ill-considered. I suspected that the humerus might be shattered and he needed an x-ray. He had to go to a hospital.

The chime of the doorbell broke the silence. Sarge backed up against the wall beside the front door, gun at the ready. "See who it is and get rid of 'em," he said and motioned to RJ who went to the other side of the door and pulled out a pistol.

My heart was pounding. Jimmy stood immobilized, his mouth agape and his face blanched. Our eyes met. I wiped my hands on a towel and went to the door. Although the porch was dark, the light from the room revealed Tom Harris's face through the beveled glass.

"It's a friend of mine. I've got to talk to him or he'll think something's wrong."

Sarge poked the barrel of his gun against my ribcage. "Don't let him in."

I opened the door a crack. The wind whistled outside and I felt the damp air. "Hey, Tom. It's kind of late."

"I know. I couldn't get home any earlier tonight. Polly asked me to deliver this fruitcake and wish you a Merry Christmas." He held up a small decorated package in one hand. "Say, did your porch light burn out?" he asked, gesturing over his shoulder.

"What?"

"Fruitcake. She's spent two weeks making them for everyone we know. Hey, is everything alright?"

"I've got to let him in," I said under my breath to Sarge. "He might be able to help you."

Tom looked worried.

"What do you think, RJ?" Sarge said.

"The doc has been pretty helpful…"

"You have to trust me," I said.

Tom frowned and craned his neck to see inside.

"All right, let him in." The muzzle of the gun pulled away from my side.

I opened the door a little wider. The smell of rain wafted in and a gust of wind blew through the porch.

"Tom, I'm doing an exam. We've got a serious situation on our hands. Maybe you can help."

"I'll do whatever I can."

"Come in slowly," Sarge said. "Keep your hands where we can see them."

"What the—" Tom's voice broke off as I opened the door and pulled him in. He dropped the fruitcake and held up his hands. I closed the door and grabbed the fruitcake off the floor.

"Give me that," said Sarge, as he and RJ trained their pistols on Tom.

Tom's eyes went wide behind his thick horn-rimmed glasses.

Sarge sniffed at the fruitcake and tossed it onto a nearby chair.

"You can trust him," I said. "He's my neighbor across the street."

Tom motioned with his palms as if to say back off.

"Believe me, he knows when to keep his mouth shut," I added. I didn't dare mention that he was a newsman.

"Sit down over on the sofa," Sarge demanded, motioning with the gun.

Tom took in the bloody body on the exam table as he backed his way across the room, his hands in front of him with his palms facing us.

"So why do you say this fella can help us, Doc?"

"Zeek needs to go to a hospital," I said. "There isn't anything more I can do for him here. He needs an x-ray. If you don't get him some serious help, he might lose that arm."

"No hospitals," Sarge said. "They're going to get the cops involved if we go to any damn hospital."

"Please, Sarge," Zeek cried. "Don't let 'em take my arm."

"That's why I think Tom can help. You know that doctor in Oregon City?" I asked Tom.

"Yes, Dr. Bjorn," Tom said. "Norwegian. Old fella. Lots of

experience. He's got his own x-ray machine. You can trust him to keep quiet."

Sarge looked at RJ. "What do you think?"

"If he could lose that arm, we gotta do something."

Sarge turned to look at Zeek on the exam table, trying to make a decision. "Okay." Then to Tom Harris, "We'd better get moving. You're coming with us."

"Wait a minute—" Tom objected.

Sarge took a step toward him, pointing the gun at his face. "You're coming with us."

"All right, all right," Tom said raising his hands higher. "Bjorn's place is a ways out of town. It's not easy to find. I can direct you. But I've got to call him first so he knows we're coming."

Sarge looked over at RJ for confirmation. RJ nodded.

"Okay, RJ, you keep an eye on these fellas and I'll make sure Fruitcake here doesn't do anything stupid. Where's the phone?"

Jimmy led them to the phone in the hall while I bandaged Zeek's arm. I could hear Tom's voice from the hallway.

Sarge returned with Tom while Jimmy hung back in the doorway. Tom and RJ helped Zeek down from the exam table and out to the car under Sarge's guard. I watched from the front door as they disappeared into the night.

I called Polly right away to tell her that Tom was chasing down an important story. "Everything's okay." I hoped that was true.

When I got off the phone, I turned to Jimmy. I was concerned that this incident would trigger a relapse into dark memories and liquor.

He spoke first. "You are so brave."

"I felt like I was back at the front line during the War."

"No Man's Land?" he said.

We had talked about my wartime experiences. "You've got the picture."

He came to my side and embraced me.

"How about a drink?" I said at last.

"Not for me," he said shaking his head. "You have one if you like."

I called Tom Harris at the newsroom the next morning. He'd had a late night.

"Yeah, I didn't get home till 3 in the morning. But everything went okay." There were voices in the background and the ringing of a telephone. "We got your patient to Dr. Bjorn and he fixed him up. Your friends drove me back into town and gave me money for a taxi home."

"They aren't exactly my friends."

"No, I hear you. And that brings up something odd. If these fellas are leery of both the vice squad and the Klan, then they must be working with some new outfit. Those two groups have had the liquor business all sewn up in Portland. Something is going on out there that I don't understand." The tapping of a nearby typewriter clattered through the line.

"Wait. The Klan is in the liquor trade? I thought they were in the business of cleaning up civic morals."

"Yes, as long as it doesn't interrupt the flow of income for some of their buddies. There's a bit of rivalry between the cops and the Klan on some fronts. Amusing, don't you think? But that's the world Prohibition has brought us. I'm curious about this new bunch trying to muscle their way into the West coast. This will be interesting to dig into."

"That's your racket. I'm glad it's not mine. Say, I hope these fellas have established a good relationship with your friend Dr. Bjorn. I can't have any more gunshot wounds showing up on my front porch."

"Right. They got along very well with the good Norwegian doctor. He's so far out in the country that he doesn't raise any eyebrows or make any news. You shouldn't have to worry about them bothering you anymore."

Despite Tom's blithe reassurance, when I hung up the phone

I was feeling deeply disturbed by this brush with such unsavory characters.

TWENTY-SIX

Just before Christmas, Joe Locke told me that his family might be in danger of losing their laundry. The property values in Old Chinatown had been increasing and the city fathers encouraged Chinese businesses to move farther north to a New Chinatown where property was cheaper. Now a white developer wanted to take over the corner where the Locke family laundry had existed for many years. The new Alien Land Law supported by the Klan had gone into effect earlier in '23 making it illegal for Japanese and Chinese immigrants to own land in Oregon. The developer thought he could use the new law to cancel the Locke family lease. If they had to relocate, it would be a serious financial blow that might force the laundry to close.

As he told me this story, Joe Locke's usual composure was gone, and he was quite shaken by the possibility of the whole family losing its livelihood. At first, I couldn't believe such a thing would happen in the United States of America. My close relationship with Joe had blinded me to the extent of anti-Chinese sentiment in my community. But the newspapers were full of anti-immigrant sentiment, mainly aimed at the growing population of Japanese in rural Oregon.

I told Joe I would look into the matter.

My first thought was to contact my real estate man, Harold Roundtree, to see if there was anything that could be done to help the Locke family. He wasn't exactly sympathetic, and he reminded me that there were restrictive covenants forbidding Chinese from residing in Sunny Grove and other parts of town. But he gave me the name of an attorney to contact. It took a week for me to get in to see him. The lawyer seemed understanding but reserved. He thought there might be ways around the law and he would look into it, but it would take some time. I informed Joe that I had set some wheels in motion, but that was small comfort to him as the fate of the family business hung in suspense.

Aside from that, Christmas was an especially happy time that year. I was glad to have Jimmy back with me. He was happy with his new work at St. Stephen's helping the choir and playing the organ, and he was making new friends in the congregation. The head organist and choir director was an older gentleman named Cassidy with whom he felt a kinship. Jimmy shared his belief that music could change the shape of a room, like when the organ music filled the inside of the church—the same idea he'd shared with me when we first met. Cassidy was an admirer of Professor Einstein's work and he introduced Jimmy to some of the geometric concepts associated with the theory of relativity.

Even though Jimmy's job kept him busy with rehearsals and special musical events connected with the holy days, we made time to decorate. He and I hung swags of cedar across the front porch, and for the first time since I'd lived in the house, I put up a Christmas tree with Jimmy's help.

Since Jimmy and I had agreed to exchange small gifts with Gwen and Charlie, I needed to do some shopping. I took a long lunch break about a week before Christmas and stopped at one of the large downtown department stores. After purchasing a few small things for Gwen and Charlie on the main floor, I headed up to the men's department to find something for Jimmy.

I followed several people into the elevator and the uniformed operator asked which floors we wanted.

"Third floor," I replied. A number of ladies requested the fourth.

We stopped on the second floor where the doors opened to reveal a young man carrying a draped female mannequin. I recognized him at once as Jerry the Fairy.

He addressed the operator. "Hi Seymour. The freight elevator's occupied right now and they need this beauty up in Ladies Wear, pronto. Mind if I ride with you?" His voice still had that familiar lilt to it.

Seymour winked at Jerry and said, "Hop in." The women behind me tittered and crowded to the rear as I stepped back and to the side, making room. Jerry got in, glancing in my direction, and I was sure that he recognized me, but he turned to face the elevator door as it closed. While he stood waiting, his cheek grew red. He kept his eyes forward. Neither of us spoke.

I could tell that his face had healed up well. If I hadn't seen him right after his injuries occurred, I wouldn't have been able to tell that he'd been beaten so badly. He was wearing his hair very short, no longer bleached but a medium brown, however he was still tweezing his eyebrows.

Seymour engaged the controls and the elevator began to rise. Jerry and I stood next to each other in silence. An observer would never have guessed that we knew each other. Jerry stood with his arms around the lady mannequin and I clutched my shopping bag, looking straight ahead until the lift reached the third floor. I squeezed past him as I got off and, turning, I gave him the slightest smile and nod. He looked away and the elevator doors closed.

I was pleased to know that he had found gainful employment.

TWENTY-SEVEN

The very next day Jerry's case and Bateson's assault again came to mind.

Vivian called to say that a Rebecca Porter was waiting in the reception area. She was a dark-haired woman in her thirties with a haggard look. She stood holding her blond 5-year-old daughter by the hand. The child clung to her arm and hid her face in her mother's hip. As I led them to my office, the little girl peeked up at me. I smiled and said hello. Her face crumpled as she let out a cry, and tears began streaming down her face.

"I don't want to go," the child said and stopped in her tracks.

The mother knelt down and hugged her. "It's all right, Sally. Don't fret. We're just going to have a talk with the nice doctor." She brushed away the girl's tears. "Come along now. Take my hand."

As we got settled in my office, the child stood next to her mother's chair and buried her face in her lap.

I began by asking about the family history.

Mrs. Porter had moved to Portland from Minnesota before the War to be near her married sister. That's when she met her husband, Marvin Porter. Not long after they were married, America joined the War, and her husband enlisted.

"While he was away in Europe, I moved in with the Batesons— my sister and her husband."

I looked up from my notes. "Does he by chance work with the police?"

"That's right. Stephen Bateson."

I felt a sinking sensation. "Go on." I wrote down the name.

"I realized I was pregnant a month after Marvin left for Europe and Sally here was born before he returned home. My sister and her husband were so helpful. After the War, Marvin and I got our own place."

"I see. Tell me what brings you in today."

"I'm worried about Sally." The child whimpered at the sound of her name. Mrs. Porter stroked the girl's shoulder.

"Has she been ill?"

"It's not that. But there are a number of things that have cropped up just recently. First, she started wetting the bed. She's never done that before."

Sally squirmed and looked up. "I do not." Her lower lip protruded.

"Hush, dear." Mrs. Porter smoothed her blond hair. "She's been quite fussy lately."

"I am not. I'm a good girl." Again tears came to her eyes. She buried her face.

"You are, Sally. You're a very good girl."

"Anything else?" I said.

"During the day she's been very quiet—doesn't want to talk or play."

I wrote down "withdrawn." "Does she play with other children?"

"Sometimes I leave her with a neighbor who has two little ones—when I need to go out for errands and such. I'm told she keeps to herself."

"No physical problems?"

"Only what I've just told you. It's more in the way she acts. Something has changed."

"Any changes within the family? A recent move to a new home?"

"No, we've been in our house for a few years now."

"And your husband? Any trouble at work or changes in employment?"

She stared down at the carpet and hesitated.

"This is all strictly confidential," I said.

Mrs. Porter took a deep breath. "My husband lost his job recently."

The child became agitated again and began crying.

I made a note while Mrs. Porter tried to quiet the girl.

When Sally was calm, I said, "Shall we do an examination?" As we stood, Sally reached up to her mother. "Oh, you're too heavy, dear. You're a big girl now. Come on."

I opened the door to my exam room and Mrs. Porter pulled the child along. Her brow wrinkled and her eyes were filled with fear. "No, I don't want to."

Mrs. Porter knelt down and took Sally by the shoulders. "Now, stop whining, dear. No one is going to hurt you. I'm right here. Dr. Holman wants to help you."

We got the child to the exam table and as I helped Mrs. Porter lift her she cried out. "No. No." At my touch Sally cowered and began to weep. As I started to listen to Sally's chest with my stethoscope, she screamed. Her small arms struck at me. Mrs. Porter tried to hold her hands. I stroked the girl's back in hopes of quieting her, but she went into another fit of screaming and fighting. Her body stiffened and twisted.

I gave up on the idea of an exam, since it seemed that the little girl's symptoms were more psychological than physical. I stood aside as Mrs. Porter comforted her. When Sally quieted down, I suggested we return to my office.

"Mrs. Porter, I think you need to see a psychiatric specialist or a social worker. I can't offer much help to you and your daughter."

The mother looked frightened. Sally again hid her face in her mother's lap and Mrs. Porter patted Sally's back to soothe her.

"I can give you some names to contact. Without some physical problem, there isn't much I can do."

"I've got to do something," Mrs. Porter sounded desperate. The child whimpered.

"Here. I'll write down the names, a psychotherapist and a social worker. I'll be glad to call them for you."

She blanched and blurted out, "No." Clutching the child to her side, she stood. "No, I'll get in touch with them. Thank you, doctor." She took the piece of paper and headed for the door.

I stood. "Please, don't hesitate to call me if there is anything else I can do."

With a hasty thank you, she left with Sally in tow.

I wished that I could have done more, but to be honest, I was glad she left before the child had another outburst.

Stephen Bateson. I remembered his cold green eyes and Jerry's story about the beating. Here was a small window into his family connections. I filed the information away in my mind as I filed away Mrs. Porter's medical notes. I hoped that the psychiatrist could do something to help her child.

TWENTY-EIGHT

Since Christmas fell on a Tuesday, Dr. Gowan had planned a party for our clinic staff on the Saturday before. He hired a small banquet room at his club for a sit-down dinner. He insisted that I bring Gwen. I stewed over the invitation for a day before I forced myself to call and see if she would join me. We discussed different excuses for not going, but in the end there seemed no way to get out of it. After arranging to rent formal wear, I let Gowan know my fiancée and I would attend.

When the evening rolled around, Gwen and I arrived at the club feeling ill at ease regarding our fellow guests. The group was small: Gowan and Bleeker with their wives, Vivian and her husband, and Gwen and I. In such an intimate group, we felt exposed and deprived of the cover of anonymity that a larger gathering might have afforded. The situation was very awkward at first, and everyone seemed a bit standoffish, Mrs. Gowan in particular, who had always struck me as rather cold and aloof. They all appeared to be eyeing Gwen as if she were some odd lab specimen that might be dangerous. But Gwen was friendly and engaging, as usual, and played the part of my fiancée perfectly. At one point I forgot we'd let on that the wedding would be in February, but Gwen took up the conversation and glossed over my blunder. Mrs. Bleeker warmed to her when the conversation turned to children, and Gwen mentioned that she worked with newborns.

"You know, Miss Cook," Gowan said, "that we are planning a maternity wing for the new hospital. You should consider coming to work with us there."

I felt my blood rise. Why did he have to bring this up here in front of all these people? He could have arranged a private conversation. I gave him a stern look, but he had turned to face Gwen.

Vivian's husband said that he'd heard Gwen was Catholic. I'd never met him before that evening, and rather liked him at first. Now I felt an additional wave of irritation. The dinner table fell silent. Gwen said that she was raised in the Methodist church.

"But I understand you work at a Catholic hospital," he said. Did he have to persist?

"Not everyone who works for the Catholics shares their faith," she replied. "Many of us are more interested in nursing people back to health than what religious beliefs they hold."

I could have hugged her. Touché, I thought.

"Ill health knows no denomination," I added.

Mrs. Bleeker broke in. "And aren't we all fortunate to be healthy today and able to enjoy this splendid meal that the club has provided for us. And what a lovely little Christmas tree your club has provided here as a centerpiece. We've decorated our tree in a very traditional manner this year, but I hear you've tried something rather daring at your home, Mrs. Gowan."

Bless you, Mrs. Bleeker, I thought. The conversation turned to Christmas doings, and religious affiliations did not resurface as a topic of discussion, much to my relief. Nor did Gowan return to the subject of the maternity wing at the new hospital.

The next morning, when Jimmy was at the church, Gwen and Charlie came over and helped me bake and decorate cookies in the shapes of Christmas trees and bells and snowmen. As assistant choir director at St. Stephen's, Jimmy had come up with the idea that we go caroling in our neighborhood, and Gwen suggested giving the neighbors cookies. We all agreed to make this another good-neighbor campaign like the one back in the summer when Jimmy and I had taken fresh tomatoes to the Mitchells.

We were feeling festive as we sat around the dining table, drinking cocoa and packaging up the cookies in decorative gift boxes. "I've been wondering about Minnie Mitchell—" Gwen began, when Jimmy burst in the front door, back from St. Stephen's.

"I've got to tell you what happened after church." He looked unsettled as he took off his overcoat and tweed cap. "Cassidy and I got carried away talking about Einstein's geometry so I didn't get away until most everyone else had gone. There was a man standing on the sidewalk in front of the church, and he came up and handed me a flier. He had a stack of them. And he started in on me about why was I a Catholic and didn't I know what a danger they were to the country."

"I can guess what's coming," Gwen said.

"He asked how I could support an organization that was sworn to destroy Protestants and take over the US government. 'That's bunk' I told him. 'No,' he says, 'it's in the Congressional record.' Then he read to me from this flier," Jimmy took a leaflet out of his suit pocket. "He was talking about how the Knights of Columbus swore to—what does it say here? '…to wade through Protestant blood up to their knees in order to destroy them.' Here, read this thing."

Charlie took the flier and began to look it over, while Gwen said, "Yes, I've heard this before. I was confronted by some LOTIE women outside the hospital with the same message. What happened is that the Knights of Columbus took their case all the way to the Supreme Court to discredit this lie about their oath. The official oath was entered into the Congressional record alongside the false one. But now these knuckleheads are going around saying that since the fake oath is in our country's official record, it's got to be true."

"We're lucky that the courts can see through this kind of

chicanery," I said, "since the general public is fooled so easily."

"We shouldn't pay this sort of thing any mind," Charlie said, flinging the flier across the table. I picked it up and began reading.

"We may not be able to change any minds," Gwen said, "but we can at least show the Mitchells that we are decent people. Here, Jimmy, try one of our cookies." She gestured to a plate on the table.

Jimmy sat down for cookies and cocoa. Then as our own personal choir director, he led us through a few carols we'd been practicing for the neighbors. With our voices all warmed up, we put on our coats and went out into the neighborhood to sing and deliver cookies.

Our first stop was the Mitchells'. Jimmy had chosen a religious carol for them and they stood in glum silence at the door while we sang "Hark the Herald Angels Sing." I remembered introducing Minnie Mitchell to Gwen at the eugenics lecture the previous spring, and after we finished singing, I made a point of introducing Gwen again, this time as my fiancée. Mrs. Mitchell's demeanor was characteristically chilly. We didn't expect the Mitchells to invite us in, but they did accept a box of cookies. As we turned to leave, Jimmy took Charlie's gloved hand and kissed it, and they continued to hold hands as we walked away. He was putting on a show to let the Mitchells speculate about their relationship. After we turned the corner, Jimmy winked at me and he and Charlie laughed as he let go of her hand.

"Not the friendliest Christians on the block," Jimmy said. I knew he was remembering the cold fury with which Minnie Mitchell had met us when we delivered the tomatoes to her family late in the summer—along with the announcement of my engagement.

Maude met us with a warm greeting, and after we sang a rendition of "God Rest Ye Merry Gentlemen," she accepted our cookies and invited us in for coffee. Although her cast had come off a few weeks before, Jimmy insisted on helping her serve, and after a bit of grumbling, she acquiesced. Settling back into her chair with a cup of coffee, she again thanked Gwen for helping get her to the hospital. They hadn't seen each other since that day.

"I've never told you, Doctor," Maude said, "but I was so sorry to hear about the Haskell boy. Such a tragedy."

"How did you hear about that?" I asked.

"Lloyd Haskell's mother, Naomi, is an old friend of mine."

I felt a chill at the sound of Lloyd Haskell's name. Jimmy and I exchanged glances. "I don't know her," I said.

"We knew each other when we lived in Southern Oregon," Maude said, "way back before she met George—Lloyd's dad. Naomi Picard was her name then. She met George in Bayfield, which was the closest town to our farm. They lived there until George took sick and died several years ago. Lloyd made her sell the feed store. She could have kept it going. She was always so smart."

"He made her?" Jimmy said. Charlie leaned in listening with curiosity. Gwen and I had summarized the Haskell case for them, including Lloyd's angry outburst. But I'd only told Gwen about the delayed medical treatment—and I hadn't mentioned my suspicions about Lloyd's sexual practices with anyone.

"He wouldn't let her be," Maude went on. "And she loved that big old house and garden there and wanted to stay on. Even though she was all alone, she still had good friends nearby. But Lloyd wouldn't let up until he badgered her into moving to Portland. He was so headstrong about it. I've known that boy since he was a child, and my, but he had a temper—even as a little tyke."

Gwen cocked her head at me with raised eyebrows. I would have liked to talk privately with Maude about the Haskell family, but I didn't want to broach any aspect of the distressing subject right then.

"Guess he still tends to fly off the handle," Maude went on, "according to Naomi. Now that we both live here in town, she and I talk on the phone. Back in Bayfield, we spent lots of time together."

"It sounds like you were pretty good friends," Jimmy said.

Charlie seemed about to ask Maude a question.

"I think we need to be moving along," Gwen said. I suspected she wanted to forestall any further talk of the Haskells. It dampened the holiday cheer. "We've got some other deliveries to make."

"This box goes over to the Harris family across the street," I said as I stood, holding up the last box of cookies.

"Merry Christmas to you, Maude," I said and avoided looking in Gwen's direction. "I'm glad to see your leg is all healed up."

Jimmy and Charlie seemed a bit puzzled by Gwen's abrupt move to leave.

We said our goodbyes and headed across the street. Charlie took Gwen's arm and gave her a quizzical look.

At the Harris's their children, Will and Rachel, watched us with wide eyes as we stood on their front porch and sang "Jingle Bells." Tom and Polly asked us in and offered us brandied eggnog. The youngsters pointed out special packages waiting for them under the tree, and while the rest of us chatted, Jimmy played with the kids, joking and laughing while asking them which of the Christmas tree ornaments were their favorites. He handed them their box of cookies and let them unwrap it. The children were thrilled with the sugary treats.

From there, we went to the house next door where we finally got to meet Mr. Postlewait, whom I had only waved to in passing all these months. He had to quiet his dog first and close it up in another room. Although he did not invite us in, he was very friendly and gave us a hearty thank you for the cookies. "You all have a very merry Christmas," he said.

TWENTY-NINE

That evening after dinner, we played Halma and listened to some of Jimmy's jazz records on the Victrola. In the middle of the game, Charlie exclaimed, "Oh, I nearly forgot. We've been invited to a New Year's Eve costume party. Do you have any plans yet?"

No one did.

The party would be held at a popular speak in a warehouse near the river. Charlie's friend Barb from the telephone company had invited her and told her to bring some friends. There would be prizes for the best costumes and a talent contest.

"I was going to go as Charlie Chaplin, but Gwen suggested we go as Gallagher and Shean. We wanted to ask if you have suits we could borrow."

I'd seen Gallagher and Shean on the vaudeville stage when I was passing through New York. "That would be hilarious," I said.

Jimmy sang a few lines from their hit record "Absolutely, Mr. Gallagher? Positively, Mr. Shean!" causing a burst of laughter.

I remembered hearing about a raid on a big party during the summer, so I thought twice before committing myself. Getting caught up in a raid wouldn't look good for someone in my position. Established speaks made regular payoffs and got protection from the cops. They were fairly safe in general. But a big party thrown together by the wrong people might be a risky proposition.

"Have you heard anything about the police being paid off not to raid this party?"

Charlie said her friend Barb had a boyfriend who was a policeman and she suspected the festivities would be safe. I said I would check with Tom Harris to see if he could confirm that.

As we finished the game, we speculated about costumes for Jimmy and me, and while we put away the Halma set, Charlie suggested that Jimmy could play the piano for the talent contest.

"Let's see what we can find for you girls in the way of duds," I said.

Gwen and Charlie followed us into the bedroom, where I began pulling suits out of the closet for them to try on.

Jimmy remembered an old pith helmet he had that Charlie could wear as Gallagher. "My father handed it down to me," he said and ran upstairs to look for it. After rummaging in the attic for a time, Jimmy returned with the hat, to find Charlie dressed in a huge tan double-breasted suit.

"This will never do," Charlie said. "Where did you ever get such a big suit, Carl?"

"It belonged to one of my patients. He lost weight during a long illness and he insisted I accept it as a gift, thinking I could have it tailored to fit me. I just never got around to it. Besides, it's not my color."

Jimmy put the helmet on Charlie's head, and we all laughed at how well it fit her face. Jimmy explained, somewhat wistfully, that when the band first got together, Diggs had used the pith helmet as a gag for muting his cornet.

"I'll need to find some spectacles, too," Charlie said.

A moment later Gwen emerged from the bathroom dressed in one of my suits. It fit her better than the one Charlie was wearing. She had drawn a mustache like Mr. Shean's on her upper lip, which made us laugh.

"The pants will work with a little hemming," Gwen said, "but I'll have to find a coat that looks more like Mr. Shean's. And a fez."

Jimmy brought down his light-colored summer suit for Charlie to try on, and she marveled at how good the fit was. "Maybe you'd like to borrow one of my dresses," she joked to Jimmy.

A curious expression passed over Jimmy's face before he laughed. "Maybe I'll take you up on that."

"Charlie has a wig," Gwen suggested.

"Hmm," Jimmy said tapping an index finger against his lips.

"What will you wear, Carl?" Gwen asked.

I disappeared into the closet, to hunt through a box from the top shelf. A moment later I emerged from the closet wearing a gas mask. Gwen let out a little cry at the sudden appearance of the bizarre elephant-like creature. Charlie put her arms around her and hid Gwen's face from the bug-eyed monster. Jimmy laughed. I pulled the mask off and said I still had my soldier's uniform up in the attic.

"Bravo." Charlie applauded.

We spent the rest of the evening offering each other suggestions and trying on different clothes. Charlie kept teasing Jimmy and suggested that he come over to look through some of her gowns.

"I don't know. I'll have to think about this. But what I will do is pick up the sheet music to 'Mr. Gallagher and Mr. Shean.'"

Gwen said she could sew a temporary hem in my suit pants, but she wondered where she might find a fez.

"Maybe you could kiss a Shriner," Charlie suggested.

Since Jimmy was busy with music at St. Stephen's on Christmas morning and again that evening, we planned to have Gwen and Charlie over for a feast in the early afternoon.

I gave Joe Locke Christmas day off as I'd done in years past. The girls came over to our house early, so we could get the turkey in the oven. When Jimmy returned from the morning service, we exchanged gifts before sitting down to an abundant table.

During the meal Gwen said that after Gowan's dinner party, she was concerned about our plans for the costume ball. "If we want to keep up the appearance that Carl and I are engaged, we should go as a couple and wear some costume that makes it clear we are together."

"Like Anthony and Cleopatra," Charlie said.

"Too tragic," Jimmy chuckled. "How about Vernon and Irene Castle?"

"They don't have an identifiable costume, really," Charlie said. "Besides Gwen can't dance like they do. No one can."

"If Carl wears his military uniform," Gwen said, "I could wear my nurse's uniform and borrow a Red Cross cape—like in the War. That would impress the patriots."

"I've been worried about this, myself," I said. "I did check with Tom Harris to see if the party would be safe and he looked into it. His contacts say the cops will be strictly hands off. But your idea is a good one. It would be more dignified for a young doctor and his fiancée. Charlie and Jimmy should also figure out costumes that go together—so folks will think they're a couple, too."

"I think I have an idea," Jimmy said. "But it's a secret. Let's you and I get together in the next few days, Charlie, and talk it over."

"Come over tomorrow evening," Charlie said. "I've been giving this some thought and I have some ideas as well."

After our feast, we put on our winter coats and took a stroll through the neighborhood, admiring the Christmas decorations.

THIRTY

During the week that followed, we became more preoccupied with the costume ball. Jimmy began practicing some of his blues songs on the piano. He and Charlie spent a great deal of time together secretly planning their costumes. Gwen borrowed a Red Cross cape from a friend who had gone to France during the War. My costume was the only one that did not require rustling up special parts.

On the eve of the New Year, we all gathered in our house. I was the first one ready in my captain's uniform. The gas mask was so cumbersome that I had decided to leave it at home. Instead, I wore my overseas cap since I didn't have a metal doughboy's helmet. Gwen joined me in the living room looking the perfect Red Cross nurse. Charlie and Jimmy had banished us from the back of the house as they bustled about with the excitement of last-minute costume adjustments and other secret preparations.

Finally, Jimmy called from the hallway that they were ready and sounded a drum roll on the closed door. A woman in a white evening gown walked into the room at a sultry pace. "She" wore a blonde wig with a rhinestone tiara and expertly applied make-up. Jimmy was barely recognizable. He was escorted by a gentleman in white tie and top hat with a mustache drawn on "his" upper lip. Charlie had her hair slicked back and looked the part of a young man-about-town. Jimmy curtsied and Charlie bowed. She stood aside as he strolled to the piano and struck a pose, before he sat down and played the opening bars of a blues song. At last his voice rose, transformed by this new guise, singing out the lyrics with an expressive power that startled us all. At the close of the song, we burst into enthusiastic applause punctuated with shouts. "Bravo! Encore!"

Jimmy stood and bowed graciously.

"Oh, Jimmy, you look beautiful," Gwen said, as our clapping died away. "I hardly recognized you." She went to Charlie's side. "And who is this handsome gentleman accompanying you?" She took Charlie's hand and kissed her cheek.

"But we can't call you Jimmy tonight," Charlie said. "You must have another name."

"Call me Velma LaRuse," he said. "The Vamp of the Blues." He made a grand theatrical curtsy, as we laughed and applauded. "That's the name I'll use for the talent contest."

We had coffee and cookies and made last-minute adjustments to our costumes before we donned our coats and piled into the Ford.

The site of the costume party was just as Charlie had described, a warehouse near the river. This industrial part of town was not where you'd expect to find a speak, less still a fancy-dress costume ball. It was past 10 when we parked on a side street near the warehouse. We caught sight of three men dressed in three-cornered hats and colonial American garb and a couple who appeared to be Anthony and Cleopatra.

"What did I tell you," Charlie joked.

A line of other folks in costume had formed at a doorway on a loading dock stacked high with crates and sacks of grain. A doorman admitted the revelers one by one, collecting admission. We could hear jazz coming from upstairs as we waited in line.

Once indoors we were directed up a flight of stairs where we were greeted by the full volume of the band. Their music rang out above a roar of conversation and laughter from the large crowd.

The musicians played at one end of the room that had been decorated with Japanese paper lanterns. The other end of the room was piled to the ceiling with a wall of crates and grain sacks next to a freight elevator. Two bars, one on either side of the room, served the pressing throngs, as waiters in white coats squeezed through the crush, carrying trays of beverages. We found a table and got settled. On the dance floor a gorilla danced with a hula girl, an Abe Lincoln in a stovepipe hat escorted a Chinese princess, and a male Ariel sprite with gossamer wings embraced a caveman in animal skins. I wondered if this was anything like the Chicago nightclub that Jimmy had described to me—the club where he met Eric.

Jimmy and I took drink orders from Gwen and Charlie and we began negotiating our way through the crowd to the nearest bar. Jimmy held my arm and pressed against my shoulder as if we were a soldier and his gal, out on the town. As we stood waiting to get the attention of one of the scurrying bartenders, I felt Jimmy's hand tighten on my arm.

"Oh, God," he gasped and a shudder went through him. He leaned in close to me and spoke into my ear. "That fellow at the end of the bar—down to your right—the one in white tie—that's Danny Felton. That's the man who killed Eric."

He stood about five yards away under a lamp above the crowded bar. I couldn't tell if his hair was blond or white. Even his eyebrows were light in color. There was something mesmerizing about him with his cold smile and smooth manner, as he joked with a good-looking young bartender.

"You're sure it's him?" I could feel Jimmy's fingers tremble on my arm.

"Without a doubt," he replied. "I'd recognize him anywhere."

"What the hell is he doing here in Portland?" I had a queasy feeling.

"What'll it be?" called the bartender.

I ordered drinks, including a Coke for Jimmy.

"Change that Coke to a gin and tonic with a double shot of gin," Jimmy called over the din.

The bartender turned back and smiled at Jimmy. "Anything you say, gorgeous." There was no way to tell if he was taken in by Jimmy's disguise or if he was just playing along.

As we waited for the drinks, I slid my arm around Jimmy's waist. His whole body was trembling. He positioned himself so he could keep an eye on Felton. He must have calculated that neither Felton nor anyone else would recognize him in his disguise. I judged he was right.

When the bartender set out our drinks, Jimmy downed his in a series of gulps without pausing for a breath. "I'll take another," he said, setting the glass on the bar.

The bartender laughed and said, "Yes, ma'am! Anything you say."

While we waited for Jimmy's second drink, I leaned in and suggested that he take it easy.

"Just fortifying myself," he said.

Carrying drinks for the four of us, we made our way toward Gwen and Charlie along the wall of crates. There attendants were seated at a long table registering contestants for the costume and talent competition.

"I'll have to come back and sign up," Jimmy said looking over his shoulder to where Felton stood at the bar.

I glanced back a couple of times to keep an eye on the man, but it became more and more difficult to see him through the crowd.

We sat down with Gwen and Charlie, who had been joined by their friend Barb and another young woman from the phone company. They were dressed in identical black and white dresses and wore necklaces and earrings made of dice. They laughed when they introduced themselves as the Good Luck Twins, Dicey and Lucky Craps.

Jimmy took a long swig from his drink before asking Charlie to accompany him while he registered for the talent contest. As I sat next to Gwen watching the crowd, a noisy group of queens in drag passed behind our table and jostled the back of my chair.

"Oh, excuse me, darling," one of them said as she passed, before turning back to her conversation. I thought I recognized the voice and watched as they passed on through the crowd, absorbed in their chatter. It was Jerry the Fairy. He was wearing a blonde wig and a stunning red evening gown. He appeared so comfortable and natural in his costume that if I had not heard him speak, I would not have recognized him as a man at all. He was in his element. Jerry and his friends disappeared into the crowd. Soon Jimmy and Charlie returned carrying a large yellow card with his talent contest number.

The band introduced a chorus line of jazz babies in skimpy little dresses who performed a dance number. The crowd near the bar thinned out as people took their seats or moved closer to the bandstand to get a better vantage point for the show.

Now I had a clear view of Felton. Jimmy was watching him, too. Felton had been joined by a handsome young dark-haired man in a business suit and a tall, bulky fellow wearing an overcoat.

Jimmy looked pale and he appeared shaken. Leaning into my ear, he said, "I recognize those two. They were with him in Chicago."

I watched the men talking. They looked dead serious.

Jimmy took a swallow of his gin, his hand trembling. He stared at Charlie across the table. She leaned toward him with concern and reached out her hand. He held it tightly. Gwen and I exchanged wary glances.

"You're shaking," Charlie said.

He continued to look at her, his eyes troubled.

The dancers wound up their number to wild applause. After bows, the shortest of them came forward and in a baritone voice announced the beginning of the costume contest. The first five costume contestants were instructed to line up in order beside the stage.

"Come sit next to me," Charlie said to Jimmy, "where you can see the show better."

The crowd began repositioning for the contest. Jimmy let go of Charlie's hand and moved his chair beside her. He kept glancing around to where we'd seen Felton, but the crowd obscured our view. Charlie put her arm around Jimmy's shoulder and pulled him close to her. They looked very much the well-dressed couple out on a date. She pointed to the Dicey Twins, who were making their way forward for the contest. He relaxed into her shoulder and focused on the stage.

I could just make out Felton through the crush of people. I felt Gwen's hand on my arm. She looked worried. I smiled to reassure her, but I don't think my smile was convincing.

The costume contestants began crossing past a table of judges and on around the room. For each entry, the baritone-voiced Master of Ceremonies announced the contestant's number and the title of each entry, making wisecracks and commentary as they passed in review. The band played in the background.

"Number three: Napoleon Bonaparte." Applause as a diminutive man, looking very much the part, crossed before the bandstand with one hand thrust inside the front of his coat. "Ooo! What a handsome chap you are," said the MC. "Give me a call if you need a Josephine. I'm always a sucker for a man in a uniform."

During the costume parade, I looked around for Felton. He had been joined by a short, heavyset bald man dressed in a tuxedo and smoking a cigar. They were deep in conversation with the dark-haired fellow. Behind them the tall, bulky man in the overcoat kept a watchful eye.

The MC called the first five talent participants forward.

A Little Miss Muffet acted out her breakfast of curds and whey while her companion, in a spider costume, sang a musical version of the nursery rhyme in a menacing voice. Next, the hula girl did a Hawaiian dance and sang a song with ukulele accompaniment by the gorilla.

This was followed by a blonde in a red dress who sang a blues song about a man who treated her mean. I leaned in toward Jimmy. "That's Jerry—that blond fellow who showed up on our front porch."

"You're kidding." He listened more intently. "He's got a

good voice—and he's sure got a knack for the blues." The piano accompaniment launched into a brief solo. "And, look, that's Vance playing the piano for him."

It was Vance, all right, lively and alert, playing the blues tune. I was glad to see that they both seemed to have made a full recovery.

During the next number, Jimmy insisted on ordering more drinks from a passing waiter. Again I suggested he go easy, but Jimmy ignored me. After this part of the talent contest, the band played a few tunes and Jimmy insisted we dance while Gwen and Charlie held our table. Whether it was our costumes or the unconventional setting, we were both at ease dancing in each other's arms, the first time we had ever done so where we could be seen. The feeling was exhilarating. While we were dancing, Jimmy kept looking around for Danny Felton. I wasn't able to spot him. When the tune ended, the next five costume contestants were called.

By the time his number was called for the next portion of the talent contest, Jimmy was well on his way toward tipsy.

"Are you sure you feel up to this?" I asked.

"Never felt better," he replied with more than a hint of irritation in his voice as he rose from his chair, teetering. "It's just these damn shoes. Gwen's feet are smaller than mine."

I felt anxious for him as I watched him make an unsteady trip to his place in the lineup of contestants. Gwen asked if he was going to be okay. I shrugged. Jimmy took his place in the line and stood with a commanding poise that seemed to overcome the effects of the alcohol.

The MC reminded the gathering that it was 11:04, less than an hour until the New Year, before he announced contestant number 11, a Charlie Chaplin imitator, who mimed a routine to a fast-paced piano accompaniment. The line moved forward and the next contestants took the stage, a man and woman in blackface who did a song and dance.

During the number, Danny Felton passed near my table. I was struck by the slight limp in his gait as he made his way through the crowd. He accompanied the short bald man with the cigar. Behind them the bulky fellow in the overcoat shepherded them along. The bald man appeared troubled, waving his cigar as he chattered on. But Felton was cool and calm in his white tie and tails, listening to his companion with a half-smile and observing the crowd as he passed. For a moment I met the icy glint of his eyes, as the threesome moved to a door at the end of the room by the freight elevator. The tall man in the overcoat knocked and opened the door, holding it as Felton and the cigar smoker went in. Casting a glance around, the tall man disappeared inside closing the door behind him. I felt vaguely uneasy.

Turning back to the talent contest, I could not find Jimmy in the line of contestants at the front of the room. I was relieved when I spotted him, partly obscured by a group of women in tutus who were standing around a table of Russian Cossacks. The contestants' line had moved up, and a new act had taken the stage. A young man with a shrill, nasal voice was dancing and singing a clever song about the dangers of modern life as he took off his business suit to reveal a caveman costume.

A couple of uninspired acts followed before Jimmy was announced as Miss Velma LaRuse, the Vamp of the Blues. He moved onto the bandstand and toward the piano with a stately walk. It appeared as if some other character had taken possession of him. His noble demeanor grabbed the attention of the audience, and a hush fell over the crowd. He struck a graceful pose next to the piano before seating himself at the keyboard. After a pause, Jimmy began to play.

As he sounded the first chords, establishing a languorous tempo, a shiver passed through me. I recognized the introduction to "You Need Some Loving"—the song he was playing when Eric was killed.

For the past week he had been practicing another song, and I expected to hear that when Velma LaRue took the stage. I guessed that seeing Danny Felton had taken Jimmy back to Chicago, and on the spur of the moment, he decided to play something different. Or maybe the song chose him.

Jimmy played the intro at a slower tempo than I was used to and a voice sang out that I'd never heard from him before. The moan of the lyrics colored the room blue. A passionate anguish struggled up out of some deep source. Electricity crackled through the room as Jimmy intoned the lyrics to a rapt silence.

> *"I went to see the doctor today*
> *To see what he had to say.*
> *Something must be wrong,*
> *I'm worried all day long."*

Then all hell broke loose. Flashes of red light shattered the fixed attention of the crowd. An alarm bell clanged. Pandemonium flooded the hall.

"Raid!" someone shouted.

All across the room people leapt to their feet. Confused revelers scrambled for the doorways. The man in the winged Ariel costume tripped on an overturned chair and fell down with a cry. A table tipped over. Glassware crashed, followed by the tinkle of shards scattering across the floor. Screams and shouts split the air.

I dodged through the confusion toward the bandstand. Jimmy was seated at the piano, still playing, as if in a trance. Gwen and Charlie had followed and were calling to Jimmy, who seemed not to hear them. I jumped onto the stage and grabbing Jimmy's shoulders, I called his name and gave him a shake. He didn't respond.

"Jimmy, listen. It's Carl. We've got to get out of here!"

He seemed to return to himself and looked around. Trying to stand, he stumbled, and I steadied him. With my arm around his shoulder, I led him down from the bandstand to where Gwen and Charlie were waiting.

The whole place was in chaos. Crowds pressed at each exit

door. There was the sound of breaking glass as a Russian cossack threw a chair through a window to create another way out onto a first-floor rooftop. Several patrons tripped over a fallen drunk who was unable to get up.

The four of us made our way toward the nearest door, trying to keep moving forward without panicking. More people crowded in behind us, pushing.

While we waited to get out, approaching police sirens wailed in the streets. I asked myself why, of all the speaks in town, the police chose to raid this one. I considered taking a seat at the nearest table and waiting for the inevitable arrest but decided there was still a chance we might slip out unnoticed amidst the confusion. If that possibility existed, I had to do what I could to avoid being caught in a situation that would jeopardize my career.

"Well, the jails will be filled with an interesting crowd tonight," Gwen said.

"I wonder if they'll lock us up in the men's side or the women's," Charlie said. She chuckled and gave Gwen a comforting little hug.

I pulled Jimmy near. "Don't worry. I'll keep you close to me."

Jimmy didn't speak. He still had a dazed expression and a blankness in his eyes. I hoped the alcohol was responsible for this effect, but I feared something more dangerous.

Once we got onto the stairway, there was no thought of escape. We were hemmed in by the press of bodies. A woman in a clown suit was weeping. Somebody called out that a man had jumped out of a second-floor window and smashed his skull on the sidewalk. No, another voice said, he landed on his feet and only twisted his ankle. Someone else said the proprietor was a Jew, who was too stingy to pay off the cops. A voice started singing "Auld Lang Syne" and we took up the song, which seemed to lighten everyone's spirits. Our progress down the stairs moved at a snail's pace.

After what seemed like an eternity but was maybe ten minutes, we emerged into the fresh, cool air of the New Year. A string of paddy wagons lined the street, and policemen herded revelers into the vehicles. There was no slipping away. I urged Gwen and

Charlie to stick close to us so we wouldn't get separated, and we all ended up crowded into the same wagon. Charlie insisted that Gwen take the last seat, and the rest of us stood as the remaining space filled up.

A heavyset man dressed in a tuxedo and reeking of alcohol crowded in next to Jimmy. With slurred speech and exaggerated compliments, he insisted that Jimmy was the most beautiful woman he had ever laid eyes on. Jimmy and I changed places, and I told the gent to watch what he said to my girl. This sent Gwen and Charlie into an explosion of laughter which they struggled to suppress.

A man in a monk's hood who was accompanied by a young blonde dressed as a nun began singing "Auld Lang Syne" again and the rest of us joined in.

THIRTY-ONE

It turned into a much longer night than we had planned. We were taken to police headquarters, but no one was jailed. Jail might have been preferable to the interminable wait to be booked and fingerprinted. When we could find a seat, we dozed while we were able. But much of the time we were on our feet shuffling forward with the queue or being marshaled from one room to another.

Some of the policemen were less than gracious in their treatment of Jimmy. There were the inevitable catcalls and whistles. One particular pair of officials in street clothes focused their malice on him. I recognized Bateson with his cruel green eyes. I sensed that he recognized me in spite of my captain's uniform and overseas cap. They razzed Jimmy for a while until, out of fatigue, I lost patience and told them to knock it off. They started in on me, baiting me with abuse about "my girl." When they saw that Gwen and Charlie were with us, they began to harass them with remarks about "who wears the pants in the family."

A police sergeant passing through noticed the abusive pair and called out, "McConnell and Bateson, you're needed in dispatch." The two exchanged glances and made gestures toward the back of the departing sergeant, before bidding us good night with "So long, gorgeous," and "Sleep tight, lover boy." Their derisive laughter faded into the crowd.

Later a commotion at the entrance to the room caught my

attention. There were loud voices as two policemen escorted a bearded man about 40 into the room. Bateson followed with a teenage boy. It was Billy Butler, whom I'd met in Pioneer Park so long ago. He was taller now and more handsome than back then. But, as before, his dark curly hair needed a trim and he wore an old brown workman's coat. The bearded man kept trying to turn around to call back at the boy.

"Don't tell them that, Billy. I never done nothing bad to you. I only tried to be your friend and help you out. Tell them so, Billy. Don't believe what they tell you. They don't mean you no good. Not like I did, Billy. Tell them I was your friend. I never tried to hurt you. Remember I gave you my coat, Billy lad. Remember that."

"Shut your trap, you degenerate," one of the cops said as they took the man off into a passageway at the back. Billy followed Bateson through the doorway of an office at the other side of the room.

After the booking and fingerprinting, we were finally free to go. A dim morning light was just beginning to filter into the sky by the time we descended the front steps of the police headquarters. We were a comical sight as we approached a taxi cab—a disheveled man in drag with a woman in a tux, and a rumpled Red Cross nurse with a weary doughboy. The cabby seemed unfazed by such an incongruous entourage and drove us back to my car near the warehouse.

"I hear there was a big raid down here last night," the driver said. "There must be a new gang of rum runners around town who made it worth the coppers' time."

We were all too tired to ask about his conjecture, but Jimmy elbowed my ribs and gave me a knowing look. We dug through our pockets to pay the cab fare including a good tip for the driver.

When we arrived at Gwen and Charlie's, they invited us in to change clothes and have some breakfast. Gwen changed first. After Jimmy got out of the dress and makeup, he put on the tux that Charlie had been wearing. Charlie changed into a pair of tan slacks that she had planned to wear as Gallagher. She said she felt more comfortable in them. Breakfast was a silent affair. We were all too sleepy and dispirited to talk. Day was dawning under an overcast sky when Jimmy and I drove home and tumbled into bed.

THIRTY-TWO

It was past 2 in the afternoon when I woke to Jimmy crying out. He lay beside me breathing heavily. I wrapped an arm around him and waited for his respiration to calm. He gave a little groan, opened his eyes, and covered his head with his hands. "Oof."

"You okay?" I asked.

He took a deep breath. "Oh, my head."

"Hung over?"

"Shh. Not so loud," he moaned and rolled over. I watched him go back to sleep.

Later in the afternoon I was reading in the living room when Jimmy emerged wrapped in a terry cloth bathrobe and looking pale. He sat down on the couch and stared out the front window.

I closed the *New England Journal of Medicine* and laid it on the floor beside my chair. The house was quiet.

Jimmy sniffled.

"Coffee?" I said.

"Maybe a weak cup of tea."

After I returned from the kitchen, he sat sipping the tea.

"You had a bad dream."

"I don't remember."

"You woke up making a noise. Like a little cry."

His brow wrinkled. "Oh?" He took another sip of tea. "Oh, yeah. It was one of those falling dreams." He set his teacup down.

"I don't remember the details. But I could feel the floor drop out from under me." He shook his head. "That's all I can remember. That sensation of falling."

"We had a rough night of it."

"Yeah." He rubbed his face. "Felton."

"You're concerned."

"Damn right." He fidgeted with the belt of his bathrobe.

"What can he do to us?"

Jimmy looked at me with astonishment. "You're not serious."

I shrugged. "What are you thinking?"

"He could do anything." He was agitated. "You don't know him."

"You're right. I don't know the man. But he does seem to have a peculiar…presence."

"Yeah, he gives me the creeps." Jimmy looped the terry cloth belt around his finger. "Last night I remembered some things I told him in Chicago—things that maybe I shouldn't have. I thought we were just having a friendly conversation, but now I see he was pumping me for information. I told him you were a doctor—he said it was always good to know someone in the medical profession." He looked at me.

I felt that same vague uneasiness I'd felt the night before. "And I mentioned that Diggs' father was in the shipping business."

"Holy cow." My uneasiness was becoming less vague. "Do you think he would try to get Mr. Monroe into shipping liquor?"

"Exactly." Jimmy frowned as he looked out the window. He took a deep breath. "There's something else I've never told you."

"What is it?"

He twisted the belt and shook his head. "Jesus." He sighed. "I don't know where to start."

"Start anywhere."

Jimmy reached for his tea and collected his thoughts as he cradled the cup.

"He told me he could get me a job. So I was considering playing piano there at Eric's club—which Felton was backing. But when things started to go south with Diggs and the band, I thought I could get back in their good graces by seeing if Felton could get something going for them. I met him for lunch…"

I waited. "Go on."

He rotated the teacup between his palms.

"He wanted to have sex." Jimmy glanced at me and looked out the window again. "I didn't understand…I wasn't sure what was going on. I just hadn't thought about it before." He sighed again. "So he took me to a hotel room and I was just sort of going along with everything but before I knew it…I don't know…he was forcing himself on me." He set down the teacup and rubbed his palms against his thighs. "That dark-haired man that was with him last night—Herman's his name. He was in the other room, so I figured there was no way out of it."

"So he raped you?"

"I didn't fight him off. What could I do?" Jimmy shook his head. "That's why Charlie's story hit me so hard. I knew what she'd been through—when you feel like there is nothing you can do to stop it so you just give in."

I went and sat beside him and put my arm around his shoulder. A flock of small birds swooped past the picture window.

"But it got worse." He took a deep breath and turned his palms up in a shrug and let them drop onto his lap. "Before I could dress, Herman came in and held a gun on me while Felton made me take a shot of dope."

I squeezed Jimmy's shoulder and took his hand in mine. He clasped my fingers.

"That's why I had to help Vance."

I leaned my head against his. "You're a brave man, Jimmy Harper."

The next evening after work, Tom Harris knocked on our door. He'd heard about the raid. A fellow reporter covering the story had learned that the editor wanted to print the names of some prominent citizens who had been arrested, thinking it would sell more newspapers.

"I did some arm twisting and negotiating," Tom said, "and got the editor to agree to keep all the names out of the story. I saw your names on the list and wanted you and Jimmy to know about it."

"Has the Klan got anything to do with this? Was that the only party raided on New Year's Eve? It couldn't have been the only place in town serving liquor."

"Just between you and me, it seems someone paid the cops to raid the place." Tom pulled out his little notebook. "I can tell you that the speak is run by a man named...uh," he flipped through a few pages, "....Maldini. It may be that the Klan had it in for him because he's foreign. The cops who belong to the Klan, like McConnell and Bateson, could have been behind it. But I'm still looking into it. It smells fishy to me. I have a hunch there's something else going on."

"Our cabby last night said there must be some new rum runner in town. That's who he thought paid the cops to raid the place. What do you think?"

"Hmm. That's an interesting angle. I don't know. I don't have a clear picture yet."

"Ever hear of a fellow named Danny Felton?" I asked.

"Can't say that I have. Why?"

"Oh, it's nothing. Just thought I'd ask. If you should hear anything about him, please let me know."

He nodded. "F-E-L-T-O-N? Danny?"

"I guess so."

He wrote down the name. "I'll keep you posted. Meanwhile, I know you'll keep all this under your hat."

I assured him I would and thanked him for keeping me informed. I normally locked up at bedtime, but as I closed the front door, I had a sudden urge to lock the bolt. The whole thing was making me more and more uneasy.

THIRTY-THREE

During the first weeks of the new year, I was confronted with a number of cases that troubled me.

A few days after the New Year's raid, I was called in the afternoon to see a man at the Lutheran Hospital. I had gotten my admitting privileges around the end of November and had been doing more surgeries there. The man in question had been booked into the local jail for vagrancy, and when he was found in his cell, unable to walk, he was sent for care.

I entered the exam room where the nurses had left him alone, lying on the table, his wheelchair in the corner. He was the same man the police had brought into police headquarters with Billy Butler. He had a gaunt face with a grizzled beard, and there were purple bruises on his cheek and forehead. His skin was tanned and weathered as if he had spent time out in the elements, and the furrows on his brow heightened a sadness in his eyes.

He had been walking just fine at the police station, so if he could not walk now, something must have happened while he was in custody. I had to gain his trust so I could learn what happened.

I began by smiling at him. "It says here that your name is Sam Patterson, is that right?" I set down his paperwork and extended my hand. "I'm Dr. Holman."

He raised his arm with a soft groan and shook my hand. "Hi, Doc." He winced.

"Got some pain in your arm there?" I held on to his hand and supported the arm as I lowered it gently to his side.

"Hit my shoulder when I fell."

"Tell me what happened."

"I know it probably says vagrancy there in your papers, but that ain't true. I was trying to help that kid. I felt sorry for the lad. I've been on the road long enough to know how things are. And when he told me his folks was dead, I took pity on him." He grimaced as he lifted his head to look up at me.

"I can't speak to your legal case, Mr. Patterson, but I want to know what happened in the jail."

"They kept me locked up with a bunch of other fellas for a day or so before these two men from Vice came and took me to a room to talk. They started asking me a lot of questions that didn't make any sense and I couldn't answer them. Least I couldn't give them the answers they wanted. And they started to rough me up."

"Is that where you got those bruises on your face?"

"I guess so. They punched me in the mug a couple times. That's when I fell out of the chair and landed on my shoulder. Then the tall guy kicked me in the back. Down low. I heard something crack and I felt a pain like nothing I ever felt before. I'm not sure if I blacked out or what. But after a bit they were hollering at me to get up and I couldn't. My legs weren't working."

"Are you still having the pain in your back?"

"If I don't move, it's okay."

I examined him and ordered x-rays. A nurse, an orderly, and I eased him onto a gurney and they wheeled him away.

It turned out Patterson had a spinal fracture and would need physical therapy at a sanitarium. But there wasn't much hope that he would ever walk again.

Now I had the problem of figuring out how to write my report. I decided to consult with Dr. Ferguson, even though I wasn't sure how far I could trust him. I'd overheard him talking with Bateson last year, but it hadn't sounded like they were well acquainted. I'd never been in this position before. I had to talk to someone.

I told Ferguson I'd seen a patient from the jail who had suffered an injury.

"That happens from time to time," he said. "The prisoners fight among themselves." He was filling out a form on his desk.

"I'm not sure what to make of the patient's story."

"How's that?" He pulled a paper from the other side of his desk, glanced over it, and continued writing on the form.

"He suggested that some officers might have been involved in the injury."

Ferguson looked up from his paperwork. "I see."

"I'm not certain how I should word my report."

"Is the patient still here?"

"He'll be here a day or so."

"Give me your notes and other papers from the case. I'll take charge of it."

"I'd like to follow this patient myself."

"That won't be necessary. I'm sure you have other patients who need your attention."

"I have a personal interest in this case."

"Leave this to me, Holman." His voice was neutral but firm. "I will see that things are taken care of."

I sat for a moment staring at him. I wanted to be sure Patterson was well cared for, even though there didn't seem to be much that could be done for him. I wanted to find out more about Billy Butler and his relationship with Patterson, but it sounded like Ferguson didn't want me to know any more.

"You can go now. I have paperwork to finish."

As I left Ferguson's office and walked down the echoing hallway, a cold, hollow feeling came over me. I realized how much was out of my control.

"100%." That's all the sign said in the doorway of my regular barbershop a few blocks from the clinic. The sign had never been there before. I'd been trying to make time for a haircut since the holidays but wasn't able to get away from work until the second week of the new year.

The "100%" signs were not new to me. The first one I'd seen was at Hamlin's grocery store before Jimmy left for Chicago, and when that ugly incident happened, I took my business to Klaus Dietrich. After that I began noticing the signs at other businesses around town.

I just needed a trim and I didn't want to have to search out another barber right then. It was just a haircut after all. I'd been going there for over a year. What could happen in a barbershop?

There were four barber chairs, one for each barber, facing a row of chairs for waiting customers along the opposite wall. I knew all the barbers, but I usually waited till Max was available. He was just finishing up with a customer when I came in. He gave me a nod and I took a seat in his empty chair. As Max got me draped and ready, who should walk in but Vice Officer Bateson. He took a seat facing me in the row of chairs along the wall directly in front of Max's chair.

His piercing green eyes fixed on me. I sat perfectly still, looking at my reflection in the wall mirror above his head. I got the distinct feeling he had followed me in.

"And what can we do for you today, Dr. Holman?" Max asked. I stiffened, wishing he had not used my name. But Bateson had already recognized me and my name was no secret to him.

"Just a quick trim around the back and sides," I said. I wanted to get this over with.

I glanced in Bateson's direction, before looking away. A smirk had spread across his face.

Max started in on the back of my neck. A gray-haired customer came in and sat down next to Bateson. The older gent picked up a newspaper and opened it.

Bateson turned to him. "Did you see the story the other day about that raid on New Year's Eve?"

I kept my eyes on the wall mirror above his head

"I missed that one," the gray-haired man replied into his paper.

Bateson turned to look at me. "Seems a crowd of sexual deviants held an illegal drinking party."

"You don't say." The man looked up from his paper.

"At a warehouse by the river." Bateson stared at me.

"I hope they shut the place down. Especially if it attracts degenerates." The man went back to his reading.

"Oh, it got shut down, all right." Bateson held his eyes on me.

"Good," the older man said.

Max began to trim around my ears.

"Say, Dr. Holman," Bateson called across to me. "How's your little girlfriend?" The smirk was still there.

I couldn't believe he was addressing me. I tried to ignore the comment.

Max said, "I heard you were engaged, Doc."

"To a very fine nurse." I wanted to deflect Bateson's remark.

"I thought you were engaged to that little fairy," Bateson said.

How was I supposed to respond? I had to say something to defend myself. "I'm engaged to a very fine woman who works as a nurse."

"Was she the one wearing the pants that night? While your boyfriend was wearing a dress?"

The barber's scissors stopped clipping. All eyes in the shop turned on me. The gray-haired man lowered his paper. The shop went quiet.

I forced a laugh. "You've got it all wrong, fella. It was a costume party. All in good fun. One of my fiancée's friends invited us, along with her boyfriend. Only an ignorant ass would take it all wrong."

The silence continued while Bateson and I stared at each other. Max let out a laugh and resumed clipping. "My wife and I went to a costume party a few years back and we exchanged clothes for it. That was the most fun we ever had. I don't think we ever laughed so hard." He continued to chuckle and shake his head.

Bateson stared at me with a cold rage but didn't say anything more.

The man with the newspaper said he had been in a show while in the army during the Spanish-American War. "I dressed as a woman and sang a duet with a young officer who played the part of my suitor." He laughed. "I think the troops got a big kick out of it."

A rotund fellow in the next barber chair told about going to a club in New York City where there were female impersonators. "They were as good as anything I've ever seen at Keith's or any of the other vaudeville houses. Told some of the funniest jokes I ever heard."

Max finished up and I paid. While I went to retrieve my hat and coat from the rack, Bateson kept his eyes fixed on me. It felt like a warning.

As I put on my coat, I turned back to him. "Have a good afternoon." I donned my hat and left.

Walking away, I heard someone behind me and felt a hand fall on my shoulder. I spun around. Bateson's eyes were boring into me.

"Listen, Holman. I just want you to know the score." He spoke in a muted voice. "I know you examined that old geezer at the hospital. Ferguson told me all about it. I suggest you keep that to yourself. Just remember that I know about you and your boyfriend at that New Year's Eve party. And I also know that you've been dispensing birth control information. That's not a very popular subject with a lot of my friends."

I couldn't believe he would threaten me right there on a busy street. But no one passing by seemed to notice. Maybe an anonymous public sidewalk was the best place to hold such a private conversation. His message was clear.

"The case you refer to—I turned it over to Dr. Ferguson. It's completely out of my hands."

"Keep it that way." He glared at me, then turned and went back to the barbershop.

I glanced back at the "100%" sign then walked away. The encounter was not something I dared risk repeating. There must be other barbershops around that aren't aligned with the Klan, I thought. Maybe something on the east side closer to our house. I would ask some of the doctors at St. Mary's.

THIRTY-FOUR

I had been doing charity work each week at the lying-in hospital for indigents run by the Catholic sisters. Although I did not specialize in obstetrics, I enjoyed the challenge and continued to learn with each case. But I knew that I might have to give up this volunteer work in response to Gowan's crusade against the Catholics.

That's where I met a 17-year-old girl who had come from New Jersey with her boyfriend to find work. She was supporting them both on her meager wages as a shop girl while he hunted up a job. When he found out that she was pregnant, he abandoned her.

She was one of the sweetest people that you would ever want to meet, radiating an innocence and hopefulness, and the nuns working there recognized these special qualities in her. She would move through the wards and cheer up other women who had been similarly abandoned, offering solace and support.

That same week a local Catholic orphanage brought a male infant to St Mary's and I was asked to examine him. The baby was a six-month-old that Gwen and I had helped deliver. The parents, a couple in their 30s, had gone out on a drinking a binge, leaving the tot locked in a closet for several days. When he was found by a neighbor, he was suffering from malnutrition and neglect and they took him to the orphanage. Upon examination I discovered he had a skin rash from unchanged diapers. But the most disturbing thing was that the child's body bore numerous cigarette burns. The infant survived all this and after a week of care by the Catholic nuns, he was doing well.

About a week later Rebecca Porter returned with her daughter late in the afternoon. Mrs. Porter had a black eye, which was a day or two old. When I asked if that is why she had come, she said no, it was nothing, she had simply bumped into a door in the night. Her daughter Sally seemed more withdrawn than before and kept her face hidden in her mother's lap.

"Why are you here?"

"I…I'm sorry. I'm bashful about discussing women's problems. I believe Sally is showing early signs of the curse." The child peeked up at me, then buried her face again.

When I said that would be unusual in a child of 5, she said Sally had been injured in a fall while playing. The little girl whimpered but kept her head down.

"Sally, can you tell me what happened? How did you hurt yourself?" I said.

Fear filled the mother's eyes. "She…she slipped getting out of the bath. And fell on the rim of the tub, you know, down there."

Sally looked up at her mother and began to cry. "I did not," she blurted out between sobs.

"There, there, dear. It's all right. The doctor will understand. I've brought you here so he can help."

"Mrs. Porter, I'm going to have to examine her. Okay?"

"Of course."

"I need your help."

"I'll do anything I can. I've been so worried."

"I understand." I got up and went around my desk toward the child. In a gentle voice I addressed her. "Sally, I'm going to need your help too." I squatted down to be at her eye level. Again she peeked out at me, her brow wrinkled, as she pulled back against her mother. I smiled at her. "Will you let me help you? You came to see me before, remember? We're old friends. I'm not going to hurt you."

"Don't be afraid, Sally," her mother said. "Dr. Holman wants to help."

Sally began to cry again and hid her face.

I waited till she quieted down. "Will you play a game with me?" She peered out. "Do you like perfume? You must have smelled your mother's perfumes, right?"

The child turned to face me and nodded.

"I've got some perfumes in the other room that you might like." She sniffled. "Will you come and see?" She looked up at her mother.

"It's okay, dear. Let's go with Dr. Holman."

"Okay," Sally nodded.

I stood and backed toward the exam room.

Mrs. Porter got up from her chair and took the girl's hand. "Come along then."

I left them standing by the exam table while I took some bottles down from a cabinet. "I think you'll like these, Sally." She watched with interest. I'd left some shaving lotion there, and there was also the rubbing alcohol, and the chloroform.

I sprinkled a bit of shaving lotion on a wad of cotton and held it out for Mrs. Porter to smell.

"Mmm. That's lovely."

"Do you want to smell?" I said. I didn't want Sally to feel pressured. I paused. The girl hesitated and looked up at her mother.

Mrs. Porter nodded. "Go ahead, dear. It smells very nice. Take a sniff."

Curiosity got the best of her and she took a tentative step forward.

I squatted down and held out the cotton at arm's length.

Sally leaned forward and smelled. She smiled and looked up at her mother.

"See," Mrs. Porter said. "Isn't that nice?"

Sally nodded. "Uh-huh."

"Here's another," I said holding out a sample of rubbing alcohol to the mother.

"Yes, that's nice too," she said. "Very clean. Try it, dear."

Again the child responded well. Next I soaked some chloroform on a piece of cotton. This time I gave Mrs. Porter the barest whiff before offering it to Sally.

"Take a deep breath as you smell this one," I said. "It's very sweet." She did as I suggested. I could smell the odor of the chemical even at arm's length. Again she smiled up at her mother. "Try it again," I urged after dousing the cotton again. She took another long sniff.

"Hold her hand now," I said to the mother. She took Sally's hand. The girl's eyelids fluttered and I reached out to support her.

"Let's lay her on the table," I whispered to Mrs. Porter. The child was becoming sleepy. Once we laid her flat, I held the cotton over her face. She murmured and squirmed a bit but soon became still.

"Now you hold this cotton over her face while I do a quick exam."

I raised her skirt. There was blood on the girl's underwear. In the course of the examination, I was convinced that the child had been raped. I finished quickly, taking a swab from her vagina to make a wet smear on a microscope slide.

"Mrs. Porter, I want you to witness this so you will know what I am doing." She watched as I prepared the slide and wrote in grease pencil on the end of the glass. "It has her name and the date on it."

I discarded the chloroformed cotton and asked Mrs. Porter to readjust the child's clothing and wait at her side. Meanwhile I stained the slide and looked at it under the microscope. Spermatozoa were scattered throughout the smear, their tails whipping and squirming amidst the background of red blood cells. The motile sperm cells indicated that less than 48 hours had elapsed since the assault.

I felt a vague nausea. What goes on in men's minds, I asked myself, that causes them to do such things? What must the child have suffered?

I recalled my first experience with anal intercourse while in the military. The pain at first... But a small child? I shut out the thought.

Opening a small bottle of formaldehyde, I eased the glass slide into it.

This was a case that would require delicate handling. I knew that contacting the police would bring nothing but trouble for Mrs. Porter and her child. No one would believe the child's word against a grown man's, even if Sally were able to tell her side of the story.

I remembered the family connection with Bateson. The thought of involving him made my skin crawl. All at once it occurred to me that Bateson might be responsible for the rape. I shuddered.

I had to talk to the mother alone. I asked Vivian, the receptionist, to come into my examining room and watch Sally while I spoke with the mother in my office. Vivian frowned but acquiesced.

When I told Mrs. Porter my diagnosis, she became agitated and tears filled her eyes. She begged me not to tell anyone. I asked if she had any idea who might have violated the child. She shook her head.

"Could it be a friend of the family...or a relative?" She covered her face with her hands. "Could it be Mr. Bateson?" I was praying this wasn't the case.

She shook her head. "No, Gladys and Steve love Sally." She was adamant in her denial. "They were there when she was born and helped me get back on my feet. They would never hurt her."

It was a relief to hear that. I hoped she was telling the truth. I waited. "Is it the girl's father?"

Mrs. Porter could not hide her fear. She recognized that I understood what she was thinking and nodded. "I went out to do some errands and left her with Marvin. When I got back and figured out what had happened, I confronted him." She pursed her lips and took a deep breath. "That's when he hit me." It was all she could say before she broke down.

I waited while she got hold of her emotions.

She took out a handkerchief. "Marvin was never the same after he returned from the War." She blew her nose.

"I understand," I said. "May I call you Rebecca?"

She wiped her cheeks and nodded.

"Rebecca, I want to help you. My first concern is for the safety of this child. Now, do you think that your husband will become violent again?" She hesitated. "Or do more harm to the child?" I could see the fear in her eyes. She nodded her head slowly.

"Does your husband know that you've been to see me? Today or the last time?"

"I haven't told a soul."

"Good." I asked if she had any relatives or friends she could stay with.

She said the only people she was close to out here were the Batesons and she couldn't impose on them any further. She wished she could return to her family in Nebraska. "I don't know where to turn," she said and began to weep again.

I gave her a moment before telling her I had a plan if she would trust me. I asked if she was willing to go somewhere to hide for the night. She paused a moment and gave me a curious look, before nodding.

"Is it safe for you to go home and gather up a few things, if I have someone drive you there?" She said she could. Her husband had gone to his local speakeasy and never came home before dinnertime.

"Do you have any money?"

"I have a little tucked away at home."

I showed her into the examining room so that she could wash her face and freshen up. Vivian returned to her desk, and I sat and watched Sally begin to come around. When the child was able to stand, Rebecca and I helped her to a seat in the reception area. I phoned Gwen to explain the situation and ask if Rebecca and Sally could spend the night in the extra room at Gwen and Charlie's. We would send the two on the train to Nebraska the following morning. Next, I called Jimmy at home and asked if he was free that afternoon. When he said yes, I asked him to take a cab over and run an errand for me in the Ford.

When he brought my car back, Jimmy told me that Rebecca and the girl were settled at Gwen and Charlie's, and he had sung a few songs for Sally and finally got her to laugh. He taught her a funny song and told her she could sing it on the train ride to her grandmother's. As soon as Gwen got home, he left them in her care.

Jimmy was planning to drive Mrs. Porter and her daughter to the train station early the next morning. We decided that I shouldn't be seen with them in case someone might be following the two. Just before Jimmy left to pick them up, Gwen phoned to tell us that Rebecca and Sally had slipped out of the apartment before dawn. Gwen had heard someone using the telephone before they left. "Rebecca told me last night that we shouldn't have gotten involved," Gwen said. "She fretted that it would make trouble for us. I think she was worried about what Bateson and her husband might do."

Gwen guessed that Rebecca had called a cab to go to the train station. I hoped she was right. But after I hung up the phone, I speculated that Rebecca's husband would have discovered them missing the night before. If he told Bateson, which I assumed he would, I wondered if there was any way they could trace Rebecca and Sally's movements. Could Mrs. Porter have taken one of my business cards and perhaps left it behind inadvertently? Or written my phone number somewhere it could be found? Were there other ways Bateson could connect me, or—Gwen and Charlie—to their disappearance?

The fate of Mrs. Porter and her daughter troubled me throughout the day. I kept wanting to find out if they had escaped. But there was no way to ask around without implicating myself. What that child must have suffered continued to haunt me.

THIRTY-FIVE

The next evening the sweet-natured 17-year-old at the lying-in hospital went into labor. I had already put in a full day's work when the sisters called me in because of serious complications. The baby was breech, something I had not encountered before. The labor went on for hours as I tried to turn the infant. By the time I decided to do a C-section, it was too late. Both the mother and the child died on the operating table.

It was dawn when I cleaned up and changed back into my suit. I was exhausted. I knew I had done all I could, but I still blamed myself. Maybe Gowan was right. I'd been working too hard. I should have called in a more experienced obstetrician. I should have called Gwen. Compounding that, the girl's gentle personality made her death all the more terrible for me.

I checked my pocket watch. There were morning appointments scheduled for me at the clinic, so before leaving the hospital, I ate a quick breakfast with two cups of coffee and drove to my office.

After my first patient, I felt my hands trembling as I washed up. Just exhaustion, I told myself. The water faucet continued to drip in the sink while I dried off. Tightening the handle stopped the water, but it did not make the dripping sound stop. It was that same drip-drip-drip from the Berlin morgue when I knew I had lost Gerald in 1919. And now I was shaken by the loss of this girl and her baby.

My concentration flagged as the morning progressed, and all through my next appointment that dripping noise continued in my head.

After the patient left, I went into my office and slumped at my desk, alone, feeling weary and sick at heart. The dripping continued. I remembered feeling the same way at the dressing station near Meuse-Argonne.

"Can't you help me, Doc?" The look of terror in the eyes of the young soldier holding his intestines in his hands. There were so many casualties. Forty-eight hours straight trying to patch up the worst of the wounded. Trying to stop their bleeding—just as I had tried to stop the 17-year-old mother from hemorrhaging. The memory of removing the dead baby from her uterus tormented me.

An image of the bruised and bloody face of Jerry the Fairy floated in front of me. At least I had been able to recognize him. Gerald had been beaten so badly there was no face to recognize. I hadn't been able to sleep for days after Gerald was murdered in Berlin.

I closed my eyes for a moment.

Jerry's discolored face hovers before me, slowly merges into the pulpy mass that constitutes Gerald's shattered features. The overhead lamp in the morgue gleams on the metal examining table, the water drips in the sink. His face is no longer a face but a swollen, purple, bloody gash. German voices murmur in the background. The face begins to move and change. The strong odor of carbolic acid assaults me. I feel my hand squeeze into the bloody opening, wedging between the baby's body and the wall of the uterus. Sally Porter's voice cries out, "No. No!" The uterus begins to writhe and bursts open with the stench of putrefaction, oozing white maggots and squirming spermatozoa.

The jangle of the telephone jolted me awake.

It was Vivian. Gowan wanted to see me. I rubbed my face and stretched. The dripping had stopped but I was unsteady as I walked to the door, and I held the knob for a moment. Taking a deep breath, I headed to Gowan's office.

"Dr. Holman, I must talk to you about some things." He sounded solemn, leaning back in his chair.

My antennae went up.

"Dr. Bleeker and I have been discussing several troubling circumstances that have come to our attention over time."

I was fully awake now.

"First there is the problem of your continued association with St. Mary's Hospital. I've encouraged you to cut your ties there and bring your patients to the Lutherans. But your activities at St. Mary's have persisted. And you refuse to use Dr. Adrian's place—a perfectly fine facility."

I sat staring at Gowan and struggled to remain calm.

"We've already lost a number of patients from the clinic," Gowan went on. "I told you about the Hamlins. And last week the Denishoffs and the Norlens took their business elsewhere. You're no longer an asset here. Even Iverson doesn't want you working at the new hospital. You stir up too much trouble with all your new ideas."

"But it's not just me," I said. "It's the College of Surgeons. The world is changing around us. Are we to stay mired in the past, like fossils? Should we stand still while science marches on? I can't do that."

"There are other more serious matters. As you know, this profession is a highly public one. A doctor must be held to the highest moral standards in any community. Without the public's trust, we can't carry out our important calling."

I guessed what was coming.

"A number of incidents have concerned us recently. There have been some rumors over the months about the nature of the people you spend your time with. Then, just recently, it was brought to our attention that you were arrested in a raid on a tawdry speakeasy on New Year's Eve. Not only that, but I have it on good authority that you were in the company of some of these questionable individuals at the time of the raid."

This was what I had been expecting.

"Normally, what you do outside of work is your own business. But when outside behavior becomes public knowledge, it reflects on the clinic. And frankly, Dr. Holman, I'm afraid that having your name associated with our clinic has become a liability."

Gowan paused and leaned forward with his elbows on his desk, fingers spread, tapping his fingertips together. The family portrait with its smiling faces stood nearby. The tapping stopped. He kept his fingertips poised and brought his palms together, almost as if he were praying, and lowered his hands onto the desk.

"Dr. Bleeker and I have decided that it is necessary to ask you to separate yourself from our surgical group."

So, it had come to pass. Drs. Bleeker and Gowan had deliberated and Gowan had made his decision. To my surprise, my very first reaction was one of relief. I no longer owed any allegiance, nor now, even lip service, to them.

I knew that the names of those arrested in the raid had not been published, at least not by Tom's newspaper. But I was sure that with all the connections between the police and the Klan, Gowan had heard plenty. All that must have influenced his thinking, besides the complaints and innuendoes from Minnie Mitchell and the Hamlins, which had no doubt continued.

I looked Gowan in the eye. "This is about Jimmy, isn't it?" I said calmly.

Gowan feigned incredulity. "I'm afraid I don't know what you mean."

The slippery bastard, I thought. Questionable individuals, he'd said. Who else could he mean?

"Bob Gowan, you know exactly what I'm talking about."

He folded his hands on his desk as he lowered his eyes. "Carl, this is about professional decorum."

"This is about Jimmy. And about what you call manhood, isn't it? Well, Gowan, there is more to manhood than fathering children." I gestured toward his family portrait.

"This is about some serious allegations of unnatural acts."

Unnatural acts?

"You think my friendship with Jimmy Harper is unnatural? No. It's not. I'll tell you what is unnatural. Fathers who abandon their teenage girlfriends to die alone in childbirth. And fathers who…" I stopped myself. I couldn't mention Lloyd Haskell. I was still uncertain. Besides, Gowan might guess which 12-year-old boy it was. "…who rape their 5-year-old daughters."

I stood up abruptly and leaned on his desk, looking him in the face. He looked away.

"Unnatural is men who beat their wives. And mothers who burn their 6-month-old infants with cigarettes—"

I began pacing.

"Unnatural is teenage soldiers with their limbs blown off and their intestines hanging out from wounds caused by so-called civilized nations—but not having been there, I guess you wouldn't know about those kinds of unnatural acts, would you, Gowan?"

I paused to take a deep breath and stared him down.

"There are a lot of things in this world that are more unnatural than my friendship with Jimmy Harper. And one of those things is bigotry."

"Watch yourself, Carl."

"And another is hypocrisy."

"Tread softly. Don't say anything you will live to regret."

"I have to say what I know is true. And I must do what's right."

"Do whatever you see fit. But you will not do it at this clinic. We can't have you working here." He looked me in the eye. His voice was quiet and firm, but his face was like steel.

I was silent for a moment as the ramifications of his finality began to sink in. The stubborn irrationality of it all. All I could feel was a rising anger.

"Very well then, you won't have to wait for my resignation." I tore off my white coat. "I quit. I've had it with this goddamned clinic." I threw the exam coat down on the chair and stormed out.

I was in such a blind rage that I didn't even think to slam the door behind me but left it swinging open, clattering against the bookcase.

I went straight to my office, collected my hat and coat, and left the clinic.

THIRTY-SIX

As I drove home, my hands were shaking. I was still in a rage. I tried to concentrate, to formulate some kind of future, but my thoughts were a jumble. The only thing I was sure of was my relationship with Jimmy.

Although my fatigue weighed on me, I was too agitated to sleep and I wanted to be alone. I knew that Jimmy and Joe Locke would be at the house, and I couldn't bear to face them. Not just now. So I drove through our neighborhood to the local park and took a long walk under the leaden sky.

I began to regret my tirade. I was glad that I hadn't gone into the unnaturalness of unnecessary hysterectomies—or of circumcisions. An old French proverb came to mind. "Noise never does any good. Good never makes any noise." Too late now. There was nothing to be done. By the time I got back to the car, I felt calmer, but my mind was not clear.

My route home took me past the Beasley house on the back side of our block, right behind us. I noticed a truck parked in front and workmen carrying furniture out and loading it up. As I drove by, I took note of the name of the moving company on the side of the vehicle. I would soon have to think about moving things out of my office at the clinic.

My pocket watch read half past 3 when I got home. Jimmy and Joe Locke were in the kitchen.

"What are you doing home in the middle of the afternoon?" Jimmy asked.

I avoided his eyes as I entered. "Oh, I didn't have any afternoon appointments." I took off my overcoat. "So I thought I'd come home and work in the garden."

Jimmy and Joe exchanged looks.

"I've got to be leaving soon," Jimmy said. "I'll be breaking in my new tux at this do tonight."

I didn't reply but went into the bedroom to change into work clothes before slipping out the back.

The January sun was still hidden by a thick cloud cover and the garden soil was damp from recent rains. As I surveyed the dead stems in the vegetable beds, I heard bumping and banging and the sound of voices from the Beasleys'. Moving. A time for moving on. Gowan.

During months of neglect, the garden beds had been overtaken by weeds, crowding out the dead vegetable stems. I began ripping the weeds out by the roots.

So Gowan and those bastards in the Klan were singling me out. The Invisible Empire was crowding out anyone who was not like them. And not just in small rural communities like Bisby. Shopkeepers and small enterprises all over Portland were affiliating with the Klan to enhance their businesses and discourage anyone who disagreed with them. The city police department, the county government, state officeholders. All allies. What could I do but tend my own garden?

Too many of the weeds broke off at the base, leaving the roots below ground. I got a shovel out of the garage. As my boot pushed the rounded point of the blade into the wet earth, a feeling of satisfaction came over me. I continued turning the heavy clay soil and bending down to shake out the clotted roots before tossing them aside. I tried not to think, but thoughts crowded in anyway.

I kept digging. Gowan's words *unnatural acts* kept turning over and over in my mind. Was my digging in the soil a natural act? Was there anything natural about human beings? Huh, Gowan?

I rammed the shovel into the earth with all my force. What is natural about human agriculture—besides the sunshine and the plants themselves? Where, Dr. Gowan, do you draw a line between the natural and the unnatural? Didn't humankind make up the word "natural" to distinguish between us and the world of nature? How natural was wearing white hoods and lynching Negroes and frightening yellow men, eh, Gowan?

I had reached the middle of the bed when Jimmy came out the back door in his new tux.

This is about Jimmy, isn't it?

I paused and wiped the sweat off my brow with the back of my glove. Jimmy crossed the patch of lawn, watching me. I leaned on my shovel.

"Carl, you didn't come home last night. You must have been called into surgery."

...separate yourself from our surgical group.

"Yes."

"Have you slept?"

"No."

A dog barked in the distance.

"Is everything okay?"

"I'm all right." I wasn't up to talking. My thoughts and feelings were too confused.

I could tell Jimmy wanted to come closer but didn't want to get mud on his new patent leather shoes. "You sure?"

I nodded.

"I've got to catch the streetcar downtown." He studied my face. "Mr. Cassidy from St. Joe's wants me to play jazz at this gathering." He paused. "It's that wedding anniversary party I told you about."

Well, Carl, I think matrimony will do you good. You need to have some kids.

"Oh, I'd forgotten." I forced a smile. "Well, don't let me keep you."

"I won't be back before 11."

I nodded.

Jimmy waited. "It's getting dark. Why don't you come in?"

"In a minute. I'm almost done here."

"Okay." He hesitated, surveying my face. He seemed to know something was wrong but he must have sensed that I wasn't ready to talk. "I'll see you later, then." He turned to leave and paused, looking back at me, then went on his way.

I kept digging. Jimmy. *Unnatural acts.* Isn't it humans, Dr. Gowan, that are the most unnatural animals? I thrust the shovel in again.

Turning over a spadeful of heavy soil, a fat earthworm squirmed and disappeared back into the earth.

But we are animals, after all, aren't we, Dr. Gowan? Just like this earthworm? We may have the sciences and the arts and spiritual aspirations, but we must accept the fact that we are all animals connected to this physical world. It's earth's web of life that sustains us. I remembered Darwin's treatise on earthworms from undergraduate biology. How profoundly the whole world of plant life depends on these humble creatures.

Cawing overhead caught my ear and I looked up to see a flock of ragged black shapes flapping above me. I rested a moment, leaning against the wooden handle of the shovel while the crows circled once and flew on.

Are we so different from these "lower" animals, Dr. Gowan? We have the same curiosity of crows, the industriousness of bees, the loyalty and affection displayed by dogs, the courage and tenacity that other animals show in defending their young, the grief shown by various species when they lose a mate. No, Dr. Gowan, I have never had any qualms about being descended from animals that have tails. My qualms are about being part of your human race.

The light was fading. Jimmy was right. It was time to go in. But I kept digging. My shovel uncovered another earthworm but peculiar in form. I knelt down to see better in the gray light. The creature wriggled and split in two. I had disturbed two earthworms copulating, lining up their hermaphroditic bodies to exchange genes between the paired male and female genitalia on each of the two.

Part female and part male. Combined. No dichotomy. Was this unnatural, Dr. Gowan? You bastard. You and your perverted Klan.

I went back to digging and my shovel struck something hard and immovable. I probed its edges, working it loose from the heavy clay soil. Finally, I was able to dislodge it from its burial site, freeing it into the light. In that shovelful of earth I had found a stone about the size of my fist. Brushing it off with my glove, I could just make out by the fading daylight that it was sedimentary rock, composed of striated layers, smoothed and rounded over time, with the small white curling shape of a fragment of seashell embedded in the layers. Darwin again, I thought. Those fossils in college geology class.

Are we to stay mired in the past, like fossils? Should we stand still while science marches on?

Joe Locke came out the back door. I stood looking at the rock in my hand. He was leaving to catch the streetcar home. "I left dinner for you next to the stove." He hesitated for a moment before he told me it was too dark to be working in the garden.

I agreed. "I was just headed in."

He said good night and disappeared around the corner of the house.

How could I explain my situation to Joe? How would I keep him on if I couldn't work? How was I going to explain all this to Jimmy?

I went to the garage carrying the rock in one hand and the shovel in the other. After I closed up the garage, the rock was still in my hand. I couldn't put it down. It was like some kind of talisman.

After changing out of my muddy clothes, I washed the rock clean in the kitchen sink. It glistened with the water, its layers prominent now and the white arc of shell visible in the electric light. *Darwin.*

I dried the rock and laid it on the kitchen counter, while I poured myself a glass of gin, almost without thinking, and took a swallow. It seared my throat. I was in a peculiar state of mind.

I left the stone and the glass of gin on the table in the breakfast nook, while I went to a bookcase in my study and searched the book spines on the bottom shelf. There it was. I hefted *On the Origin of Species*, lugged it back to the breakfast nook, and sat down to read.

It must have been an hour or more before I remembered that Joe Locke had left a meal for me. The glass of gin was long since empty and I refilled it and took another healthy swallow. I found the dinner tray beside the stove, but the food was cold and I had no appetite. It didn't matter. I went on reading and drinking gin until I began to nod off over the book. Go to bed, Carl, I told myself. You need to rest. I went to the bedroom, but once I lay down, my thoughts surged like a river at flood stage.

Would I ever do surgery again?

Jesus, it's Gowan's fault. No, there is no Jesus. That's just mythology. There is no help. But I love my work. Now Gowan says Iverson doesn't want me working at the new hospital. Oh, to hell with Iverson. Adrian, too. I hear that Adrian's made innuendoes about me being effeminate. Is that what he really thinks of me? Will Adrian and Gowan block me from ever operating again? They could smear my reputation—while they do unnecessary hysterectomies. My God. Their greed is grotesque. But what about ethics? Can I possibly lead an ethical life in this kind of society? Those Klansmen at the Bisby Grange when I was first getting acquainted with Jimmy. Their bigotry. The violence of brute force. Raw power. 100% Americanism? Is that ethics? Grocer Hamlin standing there in his bloody meat case apron while he insulted my "character." Was all this because Minnie Mitchell started some rumors about Jimmy and me last summer? *Unnatural acts.* Gowan's words. What isn't unnatural? Is surgery natural? Gowan says, *"Matrimony will do you good."* Gwen. My dear old friend. Having babies? That unmarried 17-year-old girl. I should have called in an obstetrician. So much blood. Gerald's demolished face. The dripping. No. The German officials in the morgue. No! Was my love for Gerald deviant? Tom said Bateson had it in for deviants. That's why they passed the human sterilization laws. Would I end up being castrated? Is castration natural? Can love be *un*natural? "You need some lovin' when you feel sad," Jimmy sang. Oh, Jimmy. "Noise never does any good, good never makes any noise." Jimmy tossing pebbles in water at the park. Not Pioneer Park. The loneliness. I can't go back there. Jerry the Fairy. Billy Butler. What's he doing with Haskell? *Haskell's a hot head*. Was Henry Haskell violated? His dead body on the operating table. Poor kid. And that dead baby. "Can't you help me, Doc?" That young soldier at Meuse-Argonne. Maybe I'm no good as a surgeon—or as a man. I'll never be a pillar of the community. Like Gowan's Klan members. Should I move to another town? Start over. Evolve. *Are we to remain mired in the past, like fossils?* The human family has not evolved so very far. Move on. But what about Jimmy? *This is about Jimmy, isn't it?*

Oh, forget it, Carl, I told myself. Let it go. Don't think about it. No good comes of all this rumination. But the jumble of thoughts continued. Darwin. Gowan. The Klan. Our lack of evolutionary progress. Maybe that's what's bothering me. But no. It's my career. And my relationship with Jimmy. Do I have to choose between them? What kind of choice is that? That would tear me apart.

I couldn't bear it. I got up and paced. The mental chaos persisted. I poured more gin and went back to the breakfast nook. Back to Darwin. As I focused on the words and concepts, my wild thoughts began to recede. Just like when I read medical texts, the rest of the world melted away.

When Jimmy got home, I was still in the breakfast nook, scribbling notes on papers scattered about the table beside the open volume of Darwin.

"What on earth are you doing up?"

"I couldn't sleep. I couldn't stop thinking. I had to do something. I've been reading. You've got to see what I've found. Darwin has it right. It's all here. This is…"

"Carl," he shook my shoulder to get my attention. "Calm down."

I looked up at him.

"What is it?" Jimmy asked.

"Oh…I don't know. It's nothing. I guess I got carried away." I took a deep breath. "Maybe I've just been working too hard."

"You've been pretty quiet today."

We were silent for a moment.

Now, with Jimmy there, I was able to focus my attention. Without considering, I blurted out, "Gowan fired me."

"What?" He sat down across from me. "He fired you?" He was speechless as he took it in, and I couldn't think what else to say.

At last I spoke. "He heard about our arrest…after the raid. Said I was keeping company with questionable individuals."

"Carl, I…" Jimmy stared at me with his mouth open.

"I asked Gowan right out if it was because of you, and he wouldn't answer. He said it was a matter of allegations of unnatural acts. Ha. Unnatural acts. That's what's got me so riled up." A fly buzzed over the table and I shooed it away. "While I was working in the garden, I kept wondering if there's *anything* human beings do that is natural. Why, modern man has developed to the point where we have completely transcended the natural world. There are thousands of things that humans do that are unnatural— wearing corsets, driving automobiles, flying in airplanes… plunging the whole planet into a great war. I saw it with my own eyes. Unbelievable weapons and unbelievable destruction. The war to end all wars. Next to all that, what is so unnatural about two men loving each other?"

"I've never seen you so agitated," Jimmy said, but I barely heard him. He looked disturbed, but I was too intent on my own obsessive thoughts to pay attention.

"I think people like Gowan believe that some final perfection has been achieved with modern man. Some ideal state of the world has been realized. He and Minnie Mitchell and the Hamlins and Dr. Adrian—all of them. Their kind think this is the way things are. This is the way the world is completed. But everything changes. The geology is always shifting. All the species continue to pass on and become extinct over time. Even stars and galaxies are born and disappear over the eons." I turned to the book. "Here, I have to read this to you. Let me see, where was that…?"

"You've been reading Darwin all evening?"

"I kept thinking about it while I was digging in the garden. Look what I found." I pointed to the striated stone sitting near my notepapers. "It shows exactly what I've been thinking about all afternoon."

Jimmy picked up the rock with a dubious look and examined it, as I thumbed frantically through the volume.

"Here. Here it is. Chapter 14. Listen to this." I leaned in, excited.

"'Nature may be said to have taken pains to reveal, by rudimentary organs and by homologous structures, her scheme of modification, which it seems that we willfully will not understand.' You see? Don't you see? Gowan and the Klan and all of them. They are not just blind. They are willfully blind. They refuse to open their eyes and look around themselves at the world we live in, and see what's right in front of their eyes. See it for what it is. We must jolt humanity out of its everyday catatonia. Its willful blindness." I brought my fist down on the text.

"Carl!" Jimmy reached out and placed his hand on mine. "You remind me of one of those Bible thumpers." He lifted my clenched hand and closed the book. The pages slid together with a quiet thump.

"What are we blind to?" Jimmy cradled my knotted fingers in the palms of his musical hands and looked into my eyes.

I stared at him.

"What are you blind to?" he asked again.

I realized how wound up I had become. We sat there in silence, the quiet of the midnight house and the sleeping neighborhood surrounding us. The fever broke. My mind cleared and something turned.

"…Good never makes any noise," I said, staring off into space.

"What? I don't follow you."

"Oh, nothing. It's just…something I have stuck in my head."

I remembered Gowan's steely face. *Carl, you can't work here.*

"I'm afraid. I can't bear the thought of losing my career. And now with Gowan…and the Klan…I'm afraid I may never do surgery again. I've been through so much…all those years of school…the sacrifices during the War. All the experience I've gained…I can't let all that go to waste. I love this work. I love seeing that I can make some small difference in lives that are so full of suffering. And lately I've seen so much suffering…so many damaged people. I want to heal them all."

Jimmy took a deep breath. "Carl, I'm the reason all this is happening. I hate to be the cause of so much misery for you. Maybe I should move to an apartment. Or go away somewhere, to another town…" His face was sincere and intent, with no hint of anger or irony.

I realized that he was serious. "No, Jimmy. No!" I felt a rising panic. "You can't leave. You're all I've got." I remembered how I felt after Gerald in Berlin…after the War….that desperate loneliness… my visits to Pioneer Park. Those empty years. "You mean the world to me. I don't know what I'd do without you." I raised my fist from Jimmy's hands and beat it against where my sternum shielded my heart. "I lost Gerald. I couldn't bear it if…"

Jimmy got up from his chair and knelt next to me. He took my clenched fingers in his hands. "Carl, I can't hold your hand when it's all bunched up like that. Please, take my hand."

As he continued to hold on, I began to loosen my fingers.

"I wouldn't leave unless you asked me to," he said.

I felt something give way inside. I let go and gave in to it. The dam broke, and a flood of tears flowed forth followed by wrenching sobs. This was no longer the simple physiology of lacrimal glands and saline secretions. Pain gushed out from some subterranean reservoir.

Jimmy held me in his arms as he knelt beside me. The house was quiet except for a moaning that accompanied each sob, a voice that at first I didn't recognize as my own.

I buried my face in his shoulder. Soon the flood began to ebb.

"I'm sorry." I tried to sit up. "I don't know where that came from." I took a deep breath and it quivered as I let it out.

"Maybe you have a secret drawer in your heart where you keep all those tears locked away." Jimmy handed me his handkerchief. I blew my nose and began to regain my composure.

"All these messy bodily secretions," I said, trying to laugh, but more tears came.

Jimmy said, "Do you remember what you told me? Tears are the body's way of getting rid of all that pain so that you can see clearly again."

"Did I say that?"

"When I first got back from Chicago. You were talking about Gerald."

I blew my nose again. "Who says men don't cry?"

"He-men without hearts," Jimmy replied, "that's who."

I tried to laugh but another little sob came out with it.

Jimmy pulled his chair up and sat close to me. "You know, I've been thinking this over…for quite a while actually…and I wonder if you don't…well, try too hard…to make up for the fact that you're different." He paused to see if I understood. "You don't have to be the greatest doctor in the world in order to make up for loving another man. You're a good doctor. Isn't that enough?"

"Is that what I've been doing? Compensating?" I wiped my eyes with his handkerchief. "Maybe you're right."

"You can't heal the whole world, Carl." He took a deep breath. "If you're lucky, you can heal yourself."

I blew my nose again. "Maybe I *have* been working too hard." He nodded.

From the living room the clock began to chime midnight.

"You know what else I've been thinking?" he said with an impish grin.

I shook my head.

He tapped his chest. "The shortest distance between here and there," he reached out to touch mine, "…is a curved line."

"What?" I was puzzled.

"The gravity of our love bends space and time."

After the final chime sounded, the house was quiet again.

I couldn't help laughing. "You've been spending too much time with that Cassidy fellow." I handed back his handkerchief. "Thank you."

"You must be exhausted."

I nodded.

"Come to bed."

"Yes. I think I can sleep now."

He got up and reached out to me. I took his hand and let him lead me down the hall to bed where he held me until I fell asleep.

THIRTY-SEVEN

By morning, the gray skies had given way to bright sunshine. I felt an odd sense of liberation and a twinge of discomfort too— even shame—at my behavior the day before. Not my behavior with Gowan—I was still angry, and I felt I had a right to be, though I thought I should have been more diplomatic. But with Jimmy. He was right. I had worked myself into a frenzy. And he was right on the other counts. I had been working too hard. Now maybe I could take a rest. And maybe I had been compensating, trying to make up for...for what? For not accepting myself as I am? I felt a sense of deep gratitude and love for him as we sat together over toast and coffee in the sunny breakfast nook.

"Thank you...for putting up with my tirade last night." I set down my coffee cup. "And for everything else."

He smiled and placed his hand on mine. "It's okay."

Soon he was off to the library to research a new choral piece for St. Stephen's, and I was left to figure out how to pick up my life and keep moving forward. A whole agenda of items confronted me, but it didn't feel like a burden of obligations. Being unemployed and unencumbered, I felt relaxed and calm. This was like a vacation. In orderly fashion, I began to deal with each thing that required attention.

First, I telephoned the clinic and asked Vivian to cancel the remainder of my appointments. I wasn't sure what, if anything, Gowan might have told her yet, but I wanted to give her my version. I said that circumstances forced me to take a sudden leave of absence and that I would be in to clear out my office later in the day.

Since Gowan and Bleeker normally ate lunch at their club, I went to the office a little after noon and began packing up my personal belongings. After separating out the few pieces of furniture that were mine and the books and other items that I had brought in over time, I labeled them for the movers. Next I called the company that I'd seen at the Beasleys' and arranged to have my things picked up the following day. Before I left, I grabbed my patient index cards. If I was starting over, I would need to have patients. As I left the lobby of the office building, I felt relief, not sadness, and I was thankful that I had managed to avoid running into Gowan or Bleeker.

Now, I had nothing pressing to attend to. After a bite of lunch at home, I took a long walk. My feeling of liberation from earlier in the day was tightening into anxious concerns about my future. On the bright side, I had Jimmy and Gwen and Charlie, along with other casual friends and acquaintances. I had a roof over my head, food in the pantry, and a reasonable amount in savings. I had a profession and considerable skill and experience. And a good reputation. Or did I?

Had my medical reputation been called into question—along with all the rest of it? I knew my status was tarnished with Minnie Mitchell and the Hamlins, with Lloyd Haskell and Bateson and the Klan, but now with Gowan and the medical establishment also. At least I was still in good standing with St. Mary's. Wasn't I? I walked to the park, brooding over the possibility of starting a medical practice on my own and fearful of being the target of a Klan boycott like Klaus Dietrich's grocery.

On my way home, lost in thought, I passed the trolley stop just as a car was pulling up.

"Hey, Carl," a voice called out.

Jimmy dismounted and crossed the street to meet me. He was carrying a couple of books. "Nice surprise, running into you," he said, smiling. "I found some great stuff about that choral piece. And a book about Einstein. What are you doing out here?" His face darkened as he noticed my dismal expression.

I didn't realize how downcast I had become. I made an effort to buck up and look more chipper. "I…just walked to the park." I made an offhanded gesture in that direction.

Jimmy sensed my mood. "Do you mind if I walk with you?"

"No, I'm headed back." The trolley pulled away. "I just needed to think."

We walked without saying anything for a few blocks before Jimmy broke the silence. "I understand how you must be feeling." He shifted his books to the other hand.

"I know you do." We came to a corner and waited as a car turned past us. "I just need some time…to sort things out."

We were coming up the back side of our block. The moving truck was gone from the front of the Beasley house.

"Looks like the neighbors are selling," Jimmy said, pointing to a "For Sale" sign on the lawn. "I wonder where they're moving to."

"So that's what all the commotion was about," I said. "I heard them banging around while I was working in the garden yesterday. There was a moving truck there."

When we got home I decided to work some more in the garden. As I cleared away the weeds I had uprooted the day before, I recalled Jimmy's curiosity about where the Beasleys were off to. I wondered if I should consider moving away. No, I mustn't think that way. I tried not to think about anything. The weeds became my sole concern.

When I came in from the garden, I was feeling less gloomy. Jimmy came into the kitchen while I was drinking a glass of water. He suggested we invite Gwen and Charlie over for dinner that evening. "Do you want to call them?" he said.

I guessed that he thought it might raise my spirits. He was right. The notion of talking to Gwen cheered me up, but I was not ready yet to tell her about my rift with Gowan.

"Sure," I said, "but I'd better check with Joe Locke first."

I found him dusting knickknacks in the living room. When I asked him about dinner plans, he nodded a perfunctory okay, but he was too preoccupied and upset to listen. He said his mother had taken to her bed with a case of nerves over the possibility of losing the family business. The developer who had his eye on their corner location in Chinatown was demanding that they vacate. Discouraged as I felt about my own situation, I did the best I could to reassure Joe, and promised to call the attorney that Roundtree had recommended. Thinking of Roundtree, I wondered if he knew anything about the Beasley house.

It had been a few weeks since I had talked with the property lawyer, and he hadn't gotten back to me, so I felt the need to follow up. When I phoned, he said he was making headway and had started drawing up papers for the Locke family. I told Joe that the attorney was optimistic. "Tell your mother there's reason to be hopeful." Providing this small service to Joe and his family was a gratifying distraction.

Next I telephoned Gwen at St. Mary's. Her genial voice was comforting. She said they'd love to join us for dinner, but they were both busy that evening. "How about tomorrow night?" she suggested. "We've been wanting to have you fellows over. Would you like to come to our place for dinner? Say around 8?"

"A fine idea. We'll be there." Now I had something to look forward to—and time to think about how to break my news to Gwen and Charlie. Jimmy had been astute in proposing a get-together.

Over the next day, all the obstacles to continuing my medical practice kept swarming through my mind. The Klan. Gowan. Society. I looked forward to discussing all this with Gwen and Charlie. And I needed to hear Jimmy's thoughts. Sooner than later, I had to do something.

In the afternoon the moving truck showed up with my belongings from the clinic. Rearranging my study in order to accommodate all these possessions was one more welcome diversion. I was taking one more step in freeing myself from Gowan.

THIRTY-EIGHT

As we arrived the next evening, Gwen and Charlie's warm greetings consoled me. The aroma of roast pork and freshly baked rolls filled their cheery apartment. They had set out a beautiful table with white linens and their best china.

After some preliminary chatting, we sat down to dine. It took some time for me to summon my courage.

"I'm afraid I have some disturbing news to share," I began after a lull in the conversation. "I am no longer working with Gowan and Bleeker."

"Bravo!" Gwen said, clapping her hands. "I never liked that weasel."

"Congratulations," Charlie said, smiling and raising her glass.

I was not feeling celebratory which must have shown on my face.

Gwen's expression turned serious. "Did you quit or did he give you the sack?" she asked, putting down her fork.

The memory of my regrettable outburst was still painful. "A little of both. I lost my temper when Gowan told me that my character was hurting his business. It seems word got around about our getting caught up in that raid on New Year's Eve. He doesn't like the company I keep."

"I guess that would be us," Gwen said. "Well, I don't think much of Gowan's company."

"Oh dear," Charlie said, "it was my idea that we go to that party."

"It wasn't your fault. This is no time for assigning blame. I want to know what you think I should do going forward." I turned to Gwen. "I'm concerned about salvaging my career."

She gave me a sympathetic smile. "You're a fine surgeon, dear. Your skills are in demand."

"We've talked before about you starting your own private practice," Charlie said. "The friends I've sent to see you for birth control have spoken highly of you."

"And you're still in the good graces of St. Mary's," Gwen said. "Even though they filled that head surgeon position back in December, you still have admitting privileges there and they respect your abilities."

"And you have a great bedside manner," Jimmy said.

Charlie laughed. Gwen tried to stifle a chuckle unsuccessfully.

I couldn't rally myself to join in the amusement. "What I'm worried about is my social standing. Gowan made reference to 'unnatural acts.' I'm afraid that even my engagement to Gwen is not going to protect my reputation."

Charlie turned to Gwen and sighed.

"And we all know about the sterilization laws," I added. "Jimmy and I are at risk of being prosecuted for sodomy."

A pall fell over the table.

"I mentioned this to you the other night," Jimmy said, "that I could find an apartment. If we weren't living together, wouldn't that change the way things look? Maybe I could find somewhere nearby and we could still spend time together."

"No, Jimmy…" I said, alarmed at the idea.

"What if Jimmy moved into our guest room?" Charlie suggested, glancing at Gwen.

"Hmm." Gwen sat reflecting. She smoothed her napkin. "The logical thing to do would be for us to go through with our engagement and marry."

Again we fell silent. No one touched their food. We were all digesting Gwen's proposition.

"That would help solve the problem of social appearances," Charlie said, "with you two living together."

"Would that leave Charlie and me living together at their apartment?" Jimmy asked.

"Having Carl and me married would avoid a lot of the trouble," Gwen said.

This shift in conversation made me uncomfortable. I looked down at my plate.

"Except people would think Charlie and I were living in sin," Jimmy said.

"Yes, it wouldn't look right with us living together out of wedlock," Charlie said with a laugh. "Jimmy and I would have to get married as well."

Jimmy laughed.

I wasn't laughing, and I couldn't look at Jimmy. This was all too complicated and consequential. I pushed the food around on my plate.

"Wait," Jimmy said, his eyes lighting up. "We just saw a 'For Sale' sign on the house behind us here. What if Gwen and you pretended to live here and Charlie and I pretended to live back there?" He paused, looking around the table. "For the sake of appearances."

"Wouldn't that be convenient," Gwen said. The idea seemed to tickle her.

"I've been suggesting to Gwen that buying a house would be a good investment for us," Charlie said.

"I agree with you, dear, but we are so comfortable in our apartment."

"We could at least look at the house," Charlie said. "Wouldn't it be fun to decorate a new home together?"

"But can we afford to buy a house?" Gwen asked.

This idea was beginning to work on me. "I have some savings. I could help you out." But I had doubts as I considered that I would need money if I decided to start a private practice.

We all looked from one to another around the table.

"Well, these are interesting notions," Gwen said, "but I believe we need to mull things over a bit."

"Still, you've piqued my interest about this house for sale," Charlie said. "Let's take a look at it."

"The Beasleys moved out a couple of days ago," I said. "Do you want me to contact the real estate agent? Harold Roundtree sold me my house. He knows the neighborhood."

"I guess there's no harm in looking," Gwen said. "But I want to get back to the idea of you opening a private practice. How serious are you, Carl?"

"I need to keep working."

"You know other doctors in private practice, right?" Gwen said.

"I guess I could ask around to see if anyone is looking for a partner."

"No, I mean opening your own practice. That would give you the most freedom and flexibility," Gwen said.

"But I'd have to find office space—and invest in new equipment and…well, it would be a complicated undertaking. I'll have to think about it."

We continued to talk over various considerations until Charlie said it was time for dessert.

"I like the Beasley house," Gwen said as we gathered for dinner on Monday evening at our place. We had all toured the house on Saturday and over the weekend there were many phone calls between us discussing its pros and cons. "The more I think about all this," Gwen went on, "the more it seems like the best thing for all of us. It would solve a lot of problems if Carl and I got married."

"What about Charlie and me?" Jimmy said.

"I think you should at least announce your engagement," Gwen said. She turned to Charlie.

"But there's more to it than an engagement," Charlie said.

"Gwen and I have been discussing this. Buying the house and all will only work if there are two marriages."

Although the disruption to their lives posed by moving and adjusting to new routines concerned them, they both agreed that there were advantages to having husbands, at least on paper, because of financial matters that posed a legal problem for single women.

We all turned to Jimmy. At first he looked serious, but then he smiled. Glancing over at Charlie, he broke out in a laugh. "I've been mulling this over during the weekend," he said.

On Sunday, Jimmy and I had discussed the possibilities. He liked the idea of telling his family that he was getting engaged. They had been after him to get married since he left college. He was fond of Charlie, he said, but he was hesitant to take such a big step.

"Well?" I said, looking at him.

"What do you think, Charlie?" Jimmy said.

Gwen and Charlie turned to each other.

"I think it could work," Charlie said.

"Charlie and I have been doing some accounting," Gwen said, "and we can manage financially. Charlie thinks the Beasley house is a bit small, but it's larger than our apartment. I think we can make it work. I bet you'll love it, honey, once we move in. It does have one more bedroom. For my part, I fell in love with that kitchen, the way it looks out over the back yard toward this house."

Charlie said she'd been thinking we could landscape the backyards so there is a gate between them. "We can come and go after dark, and the neighbors will be none the wiser."

Jimmy turned to Charlie. "So does this mean we're getting engaged?"

Gwen let out a titter.

Charlie placed an open hand on either side of her face, like petals of an unfolding flower, and cocked her head at a comical angle toward Jimmy, fluttering her eyelashes. He reached out, and she put her hand in his as he sang a line about wedding bells from a popular song.

"Oh," Gwen moaned, "Jimmy gets to marry my pussycat."

Charlie jumped up and gave her a hug. "Don't worry, dear heart," she said. "I'll always love you best."

"I can help with the down payment out of my savings," I said. I had decided on getting a separate business loan. "Jimmy and I have been reviewing our finances, too. I think if we all pool our resources, we can manage the monthly payments on both of these houses comfortably—but we'll have to keep up the rent on your apartment until the weddings are behind us."

"Yes, it will cause some disruption," Charlie said returning to her seat, "but I think this plan is going to simplify all our lives in the end."

"My thought is that I keep this house in my name. Jimmy's name can go on the Beasley house—for Charlie and him after they marry. No one needs to know that Gwen and Charlie will live together at the Beasley house while Jimmy and I live here."

"That all sounds reasonable," Gwen said.

Joe Locke came in and cleared away the salad plates.

"Now, about my medical practice, I've been thinking it over. I could open my own office on the east side, where Roundtree tells me office rentals are less expensive. I would need to borrow some money to start with—invest in new equipment and get myself set up—but I believe there are plenty of patients who don't want to go downtown to see a doctor."

"That's a great idea," Gwen said.

"You've put a lot of thought into it, haven't you?" Charlie said.

"Gwen, what would you say to working with me in my new clinic?"

"Oh, Carl, I would be love to work with you…but what about St. Mary's?"

"You can stay on there until you feel ready to leave. But I can offer you better hours. Jimmy and I have been talking, and I've decided I need to slow down. I have been working too hard." I glanced at Jimmy. "I propose that my new office be closed on Sunday and Monday, and that we only work from 9 to 5 the rest of the week."

Jimmy gave me a curious smile. "So you're taking my suggestion seriously."

"Almost bankers' hours," Gwen said.

"And we'll be working for ourselves so we can schedule vacations," I added.

"My, what a luxury!" Charlie said.

"Maybe the Sisters will allow me to work part time and I could work the rest of the time with you," Gwen suggested. "Until you get established. Then I could quit the hospital altogether."

"Sounds good to me," I said.

Gwen pondered for a moment and said, "I'll start dropping some hints at St. Mary's."

"Those are my thoughts about a new medical practice," I said. "What do you think?"

We all seemed to understand that these were big decisions.

"I think we should give it a try," Gwen said. The others nodded.

"Looks like January could be the month when everything changes," Charlie said.

The rest of the meal was consumed with plans and cautions, but we all basically agreed. Then there were all the wedding plans. I prevailed upon Gwen to have a large wedding, so as to publicize our marriage in the community. Charlie thought a very small ceremony with a justice of the peace was more appropriate for them. Jimmy agreed. By the time we had finished dessert and coffee, we were guardedly hopeful about our plans.

After dinner, Jimmy found sheet music for Mendelssohn's "Wedding March" and began practicing it. Then we decided we had time for one round of Halma—to celebrate our engagements—before it was time to break up the party and think about going to work in the morning at our various endeavors.

THIRTY-NINE

My life, which had been a routine of daily medical exams and occasional surgeries, became a whirlwind of plans and activities in the commercial and social worlds. I was glad for the change. Gwen and I began meeting often to discuss the wedding and the new medical office. We wanted to get the business going as soon as possible, and we set the wedding for late February. The purchase of the Beasley property was in process, and the house would be ready for possession in February as well. Jimmy would pretend to take up residence there as soon as it was available, in advance of his anticipated wedding to Charlie. Charlie would keep the apartment, and Gwen and I would make a pretense of occupying my house.

At first I had difficulty getting a business loan to set up shop. This held up the lease on an Eastside office space that Roundtree had shown me. It was a small one-story building with a storefront window, suitable for a reception area, and a number of back rooms that could be used for exam rooms, lab work, offices, and storage. Located on a pleasant commercial street near a recently developed residential neighborhood, the property had the added advantage of being down the block from a pharmacy, all of which made the site ideal. I liked it very much, as did Gwen, so I put down a deposit with Roundtree, and he said he would hold the place until I could set up a loan. After being turned down by three banks and more than a week of delays, Roundtree told me he couldn't hold up the lease for much longer—he had other offers.

Around this time, Tom Harris stopped by one afternoon to let me know he had run across the name Danny Felton. I offered him a seat and said I was all ears.

"I found out that there was a lot going on behind that New Year's Eve raid on Maldini's," Tom began. "Not only is Maldini a recent Italian immigrant but, just as you might expect, a Catholic to boot. That's two strikes against him. Then it appears his nightclub was taking away business from some local bootleggers because he was importing Canadian liquor from another supplier and undercutting the local prices. The local runners who are paying off the police in the Klan get the short end of the stick. That's another strike. It seems the locals have been trying to put Maldini out of business with a boycott for a while, but it never worked because his place had become so popular with the younger set. So this shadowy figure named Danny Felton shows up in town and I'm not yet sure of all his connections but it looks like maybe he pulled some strings and Maldini got raided."

"Egads! You know Felton is from Chicago. Jimmy got tangled up with him and his Italian gang back there. There were some murders, I guess."

"That all checks out with what I've found."

"So you think Felton is here to stay?"

"It's hard to say. But I found out Felton has some dealings with another fellow you are familiar with. Lloyd Haskell."

"Jesus." My stomach churned. "You remember those black bootleggers were working with Haskell." I tried to fit the pieces together in my mind, but the picture didn't make sense. I was left with a feeling of dread.

"Yup. I suspect Felton and Haskell may be working together. Probably narcotics and booze. I thought you should know." Tom registered my reaction. "Sorry to be bearing more unwelcome news. It's a bad habit of mine." He tried to change the subject. "So how is the new medical office progressing?"

"The office? Oh yes, my new medical practice. It's been a major frustration." I launched into the tale of my loan rejections.

He listened patiently and nodded. "I suggest you try the Taylor Savings and Loan Bank."

I could tell he was onto something and, when I pressed him, he confided that two of the banks I applied at were connected to the Klan through their boards of directors. He wasn't sure about the third. But Taylor Savings and Loan was run by a Catholic, and Tom assured me that I would not find the same bias with them.

"So you think the Klan is behind my not being able to get a business loan?" I was skeptical.

"Look, Carl, you know full well that Gowan and Bleeker are both connected with the Klan. Your refusal to join didn't endear you to them. And you can be sure they didn't keep it a secret. Businessmen talk. Word gets around."

I shook my head in disbelief. "It's hard for me to accept that those thugs have so much clout. I admit I'm pretty green when it comes to running a business, but is this the way things work today? I know the Klan is boycotting grocery stores like Dietrich's and other shops that don't fall in line. I've seen the 100% signs at Hamlin's and elsewhere. But banks?"

"Welcome to the twentieth century. Oh, and by the way, when you talk to Taylor, be sure to mention that you are good friends with the organist at St. Stephen's Church."

I looked at him in disbelief.

"Just a helpful hint," he said.

Tom knew what he was talking about. Within a week I was approved for a loan and Roundtree obtained the lease for the Eastside office space I wanted.

That same week I received a letter of thanks from Rebecca Porter accompanied by payment for my medical services. The letter was postmarked Omaha. Rebecca and Sally had taken a cab to the train station, she wrote, because she didn't want my friends and me to get in trouble for helping her. They had gotten on the train without any problems, and her Nebraska family met her when she arrived.

FORTY

While we were planning the wedding and getting the office up and running, I received an occasional call for my services.

One night I was awakened by a call around 3. I could hear rain pounding on the roof as I hurried to the phone. A woman's voice implored me to come to a café where there had been a fight. She sounded frantic and I could hear shouting in the background. The address was in the old vice district north of downtown, a rough neighborhood I'd heard stories about. I hesitated, wondering how safe the situation would be. "Have you called an ambulance?" I asked. When she said she was afraid to get the police involved, I paused again, unsure how best to proceed. I felt a growing apprehension. Then she told me Billy Butler had given her my name.

This information was not reassuring, but it roused my curiosity. I asked about injuries. The woman said her sister had been cut up in a fight. I told her I would get there as fast as I could, but I insisted that she call an ambulance while she waited.

Jimmy had rolled over when I got out of bed, but he was sleeping when I went back to dress. I wrote him a quick note and went to the car.

It was still raining when I arrived at a dingy café. Under the awning of the entryway, two men were arguing. Hurrying toward them, I saw that one was not a man but a teenage boy. It was Billy

Butler. His dark curly hair was wet with rain. In spite of his old brown workman's coat and scruffy appearance, he was developing into a handsome young man.

The other fellow, a tall gent in a raincoat, was shouting at him. "This is all your fault. I seen what you been up to."

"Someone called for a doctor," I said over the splatter of raindrops.

"Dr. Holman," Billy said. "Quick, in here."

"Don't trust him," the tall man shouted, grabbing my shoulder. "I seen him sneaking cash out of the till."

"That ain't so," Billy said, raising a fist at the man. "Theresa was just helping me out."

"She's been turning a blind eye to your thieving, you little bastard, that's what she been doing."

Billy lunged at him but I stepped in between them.

"I'm here to see to an emergency," I shouted, pushing the man away from the door.

Billy pulled me inside.

"Luke, lock the door and don't let Al back in," Billy said to a small Negro man near the front. "She's back here," he said, leading me across the sawdust-covered floor past some tables to the rear of the café.

A woman with long black hair knelt over a supine body. She appeared to be an Indian and I wondered if she might be from the Warm Springs tribes that lived near my childhood home.

The figure on the floor was clad in a blood-splotched dress. I knelt down for a closer look. The face was unrecognizable— like Gerald's face in that Berlin morgue. I felt like I'd been slugged in the gut.

I forced the image out of my mind and said in my best professional voice, "Turn on the lights and bring me a lamp."

The woman hovered over the body, and I asked her to move aside. Billy brought a floor lamp and plugged it in.

The patient was female and had been severely beaten about the face. Shards of glass were embedded in her cheek. I smelled the strong odor of whiskey. A small gold cross hung at her collarbone, glinting in the lamplight. Behind the woman's head, a single gray braid snaked out, soaked with the blood on the floor. Her pulse was weak but she was still breathing.

"Did the ambulance say how soon they'd get here?" I asked. The other woman and Billy looked at each other. "Have you called an ambulance?"

"I was scared to," she said.

"Dammit. You must call right now. You have a telephone, don't you?"

She nodded. I took a card out of my bag and handed it to her. "Call St. Mary's at this number and give them my name. Tell them there's no time to waste."

As the woman scurried off, the Negro sidled closer. Billy Butler looked on. I took forceps and cotton from my bag and tried to determine where the bleeding was coming from. I began trying to stanch the blood. "Tell me what happened."

Between Billy and the Negro, I was able to piece together that Theresa Littlefoot and her husband had been drinking heavily when they began arguing. He flew into a rage and started beating her, ending with a lunge at her face with a broken whiskey bottle. At that point, two of his pals pulled him off and took him away to a hotel down the street.

I heaved a sigh of relief when I heard the ambulance siren. Soon the attendants had Theresa on a stretcher. As they carried her out, I said I would meet them at St. Mary's.

I gathered up my things. Billy begged me to let him ride to the hospital in the ambulance. He was afraid that Theresa was doing to die. I didn't want him bothering the attendants, but he was so insistent that I told him he could ride with me.

On the way, I asked Billy where he was staying. He told me Theresa let him sleep in a small storage room in the back of the café. "She's been like a mom to me," he said as he hugged the old coat around him. "When I first met her, she'd slip me a dollar or two once in a while."

"Why don't you go home to Idaho, to your folks?"

"You kidding? My mom never treated me no good, not like Theresa. Besides she left us. That's part of why I run away."

"But how do you get by?"

"Oh, I get little jobs here and there."

"Like what?"

"There's this pharmacy fella, he pays me to make deliveries for him. I guess his son died and he lets me ride his kid's bike to take stuff to customers. Honest, I ain't been stealing from Theresa and her old man. Theresa told me to take money out of the till to pay Mr. Haskell. He had some whiskey left off at the café last week and there wasn't no one else around to pay for it."

Lloyd Haskell. There he was again. He seemed to be everywhere I went where there was trouble. I remembered Henry Haskell's venereal warts. Could it be that Haskell was also demanding sexual favors from Billy? Disgust rose in my gut. There was no way I could protect Billy from Haskell.

"You know Haskell could hurt you," I said.

"Aw, I can take care of myself."

I left it at that.

"I saw you at the police station on New Year's Day," I said. "Were you in some kind of trouble?"

"Hell, those damn coppers double-crossed me. The bastards. Bateson said they'd give me money to turn a fella in and they never paid up. What were you doing there?"

"Never mind. So you know that fellow named Sam Patterson? The man with the beard?"

"Hey, how do you know about him? I never knew his last name."

"You don't know what happened to him?"

"Naw. Except for that night, I never saw him again."

"He said he was your friend."

"I had to get friendly with him in order to turn him in. That's how it works."

"Did he give you that coat?"

"That's a lie." Billy gave me a hostile look.

I shifted gears and turned a corner. "Sam Patterson isn't doing so well. It seems Bateson and his friend roughed him up some. He ended up with a broken back and now he can't walk."

"He can't walk?" Billy stared out the window. "Holy crap!"

We were quiet while I turned another corner toward St. Mary's.

"That's why I talked Theresa's sis into not calling the ambulance," Billy went on. "I was afraid they'd get the cops down to the café. I don't trust the lousy rats any more. And I didn't want the cops to find out about the whiskey and Haskell and all. I remembered your name—from that business card you gave me way back—and I thought you'd be able to keep the cops out of it. And now with the Klan fellas all over town, I never know what those assholes are gonna do."

"You know the hospital will talk to the police. They'll have to."

"Son of a bitch. Maybe I better head back up to Seattle. You know, I followed this jocker up to a logging camp in Washington last spring, and we went to Seattle when the snow came on. But I hated Seattle. That's when I come down here. Maybe I'll go down to California."

When we got to the hospital, I left Billy with a nun at the front desk and told her he was a friend of Theresa Littlefoot. I went to the surgical suite.

Theresa was on the operating table for more than three hours as we tried to put her face back together and save her injured eye. She had lost some front teeth and a couple of her facial bones were fractured. It would take months for her to recover.

It was dawn by the time I cleaned up and changed. I was exhausted, but I wanted to check in with Billy and let him know that Theresa would survive.

He was nowhere to be found. The nun at the front desk told me that he had been wandering the halls near the supply room where the narcotics were kept. She and the security guard had thrown him out.

So Billy proved to be as devious as I suspected. I had let him take me in again. But I was also dismayed at his revelation that he and Lloyd Haskell had a business relationship. Would Billy use his knowledge about me in Pioneer Park for blackmail? Would he share that knowledge with Haskell? Maybe he already had. And I continued to worry about whether Billy was having sex with Haskell.

FORTY-ONE

Gwen and I were married in February. All in all, the lead-up to the wedding went without major difficulties, although there were moments when both of us became exasperated with one another and wanted to call the whole thing off. We disagreed about the guest list and what we should wear. Charlie kept bringing up details from her etiquette book, which we took issue with, and Jimmy had his own ideas about music for the ceremony. The situation was further complicated by Jimmy and Charlie wanting to spend more time alone with each of us, but planning sessions for the wedding and the new medical office kept Gwen and me busy.

Meanwhile the demands of wedding events made it hard for us to spend much time at home. With Gwen's parents living so many miles away, we needed to make numerous visits there, first to announce our engagement and later to include them in the wedding plans and to attend an engagement party. We also spent a weekend visiting with my mother and father in eastern Oregon. The wedding announcement was in all the local newspapers. Later on, the wedding, which was held at a small Methodist church in Gwen's hometown, was covered as well. While Jimmy and Charlie stayed home to keep an eye on things at our three homes, we took a brief "honeymoon" to the new Columbia Gorge Hotel on the recently completed scenic highway. This was all for show—we reserved a room with separate beds—but the trip was a welcome relief after the hectic weeks of preparation, and it was my first real vacation since the War.

When I returned, I got some good news. The attorney who was looking into the Locke family case called to say it would take a week or so and a few hundred dollars, but I would be able to get the Locke property lease transferred to my name, as a native-born American citizen. The arrangement was all worked out by legal contract and the lawyer assured me that it would stand up in court. He suspected that Oregon's Alien Land Law would be overturned by the US Supreme Court, but until then, the Locke family business could safely continue operating. Of all the wedding gifts Gwen and I received, that was the best.

It wasn't long before Gwen and I had the medical office up and running. Jimmy helped us repaint the interior. Charlie referred women from the phone company. I phoned former patients, and Gwen's contacts from her years as a nurse were also a help. Soon I had enough patients to pay the bills and keep the home and office going.

Since our wedding, Gwen had been coming to my house each night after work. Jimmy had been making a pretense of living at the Beasley house. Charlie was keeping the apartment, but she and Gwen still ended up spending much of their time there as before. The logistics were difficult, and we were all looking forward to April when Jimmy and Charlie would be married and could officially "take up residence" in the Beasley house.

FORTY-TWO

One morning in late February while sitting at my desk in the new office, Gwen knocked on the door. There was a man in the reception area who insisted on seeing me, saying it was urgent. "He says his name is Roy Underhill."

I didn't recognize the name.

"What about Mr. Hiram? He's scheduled for 10 o'clock."

"Yes, he's here. I'll tell Mr. Underhill he'll have to wait till you're done with Hiram."

Gwen was back in a bit. She closed the door behind her, looking a bit rattled, which wasn't like her. She was not easily put off balance. "Mr. Underhill is demanding to see you immediately. He won't take no for an answer."

I set aside Mr. Hiram's records. "All right. Ask Hiram to wait and show this fellow in."

A moment later she opened the door and ushered Underhill in. He was a man of average height and build with nearly white hair and icy blue eyes. In spite of his alias, I knew who it was at once. I recognized him from the New Year's Eve party at Maldini's. It was Danny Felton.

As soon as he walked into the room with that distinctive limp, the hair stood up on the back of my neck. But the feeling arose from more than just recognizing him. As Gwen left, the look she gave me was one of a similar discomfort. Jimmy and I hadn't said anything about Felton to Gwen or Charlie, either at the Maldini's or later, so I knew Gwen's discomfort wasn't from prior knowledge. Something about Felton's presence was unnerving.

He hung his overcoat on the coat rack and sat down across from me. His hair looked lighter now in the daylight—even his eyelashes were blond. A diamond stickpin glittered on his necktie. He fixed me with his cold gaze before he told me that he had kidney stones. He had suffered from this in the past, he said, and usually passed the stones in a day or two. If he could just get some morphine to see him through the pain, he was sure everything would be fine.

Besides what Jimmy had told me about Danny Felton, I had already heard this ploy from Vance, so I was wary. Felton's demeanor failed to show the kind of pain that I would expect in a patient with kidney stones. I hoped to discourage him, saying I would have to do an exam before I prescribed narcotics. He showed no reluctance.

I led him into the exam room, pointing out a rack where he could hang his clothes and asked him to undress and sit on the examining table.

"Ah, I've always liked the smell of a doctor's office," Felton said, loosening his tie. "Such clean places."

I was not looking forward to this exam.

I told him I would be back in a minute and returned to my office to make notes on his index card while he undressed. I hadn't asked his age and as I filled out the card, it occurred to me that he could have been anywhere between 20 and 50. When I returned to the exam room, he sat on the table wearing only men's hose with garters and a white shirt.

"You'll have to remove your shirt so I can examine your belly," I said.

Felton raised his shirt, revealing an erection. A drop of seminal fluid glistened at the tip of his penis.

"Sorry, Doc. You caught me between a cock and a hard place," Felton said, smiling. His penis was scarred and the foreskin was ragged and uneven. "Don't laugh, Doc. It's not what you think. It's not a bad circumcision, it's what the Germans did to me in the War. Land mine."

"Just hold it aside," I said.

I observed that he had scars running across his abdomen and down the inside of his thigh. Additional ones crisscrossed his left knee.

"God, I hate the Krauts," Felton said. "You know, Doc, those archeologists found that Neanderthal skull over there in Germany—near Dusseldorf. Hell, I think the damned Huns all descended from Neanderthals."

I asked him to lie back on the table while I checked his abdomen. He did as I asked, but he proceeded to stroke himself while I felt for his liver.

"It would be better if you kept your hands at your side," I said. He accommodated my request but fixed me with that cold smile.

As I continued my exam, his skin gave off an unpleasant odor that I could not identify. I asked him to turn over, and as he did so, I saw that he had only one testicle. I finished the exam, and as I washed my hands, I told him to dress and meet me back in my office.

Waiting at my desk, I noted in his record that he showed no evidence of pain and nothing to suggest kidney stones. While I described the extensive scarring, I couldn't help thinking about that young soldier at Meuse-Argonne with his belly torn open. I tried to recall his face but could not. No one could remember all those young faces, splattered with blood and muddy from the battlefields. My attention had been focused on saving lives that hung by a thread in those shattered bodies. It could have been Felton that I sewed together that day. I thought of all the soldiers for whom I wished we'd had morphine. If Felton had told me the truth about being addicted and if he had convinced me that he actually was in the War, I might have taken pity on him and considered giving him a prescription. But pity can be dangerous. Besides I didn't believe his story. And prescribing narcotics could be dangerous, particularly with a man like Felton.

I shook my head. His war story was as bogus as his claim of kidney stones. No, I couldn't prescribe him narcotics. That would give him a pretext to blackmail me. But who could say what he had up his sleeve. Knowing what I did about Danny Felton, I decided to have nothing to do with the man.

When he returned to my office, I told him I could find no evidence of kidney stones and could not prescribe narcotics for him.

"Aw, come now, Doc. Make this easy for me. I'm traveling here from out of town, and I'd normally see my regular physician who knows all about my condition. Maybe I could have him phone you to explain things."

"Have you been addicted to this stuff since the war?" I asked.

"I don't know what you mean, Doc."

"I'm sorry, Mr. Underhill," I said. "I can't help you."

"Look, Dr. Holman." Felton's tone was grave. "I'm acquainted with your little pal, Jimmy Harper." He paused for effect.

"A lot of people know Jimmy," I said.

He smiled. "When he was in Chicago, he told me all about you. He said you were a sympathetic type." His voice became steely. "Please understand my position. If you make things easy for me, I can make things easy for you."

"As I told you, *Mr. Felton*, I can't help you." Using his real name was not a slip of the tongue. I wanted to let him know that I knew precisely who he was. He chuckled. I could see we understood each other.

"You realize, Doc, I can make trouble for you."

"I can refer you to a discreet clinic in California that specializes in the treatment of drug addiction," I said.

Again, he chuckled and said, "But this is such a pleasant little town. I think I'll stick around for a while. I was hoping we could do business." He paused, waiting for me to change my mind.

When I said nothing, Felton took a money clip out of his pocket, peeled off a 100-dollar bill, and laid it on my desk. I didn't move. He laid another 100 on top of it. I stared at him in silence. Felton continued peeling off bills, one by one, until there were ten of them lying on my desk.

"It's out of the question," I said and stood up. "Now, you must excuse me. I have other patients waiting."

Felton took a cigarette from a jeweled case. "Please sit down, Dr. Holman. I'm not through yet."

I remained standing behind my desk.

"Do you think that raid on New Year's Eve at Maldini's was an accident?" Felton continued. "You see, he refused to do business with me, too." Felton took a puff on his cigarette and stared at me. "Do you think Gowan sent you packing just because of that Haskell kid?"

"What do you know about the Haskell case?"

"I know enough to put the knowledge to use," Felton said.

How could he have influenced Gowan to give me the sack? I suspected that he was bluffing—at least I hoped he was.

"I'm sorry, Mr. Felton. I must ask you to leave. I have patients to attend to."

Felton took another puff on his cigarette and exhaled. "Very well, doctor." He uncrossed his legs, stood, and strolled to the coat rack. Holding the cigarette between his teeth, he put on his overcoat. He straightened his clothing and taking the cigarette in his fingers, he said, "Think it over, Doc. Your nurse has my phone number. Give me a call."

I gathered the hundred dollar bills from my desk, went over to Felton, and stuffed the money into the pocket of his suit coat next to a neatly folded handkerchief.

"There is nothing to think over, Mr. Felton," I said and opened the door for him to leave. "Goodbye."

He stared at me while he took a puff from his cigarette. "I'll be in touch," he said and smiled. With that, he walked out the door.

I returned to my desk and sat frozen. So everything Jimmy had told me about Felton was true—and then some. Was there anything we could do to protect ourselves from a man like this? I was anxious to tell Jimmy that Felton had come to my office, but I did not want to discuss it over the phone.

I also needed to explain the situation to Gwen. I arrived at the reception desk just in time to watch her eyes following Felton out the door. The patients in the waiting area were all staring after him as well. Gwen looked worried. I couldn't discuss this with her at our busy office so I suggested she and Charlie join us for dinner.

FORTY-THREE

At home, Joe Locke had the day off and Jimmy had started dinner. Gwen and I were helping him in the kitchen when Charlie arrived from work. She was riled up like nothing I'd ever seen. At work that afternoon, a co-worker had tried to recruit her to join the women's auxiliary of the Klan. But what upset her most was a Klan publication that she had been given. Before she even removed her coat, she was off on a rant.

"You will not believe what this thing says. Just listen to this." She began reading aloud.

"'Never before in the history of our great movement have the hearts and souls of manly men been thrilled with such emotion for our righteous cause. The spirit of Klankraft is bringing untold thousands of big, virile men into the fellowship. We seek to become the masculine arm of Protestantism in the interest of cleaner local politics and a more moral community.'"

Charlie looked up from the pamphlet. Jimmy and I exchanged glances and chuckled.

Gwen came over and put an arm around her. "Charlie, honey, calm down and take off your coat."

"Oh, I'm sorry. This is just so beastly. And that was the funny part. Wait till I get to the scary part."

Gwen took the pamphlet and leafed through it while Charlie hung up her coat.

"They've included some recipes," Gwen observed.

"Yes, they're probably recipes for poisoning Catholics and Jews," Charlie called from the hallway.

Jimmy couldn't help laughing. "Charlie, I've never seen you so wound up."

"You should be too," she said, returning to the kitchen. "We should all be angry. I can't believe those ninnies at work would even consider joining the Klan, let alone suggest that I should. No one with an ounce of sense would have anything to do with such an organization."

"They haven't got an ounce of sense," I said as I chopped vegetables at the kitchen counter. "Do you think Gowan and Bleeker have any sense? Disassociating themselves from an excellent colleague like me?"

"I couldn't agree more," Gwen called out, stirring a pot on the stove.

"Now listen to this. This is the bone-chilling part..." Charlie flipped through the tract. "'Our devoted squad of whispering women is our secret weapon for 100% Americanism. Together we strengthen our moral communities and rid ourselves of foreign pests simply by shopping at and supporting only 100% business establishments.' After that they have a listing of Catholic and immigrant businesses that no one should patronize—with street addresses—including Dietrich's Grocery. No wonder that poor man is going out of business."

"Let me see," I said, stepping to Charlie's side. She pointed to the address. I stood there reading, still holding a kitchen knife in one hand and a parsnip in the other.

"Jesus," I said. "That's a damned crime. Who else do they list?" I examined the page. "Holy Toledo. Walter Austin? He isn't Catholic. I treated his wife a while back and they're no more Catholic than I am."

"And," Charlie continued, "there is a perfectly disgusting article about an ex-nun and her allegations about parochial girls' schools and convents. I can't even read that stuff."

"Where?" Gwen said, taking the pamphlet.

Jimmy stepped in and read over Gwen's shoulder.

I returned to the cutting board. "What does it say?"

"Oh, it's not proper dinner conversation," Charlie said, going to the stove and lifting a lid to see what was cooking. The aroma of braised onions permeated the air.

"My word," Gwen said. "It says 'They were forced to lie in bathtubs where menstrual rags were soaking?'"

"I don't want to hear it," Charlie cried. "I'm going to the living room."

"And this nun claims she was forced to lie in a coffin full of feces," Gwen continued. "That's absurd. Who invents this tripe?"

"Of course, it's absurd," Charlie said over her shoulder. "I was raised Catholic and went to a Catholic girls' school. I never heard of such goings on." Her voice trailed off into the other room.

Jimmy took up the pamphlet and began perusing it. "'My word' is right. Here it says that the priests imprisoned and raped the school girls. And later some of the girls committed suicide."

We heard Charlie begin to play the piano in the front room as Jimmy read to himself. "And here they talk about the priests forcing the nuns to, and I quote, 'submit to their unnatural sexual desires.' Unnatural desires?" He shook his head. "Then when the nuns became pregnant, they were forced to have abortions. Good God, this is incredible. My guess is that more priests are interested in the altar boys than in the nuns." Jimmy and I laughed.

Charlie's playing rose to a ferocious volume as she plowed into a rendition of the final movement of "Moonlight Sonata."

"Boy," Jimmy said to Gwen, "she really is upset by this, isn't she?"

"I think this all must have touched on some things from her childhood," Gwen said. "I'll go talk to her. Stir the soup, will you, Jimmy?"

I finished with the vegetables and dried my hands. "Let me see that booklet," I said.

"It's hard for me to think that anyone buys that stuff," Jimmy said, turning to the large pot on the stove. "It's so unbelievable."

"Tom Harris says all bigotry is irrational," I said. "Why do you think people are so afraid of folks like us?" But I was thinking of folks like Jerry the Fairy.

"Because of folks like Danny Felton," Jimmy replied in a tone thick with disgust.

His remark took me aback. "Because you think he's like us?"

"He seems to prefer young men—sexually."

"Well, I may as well tell you. That's the reason I wanted us all here for dinner tonight. Speaking of the unbelievable, I gave Danny Felton a medical exam today. He wanted me to prescribe morphine for him."

Now it was Jimmy's turn to be taken aback. "My God." He covered his mouth with his hand.

"It's okay. I refused to deal with him. What can he do?"

"Anything," Jimmy said. "He's not human."

"Or maybe he's all too human," I said. I could see the worry in Jimmy's face. I put my arm around him. "Try not to think about it. We'll lie low for a while and keep our eyes open."

Jimmy didn't reply.

When we sat down to dinner, I recapped my encounter with Felton. Jimmy, with my prodding, told about seeing Felton on New Years' Eve and shared some of what he knew about Felton's business in Chicago. I stressed that we all needed to be careful. "If we feel that we are being followed or observed, we need to be cautious. Take a different route to work every day. Keep the doors and windows locked. Phone me for a lift, if you need to, or take a taxi." I wasn't sure any of this could help protect us, but I felt the need to say something reassuring.

We were all feeling a bit glum by the time dinner was over, but Jimmy sat down at the piano and played some upbeat music, which helped lift the mood. Charlie suggested we play a round of Halma, and the familiar ritual of the game comforted us a bit.

FORTY-FOUR

It was sprinkling when I drove up to our office the next morning. Gwen had taken a cab in early to open up, while I stopped by Roundtree's to sign some real estate papers. A small crowd had gathered in front of the building. A police car was parked out front and Gwen was standing next to it in her nurse's uniform talking with an officer.

I pushed through the crowd. Broken glass was scattered across the sidewalk. Our storefront window was reduced to jagged fragments clinging to the window frame.

"What the hell...?" I said.

Gwen was explaining to the policeman that this is how she'd found things when she got there. She introduced me to the officer.

"We'll need you to sign a report," the policeman said.

I nodded. Looking around at the glass shards, I shook my head. Felton, I thought.

"Let's go inside out of the rain," Gwen said.

It took all morning to get some workmen in to board up the window and clean up the glass. We tried to carry on as normal, but the reception area was cold and drafty. Gwen sat at the front desk wearing her coat, answering the phone and trying to reschedule appointments.

In the middle of the afternoon, Bateson showed up. Although his cold stare was not a welcome sight, I preferred a visit from him to a visit from Felton.

He wanted to speak with me privately. Despite feeling a strong dislike for the man, I invited him to my office in the back.

"So who has it in for you?" he asked with an irritating smile.

It could just as well have been him, but I knew that was not a prudent response, and I didn't want to say anything about Felton.

"I have no idea," I said. "Do you?"

"We have no clues. That's why I'm asking you."

"I've only recently opened up for business here. I can't see that I'm a threat to anyone."

"Do you think your old friend Gowan had anything to do with this?" His smile did not change, but the tone was more menacing.

I hadn't considered that the Klan might be involved. Now, coming from Bateson, the possibility loomed perilously large. But after my threatening visit from Felton the day before, I was still betting that he was behind this attack.

"What are you suggesting?"

"Oh, I don't know. Perhaps having invisible brothers could be an advantage."

He had taken me by surprise. I stared at him in astonishment.

"I have no beef with Dr. Gowan."

"But he might have a beef with you."

"I don't know what you're getting at."

"If you joined up with the right sort, now that you're a married man, you could get the protection you need."

Although I should have expected this, I wasn't ready for it, and I responded the only way I could think of. "I'm not a joiner."

"I see. Let me put it this way. If you aren't feeling brotherly, maybe you will consider a monthly donation to the policemen's benevolent society. We're interested in keeping our neighborhoods safe. Especially from outsiders."

"Are there outsiders I need to be protected from?"

"It could be. That's what I'm here to find out. Just look out front there."

"So you have an idea who was responsible for this attack on my business?"

"No. There are suspicions though. We might be able to exert some influence to keep you safe."

I felt my attitude solidify against these strong-arm tactics. Although I was alarmed by my circumstances, coercion was not a winning strategy with me. Besides I was losing patience.

"I think our little chat has gone on long enough," I said. "I will not let you intimidate me."

He looked surprised and for the first time his smirk softened for a moment before it turned angry. But he caught himself and gave a sneering laugh. "Suit yourself, Doc," he said. "It looks like you're on your own."

Considering this a small triumph, I stood and said, "I will see you out."

"I can find my way." He put on his hat and left.

I took a deep breath and sat down. My shirt was soaked under the white coat and the cool air from the boarded-up window made its way into my office and gave me a chill.

So this was how Bateson was extracting money from the speakeasies in town. I felt a sense of satisfaction. Maybe I was foolish. Maybe I was leaving myself and my business—even my friends—open to more serious harassment. But at least I had taken a stand.

FORTY-FIVE

Late at night a day later, I received a call from a Mrs. Swanson, who told me there had been an accident. She was calling me at home, she said, because the situation was somewhat complicated. She gave me the address of a house that she rented out to the Molloy family.

I arrived after midnight at a shabby building in a neighborhood where immigrant families had settled south of downtown. Edna Molloy, wife of an Irishman named Patrick, had fallen down the stairs. "I've taken the children over to my place next door," Mrs. Swanson said as she closed the front door and led me upstairs.

"How many children?"

"There are six."

I stepped over a patch of blood on the stairway. "What's this?"

"I did my best to clean up in short order. But you must come see Mrs. Molloy."

"And the father?"

"My husband and a neighbor fellow carried Mr. Molloy over to my cousin's home—just down the street." She gripped the newel post as she reached the top step. "We found him sitting right here blubbering. They had a time of it getting him down the stairs."

"Carried him?"

"He was drunk again."

The scene in the bedroom was not encouraging. Edna Molloy's

face was bruised and bloodied, but of most concern was her heavy vaginal bleeding. Except for that pregnant 17-year-old, I hadn't seen such hemorrhaging since the battlefield at Meuse-Argonne. Mrs. Swanson had spread towels on the bed and used diapers as best she could to pack Mrs. Molloy's vagina but the bleeding would not stop. I sent Mrs. Swanson next door to call for an ambulance.

I tried to talk to Mrs. Molloy but she was in shock. "He didn't mean it" were the only coherent words I could make out. I attended to her face and found that she was not as badly hurt as she looked. There were a couple of bruises, but the worst injury was a small cut on her eyebrow, which didn't require suturing. However, on further examination, I found extensive bruising on her abdomen.

When Mrs. Swanson returned, I asked her what had happened. One of the Molloy children had come to fetch her. She and her husband found Edna lying at the bottom of the staircase, while Patrick sat bawling at the top. I felt sorry for the children.

I did what I could to control the bleeding while we waited for the ambulance to arrive. Mrs. Swanson laid fresh towels on the bed and deposited the bloody ones in a washtub at the bedside. She gave a little cry and said, "Oh, dear God. Doctor, come look."

There in the washtub, like a heap of twisted entrails, lay the bloody towels lit by a lamp on the bedside table. Mrs. Swanson pointed to a small clot on top of the crimson mound. It was an embryo. I picked it up and held it in my palm, examining it under the lamp.

The embryo would have fit inside a thimble and could easily have been lost in the mess of towels. But there it was in all its pathetic presence, this primordial creature with its enormous head and bud-like unformed limbs. And most striking of all, curling down at the end of the miniature body, was the vertebrate tail— that inherited vestigial tail, handed down out of the endless ages of our evolutionary past.

Standing there confronted by the results of what appeared to be alcohol-blinded violence, I couldn't help thinking once again that we, the human family, had not evolved very far.

I placed the embryo in a small jar of formaldehyde that I kept in my medical bag.

"Mrs. Swanson, did you know that Mrs. Molloy was pregnant?"

She said she had not heard anything of it. "But I was not so very close with her. You see, we're not Catholic."

"Please be honest with me. Do you think that the Molloy children will be safe?"

"At my house? Of course."

"I mean around Mr. Molloy."

"Well, Doctor, I really can't say. He seems to be a very good father. But, like I said, we don't know the Molloys all that well. He's never beaten her like this."

"I take it this sort of thing has happened before?" I said.

"Oh, no. Nothing like tonight. He's never been this far gone. Usually he comes home drunk, singing at the top of his lungs in that thick Irish brogue, and falls asleep. Oh, I guess on one occasion he struck her. But it's only when he's drunk. And when she came over to my place to get away from him, he came knocking on our door, blubbering and weeping and full of apologies and begging her forgiveness. Then me and her helped him home to bed and he fell asleep. He's always shamefaced the day after. And we see him going off to Mass every Sunday. Never misses. He'll be at church again this weekend, mark my words. But, I swear, he was drunk out of his mind tonight. Why, he wasn't even singing."

"Where does he work?"

"Well, you see, he has trouble holding down a job because of the drink, you know, and I think that causes him to drink all the more."

It occurred to me that perhaps Patrick Molloy had just learned of his wife's pregnancy that night. Maybe the knowledge of one more mouth to feed had sent him into a rage. I hoped that was not the case. If Patrick Molloy was a good Catholic and a good father, maybe when he understood what had happened to his wife, he would be shocked into mending his ways.

The ambulance arrived and while the attendants took Edna

Molloy downstairs, Mrs. Swanson changed the bedding and I packed up my medicine bag.

"Mrs. Swanson," I said, "I think it would be best if you didn't tell anyone about this thing we've found. The consequences of a physical assault are serious enough as it is. We must consider the rest of the family. Maybe they can get help through the church."

Mrs. Swanson promised me it would not pass her lips.

The ambulance took Edna Molloy to St. Mary's. Eventually we stopped her bleeding and she was transfused. Once she was stable, I turned her over to the intern on duty. All I could do was to wait and hope. Praying was not my area of expertise, so I left that to the Catholic sisters, and around 3 in the morning, I went home to bed.

The next day at the office, we were able to get the front window replaced. It was a busy day of appointments, made more hectic by workmen coming in and out.

By late afternoon I was able to get away to St. Mary's to see how Mrs. Molloy was doing. In one of the large indigent wards, the head nurse told me that she was much improved. She was sitting up in her bed across the ward, speaking with Father Poitiers from her parish. I knew him from occasional encounters there. While they finished talking, I waited, and as he left, the priest and I exchanged greetings.

I examined Mrs. Molloy and noted that she was doing well. She said her husband had come by with one of the older children to look in on her.

I brought up the subject of her pregnancy. She said she was aware that she had been pregnant and knew that it had ended. I asked her to tell me what had happened that night.

She said she was helping Patrick up the stairs to bed. He was in an especially bad way and could barely walk. They had gotten to the top of the stairway when she said he became belligerent and took a swing at her. She swore that he didn't know who she was or what he was doing. She dodged his blow but lost her balance and fell down the stairs. Nothing would have come of it if she hadn't been at the head of the staircase. The next thing she knew she was in bed with Mrs. Swanson trying to help her.

Edna Molloy's story that her husband had not struck her was not entirely convincing. It didn't line up with Mrs. Swanson's report that Mr. Molloy had struck her in the past. But I didn't press her.

I was not sure that the fall was the cause of Edna's aborted pregnancy. The bruising on her lower abdomen did not fit with her version of the story. Had her husband kicked her? Was Edna Molloy willfully blinding herself to her husband's brutality— whiskey-soaked as it was—in order to bear that intolerable reality? Or was she just trying to protect her family. There was no way for me to know.

She acknowledged that her husband had a problem with drink, and I told her I would speak with the hospital staff and have a social worker visit her. With the help of the hospital and her parish, I said, I was sure her family would come through this. She thanked me for my help, and I told her she should be able to go home in a day or so. On my way out, I found Father Poitiers and reassured him that Mrs. Molloy was recovering well.

Before leaving the hospital, I took the embryo to the office of Dr. Hazlitt, the hospital pathologist, whom I'd gotten to know while doing inspections for the American College of Surgeons the year before. He had struck me as a decent sort, trustworthy and straightforward, and I'd always liked him. But I knew I would be placing him in a ticklish position asking him to examine this kind of specimen—even more so, asking him to keep it off the record, which contradicted the mandate of the College to keep complete records.

But I needed to put my mind at rest. If there was a developmental abnormality, perhaps the embryo could have spontaneously aborted. And if that was the case, I could report that Patrick Molloy was not responsible. I worried that Mrs. Swanson would not keep our secret, and the possible legal, even criminal, problems connected with an aborted pregnancy would complicate matters.

"I need to ask you a professional courtesy," I began. Without telling him anything about the case, not even the name of the family, I asked him to examine the specimen.

He took a glance at the bottle and stared at me over the top of his eyeglasses.

"I don't want anyone to know about this," I said.

He pursed his lips and looked away.

"As a personal favor to me. I want to protect the family. If there are any abnormalities that would have caused a spontaneous abortion, I need to know."

He paused. "All right."

Inspecting the embryo in the jar, Hazlitt told met it was no more than six weeks old. "I couldn't even tell you if it's male or female at this point." But he agreed to keep the specimen and take a closer look at it when he had time.

I reinforced the point that we needed to keep this out of the records. He sighed and again looked at me over his glasses. We both knew my request was irregular. I hoped he would not be offended.

"Okay, Holman. I admired your work with the inspections. I'll keep this one to myself."

As I left the hospital, I wondered if it would be possible to keep the Molloy family together. I had to hope that the possibility existed. If Patrick Molloy was the sort of man who was contrite in the morning, perhaps he and his family could be helped. There wasn't much that I could do, but St. Mary's with its social workers and charity organizations could help. Maybe the Molloy family had a chance.

FORTY-SIX

Charlie and Gwen had arranged for the four of us to dine out at the end of the week. The occasion was a celebration of sorts. We felt good about the success of our arrangements. The medical practice was up and running, and Gwen and I were relieved to have our wedding over with. So the girls wanted to celebrate and they thought that an elegant setting was called for. The Chandler Hotel was the perfect choice since Jimmy and I had first met there at the Iverson wedding reception.

Over dinner Jimmy and Charlie talked about various plans for their marriage. They hadn't settled on a date but discussed late April or early May. Charlie suggested they should avoid all the fuss and elope. But Jimmy wanted to include his parents somehow, at least with a brief visit after the ceremony, however small and private it was. They both thought they should have a small wedding party later on, maybe after a short honeymoon trip. We discussed the move to the Beasley house, and the girls were excited about the decorating they planned to make the place their own. As we left the hotel, we were all feeling gay. There had been several days of fair weather, and the fragrance of spring was in the air. It was dusk and the street lights were coming on.

Out on the sidewalk, a large crowd had gathered. In the distance we heard the faint sound of a marching band. We moved down the block to a place where we could get closer to the curb, but we still had difficulty seeing through the crowd. All up and down the thoroughfare, people lined both sides several bodies deep. Traffic barricades blocked the cross streets, and foot patrolmen were stationed at the intersections. The crowd was abuzz with excitement.

"What's going on?" Gwen asked a young woman standing next to us.

"Oh, there's big doings," she said. "The Klan is having one of their biggest initiations yet—200 men and 100 Klan ladies. They are marching from the park down to the armory where they'll hold the naturalization ceremony. This is the first time men's and women's Klans are marching together. It's going to be quite a show."

I felt a growing anxiety.

Horses' hooves could be heard from up the street. A fiery glow approached, casting a rippling light that reflected off the buildings opposite. A couple of city police vehicles led the way. Beyond them, we glimpsed the white robes and pointed hoods of the two horsemen at the head of the parade. One carried a flaming cross, and the other a large American flag. At the intersection, the horseman with the flag jerked back on his reins, and his horse reared up on his hind legs. Behind followed more riders, and a short distance back, two robed figures on foot carried a Klan banner and another American flag. In the wake of the flaming cross, I smelled the oily stink of kerosene smoke.

Next came a marching band in robes, many with their masks pulled back so they could play their instruments. The staccato rhythm of the band's drum corps electrified the crowd. I felt it too. A smattering of applause rippled through the onlookers. Behind the band flowed a river of white-robed figures, all masked with pointed hoods, eight abreast, marching in solemn rank and file.

Near us, jumping up and down on the curb, a young boy shouted, "Aunt Betty, there's Uncle Lloyd! Over there! I see his shoes."

The woman swatted the boy's bottom and shushed him. The boy looked up at her, his cheeks red, fighting back tears.

I looked in the direction the boy had pointed and recognized a pair of brown-and-white spectators under one of the passing white robes. Lloyd Haskell. My heart hardened with dread. From behind I couldn't see the face of the woman with the boy. She was wearing a cloche that concealed her hair, but judging from her height and size, she could have been Haskell's wife. I suffered a wave of sadness thinking of the dead boy on the operating table.

After the endless ranks of white-robed men, there followed a pick-up truck carrying a masked figure in a scarlet robe seated on an ornate throne backed with a large cross of electric light bulbs. A man near us whispered to his companion that the fellow on the throne was Oregon's Grand Dragon.

A couple more police vehicles were followed by another male color guard carrying the American and Oregon flags and a large banner announcing the women's Klan, "Our Honored Mothers, Wives and Sisters."

As the robed and masked women approached, there was a wave of movement through the onlookers. Men all along the parade route were removing their hats. When the color guard reached us, I understood why. Groups of two and three robed Klansmen walked along the curb on both sides of the street. They carried billy clubs like I'd seen at Bisby Grange. If they spotted a man who had not removed his hat, they called out, "Honor the Women of the Klan." If he did not comply, they would approach him, threatening with their clubs.

I removed my hat but heard the hooded Klansman passing near us call out in my direction. "Honor the Women of the Klan." Confused, I looked around. All the men surrounding me were bareheaded except for Jimmy, who stood firm with his tweed cap squarely atop his head. I elbowed Jimmy, but he didn't move. Two white-robed figures approached us pointing with their clubs.

"You will remove your hat in honor of the Ladies of the Invisible Empire!" one of them shouted. Jimmy did not move.

People turned as we became the center of attention. I recognized Betty Haskell's face.

"Hey, buddy, show some respect," called a voice behind us. A chorus of male and female voices around us shouted assent.

Quick as a flash, Gwen reached up and grabbed the cap off Jimmy's head.

One of the club-wielding Klansmen approached and shouted, "The little lady knows what's healthy for you, buddy. Take a lesson from her." A riffle of laughter spread through the crowd. Jimmy did not move, but in the light of the street lamps I saw that he had gone red in the face.

The four of us stood silently for a long time, afraid to move, watching as the Klanswomen filed past.

When another group of horsemen approached carrying another flaming cross, evoking a wave of whoops and cheers, I leaned toward Jimmy and without turning my head, said in a low voice, "Let's go."

I took Gwen's arm and escorted her out of the crowd, which filled in the space we vacated. Jimmy and Charlie followed. But before we had separated ourselves from the crush, a man at the back of the onlookers called after us, "Go back to your stinking Pope church where you belong. We only want 100% Americans here."

We walked down the nearest side street. Once we were a block away, Gwen handed Jimmy's cap back to him.

"Bastards," Jimmy muttered as he put it on. "I'm sorry," he said, "but I was torn. I didn't want to make a scene and cause trouble for all of you, but I'll be damned if I'll take off my hat for a bunch of bigoted harpies."

No one spoke as we drove home. When I turned the Ford off Wilkerson Street where Thornhill Boulevard comes down the hill, we could see on the top of nearby Mount Tabor a huge fiery cross burning in the night.

After dropping the girls at their apartment, Jimmy and I went home. I was brushing my teeth in the bathroom when the phone rang and Jimmy went down the hall to answer it.

A few moments later he appeared in the bathroom door.

"Was that a medical call?" I asked, drying my hands.

Jimmy's face was pale.

"Who was it?" Now I was alarmed.

"Danny Felton." Jimmy folded his arms in front of him. "He said to tell you that if you didn't want trouble from the Klan, you should call him. He says you know his number."

"That bastard! Calling my home."

"Then he said something I didn't understand. He said, 'Tell Dr. Holman I didn't know he was an abortionist.'"

Desperate to speak with Dr. Hazlitt, I stopped by St. Mary's early Monday morning. Mrs. Molloy had been discharged on Sunday when her husband and children came by after mass.

When I was able to speak to Hazlitt in private, I asked about the specimen. He told me that on close examination he found nothing abnormal about the embryo, but as he had predicted, at such an early stage of development there was no way to determine if the pregnancy was viable.

"Forgive me but I need to ask—you haven't mentioned this case to anyone, have you?"

"Look, Holman, much as I didn't like it, I've honored your request."

"I don't mean to insult you. But I've heard something recently that sounded like word had gotten out. Maybe it's just some neighborhood gossip. I'll take the specimen off your hands."

"You'll be glad to know that I disposed of it."

I was surprised. "Thank you." We shook hands. "I appreciate your help. We won't talk about this again."

Hazlitt's failure to confirm a fetal abnormality dashed my hope of protecting Patrick Molloy. But now I worried that I needed to protect myself from the possible accusation that I had aborted Edna Molloy's pregnancy. For that I could thank Danny Felton.

FORTY-SEVEN

Even though I couldn't place the voice coming through the phone, I felt a wave of anxiety. When the man identified himself as Bateson, I understood my reaction. He said he wanted to see me in his office.

"Can't we talk on the telephone?" I asked. The last thing I wanted was to sit across from that man in a small office.

"It's of a private nature. We should meet in person."

I knew there was no use in trying to avoid this encounter. He had all the authority of the police behind him. With much trepidation, I agreed to see him that afternoon. I had to force my body to drive myself through the wet streets, downtown to the Central Precinct.

Bateson's office was at the same station where I'd waited to be booked after the New Year's Eve raid. Walking out of the cool March day and into the precinct building, I felt a chill as all the bad memories of that night rushed back.

It took some time to find the right office and get the desk officer to tell me if Bateson was in, but he finally responded when I told him I was a doctor and handed him my card.

Bateson's desk was perfectly clean and free of papers. I took a chair opposite him. Even though the room was cool, I had already begun to sweat. I had waited outside his office for longer than I expected to. Perhaps that was part of his plan to put me off guard.

I felt a knot tightening in my stomach. But he started off friendly enough, although his smile was cold.

"I wouldn't have summoned you here except for the seriousness of what I have to tell you."

A draft came from the window behind him, its sash propped open with a book.

"Something happened at the poor farm yesterday that you should know about."

I'd heard that Sam Patterson was transferred from the sanitarium to a poor farm. The physical therapy hadn't shown any effect and he was never expected to walk again. So I guessed at once that Patterson was the subject of my visit.

Hoping to get a jump on the conversation, I said, "I've told you that Dr. Ferguson took over the Patterson case. I've had no further connection with it."

"Yes, but you have some knowledge of the case, and we want to make sure you know the actual facts." His piercing green eyes held me like a spotlight.

"What are these actual facts?"

His smile turned into a smirk. A fly buzzed against the windowpane behind him, unaware of the opening below.

"Mr. Patterson was found yesterday with a gunshot wound to his head. An apparent suicide."

I felt the color drain from my face. Jesus, the poor fellow didn't deserve that. "You're certain it was a suicide?" I didn't put it past the police to cover up the cause of his condition by silencing him. They could have just as easily silenced me.

"I know what you're thinking," he said. The fly behind him flew to another pane. "There is plenty of proof that it was suicide. Reports by a social worker and a number of the residents state that he didn't want to go on living. As you know, he was a robust fellow, used to manual labor out of doors. He never accepted his condition."

Good God. Accept his condition? A condition that he neither earned nor deserved.

"I don't know why you are telling me this."

"Just stating the facts. There was a suicide note, besides the other evidence."

I wasn't sure I believed him. Such a note could be fabricated.

"You're certain it's authentic?" Maybe my question was too presumptuous.

He leveled his eyes at me. "No question about it."

Of course. He held all the cards.

"So why am I here? Can you get to the point?"

"My point is that there are stories going around that someone connected with the jail was responsible for Mr. Patterson's injuries."

"I don't know where such reports might be coming from," I said. "I've discussed this case with no one." Of course, I thought, Patterson himself could have told others what happened to him.

"And that's as it should be, doctor." He smiled.

The fly began bumping against the glass again. I was just as desperate to get out of that room.

"I expect things to stay that way. And now that Patterson's dead, there is no reason for the subject to come up. Right?"

I shifted my weight in the chair and a trickle of sweat ran down my back.

"The actual facts," he said, "in case anyone should ask, are that Mr. Patterson became uncooperative and fell down a flight of stairs. The guards were just escorting him to another jail cell."

All I could do in response was to sit stark still and stare back at him.

"We know, Dr Holman, that there are also a number of stories going around about you."

I should have expected this but he caught me by surprise. I didn't really want to know, but I blurted out, "What kind of stories?"

"Let's just say...unwholesome stories."

Was it my relationship with Jimmy? I was a married man now. Could it be Billy Butler? Was it the rumored abortion of Mrs. Molloy's fetus? I had a witness, Mrs. Swanson. But Bateson could make up whatever he wanted to and any defense of mine would be useless.

I wanted to end the conversation as soon as possible. In spite of the cold draft, I felt like I was suffocating. "What do you want from me?"

"What you need to know is that if you stay quiet about Sam Patterson, then you can expect that we will be quiet about some of the unwholesome allegations against you."

"I've already told you I relinquished the case to Dr. Ferguson and I have not—and do not—intend to say anything more about it. Now is there anything more?"

Bateson smiled and stared at me. The fly spun into another frenzied attempt to break through the invisible barrier.

"No. Nothing more. As long as we understand each other."

"I can assure you of that."

"Good." Bateson nodded. "Now get out of here. No one needs to know that we had this conversation."

The buzzing at the glass stopped as the insect took flight and disappeared out the opening at the bottom of the window sash.

FORTY-EIGHT

Shortly after I talked with Bateson, Theresa Littlefoot was released from St. Mary's. Considering her long convalescence, her face looked bad and her eye was still not functioning properly, but she was healing. Billy Butler and Theresa's sister were there to take her home.

While they finished up their paperwork, I took Billy aside and told him I needed to talk to him. The day was cool but sunny and we went out into a garden courtyard between the wings of the building.

"I seen Sam at that sanitarium," Billy said before I could say anything.

"How did you find out where he was?" I was surprised.

"I got my ways. Anyway, after his accident—"

"It wasn't an accident," I interrupted, but remembering Bateson's threats, I stopped myself.

Billy glared at me. "After that—he said they dropped all the charges against him. I wouldn't have said anything against Sam, anyway—not after they double-crossed me."

"Did you know he was moved to the poor farm?"

"I heard about that. I feel bad for him. Stuck in that wheel chair."

This expression of sympathy gave me pause. A nun walked by carrying a vase full of flowers. I shifted the subject.

"Are you still working with Haskell?"

"I'm getting jumpy about that deal. I think I'm gonna have to bail out before long."

"You and Haskell not getting on?"

"It ain't so much Haskell. It's that fella he's doing business with. Felton."

"Felton?"

"Yeah, there's some scum!"

"How do you mean?"

"I told you I don't go in for that fairy stuff. Well, Felton had his buddy pull a gun on me and forced me to suck him off. He even slapped me around a bit to get me to cooperate. He used one of those rubber things on his cock. It made me sick. I ain't proud of it, but he forced me." Billy pulled a toothpick out of his pocket and began digging at his teeth.

"What did Haskell have to say about that?"

"I never said nothing to him about it. I didn't reckon I wanted him to know." Billy started to say something more but stopped himself and continued picking his teeth.

"What?" I urged.

"Well—" He paused. I waited. He twirled his toothpick between his finger and thumb. "They made me take a shot—with a needle, you know. You're a doctor. Felton said it would make me feel good. But it made me upchuck. I don't cotton to none of that stuff. I won't even drink their hooch. That's another reason I never said nothing to Haskell."

"So you think you might pull out of there?"

"I don't know. Haskell's been pretty good to me. He pays better than Theresa can. Anyway, now when I see Felton come round, I sneak off. I'm pretty good at dodging him."

"Did Haskell ever force you to have sex?"

Billy looked at me with astonishment. "Never. He treated me like I was his own. I think after his kid died, he saw me as taking his boy's place."

I gave Billy a long hard look. "Are you telling me the truth?"

"Honest." He seemed to be leveling with me.

"How long have they been working together, Felton and Haskell?"

"Since back in December. Around then was when I first heard of him. Remember when those nigger bootleggers got run off the road and one of them took a bullet? It was the KKK that done the shooting, I guess. Haskell was real mad about it and wanted to get back at them, but I hear Felton made him put a lid on it. I never met him till after Christmas."

We watched a squirrel scamper across the lawn into some shrubs next to the building.

"It was after that deal with Bateson and—and Sam. Jesus, I never would have gone for that if I'd known he was gonna end up in a wheel chair." Billy examined the end of the toothpick, then looked off toward the gardens.

"Billy, there's something I've got to tell you about Sam."

"Yeah?"

"It's not good news."

He moved the toothpick to the other side of his mouth.

"Sam committed suicide—out at the poor farm."

Billy's eyes got wide. "You're pulling my leg."

"I wish I was."

His eyebrows narrowed into a pained frown. He hurled the toothpick into a nearby bush. "Shit!"

On the other side of the lawn a nun pushed a patient in a wheelchair along a walkway.

Tears glinted in the corner of Billy's eyes. He turned away. "The poor devil." His head jerked up with a forceful sniff.

"I'm sorry, Billy," I said and placed my hand on his shoulder.

He shrugged it away. "Damn but this world is a hellhole."

FORTY-NINE

Our medical practice had picked up to the point that we needed extra help, so we advertised for an all-around receptionist and office assistant. Gwen and I did a series of interviews and hired one girl who didn't work out, but on the first day of spring, a young woman named Cora came to see about the position. We hired her right away.

Like the season, she was a breath of fresh air. She was a lovely blonde who wore round horn-rimmed glasses and always arrived well-groomed and neatly dressed. Not only was she pleasant to work with, she was quick and capable. Gwen had checked Cora's references and found that she came highly recommended, with special praise for her bookkeeping and accounting skills. By the end of the first week, Gwen had taught Cora our billing system, and Cora took over the job with enthusiasm.

All the patients seemed to like her, and Cora soon became an essential part of the office routine. Her efficiency made life much easier for us.

One rainy afternoon in late March when Jimmy had been using the Ford to run some errands for his wedding, he came by the office at the end of the day to pick up Gwen and me. He had never met Cora, and Gwen introduced them. Cora was planning to work late finishing up some accounting, so Gwen left her in charge of locking up the office for the day. On the way home, Jimmy remarked that Cora looked familiar, but he couldn't place where he might have seen her. He decided that maybe she had been at St. Stephen's.

The next day Gwen came into my consulting room and asked if I had prescribed or administered any morphine the day before. We kept a small number of ampoules on hand for emergencies, always locked in a small cupboard in a back room. I told her I had not.

"That's strange," she said. "I must have miscounted. Anyway, I found the cabinet unlocked this morning. I must have forgotten to lock it last night in all the confusion of trying to get out of here after Jimmy arrived. I'll have to be more careful in the future."

I didn't think any more about it until a few days later when I found myself out of tongue depressors in the middle of an exam and went to the back room for more. Cora was unpacking a box of gauze and cotton, which were kept in a cabinet at the back of the room, but she was standing in front of the unlocked cupboard of medicines.

"Oh, Dr. Holman," she said as I entered, "we seem to be low on some drugs here. I was just doing an inventory, since I was back here unpacking these other things. Do you want me to order more?"

"Sorry, I'm in the middle of an exam right now. Why don't you go over that with Gwen when she's free?"

"I'll do that," Cora said, locking the cupboard.

That evening I asked Gwen if she and Cora had talked about ordering drugs.

"She's done a complete inventory of supplies to go along with the accounting. So I asked her to take care of the ordering and showed her how to fill out the narcotics paperwork. She said she would go over each order with me before she phoned it in. Gosh, that girl is a wonder."

fifTY

Edna Molloy continued to see me and I noted that she was doing well. Color had returned to her cheeks and she had more energy. I had seen her last in early April when she told me that with the help of the hospital social worker and Father Poitiers, her husband had found a part-time job cleaning trolleys for the traction company. She said she was feeling hopeful and things were looking up for her family.

We were all anxious to have Gwen and Charlie move into the Beasley house as soon as possible, so we originally planned for Jimmy and Charlie to wed in mid-April. But Holy Week fell in the middle of the month and St. Stephen's had a full schedule, so Jimmy arranged to take a few days off after those observances.

The marriage took place at City Hall on an afternoon in late April. Since Jimmy didn't want to complicate the plans by inviting his parents for such an informal wedding, he and Charlie planned to drive to eastern Oregon to visit with them afterwards. Owing to the estrangement between Charlie and her parents, they were not invited. Jimmy and Charlie decided that after they returned from the "honeymoon," they would have a small reception for friends and neighbors, maybe a garden party.

Gwen served as maid of honor, and I was Jimmy's best man. Charlie's Aunt Inez signed as a witness. We went out to an early dinner at the Chandler Hotel after the wedding, and Gwen and I presented our gifts. Charlie's was a string of cultured pearls, and Jimmy's was a gold lapel pin shaped like a musical eighth note set with a diamond.

Right after this festive gathering, Jimmy and Charlie drove off to the same hotel where Gwen and I had honeymooned, even booking the same room—with two beds. The next morning, they would drive on to visit Jimmy's parents on their orchard east of Mount Hood.

We scheduled painters to come during the honeymoon to repaint and wallpaper some of the rooms in the Beasley house. Later the movers were to bring the furniture and household goods from Charlie and Gwen's apartment, so that everything would be in place for the newlyweds to "set up housekeeping" when they returned.

One afternoon during Jimmy and Charlie's honeymoon, I was manning the reception area while Gwen was at the bank making a deposit and Cora was in the back using the powder room. The day wasn't busy and I had no appointments for a couple of hours. When the postman delivered our mail, I glanced through the letters. An invoice from our drug supplier caught my eye along with a scenic postcard from the newlyweds. Just then an old patient named Simmons came in. As he began regaling me with his aches and pains and news of his family, I tucked the two pieces of mail in the pocket of my white coat. When Cora returned to the reception desk, I told her I would see Mr. Simmons right then, since there were no other patients scheduled. When I finished with him, I remembered the mail in my pocket and sat down at my desk.

The postcard pictured the Columbia River Gorge looking west from Crown Point and on the back was a brief message from Charlie and Jimmy. I slit open the pharmacy invoice and studied it. I was surprised to see charges for a quantity of morphine ampoules. Since I knew we had not used any in the past week, I picked up the telephone and called Hal Gaston, our supplier.

"Hullo, Dr. Holman," he said. "I haven't talked to you in a

while. I usually talk to your young lady. How are things with your new office?"

"Going fine."

"Say, that was a real shame about the Haskell boy last winter."

"It was," I replied. "How did you hear about that?"

"Oh, you know, Lloyd Haskell was pretty broken up about it. Since I do business with his pharmacy, it came up."

"Of course."

"Pity about his wife too," Hal Gaston continued.

"How's that?"

"Seems she took a nasty fall. Pretty badly banged up."

This was startling news. I remembered how Haskell had treated his wife at St. Mary's and Bleeker's remark about his hotheadedness. I was suspicious that this was no accidental fall. That poor woman.

"That is a shame," I said.

"I hear she fell down the basement stairs. But, you know, just between you and me, I wonder if maybe she and Lloyd weren't having a quarrel when she had her accident. That Lloyd has a temper, you know. Why, a veterinarian down in Bayfield told me about the time that Haskell took a baseball bat to a horse that raised his ire. Imagine that. Taking a baseball bat to a horse."

As much as I was dismayed and sickened by this information, I jumped in before Gaston could veer off again. "Say, Hal, there's something I need to check on." I asked him about the recent invoice, and he consulted his files and confirmed that Cora had indeed ordered the listed items the week before.

"Boy," he went on, "I'm sorry to hear about that Wilbertson fella from Nevada. It's a shame he's taking so long to heal up."

"I beg your pardon?"

"That fire, I mean. Sounds like his burns are something awful. Yes, Mark Barnett, the pharmacist over on Nineteenth Avenue, told me all about it, how Wilbertson was visiting his daughter when it happened. Barnett said the daughter was coming in every other day to fill your prescription for him."

I thanked him for checking on the invoice and hung up.

When Gwen returned, I spoke to her in private, showing her the invoice. I told her Gaston's story about the bogus burn victim. She raised her eyebrows.

"What do you think we should do?" I asked.

Gwen folded the invoice and put it back in the envelope. "Nothing," she said, "not yet. Let's not do anything that would cause suspicion. I'll tell Cora this came with yesterday's mail. It's postmarked two days ago. I took the mail yesterday while Cora was out to lunch. I'll just say it got in with a stack of papers on my desk, and I opened it by mistake. Don't say anything to her for the time being."

I could see the wheels turning in Gwen's brain.

That evening after Cora left the office, Gwen locked up and asked me to follow her. We went to the supply room in the back.

"Unwrap one of those blades," Gwen said and took out a scalpel handle. After fitting in the new blade, she unlocked the cabinet and began counting the morphine ampoules. "For the love of Mike, there are two less than I counted this morning. She must have pocketed a couple this afternoon. And it looks like there are some prescription forms missing too." Gwen took down the small glass morphine containers from the cupboard. "Here's my plan. We'll make three little cuts on the back edge of the label on each of these ampoules. That way they can be traced back here in case any of them turn up missing. The cuts shouldn't be noticeable to anyone who isn't looking for them. We need to tell someone else about marking them though, so they can corroborate our story."

"Let's talk to Tom Harris as soon as we get home," I said.

"I'm betting that these vials will turn up missing very soon," Gwen continued. "We want to be able to follow their movement."

"You know what concerns me?" I said.

"That Cora is connected with Danny Felton?"

I nodded.

"It is morphine we're dealing with," Gwen said. "I should have suspected something sooner." She locked the cupboard. "But there's another thing."

"What's that?"

"If Cora is stealing morphine and prescription slips, she may be planning to frame you."

I felt my stomach churning.

"I'd better monitor the medicine cupboard and keep my own records of the supply," she said.

When we got home, I called Tom and urged him to drop by. When he arrived after dinner, Gwen and I described the morphine situation to him, including Gwen's marking of the ampoules. Gwen told him that we suspected Cora was planning to frame us for illegally prescribing morphine.

"Are there any authorities we can trust to investigate this before Cora springs a trap on us?" I asked.

"Whew," Tom Harris said shaking his head. "I believe they're all on the take, and the ones that aren't are afraid to speak up."

"We've sure got ourselves in a fix," Gwen said.

"Here," Tom said after a moment, "I'll give you the name of a private detective firm you can trust." He pulled out his little notebook and wrote down the name and a phone number. "And let me do some checking, too, before you think about talking to any authorities." He handed me the slip of paper with the name Lockwood and a phone number. "This kind of thing will spread like wildfire in the police force once it gets out."

Tom called the detective and told him who I was before he put me on the line. Mr. Lockwood agreed to meet with us that very night. I felt we didn't have any time to lose, so when Tom went home, Gwen and I drove straight to the detective's office. We told him about our suspicions. He agreed to have his team keep an eye on Cora and find out whatever they could. He asked if we had anything else for him to go on and I told him to keep an ear out for any information about a man named Danny Felton, alias Roy Underhill.

We agreed on a fee and hired Lockwood on the spot. Before we left, Gwen handed him a key to the office, so he and his associates could get in and do some looking around after hours if necessary.

Driving home, Gwen confided that she was relieved we had enlisted some professional help. "After all," she said, "I'm a healer, not a sleuth."

She continued to keep an eye on the morphine supply without arousing Cora's suspicions. The marked ampoules vanished, one by one.

FIFTY-ONE

A few days later Tom Harris banged on my door late at night while I sat reading. Jimmy and Charlie were still away on their honeymoon, and Gwen was at the apartment. When I let Tom in, I heard a whoosh of wind outside and felt it tug at the knob.

"Come in out of that gale," I said, closing the door behind him. He seemed agitated. I offered him a drink, but he refused and said he couldn't stay long. He wouldn't sit down.

"I've got some news you should know about right away." He took out his little notebook. "I'll trust you to keep it to yourself."

I nodded as he flipped through several pages.

"A man was found tonight with a rope around his neck, hanging from a tree outside of Bisby."

I grimaced at the thought. I couldn't help remembering the trouble Jimmy'd had with the KKK boys out there.

"The Klan left its mark," Tom said, "a burned cross."

I reminded Tom about that incident I'd witnessed driving home from the Grange dance, when the Klan was punishing that young couple they'd apparently found spooning.

He nodded. "I remember. How long ago was that?"

"Last May."

He made a note in his book. "There's no question the Klan was responsible this time too. They even set the man on fire before they left."

I winced. "But why are you telling me this?"

"I've heard that you treated Edna Molloy recently. Is that true?"

My heart sank. "That's right."

"We think the hanged man may be Patrick Molloy."

"Good God," I whispered. "That poor woman." I thought of Edna Molloy lying in her bed, bruised and bleeding. Six children, and a seventh one lost. And now her husband. I began to worry that the Klan had made a connection between the Molloy family and me.

Tom waited to see if I would volunteer any information. As far as I knew, no one was aware of Mrs. Molloy's miscarriage besides Mrs. Swanson and myself. But there was Felton's veiled threat on the telephone to Jimmy. I didn't say anything to Tom, and waited.

"I've been told that Molloy beat up his wife and caused her to lose an unborn child." Tom scrutinized me. "Some are saying that's why the Klan nabbed him—besides that he was Catholic—and a foreigner."

Had Mrs. Swanson not kept our secret? Or perhaps there was more to it than that.

"No, it's not clear that's how it happened," I said.

"None of it?"

"Edna Molloy told me that her husband never struck her. She says she dodged him and fell down the stairs." I was still not convinced this was true.

"And the miscarriage?"

I sighed and rubbed my face. "If Molloy is dead, then it doesn't matter much if I tell you that part is true."

"That's the problem. You see, Molloy was still alive when they found him. He had been cut down from the tree and left for dead. He's over at St. Mary's now. They are trying to save his life."

It took a moment for me to understand what Tom was saying. I looked at him in disbelief. "He survived all that? Dear God, tell me this isn't true."

"I wish I could, Carl," he said with a sigh. "I wish I could."

"No, it's too monstrous," I said, shaking my head.

The wind howled around the chimney and reverberated out of the hearth.

"I suspect this will go down as one more unsolved crime," Tom said. "It's outside the jurisdiction of the Portland police, and the sheriff in Bisby isn't going to investigate. With so little to go on, I'm not sure our paper will publish the full story either. I thought I should let you know—just so you'll be on your guard."

"What that family has been through," I said.

"This may be nothing—it's impossible to know what kinds of rumors might get started—but having your name associated with an aborted pregnancy...well, just be careful."

Even without Felton's phone call, I had already seen the risks. I heaved a sigh. "I've thought of that."

Another gust hit the side of the house.

"Right after that big Klan march downtown, I got a phone call from Felton. He accused me of being an abortionist."

He whistled. "I don't envy you," he said and shook his head, looking as worried as I felt. "Well, I've got to get home." He glanced at his notebook and paused. "One more thing you should know. This may be adding insult to injury. It seems that Lloyd Haskell has some buddies out at Bisby."

"Jesus." This made the Molloy story more ominous than ever. "What is Haskell's connection to Bisby?"

"I don't know any more than that. It was just a casual remark I heard from another reporter."

I frowned.

He placed his hand on my shoulder. "Keep your eyes open." He put his notebook away. "And let me know if you learn anything I should know."

"I'll be vigilant." I pursed my lips. "And you keep me posted if there's any more news."

"You know I will." He went to the door but turned back. "I'm sorry."

I nodded. "Thanks, Tom."

He left and I was alone in the house.

I dared not think about what Patrick Molloy had suffered, but I was aghast at this madness that was plaguing my world. I felt as if the earth's axis had been kicked askew.

I wanted to go straight to St. Mary's, but considering all that Tom had told me, I knew it would look bad. Besides there was nothing I could do to help. Others would be handling the case. But I wanted the answers to the many questions that crowded my mind.

Had they dragged him from his home? In front of his wife and children? How had he survived hanging? Maybe it was a mock exercise meant to scare him, and the mob had gotten out of control. I wondered what had gone through Molloy's mind. Did he ask himself why he was still alive? I wondered if he might be better off dead. What had that young soldier at Meuse-Argonne thought as he held his intestines in his hands, knowing he was still alive? But some things are just too horrible to contemplate. That is why the body goes into shock—to protect itself. It is a mercy.

I considered phoning Gwen at the apartment, but I didn't know where to start and I didn't want to burden her with the horror of it. Besides it was late. She would hear the story soon enough. But if Felton had somehow engineered this attack on Molloy, I wondered, was I safe? Was Gwen safe for that matter? I decided there was nothing I could do so late in the evening and went to bed.

I spent a troubled night fretting over the possible connection between Felton and Cora. And how did Felton know about the Molloy case? I hoped Lockwood and his associates were figuring out the answers. And what was this connection between Haskell and Bisby that Tom had mentioned? I wondered if Maude Williams would know anything.

The wind had let up when I left for my office the next morning. I'd gotten an early start so I could stop by St. Mary's on my way. I happened to pass Father Poitiers, who was in the hallway speaking with one of the nuns. When she withdrew, I approached and shook the priest's hand and expressed concern for the Molloy family.

"So you've heard," he said.

"How is Mr. Molloy?"

"I administered the last rites this morning. He died just after dawn."

It took a moment for this to sink in. I wanted to say that after what I'd heard, I was hoping for that. But I realized the priest might find it sinful for me to wish Patrick Molloy dead.

"I'm sorry," I said. Then I thought of Edna Molloy. "I'm so sorry for the family. Especially Mrs. Molloy."

He placed his hand on my shoulder and said, "It's in God's hands now."

I felt a panic wash over me. "But will she be all right? How will she get by? I've been worried ever since she lost...since her pregnancy."

"Let me have a word, Doctor." He took my arm and led me down the hall toward a private alcove. "I've heard the rumors."

He kept his voice low so as not to be overheard. Which rumors, I wondered.

"But you mustn't blame yourself." He searched my face to see if I understood. "The miscarriage was not your doing. You did all that you could."

His frankness surprised me as much as his conviction that I was not to blame. How could he know? I must have looked confused.

"Priests learn certain things..." he said.

A nun passed by in the hallway and made a little bow toward Father Poitiers. He nodded to her before turning his attention back to me.

"Be comforted. Let God heal these wounds with his infinite love."

"But Edna. Her family..."

"The church will do what it can to watch over the family." He looked at me with a calmness that I could only imagine was rooted in his faith.

"Thank you, Father." I shook my head and sighed. "Thank you." I walked down the hall.

I wanted to talk to Hazlitt in Pathology to see if he knew anything about Patrick Molloy, but one of the nuns said he was not in yet. I needed to get back to my office where I had appointments lined up so I left.

Throughout the day, I couldn't stop brooding over the Molloys. Father Poitiers' words kept circling in my mind. I thought back over my examination of Mrs. Molloy the night of her fall. The abdominal bruising. The newel post at the head of the stairs where Patrick Molloy sat bawling. Poitiers sounded certain that he knew something about the terminated pregnancy.

An intuition arose in my mind. Had Edna shared something with Father Poitiers in the confessional? My suspicions led me to believe that she had told me only part of the truth. I now suspected that her husband had not hit her—or kicked her, as I first supposed. I imagined that in her desperation Edna Molloy had thrown herself against the newel post—over and over—to end her pregnancy until she lost her balance and fell down the stairs. The poor woman. It dawned on me that the Klansmen must have assumed—just as I had—what Tom Harris had suggested, that Mr. Molloy had assaulted his wife and caused her miscarriage. That's why they had taken their revenge. In that moment I guessed what Edna must be experiencing, blaming herself for her husband's suffering. That's why she must have confessed to Father Poitiers. Dear God. I wished that I believed in prayer.

When I was able to get away from my office in late afternoon, I went straight to St. Mary's.

Ever since I had taken the embryo to Dr. Hazlitt, I had connected him with the Molloy family—even though I had not told him where the embryo came from. I didn't know what his politics were, but I felt I could trust him.

Hazlitt welcomed me into his office. "I kind of expected I might hear from you."

"Then you know why I'm here?"

"You want to know about Patrick Molloy."

I nodded.

"As a matter of fact, I did the autopsy on his body this morning."

"Father Poitiers said that Molloy died just after dawn. From what I've heard, it's a blessing he's dead."

"What have you heard?"

I told him that a friend of mine was a news reporter, and I related the bare facts of Tom's account. "How bad were his burns?" I asked.

"Extensive second- and third-degree burns."

"Good God."

"Dr. Holman, was that embryo you brought me Edna Molloy's?" he asked.

The question took me by surprise. I hesitated as my guts tighten. "What makes you ask?"

"There are some peculiar things about this case. And I've heard stories. There are rumors about Mrs. Molloy being pregnant before her accident. Some say her husband beat her and caused a miscarriage and that's why the Klan killed him—besides the fact that he was a devout Catholic. Others are accusing you of inducing an abortion."

So Tom's warning was apt. And Felton's veiled threats had come to fruition. Rumors were circulating.

Hazlitt watched me. "There is no question," he said, "that someone was trying to punish Molloy. Do you think he caused the miscarriage?"

"I don't think he did, but I can't prove that in a court of law. I can tell you there is a witness who can vouch that I did not induce an abortion."

"I'll take your word for it. Most everything that your reporter friend told you is true. Molloy had rope marks on his neck, but the neck was not broken. There is another fact that you should know about, if you will hold it in strict confidence."

I nodded.

"Molloy had been castrated."

The horror of this revelation nauseated me.

fIfTY-TWO

Jimmy and Charlie arrived home from their honeymoon around noon on Saturday. The women's furnishings had been moved to the Beasley house, which was all ready for the "newlyweds." Charlie and Gwen began settling into their new home while Jimmy helped with the unpacking and arranging.

I wanted to tell Jimmy about Molloy, but I didn't want to spoil the happy mood that having Charlie and him back home had brought with it.

Gwen wanted to have dinner at the Beasley house, but she couldn't find her cooking pans and her kitchen was still in chaos, so we prepared the meal at our house. Charlie and Jimmy told us about their trip. They'd had a good visit with his family. His father and brothers had taken them trout fishing. Charlie said she didn't fancy the fishing part, but she loved getting outdoors in the country. Jimmy told us about the anti-Japanese activities over there organized by white farmers and orchardists, including his father. Because they felt threatened by what they saw as an invasion of Japanese immigrants buying land in the valley, they were all supporting enforcement of the Alien Land Law.

Jimmy's family, in particular his mother, took a special liking to Charlie, who insisted on unpacking and showing off a set of twelve crystal wineglasses with gold trim, which Jimmy's parents had given them as a wedding gift. The set was an heirloom from

Jimmy's mother's family, but it got little use out at the orchard. The glassware was of superior quality, Charlie said.

When Gwen and I shared our story about Cora and the missing morphine, a pall fell over our reunion. I didn't even consider bringing up the Molloy case—it was too disturbing. Jimmy looked unusually worried. He believed Felton was behind the morphine scheme and he was convinced that it endangered all of us.

After dinner Jimmy and Charlie strolled around the block past the Mitchell house to their new home. Later, when it was dark, Gwen slipped through the back gate to spend the night with Charlie, and Jimmy came back over to our house.

As we prepared to turn in for the night, I tried to reassure Jimmy. I told him that I trusted the detective Tom Harris had recommended, but Jimmy remained apprehensive.

Sunday morning Jimmy returned to his organ playing at St. Stephen's Church. Gwen spent the morning arranging the kitchen in the new house, while Charlie unpacked more boxes.

When Jimmy got home, he wanted us to go visit Maude's to announce that he and Charlie were married. The girls wanted to continue setting their house in order, since Charlie had to return to work the next morning, so Jimmy and I went visiting without them.

Maude was happy for Jimmy and offered her congratulations. "But where are your wives?"

"They're hard at work tidying up the new house," Jimmy said. "We're purchasing the Beasley house behind you here. So we'll be your neighbors."

"That will be nice." She was disappointed that she had not been invited to the wedding and said so.

Jimmy explained that Charlie wanted the simplest wedding possible so they hadn't invited any guests. "But we're planning a reception party. You'll get an invitation to that."

"I'll be glad to help you celebrate," Maude said. "Now how did you and your wife meet? She's the young lady you brought round at Christmas time, right?"

"She's an old friend of Carl's," Jimmy said.

"That's nice." Maude's cat hopped up into her lap. "Hello, Blossom," she said stroking its fur. "How about you fellows? I've never heard how you met each other."

That was just the opportunity I was looking for to ask her about Haskell's connection to Bisby. "Jimmy was playing at a dance out at the Bisby Grange last year. I'd never heard him play jazz before, so I drove out to take it in."

"Oh, yes, Bisby. I heard there was some trouble out that way. Those Klan yahoos."

I was surprised that she knew about the incident but glad I didn't have to bring it up. "How did you hear about that?" I asked.

Jimmy gave me a quizzical look. I still hadn't told him about Patrick Molloy or Haskell's connection to Bisby.

"My friend Naomi. You know, Lloyd's mom. She told me he's got a childhood friend from Bayfield that lives near Bisby—a fellow she remembers from his school days." The cat lay down and relaxed into her lap. "Sounds like Lloyd heard from him about a hanging that took place out that way. A mob took some city fella. The story Naomi told me sounds like something you'd hear about Negroes down South. It's just a crime. No one deserves to be strung up like that. I sure hope the law catches whoever was responsible."

"Driving home from that Grange dance, I saw some Klansmen performing a ceremony." I didn't want to go into the disturbing details.

"Naomi claims there's a bunch of them out there." Blossom was beginning to purr loudly.

"There are plenty of them here in town, too," I said. "Is Haskell mixed up with them?" I knew the answer for myself, but I wanted to see if Lloyd's mother had said anything about it.

Maude continued to stroke the cat's back. "Naomi has mentioned it and she's not pleased. She doesn't like him associating with them. We both agree they're a bad lot—especially after my run-in with those LOTIEs."

"Has she ever mentioned a fellow named Danny Felton?" Jimmy asked. I never would have expected to hear him bring up that name until I figured out that Jimmy was probably making a connection between Felton and the fact that Haskell was supplying morphine to Vance.

The cat's tail settled alongside its body as it continued to purr. "Not that I recall. Who's Danny Felton?"

Jimmy and I exchanged glances. What could either of us tell Maude that would adequately describe Felton?

I jumped in. "Oh, he's just a man I've heard might have some business connections with Lloyd. It's probably nothing."

Jimmy found his voice. "But if you hear any mention of him, would you let us know?"

"That doesn't sound like nothing."

"It's just that we've heard some rumors about him," I said. "That's all. However, regarding those Klan boys out by Bisby, if Naomi mentions any more details, I'd sure be interested to know."

The cat continued its boisterous purring as Maude petted its dark fur.

"We happened to catch that big Klan march downtown several weeks ago," I continued. "I saw Betty Haskell there watching the goings-on." I wondered if Maude knew about the accident that Hal Gaston told me about.

"Poor Betty," Maude said.

"Why do you say that?" I asked.

"I guess she had an accident. So Naomi said. That was a few weeks back."

"That's a pity. What happened?"

"A fall, Naomi said. But, you know, just before that, Naomi told me Betty had called her—which hardly ever happens. Naomi usually talks with Lloyd—he doesn't like Betty talking to her. I think he's afraid of women's gossip. Anyway, I reckon Betty was in a state about something to do with Lloyd's business."

Jimmy looked worried. I needed to share all the news he'd missed while he was gone.

"Many marriages are troubled," I said, hoping to wind up our visit. "I suspect losing Henry was difficult for them."

"Naomi still laments the boy's passing. They're all pretty broken up about it."

The cat started to drool and pump Maude's thigh with its paws. "Okay, Blossom, that's enough." Maude lifted the animal off her lap and lowered it onto the floor. "You funny old girl."

"Well, we'd better get back home and start dinner," Jimmy said. "While our wives are busy getting the Beasley house fixed up, we've been delegated to cooking duty."

I checked my watch. "It's later than I thought. KP awaits us."

"Yes, honeymoon's over," Jimmy said as he stood. "Once we get settled, we'll bring the wives over to visit."

"Do that," Maude said. "I'd enjoy a chat with them."

Jimmy went over to pet the cat. "Goodbye, Blossom." It shook its head and trotted out of the room. "I'll keep you posted on our wedding reception. It'll probably be a home affair. Maybe mid-May."

"I'm looking forward to it," Maude said.

While we walked home, I gave Jimmy a quick rundown on the Molloy family and my phone conversation with Hal Gaston about Haskell. "I'm sure Gwen will fill Charlie in on all this," I added.

"Yes, let's not bring it up at dinner," Jimmy said. "Charlie is in such a cheery mood after getting away for a few days. We had a fun trip."

fIfTY-THREE

That night at dinner, Jimmy and Charlie told us they had begun planning their wedding reception. Jimmy had some musical friends that he wanted all of us to meet, and Charlie wanted to introduce us to some more of her girlfriends from the phone company. And we all wanted the neighbors to know that Jimmy and Charlie were now living in the Beasley house.

We picked out a Sunday afternoon in mid-May for the festivities. Jimmy envisioned a garden party on the front lawn at our house. He suggested moving the piano out onto the porch for music and setting up tables on the grass for refreshments. The girls talked him into keeping the food and drinks in the dining room and kitchen where it would be easier to manage and clean up. The guests could carry their food and drinks to small tables on the porch and at the top of the drive. Besides, they argued, if the weather turned bad, all we had to do was move the guests indoors. Jimmy liked the idea. And then there was the issue of finding a caterer.

Gwen planned to finish sewing new covers for the cushions on the porch swing. Charlie said we needed to arrange for invitations to be sent out right away and asked Jimmy and me to give them names and addresses of people we wanted to invite. I insisted that we invite the Mitchells, much as I disliked the idea. I didn't believe they would come, but we had to send them an invitation so that they knew they were included and that Jimmy and Charlie were now married. Jimmy volunteered to take charge of getting invitations printed since he was free during the day. He would talk to a stationer on Monday morning, but the girls insisted on seeing samples before a final decision was made.

Early Monday Jimmy brought stationery samples by the office for our approval before taking them downtown for Charlie to see. It was raining hard, and Jimmy was wet when he came into the office, clutching the samples under his overcoat. Gwen and I looked over the invitations and after Gwen picked her favorites, Jimmy prepared to leave.

Cora had been at lunch when Jimmy arrived, but she returned just as he was saying goodbye. She came out of the downpour wearing a dark blue scarf pulled close around her face to keep off the rain and she had removed her horn-rimmed glasses, to keep them from getting wet I presumed. Jimmy stopped in mid-sentence, when he saw her.

After a pause, he laughed, although I thought it sounded forced, and he said, "Hello, Cora. Is it wet enough for you?"

She laughed and threw off the scarf, shaking off the raindrops. "It certainly is coming down out there," she said as she quickly put her glasses on.

Jimmy slapped his hand on my shoulder and said, "I almost forgot, Carl. Let me show you these papers before I leave." He hustled me off into my office, and I knew something was up.

As soon as the door was closed, Jimmy came closer and said, "I just realized where I know her from. The first time I met her, she had dark hair and no glasses. That's why I didn't recognize her. I met her at the Checker Club in Chicago. She's Danny Felton's wife."

At first I couldn't take this in. Felton's wife? I didn't even know he was married. Then I thought of the disappearing morphine, my conversation with Gaston, and Cora's behavior. Things began to make sense. As the implications sank in I experienced a bone-chilling dread. I remembered Jimmy's description of Felton murdering Eric and the blood on the tuxedo.

I put an arm around his shoulder. We were all in danger.

"I'm scared," Jimmy said.

"I am too. But we need to carry on as if nothing has changed."

His face was clouded with worry.

I wanted to reassure him, but I was not at all reassured myself. "I'll contact our detective. And maybe Tom Harris will have some suggestions." I began to feel anxious about how much leverage Felton had over the police. If the rumors were true, he had been able to pressure them into shutting down Maldini's speak. Would they protect us?

After Jimmy left, I phoned Lockwood and told him we believed that Cora was married to Danny Felton. He said that was an illuminating piece of information. He had been hearing stories about Felton and making some phone calls. "I found out he has a marriage license in Chicago, but I never suspected he would be traveling with his wife. He's with the Italian mob back there. The Chicago police want him for murder?"

"Yes, there's a witness."

"Hmm. Interesting. That may prove valuable."

I wondered if I should have said that. Jimmy didn't need to be dragged into this any further.

Lockwood went on. "I found out Felton ran a string of brothels in Chicago during the War."

"He didn't fight in the war in Europe?" I asked.

"There's no way he could have," Lockwood replied. "The only war he did fight was with the Chicago gangs. He survived an attempt on his life by a German gang after Felton tried to muscle in on their beer industry. They planted a bomb in his car. He spent a couple of months in the hospital while a team of doctors did their best to stitch him back together."

"I can corroborate that. I examined him when he came to my office. He's got extensive scarring. Is there anything else I should know?"

"A number of puzzle pieces are falling into place, but I need a day or so to check some things out," he said. "I'll keep in touch with you."

Next I phoned Tom Harris. He was in a temper.

"I just found out that the Klan is threatening to boycott our paper—and our advertisers—if we don't stop writing unflattering stories about them. Jesus H. Christ." In the background I heard typewriters and telephones and general newsroom hubbub. "We could go out of business if no one buys our papers."

"I sympathize. Can I prescribe some booze for you?"

He laughed. That was a good sign.

"Whatever happens, I'll subscribe to your paper—even though I never have time to read it."

"I know all too well you're a philistine when it comes to news."

"Speaking of which, I've got some news for you. Jimmy and Charlie are married now. They just got back from their honeymoon. They'll be having a wedding party in May. You'll be getting an invitation soon."

"That is some good news. Tell them congratulations for me."

"There's more. Jimmy dropped by the office this morning and here's the real scoop. The girl we hired as a receptionist here—Jimmy says that she's Danny Felton's wife."

Tom didn't respond and I listened to the background noise.

Finally he spoke. "And she's the one you suspect of stealing morphine? Boy!"

I heard the rustling of papers.

"This is a tricky bunch you're mixed up with—worming their way into the heart of your practice."

"And they're dangerous. That's my big concern."

"I understand. But here's something to think about. I've been working on a story—and this may be why the Klan is so riled up. There's been talk about a number of squabbling factions in the

Klan. First, there are some tensions developing between the local and the national Klan organizations. Some folks think too much of the dues is going to Klan headquarters in Georgia. And there are some Klaverns that think it's okay to play rough, like those boys out at Bisby, while others think they ought to let the law take care of misconduct—otherwise they think it makes the Klan look bad."

A muffled voice interrupted Tom and he must have put his hand over the mouthpiece.   "Yes, I'll get to it in a minute," his voice came back on the line. "Excuse me, Carl. Then there's the police. Some are Klan members, and some aren't. On top of that, there's the booze angle—some Klansmen and some cops are content to look the other way when it comes to bootleggers so they can make some money on the side. They don't earn much salary. Others don't approve but keep their mouths shut."

"So what's all that got to do with Felton?"

"Sorry, I was thinking through my news story. Here's the deal. Bateson and his buddies are making money from payoffs to protect their network of bootleggers. Felton's working with Haskell to set up his own connections to distribute high-quality Canadian liquor underselling the locals—and that's cutting into Bateson's take. That's why Maldini's place was raided on New Year's Eve. I was wrong in thinking Felton paid off the cops to raid Maldini. The local police wanted to teach Maldini that he should do business with the local suppliers, not with Felton."

"So you think Bateson would like to take down Felton?" I asked.

"That's right, but Bateson and Haskell are both in the Klan, and that's helping Haskell stay in the clear. But loyalties are divided even within the Empire. If you've got some information on Felton, Bateson would want to know about it. He and his vice squad might help protect you from Felton—if they have a reason to."

His voice turned away from the phone again. "Be right there.

Look, Carl, I can talk more this evening if you want, but I've gotta go now."

"Sure, I understand. Thanks for the tip."

I sat mulling over our conversation. I trusted Tom's information and his judgment. He seemed to be throwing me a lifeline and I thought I saw a glimmer of hope. Cora was the key. I needed to find out if Bateson knew the whole story on Felton. I had to talk with Bateson much as I abhorred the idea of having anything to do with him.

FIFTY-FOUR

I was still traumatized by my earlier talks with Bateson. The very thought of talking to him alarmed me. But when I weighed a meeting with Bateson against a chat with Felton, there was no comparison. Besides, I had no leverage with Felton. With Bateson I had the evidence of a child rape by his brother-in-law, and I had the information that Felton's wife was stealing narcotics from my medical office. If Tom Harris was right, Bateson would want to know what I had to offer. I didn't like it, but I knew what I had to do.

I phoned his office and said I needed to talk to him right away. He agreed to meet with me as soon as I could get there.

I tried to steady my quivering knees as I drove through traffic on the wet streets to Central Precinct. The rain had let up a little, but it was cool out. Regardless of the weather, I felt myself sweating even before I parked the car.

"I have an appointment with Officer Bateson," I told the man at the front desk as I fidgeted with my hat. I soon found myself entering Bateson's office. My guts clenched and my mouth was dry.

Bateson sat at his desk, scrutinizing me with those intense green eyes. Unlike during my first visit, his desk was littered with papers. Had he cleaned up for my first visit, knowing I was coming? Maybe I'd caught him off guard this time.

"To what do I owe the pleasure, Dr. Holman?"

His office was cold, and I didn't understand why he had an electric table fan whirring at the corner of his desk. The papers, held down by paperweights, flapped about. The window behind his desk was raised. I didn't see any flies on the glass today.

Even though I'd been rehearsing what to say, that all evaporated now.

"I believe I have some information that will be of help to you." My heart was pounding. "About Danny Felton."

His expression didn't change. "Why should I care about a Danny Felton?"

"These matters are rather delicate. I'm sure you would agree."

He didn't react. I felt unnerved by the fluttering documents on his desk.

"I understand you've been investigating him," I said.

"Let's assume that we were interested in this fellow, why should I trust anything you have to say about him? Your reputation is a bit sullied."

"I know someone who has direct information about Felton from time spent in Chicago."

This seemed to catch Bateson's attention.

"Tell me more."

"And I know some things about Billy Butler."

"And why would I be interested in Billy Butler?"

"Let's be honest here. You know I was here on New Year's Eve. I saw you talking to Billy that night."

"And I saw you here with that little fairy, that night." His disdain was palpable.

I took a deep breath and steeled myself. "Jimmy Harper and I have a close friendship. But let's leave him out of this. I'm a married man now. I'm here to give you some information you may find valuable."

"I'm still not convinced I can trust you, Doctor. I have it on good authority that you were the one responsible for my sister-in-law abandoning her husband."

A trickle of sweat ran down my back. "Rebecca Porter. Precisely. This is why you should trust me." A sheet of paper in front of me flapped up and down. "Did you know Marvin Porter raped his daughter?"

Bateson let slip a momentary look of surprise.

I went on, "Mrs. Porter witnessed my examination of the little girl, and I have a microscope slide preserved in formaldehyde—besides my medical records from that day."

He stared at me a moment before his eyes wandered to the side as if he were remembering something.

"I believe you would find it to be convincing evidence."

The rigidness of his manner softened a tad. Bateson reached to adjust one of the paperweights on his desk.

"What's more, Rebecca had a black eye when she brought the child in to see me."

Bateson looked up

"She confronted Marvin about what he did to Sally, and he punched his wife in the face to get her to keep quiet."

Bateson frowned and tightened his lips while he appeared to deliberate some odious dilemma.

"The child *was* troubled," he said.

We were both quiet for a moment as a light breeze from the window mixed with the current from the fan.

Then Bateson spoke. "So what do you know about Billy Butler?"

"Billy told me that he's been working with Lloyd Haskell—making deliveries." I put emphasis on the word "deliveries" to punctuate my meaning.

"Can you prove that?"

"We were alone when he told me. But he accompanied me to St. Mary's with a friend of his who was injured. Later that night, Billy was discovered trying to get into the drug dispensary at the hospital. You can ask the night watchman there, as well as some of the nuns."

Now Bateson looked intrigued.

"And this Felton fellow?"

"I hired a young woman as a secretary in my medical office a month or so back. She's been observed by my nurse—my wife—in some suspicious activities involving our narcotics supply. She has been identified to me as Danny Felton's wife." Now I had his full attention. "Besides that, I suspect she has been cooking my books to make it look like I've been selling morphine and alcohol. I believe just the opposite is happening at Haskell's pharmacy. There seems to be plenty of anecdotal evidence that Haskell has been supplying users."

"We've been suspicious of him but…" He stopped. I guessed that he was thinking of Haskell's Klan connections.

"I believe Haskell and Felton are in cahoots." I continued. "Felton is a morphine addict. He approached me in my office for script and offered me a bribe to supply him. Of course, I turned him down."

Bateson raised his head almost as if he were about to nod. "I see."

"I also believe Felton is responsible for the flow of Canadian whiskey into town. Haskell and Billy Butler have been involved."

A sheet of paper near the fan flipped over and floated to the floor.

"One final thing. Did you know that Felton is wanted in Chicago for murder? I believe he is here in Oregon on the lam."

At last Bateson was fully engaged. His eyes darted to the side and back to my face a couple of times as he considered the implications. I was a bit dismayed that all of this seemed to be news to him, but I was relieved that I'd had my say and I didn't think there was more I needed to add. The rest was up to Bateson.

He reached down to pick up the paper off the floor. When he straightened up, he gave me a long, hard look and nodded slowly. "Would you be prepared to give us a statement?"

"Felton is a dangerous man. Would you be prepared to have some of your men patrol our neighborhood?"

I sensed we had reached an understanding.

When I got back to my office, I phoned Lockwood and told

him I'd spoken with Bateson about Felton and Cora. He said he knew some cops and would follow up to see what action they were taking. He also agreed to have his associates keep a closer eye on our office and the two homes.

That evening when Jimmy and Charlie walked around the block to the Beasley house, they saw a police vehicle cruising around the neighborhood.

FIFTY-FIVE

Cora didn't show up for work on Tuesday. When Gwen discovered that the rest of our morphine supply was missing, she phoned Lockwood. Was this just the lull before a storm? I contacted Bateson's office and relayed the news. He told me they had Felton under surveillance, but that didn't put my mind at ease. If, as Jimmy said, Felton could do "anything," he might take revenge on Jimmy or me—or the rest of our little family. We were all on pins and needles, but we resolved to carry on.

That day and the next were unnerving times with no news of Felton from Bateson or Lockwood, although we called several times to check in. Thursday morning Gwen asked me to open the office while she ran some errands. When she planned to take a trolley, I insisted she would be safer taking a cab. She agreed.

I left around 6 to get a head start on my work. It had rained during the night and the puddles in the gutters reflected the gray sky. As I drove over the wet pavement, I thought back over my meeting with Bateson. It had gone better than I anticipated. I hoped he would be able to restrain Felton somehow, but I was dubious.

When our office building came into view, I saw a person lying near the front door. "What now?" I said under my breath. I hoped it was just a drunk, but that was not typical in this part of town. I shifted down to first gear and pulled up to the curb. It looked like a male lying on his back, face turned away. I pushed down a rising feeling of alarm. Please let it just be some inebriate. I got out of the car. The figure was dressed in a familiar brown coat. It was Billy Butler. I froze as dread overcame me, but I forced myself to walk closer. He lay still, his face pale. A soft breeze stirred the dark curls of his hair. Squatting beside him, I reached out to feel for a pulse at his neck, but the skin was cold.

"Dear God." I pulled open his coat to find his shirt was stained with blood. "No," I cried. Several bullet holes had pierced his torso leaving ruptures in the flesh.

I had to force myself into action.

I knew he was dead but I placed my hand on his chest between the bullet wounds. His clothing was damp, the body cold. Rigor mortis had set in. I felt something beneath his shirt and undid the top button. Just below his collarbone lay a small gold cross on a chain. Had Billy gotten religion? I rose to my feet and stood back, looking at him. His handsome face was immobile. His shoes and pant cuffs were splattered with mud. I wondered if he had been chased down.

A lump rose in my throat as I leaned against the side of the building, looking up at the gray sky. I covered my face.

"This world is a hellhole." Billy's words. The poor kid. He may have been a scoundrel, but he didn't deserve this.

A gust of wind sent a chill through me. I pulled myself together. There were things to be done. I went inside and called Bateson to report a dead body in front of my office.

I was having a shot of whiskey from our medical supply cabinet when I heard the police sirens. I rinsed my mouth with tap water and went out to face Bateson and his men.

After a lot of questions and gathering of evidence, Bateson took me aside and thanked me for spilling the beans on Felton. The Vice Squad was moving in on the man, but he kept evading them. Bateson thought they would catch up with him in the next day or so.

What other trouble could Felton cause in that amount of time? I wondered.

Bateson wanted to know if I thought Felton had anything to do with Billy Butler's death.

"It's a good bet," I replied.

He just nodded.

I called Lockwood to tell him about Billy, but he'd already heard the news from his friends in the police department. He thought things might resolve themselves overnight. He promised to stop by our office the next afternoon to fill us in. Next I called in a workman to clean the blood off our sidewalk. I hoped there wouldn't be any more.

Late in the day Tom Harris called. He'd heard about the dead body and he wanted to know everything. He was handling the story for his paper. After I shared all that had happened that morning, I reminded him of the Theresa Littlefoot case and her connection with Haskell as a liquor supplier. He recalled the black bootleggers that came to my house.

"Billy told me he was staying at her café," I said. "She may know something. But please keep her name out of the paper. She may be in danger."

Tom agreed and thanked me for the tip.

That evening Jimmy was upset by the news of Billy's murder. "I told you Felton could do anything," he said before he sank into a gloomy silence. I tried to reassure him that Bateson was on Felton's trail, and that there were police patrolling our neighborhood, but that didn't raise his spirits. I wasn't reassured myself.

When Charlie tried to cheer us up by suggesting a game of Halma after dinner, Jimmy refused to play. That wasn't like him. We were all on edge as we cleaned up the dishes. Jimmy retired to the piano and played church music for a long time.

The next afternoon Lockwood came by and settled in my office with Gwen and me.

"I suspected that Felton and his gang had moved out of town a couple of days ago," he began.

"Yes, Cora hasn't been in since Monday," Gwen said.

"The whole bunch has been on the move, going from one hideout to another. They used every trick in the book to shake anyone trailing them—disguises, changing vehicles, and differing routes."

He said the police tracked Felton to a rural farmhouse near Bisby. They raided the place during the night, but no one was there, and from the shambles they found, it looked like Felton's gang had left in a hurry. "It seems that they were traveling with quite an entourage. Reports suggest there were at least two drivers, some bodyguards, and an assortment of others."

"At Maldini's on New Year's Eve there were a couple of men with Felton," I said.

The detective nodded. "Bateson's squad did catch up with a couple of Felton's goons, refueling at a gas station. My police buddy laughed when he told me. Then he winked and said they let the two louts go. I take it some money changed hands. But before they skedaddled, he told them there were some Klan boys around who would take care of them if they ever showed their faces again. They got the picture—after that Molloy business. The cops said, 'Tell that to your Italian friends when you catch up with them.'" Lockwood chuckled.

"Do you think that's the last we'll see of them?" Gwen asked.

"I expect so." He went on to give us a rundown on what the police found at the farmhouse. "My friend showed me some of their evidence. There were a number of empty morphine ampoules. They had your cut marks on them." Most interesting of all was a set of accounting books that the police discovered half burned in a cook stove. As we suspected, Cora had been keeping an extra set of accounts for our office, skillfully doctored to make it look as if we had been covering up large-scale sales of morphine and alcohol.

Lockwood said we should expect another visit from the police. He didn't know who had tipped off Felton that the law might raid his place in town, but he was convinced that Felton had gone underground. I hoped he was right, but my apprehension lingered.

Not long after the detective left, Tom Harris phoned.

"I finally got a hold of Theresa Littlefoot today," he said.

I heard children's voices in the background, so I guessed he was at home.

"I spent a long time talking with her. She didn't trust me at first, but I told her I'm an old friend of yours—a neighbor across the street. She was still suspicious until I told her you delivered one of my kids. That seemed to get her attention. She said you were a good man."

"How did she look? Her face, I mean. She was pretty badly cut up when I operated on her. I haven't seen her since she left St. Mary's." I fidgeted with a notepad on my desk. "She never followed up at my office like I asked. I think she didn't trust our white man's medicine."

"She's got some scars, for sure. And one eye doesn't look like it's working right."

"The whole thing is such a pity. She struck me as a kind soul. She was good to Billy Butler."

"That's what I got her to tell me about in the long run. Billy showed up at her place in a panic. Said he had to get out of town. He was hiding from Felton. She gave me the impression that Felton believed Billy was the one who had ratted on him to the cops."

"Christ!" It came out louder that I intended and I dropped my fist onto the desk with a thud.

"Don't take it too hard, Carl. It's not your fault."

"Still…"

Gwen came into my office and stood watching me with concern.

"Let it go," Tom said.

"It's Tom Harris," I said, covering the mouthpiece of the phone. Gwen took a seat.

"Okay, what else did Theresa Littlefoot have to say?"

Gwen's ears pricked up.

"She gave him some traveling money. Then she said she took off her gold cross and put it around his neck—to protect him."

The sadness I felt when I found the body rose up again. "Oh, God." I closed my eyes and shook my head. I couldn't look at Gwen for fear of crying.

Tom continued his story. "A while after Billy took off, Felton came round to the café and started asking her questions about him. She put on the dumb Indian act and wouldn't tell him anything. He started to threaten her, but a police car pulled up out front and Felton disappeared out the back."

"This is all too sad."

"I guess this isn't the end of the story yet," Tom said.

"We heard that Felton has disappeared. That's what Lockwood says. He paid us a visit this afternoon."

"I guess I'd better get in touch with him—and the police."

I thanked Tom and hung up. Gwen came to my side and put her hand on my shoulder as I sat staring straight ahead.

FIFTY-SIX

As I was getting over my sadness at Billy Butler's murder, I began to feel more confident that we wouldn't have any more trouble from Felton. Some of Bateson's vice officers came by our office to ask more questions. After Gwen and I shared what we knew, they said they thought Felton had returned to Chicago. I hoped that we'd seen the last of him.

Sunday afternoon Gwen and Charlie hosted Jimmy and me for our first meal at the Beasley house. They were settling in and Gwen had the kitchen in working order. Charlie set a beautiful table with damask linens and the wineglasses from Jimmy's mother.

During the meal, that fearful edge was gone from our little gathering. We discussed Felton's disappearance feeling more at ease.

Soon the conversation turned to the wedding party. It was two weeks off and there were still a lot of things to finalize. Charlie would get the last of the invitations out in the next couple of days. Jimmy would talk to the caterers at the Chandler Hotel. He and I told the girls about our chat over the salmon mousse pastries at the Iverson wedding reception the year before.

"I ordered some of those same pastries for a picnic when I invited Jimmy to go fishing with me. We were just getting to know each other."

"Yeah," Jimmy said, "it turned out Carl didn't know much about fishing so I had to give him some pointers." He laughed. "But that was some picnic he put together. So we should order some of those salmon pastries for our party."

We all agreed. After dinner we got out the Halma set and moving the playing pieces across the board further put our minds at ease. It was like old times.

The next Sunday we again gathered for dinner at the Beasley House. This was becoming a tradition. Preparations for the wedding party were coming together. Jimmy told us that he had been at the Chandler Hotel dealing with the caterers. He stopped at a newsstand to buy a magazine for Charlie, when he became aware of a portly, bald man next to him. The man jostled his shoulder reaching for a newspaper with a headline about the Klan. Their eyes met.

"It was Dr. Gowan," Jimmy said. "He must have recognized me, because he gave me this cold stare, like I was some piece of filth in the gutter. Then he literally growled at me, 'Watch what you're doing.' I just stood there staring back at him without saying anything. What could I say?"

"There's not much to say to that old goat," Gwen said.

I hadn't thought of Gowan or his clinic for months. I felt a wave of anger and disgust. But it dissipated, and in an effort at fair-mindedness I tried to remember some of his good qualities—his generosity to those he liked, his industriousness, his jovial side. But his intolerance and bullheadedness tipped the scales against him. I was glad to be clear of his domination.

"Yes, he can be nasty," I said.

"You can say that again," Jimmy said. "And you'll never guess who I ran into at Hansen's diner while I was having lunch? Vance."

Jimmy said that Vance didn't look so good, even though he claimed to be staying away from narcotics. "He tried to convince me to take a music job with him." Some casual acquaintance had invited Vance to play at a big Klan gathering. They were paying quite well, he said, but he needed a singer. He kept trying to entice Jimmy to join him. Because the Klan was involved and because Vance insisted so, Jimmy wasn't having any of it, but Vance kept trying to cajole him, offering him a bigger piece of the take. I was concerned for Vance.

"Here's the kicker," Jimmy said. "The big number the Klan wants Vance to play is 'Yes, We Have No Bananas,' but they want to insert their own lyrics so it goes, 'Yes, the Klan has no Catholics.' Can you believe it?" Gwen shook her head.

"Typical of those lamebrains," Charlie said. "Let me propose a toast to their rapid demise." We all drank to that. "Oh, I've got to tell you about my conversation with Maude." Charlie set her wineglass down. "I was doing some housework this morning and I decided to air out some of my dresses on the clothesline in back. I kept hearing a rustling sound beyond the hedge in Maude's garden. When I called out to her, she said, 'I'm here all right.'"

Jimmy laughed. "Sounds just like her."

"I asked what on earth she was doing over there, and she told me she was harvesting her snow peas. She said she had a bumper crop and did I want some. 'Of course,' I said, 'I love fresh snow peas,' and offered to give her a hand. She told me to come round to her gate. When she opened it, this look of dismay came over her, and I remembered I was wearing a pair of Jimmy's slacks."

Gwen chuckled. "That's my girl."

Jimmy laughed too.

"Well, it's just easier when you're doing housework or out in the garden. Anyway, she gave me a bucket and we picked snow peas for a time, talking about this and that."

Charlie wanted to know if Maude would be coming to the wedding reception—she was. Maude wanted to know how my new medical practice was going—just fine, Charlie told her. "I didn't want to mention the dead body or any of that." By the time they had picked all of the pea pods, it was getting warm so they climbed the stairs to Maude's back porch and sat in the shade.

"While Maude was in the kitchen getting us some iced tea, I sat looking out at her garden—boy, does she have some garden—and I could see over her hedge where my dresses were hanging on the clothesline, and I noticed that I'd left the back door of our house open."

"I felt the breeze through the kitchen earlier," Gwen said. "I assumed you left it open on purpose."

"While we were sipping our tea Maude commented on the gate we put between Carl's house and ours. She told me she doesn't sleep well sometimes and she'll come out on her back porch at night to sit a spell. She said she sees a lot of coming and going through that garden gate after dark."

"Oh-oh," Gwen said. She arranged her fork and knife on her empty plate.

Jimmy and I looked up. I worried about what was coming next.

"Yes, indeed," Charlie replied.

Jimmy said, "What did you say?"

"I asked her what she made of it, and she said it sure looked to her like the girls sleep in one house and the boys sleep in the other."

"Oh, boy!" Jimmy said.

I felt uneasy. I valued Maude's friendship.

"I asked if that shocked her. She sat there stringing peas for a bit and gave me a funny look. She said she's seen enough in her time that nothing shocks her, but she didn't think it was part of God's plan."

"Oh dear," Gwen said.

Charlie continued. "I said, 'Because we don't have any children?' and she said she guessed so."

"Hmm," I said, laying my fork down. Jimmy and I looked at each other.

"No, wait," Charlie said. "I asked about her children. She's got six, you know. She told me only three of them have kids. One son's wife never seems to get pregnant, she said, and they've considered adopting but never do. The oldest daughter, Betsy, here in town, doesn't want babies since she's so busy with her social climbing. And her youngest son has never married. I told her that it seemed to me like God had many different plans when it comes to having babies."

"Well put," I said, wanting to get up and give her a hug.

"She asked if Jimmy and I wanted kids."

"God forbid." Jimmy shook his head and laughed.

"I told her I never liked being around children, and she admitted that she would have been glad to leave off after three."

Charlie looked around the table. Jimmy folded his napkin and laid it beside his empty plate. We were all quiet waiting for her to finish her story.

"She considered for a moment and finally said she reckoned maybe we humans could only see a little piece of God's plan."

"She told me she was never very fond of her husband," Jimmy said.

Charlie nodded. "She also confided that she's a bit jealous of the freedoms young women like us have today."

"Bless her heart," Gwen said

"She went on to say that our sleeping arrangements were our concern and she didn't hold it against us. She feels that you've all been very good to her. She thought it wasn't any of her business anyway, she just had to get nosy."

We all laughed.

"I told her I wished all our neighbors were nosy in the same way she was."

FIFTY-SEVEN

The wedding reception was fast approaching. Charlie had sent out the last of the invitations. Jimmy made arrangements for a substitute organist at St. Joe's that Sunday. The Chandler Hotel would see to the food and provide servers and clean up. During the week before, we hired a cleaning service to help Joe Locke with the extra work getting ready. I had Clark Mitchell take special care with the lawn. His mother was still resistant to letting him do yard work for me, but the prospect of earning pocket money always seemed to persuade him, and with his father's help, Clark was able to overcome Minnie's objections. Although they were invited, I didn't expect to see any of the Mitchells at the party. Still they had been made well aware that Charlie and Jimmy were now married.

By Saturday evening, the house had been cleaned, the front windows washed inside and out, and new curtains hung in the living and dining rooms. The front porch was swept and scrubbed, and Gwen had finished the new covers for the porch swing. The lawn was mowed and edged, and the flowerbeds were in order. Jimmy had consulted with the caterers about last-minute details. Everything was set.

That night we shared a quiet dinner together. We were all tired from the day's cleaning and tidying, so we anticipated turning in early to be well rested for the party.

The ringing telephone interrupted our meal. I went to answer it, hoping it would not be a medical call. It was not.

"You owe me," said a man's voice on the other end.

"Who is this?" I said.

"And I'm gonna make you pay."

"What are you talking about? Who's calling?"

"You're responsible for the death of two boys now. And you'll answer for it."

Before I could ask another question, there was a click and the line went dead. I stood there frozen, holding the earpiece in midair.

It had sounded like Haskell, and the reference to two boys made it obvious. Henry Haskell and Billy Butler. All that sadness welled up again. And I felt a rising anxiety that I thought had departed with Danny Felton's disappearance.

I hoped Haskell's threats were hollow. What could he do anyway? I remembered Patrick Molloy and the Bisby Klan. Mounting panic knotted my stomach. No, not here. Not me. Not us. What could I do to protect us?

I hung up the phone and stood there, my thoughts racing. What about Bateson? No. With Haskell's Klan involvement, I wasn't sure what Bateson would be able to do. Besides it was too late in the evening to contact him. Lockwood? He wasn't a body guard. I heard a burst of laughter from the dining room. I felt compelled to do something. I rang up the detective and told him about the threatening phone call. I said I thought it was Haskell. He said he would look into it.

"Is there anything you can to do to provide us some security? We're having this wedding reception here tomorrow afternoon. We don't want any trouble."

"That's not exactly my line of work. I could get in touch with the Pinkertons for you. But they're expensive."

I associated the Pinkertons with labor unrest and didn't feel comfortable with that idea. Besides, I felt we'd already spent enough on Lockwood without adding another expense. "Maybe you could have someone keep an eye on our homes until the party's over tomorrow afternoon." He agreed to put one of his team on it and have them call the police if they saw anything suspicious.

I hung up, feeling helpless. Poor Billy. God have mercy. I rubbed my hand over my face and sighed. The others didn't need to know about this. We were already nervous enough about tomorrow.

When I returned to the dinner table, I said it was an old patient and that I had recommended aspirin and bed rest.

Sunday morning turned out to be sunny and not too hot, a perfect spring day. Jimmy and I pulled back the carpet and wrestled the piano out of the living room and over the threshold of the front door. Once on the porch, we could easily roll it down to the end near the driveway. Gwen pulled the new covers onto the cushions of the swing. The colorful floral pattern dressed things up and complemented the profusion of pink blossoms on the small rhododendrons below the porch. The young ash trees up and down our street were all leafing out with fresh spring green.

Jimmy wore his tuxedo with the diamond music note pinned to his lapel. He was nervous and excited, fussing with all the details.

Charlie wore a pale orange dress that she'd bought for the occasion and the string of pearls that Gwen and I had given her. She was serene, gliding from the porch to the kitchen, smoothing a tablecloth here or adjusting a tray of cookies there.

The guests began to arrive a little after 1 o'clock, and, at last having an outlet for his nervous energy, Jimmy relaxed into being a guest of honor. The first to arrive were some of his musical friends whom he'd been wanting Charlie to meet, Vance among them. Though a bit pale and thin, he seemed alert. Still I was wary. Charlie, of course, charmed them. Before long Vance began to play the piano, then one of the other musicians took over, and the music made everything more festive and relaxed.

Guests continued to arrive, some of Charlie's co-workers from the phone company and medical colleagues of Gwen's and mine. Charlie's Aunt Inez showed up, which pleased us all. She had recently come down with a cold and we didn't know if she would be able to make it. Mr. Cassidy from St. Stephen's came with some members of the church choir, and Jimmy introduced him to Charlie as the man who was teaching him about Einstein's geometry.

Neighbors began to arrive next, some of whom we had not yet met. Others, like Tom and Polly Harris, were old friends. Maude was there, and Mr. Postlewait, who lived next door to Tom, but no sign of Clarence and Minnie Mitchell. I wasn't surprised. We all engaged in the meeting and greeting and introductions and pleasantries.

At some point Gwen nudged me and suggested I propose a toast to the newlyweds. I was not prepared for a speech, but I stood on the porch, with Jimmy and Charlie on one side and Gwen on the other. I raised one of the gold-trimmed wineglasses, but before I could speak, a tear welled up and I had to compose myself. I offered a few brief remarks about Charlie and Jimmy making beautiful music together.

Later one guest or another said goodbye and congratulations and began to drift off. Vance slipped away before I could offer him an encouraging word. Soon, the party had dwindled to a few friends and neighbors. The conversation became more relaxed. I talked to one of the musicians about the best places in town to go dancing. Before she went home, Maude thanked Charlie for helping with the snow peas and wished the couple well. One of Charlie's girlfriends from the phone company introduced me to her boyfriend and thanked me for my "medical advice." The boyfriend winked. Polly Harris brought their children over to say hello to Jimmy and Charlie and to play on the lawn. Soon most of the guests had bid farewell with promises to get together sometime. The last of Jimmy's musician friends said goodbye and took off as well.

Shadows were stretching across the lawn as I settled into the porch swing, and Jimmy took a seat on the piano bench facing me. We were alone. From inside the house came the sounds of Gwen and Charlie helping the caterers clean up.

Jimmy sighed. "Well, I'm glad that's over."

"You and me both," I said. "But it was a nice party, wasn't it?"

He agreed and looked out over the lawn toward the street. Some boisterous children ran up in front of Tom Harris's house and disappeared around the corner. The shadows lengthened farther across the grass. Jimmy turned to the piano. He played a chord, then another, then launched into a little piece by Mozart. The caterers cleared away punch cups and plates and folded up the tables and chairs. As Jimmy began another Mozart composition, he seemed to be warming up to something.

A breeze stirred the air. Veils of clouds stretched toward the horizon, gathering in the golden light of the sinking sun to the tune of Mozart's sunny melodies. The wispy clouds intensified into a brilliant coral against the sky-blue vault of the heavens. A warm glow bathed the homes on Elgin Street.

Gradually the fire faded from opalescent to pink to mauve. The strains of Mozart rose and fell in the velvety air. The mauve aged, like withering flower petals, to a smoky charcoal against the pearl-gray sky.

Jimmy played the closing notes of another Mozart piece as the light dwindled. He paused and seemed to be considering what to play next. I felt content moving back and forth on the porch swing. Jimmy began a Bach piece while the heavens darkened into a deep blue.

Charlie came out and relaxed into a chair. Across the street, houses lit up inside and streetlamps blinked on. Tom Harris walked out onto his stoop and lit a cigarette. Next door Mr. Postlewait's porch light switched on and he settled into a wicker chair, while his Labrador retriever lay down beside him with its head between its paws. A gentle wind arose and rustled the leaves of the ash trees.

The Bach piece picked up momentum with its inexorable forward drive. Jimmy had a grip on something in the music that made the hair stand up on the back of my neck.

Mr. Postlewait's dog stood up and gazed toward us, tail wagging. Tom Harris rose and came down from his porch, smoking as he listened. Charlie had closed her eyes, absorbed in the sounds. Gwen came to the screen door, wearing an apron and drying her hands on a towel, her ear cocked toward the piano.

As the Bach composition knit the diverging strands of melody together, Jimmy shepherded the piece to its ordained resolution. The effect of the music lingered in the hush that followed, holding us spellbound more than the sound that preceded it.

While this enchantment hung in the air, Jimmy broke the silence with a single note, then another, and at last, a chord, feeling his way into the music. He continued in this deliberate fashion, shaping a pattern and finally a melody. When I recognized it as the song he had been playing when Felton murdered Eric, I felt apprehensive.

Jimmy was breaking the tune into pieces, musical seeds, exploring each possibility, working through one variation after another. This was the same insipid song that had been in his mind since Chicago but transformed somehow, as he confronted something head on and laid it to rest. He was reaching for something, something beyond blues or jazz, beyond music.

A flock of crows passed overhead, punctuating Jimmy's playing with their rasping calls. The light had faded and the first star appeared. A single crow turned back, silhouetted by the dying light in the west. Three more followed, and others, black shapes against that unearthly blue, circling silently above our house, as if they had ceased their cries in order to hear Jimmy's music.

Now, he had a hold of the long line, following a force that propelled the music forward. There was not a hint of hesitation or doubt in his playing.

Mr. Postlewait's dog came down onto the grass, still wagging its tail. Tom Harris walked to the young ash tree near the curb, looking at the crows as he listened. Gwen came out, still holding the kitchen towel, and sat on the front step, gazing up at the birds moving across the sky. Charlie continued to sit, eyes closed, swaying ever so slightly with the swell and ebb of the music. The crows rotated in broad loops then peeled off in twos and threes and flew away to wherever they disappear to at night.

The music was flowing through Jimmy now, rising like spring water from underground caverns to join the streams of the upper world and merging with the rolling oceans. Jimmy's music had joined the vast encompassing cycle of the world.

My initial feeling of dread, upon recognizing the melody, had transformed into the sweetest kind of sorrow and longing, and ultimately into acceptance and peace.

It was dark by the time Jimmy cradled the composition to a close. None of us spoke or moved. The silence lingered. The rest of the stars began to come out.

The intense stillness was broken by a commotion down our street. A number of automobile engines rumbled to a stop. Car doors slammed. There were voices and sounds of feet on the pavement.

Polly Harris came out onto their porch, and Tom stepped off the curb to see down the street. A man a few houses down came out onto the sidewalk to see what was happening. Mr. Postlewait's dog walked forward, sniffed the air, and turned back as if to question his owner.

A whoosh of fire flared up and a glow came from down the way. As the sound of marching feet approached, a man's voice began chanting something we couldn't make out. Other voices joined in.

A flaming cross loomed into view carried above the crowd of twenty or thirty figures in white robes and hooded masks. They marched closer, and now we could make out their words. "Sodomites! Sodomites!"

I rose from the swing, crossed the length of the porch past Jimmy at the piano, and walked partway down the drive. Charlie rose from her chair, and Gwen got up and stood beside her. Jimmy turned from the piano, looking out at the street. Mr. Postlewait stood up from his porch chair and his dog began to bark from the edge of the curb. A few more neighbors up and down the street came out of their houses to see what the commotion was about.

The white-clad crowd crossed the intersection and approached our curb. The firelight from the burning cross flickered on the white robes. Some of the Klansmen carried billy clubs and baseball bats. A couple of men had coils of rope slung across their shoulders.

"So-do-mites! So-do-mites!" The chant became angrier. Without thinking, I took a few steps down the drive toward the street and raised my hands as if to calm the mob and shouted, "Listen!"

The chant intensified as the marchers in the rear closed in, forming a sea of white that paused at the shore of the curb as if reluctant to cross the final boundary and violate our private property.

"Destruction to Sodom and Gomorrah!" someone shouted. A smattering of stones volleyed toward the house.

"Stop!" I cried, holding up my hands in a futile gesture, as if I could hold back the tide with my fingers.

A few of the men in the mob began to move across the curb and the lawn of the planting strip onto the sidewalk. By the light of the flames, I caught the flashing white of spectator shoes below the hem of one of the robes.

Jimmy descended the steps at the side of the porch and walked to the top of the drive.

One group of men, carrying the flaming cross, moved forward up the walk in the middle of the lawn toward the front porch where Charlie and Gwen stood together. Another group advanced on me where I stood in the middle of the inclined driveway.

"Carl!" Jimmy called out in warning and despair. The anxiety in the sound of his voice caused me to turn away from the threatening crowd to face him. He looked toward Charlie and Gwen on the porch and back to me. For an instant our eyes met and I could see his anguish as he hesitated, torn, trying to decide which way to rush to offer protection. But he seemed unable to move.

All at once, as if on impulse, a white figure wielding a baseball bat broke from the gang on the lawn, dashed across the grass, and leapt onto the porch. He positioned himself in front of the piano and raised the baseball bat.

The instrument, which had so recently transfixed us with beauty and mystery, gave out an agonized series of groans and shrieks with each blow of the club to the keyboard. The cacophony took everyone by surprise, holding us bewitched.

The attacker's final frenzied blow came down on the top of the piano, giving out a dull thud that resounded through the instrument causing all the strings and the sounding board to vibrate with an eerie hum. The sound was like some strange caricature of the music of the spheres.

As the reverberations died away, I sensed a great calm settle over Jimmy and the agony faded from his expression. Fixing his gaze on the hooded figure stupefied before the humming piano, Jimmy moved with a dignified assuredness to the porch. In a simple gesture, he held out his open hand.

He acted with such quiet authority that I think it took the attacker by surprise. Perhaps it was the fearlessness with which Jimmy approached him, or maybe it was the serene tranquility that manifested itself in Jimmy's demeanor that held the man transfixed. Or perhaps the figure holding the baseball bat was immobilized with confusion and guilt at his own act of violence. Whatever it was, the Klansman with the bat stood there dumbstruck.

The rest of the Klansmen fell silent as if turned to wood and rooted to the ground by the boldness of Jimmy's act. The whole scene was absolutely quiet. Even the Labrador had ceased barking. The only sound was the crackling of the flaming cross.

The hooded figure by the piano gave over the bat handle and Jimmy took it into his outstretched hand. With firm steps, Jimmy turned and walked down the drive toward me. He held the baseball bat in both hands, palms facing up, as if he were a suppliant making a holy offering. He presented the baseball bat to me.

Before he reached me, someone in the hooded gang called out to the one at the piano. "Dammit, Jenkins, don't let him do you like that."

The figure on the porch sprang to life and darted down the drive. He grabbed Jimmy's arm, whirled him around, and punched him in the face. The baseball bat clattered onto the concrete driveway and rolled down the incline. Jimmy stumbled backwards with the force of the blow and fell face down on the lawn.

A deafening shotgun blast split the night air as a blaze of light flashed from Maude's porch. Everyone jumped and froze in place. With the shot so near at hand and following so soon after Jimmy's fall, my first impression was that he had been hit by a bullet. I took a step toward him. But he rolled over and looked in the direction of Maude's house.

I looked from Jimmy to Gwen and Charlie to see if they had been hit. Another blast rang out from the direction of Maude's front porch, and Jimmy's attacker raced back to the safety of the mob. I sprang to Jimmy's side and knelt beside him. The Klansmen on the lawn backed off into the street, and a few retreated down the block.

In the silence that followed, a voice called out of the darkness. "Lloyd Haskell. You and your men take one step closer to that house, and you'll regret it. I fired into the ground at first, but I know just where to aim the next time." It was Maude's voice. I could barely make out her figure by her front door.

A sharp click echoed from her porch, the noise of the shotgun being reloaded. The crisp, clean sound seemed to cause the hooded figures to retreat another few steps, and some at the back of the mob backed farther away down our street.

"I know what you're up to, Lloyd. Your mother telephoned me and told me what you had planned. You boys ought to be ashamed of yourselves coming around here hiding behind bed sheets and pillowcases, bothering these good people with your nonsense. Now, all of you clear out of here and go back to your women and children where you belong."

The burning cross crackled and wavered. The crowd of Klansmen began to retreat. The wail of a siren could be heard in the distance.

A screen door slammed at the Harris house behind the mob. Little Rachel Harris appeared on her front porch, wearing a nightgown and carrying a doll. "Mommy, is it Hallowe'en?" she cried and ran out onto the lawn.

Maude let out a hoot of laughter and called out, "That's right, darlin'. They're just a bunch of spooks."

Polly Harris scooped Rachel up in her arms and hurried into the house.

"Get along now," Maude shouted. "I've got plenty of ammunition here, in case you have any doubts."

Some of the robed figures backed off up the street. A second far-off siren wailed in the night. Both sirens grew louder. Another blast sounded from Maude's porch, and everyone jumped again. The hail of buckshot hit the edge of our lawn and tore up a patch of sod with a burst of dust. The mass of the Klansmen began to run away up the street.

"That's right. Clear out, now," Maude called.

"Yeah," called Mr. Postlewait from his porch as his dog began to bark again. "Get out of our neighborhood."

The sirens came near, and when headlights appeared down the street, the remainder of the mob scattered in retreat up the block. The last fellow to depart hurled a final stone at the house before he ran away. The sound of breaking glass tinkled from the upstairs dormer of Jimmy's old room. We could hear engines starting up and racing off. The fiery cross lay burning on the grass beside the curb.

A fire truck pulled up in front and firemen began swarming off the vehicle, unwinding hoses and taking up axes.

I turned to Jimmy and found Gwen kneeling in the grass at his head. She was holding the kitchen towel to his bleeding nose. By the headlamps of the fire truck, I saw the blood on his face. Droplets stained his tuxedo lapel and streaks of scarlet ran down his shirtfront.

Jimmy looked up at me. Neither of us spoke. He retained that extraordinary calmness. "Hey, Carl," he said at last.

I squeezed his shoulder, but I couldn't say anything.

"It's okay. I'm all right," Jimmy said.

Gushing water sounded from the fire truck and a hissing sound arose as it doused the dwindling flames of the smoldering cross. I could smell the smoke.

"Try to keep your head tilted back, honey," Gwen said. "It will help stop the bleeding."

Charlie came across the lawn. She had gone over to thank Maude. "She told me she was going to bed."

"God bless her," Gwen said.

"How's my husband?" Charlie asked, bending down.

"I think he'll be fine," Gwen said. "Charlie, honey, would you run in the house and get us a couple of damp towels please. And turn on the porch light."

Charlie patted Gwen's back and departed.

The fire chief approached me and said, "We received a call that there was a fire here. Is there a fire in the house too?"

"Just that," I said, indicating the blackened cross. I got the impression he was disappointed. He began barking commands at the firemen.

Another siren wailed, and headlights approached as a police car pulled up to the curb. Behind it, a paddy wagon followed. Uniformed policemen began piling out of their vehicles with handguns and nightsticks at the ready. I walked down to the sidewalk.

A man in street clothes approached me. "I'm Police Detective Higby," he said. "We got a call that there was a brawl here."

"It's all over now," I replied. "We just had a little visit from the Klan." Again I gestured toward the soggy cross lying on our lawn.

"I see," Higby said, taking out a notebook. "Sure thing they didn't mistake you for niggers. What are you, Catholics? Or kikes?"

"My friend there is an organist at St. Stephen's. Maybe that's it. But none of us are Catholics."

"What else can you tell me?"

"I've been in touch with Officer Bateson lately. You should talk to him about this incident. I'm sure he'll want to know. We suspect a fellow named Lloyd Haskell was involved."

The police detective raised his eyebrows.

"And you might want to talk to the lady next door sometime," I said. "But she just turned in."

Tom Harris walked up through the milling police and firemen. "Hello, Higby," he said.

"Well, hello, Tom. You're Johnny-on-the-spot."

"It was hard to avoid," Tom said, "I live right across the street."

"Now that is convenient," Higby replied. "Have the news come to you, huh? Tell me what happened."

Tom began to tell Higby the story as a uniformed officer picked up the baseball bat from the grass. He stood there inspecting the gashes on the surface of the bat, shaking his head. " C r y i n g shame," he said under his breath. "A perfectly good Louisville Slugger like that. It'll never hit straight again."

"Excuse me," I said to Higby. "I have to go help my wife."

"I'll need a statement from you," Higby said. "Don't go too far."

"I'll be on the porch," I said.

I went back to Jimmy and helped Gwen get him to his feet, and we guided him up to a chair under the porch light.

Charlie came out of the house carrying the damp towels and handed them to Gwen, before squatting down beside Jimmy and placing a hand on his shoulder.

"You okay, sweetheart?" she asked.

"I'm fine," Jimmy said. "Don't worry."

After Gwen cleaned his face with one of the towels, I examined his nose.

"You've got a broken nose there." I prodded gently with my fingertips and he winced.

As Gwen and I attended to Jimmy, Charlie walked over and examined the piano. She ran her hand over an ugly dent in the front edge of the wooden top, then inspected the damaged keyboard. The uniformed cop with the baseball bat came up to her and began asking questions.

"No, only one of them came up on the porch," Charlie was saying, "the one that was carrying that bat. He attacked the piano."

The policeman looked from the baseball bat to the piano and back to the bat, shaking his head.

"Carl," Gwen said, applying a damp towel to Jimmy's face, "we could use an ice pack."

"I'll go make one up," I said. "I'll get some cotton too."

She handed me a bloody towel.

I went to the piano, where Charlie and the policeman were holding up the front board, inspecting the hammers and wires inside. Placing my free hand on Charlie's shoulder, I leaned over to see. Charlie reached up and patted my back.

"You okay?" I asked.

"I'm fine," she said.

"You the homeowner?" the policeman asked.

"Yes," I said. "I just talked to Detective Higby down there." I pointed.

"Damn shame about this Slugger." He shook his head. "It's ruined." He ran his hand over the gouges in the bat, as Charlie sounded one of the piano keys. He looked up and added, "The piano too." Charlie played a chord. "Was this bat yours?" he asked.

"Why, no. No, they brought it with them. Excuse me, I need to attend to my patient." I left the policeman standing there shaking his head.

I went in the house and fetched some ice and my medical bag.

Before long I had Jimmy fixed up, his nostril's packed with cotton and a cold pack against his face.

It seemed like forever before the firemen stowed their equipment and left. The police finished asking questions and drove away. Tom Harris joined us on the porch as the neighborhood settled back into silence.

Jimmy said we shouldn't leave the piano outside all night. I didn't want him to exert himself and start his nose to bleeding again, so I enlisted Tom's help, and we wrestled the piano back into the living room. While Jimmy sat on the porch holding the icepack, Gwen and Charlie went upstairs to see about the broken window. Tom told me he was sorry about all the trouble. He said he would let us know what he could find out and wished us a good night.

Gwen and Charlie came out and told us they'd covered the broken window with a piece of cardboard and they'd checked all the other rooms for signs of forced entry and made sure all the doors and windows were secure.

Maude's porch light came on and she appeared in her housecoat. "Is everyone all right over there?" she called.

"For the most part," Charlie replied. "Wait there. We'll be right over."

Jimmy started to get up from his chair. "Better stay still," I said.

"You two go ahead," Gwen said, "I'll stay here with Jimmy."

Charlie and I told Maude about Jimmy's broken nose, but that he was okay otherwise.

"I thought you were going to bed," Charlie said.

"Oh, I just didn't want to talk to the darn police. But I couldn't turn in before I was sure you folks were okay."

She said she was just sick about all this mischief. "But I'm glad my old shotgun still works good."

"Thank you for what you did," I said.

"Oh, don't mention it," Maude said. "Those Klan varmints are just a bunch of cowards. A man who has to hide behind a pillow slip and a night shirt doesn't scare me. They're only a menace as long as no one knows their names. Once you call them out, watch them slink away."

"Are *you* okay?" Charlie asked.

"Don't worry about me. I'm fine. My shoulder's just a little sore from that shotgun. But I'm about done in from all the excitement. I've had enough for one night."

Back home we drifted into the dining room and sat there without speaking. I got out a bottle of gin, and everyone had a drink except Jimmy. He sat with his head tilted back, ice pack against his face. We were sipping our drinks in silence when the phone rang. We each looked up, while Jimmy lowered his ice bag.

"So late?" Gwen said.

I went to the hallway to answer, worrying about who might be calling now.

I was relieved when Lockwood spoke. "Sounds like you had some visitors tonight."

"Yes, someone decided to have a little Klan party over here after our wedding reception."

"I'm sorry our fellow wasn't around. He went home when your party broke up."

"I understand. We can't expect you folks to spend all your time here. The police showed up pretty soon after the mob arrived. A Detective Higby was handling things."

"I know him. I'll give him a call tomorrow and see what they find out."

I told him we suspected Lloyd Haskell was involved and that our neighbor next door would have some information.

"Our detective," I explained, returning to the dining table. "No news."

Jimmy continued nursing his ice bag. Gwen said she was exhausted and wanted to go to bed. I offered to walk Gwen and Charlie over to their place. Jimmy wanted to come along, but Gwen and I insisted that he stay put and take care of his nose.

The three of us went all through the Beasley house turning on the lights to make sure that everything was the way they'd left it.

There was no evidence of intruders or damage to the house. We hugged and said goodnight.

After Jimmy and I had settled into bed, his body began to tremble. I assured him that I was right there at his side, and he made an effort to relax, but the shivering continued for a long while. I held him in my arms until he finally fell asleep, and I continued to lie close to him all night long.

EPILOGUE

Portland, Oregon – 1981

Today I sit on our front porch looking out at the ash trees and thinking back to when they were spindly young things. Over the years, Jimmy and I watched them grow, reaching up like the hands of God, filling the sky over Elgin Street. We would sit here reading, me with a book and him with his newspaper, and he would often remark about how the world was changing.

Back in the day, we didn't know if the Klan would ever lose its influence. Tom Harris continued to keep us informed of the political vicissitudes. Not long after the cross burning at our house, divisions within the organization strained its coherence. Soon the Oregon Klan began to disintegrate. Disgruntled Klansmen started speaking out against the organization. The state's Grand Dragon faced mounting charges of corruption. Also during this time, a number of local newspapers obtained lists of Klan members and printed their names. Stripped of their hooded masks and anonymity, many members dropped out—just as Maude had suggested they would. After the Oregon Grand Dragon resigned in 1925, the organization collapsed.

A crowning blow came that same year when Indiana's Grand Dragon was accused of abducting and raping a young woman, who later committed suicide. I remember Charlie sitting in our living room reading a magazine article about the case and exclaiming, "Oh, my God, he disfigured the poor girl. No wonder she killed herself. This is just the sort of thing that the Klan accused the Catholic priests of doing."

The assumed moral authority of the Klan was largely discredited with the conviction and life sentence of the Indiana Grand Dragon. By the late 1920s, the national membership had dwindled. However, Tom Harris cautioned us that the Klan might have collapsed as an organization and political force, but the feelings that fueled it would only go underground—just as Danny Felton had done.

Much later Tom told us that a rival gang in Chicago attacked Felton's car and he caught a stray bullet in the throat. Although he recovered, he was never able to speak again.

Lloyd Haskell was arrested and indicted for illegal narcotics dealings. He was given a small fine and a light sentence. His wife filed for divorce while he was incarcerated, and when he was released, he tracked her down and beat her to death. During the trial that ensued, his attorneys mounted an insanity defense, but the jury didn't buy it. Lloyd Haskell was convicted of murder and hanged.

Soon after the Klan incident at our house, Jimmy lost his job at St. Stephen's Catholic Church. He was never able to get an explanation for his firing. He was told that his services were no longer required and that another organist had been hired. Out of a job, Jimmy became despondent. Hoping to cheer him up, I suggested we take in a movie. We went to one of the downtown movie palaces where they were showing a Charlie Chaplin short along with *Blood and Sand* staring Rudolph Valentino as a Spanish bullfighter. As we sat waiting for the movie, the theater organist played a popular tune that the Diggs Monroe orchestra used to perform. Jimmy and I both had the same thought, but before we could discuss the prospect, the picture began. In the final scene of the feature, a close companion of Valentino's, a fellow bullfighter, was gored in the bullring. As his blood spilled onto the sand, Valentino gave the beloved friend a farewell kiss on the lips. Jimmy elbowed me, and I tapped my knee against his.

When the movie was over, Jimmy approached the theater manager and by the end of the following week he began work as relief when the main organist took his regular union-sanctioned breaks. The appointed hour for the switchover often took place in the middle of the movie. So, as the regular organist played, Jimmy would slide onto the bench beside him and, one hand at a time, Jimmy would pick up the melody accompanying the flickering images on the screen. And just as smoothly, Jimmy eased himself into a new career.

When the first major talking picture, *The Jazz Singer*, appeared in 1927, Jimmy was irritated with the film's title, claiming that there wasn't a note of jazz in the whole movie. But the "talkies" were here to stay, and Jimmy saw that the days were numbered for silent movie organists. Now working evenings, Jimmy went back to school during the day. He earned his teaching credentials, specializing in mathematics and music, and before the last movie house in town installed sound equipment, he was teaching in the public schools.

At Christmas in 1929, Charlie gave us a new board game called Chinese Checkers. It was played the same as Halma, but the playing surface was reconfigured from squares into triangles, forming the now-familiar star. After playing Halma for all those years, the novelty of the new game fascinated us. But Joe Locke never understood why the game was called Chinese Checkers. As we played, he would leave the room shaking his head.

Jimmy bought a camera around that time and began taking snapshots of us, preserving the photos in scrapbooks alongside news clippings and memorabilia. He included old photos from his time as a movie organist, and later ones with Gwen and Charlie on fishing trips and at her parents' farm, celebrations after VE Day in 1945, wedding invitations from straight friends, a clipping about an award he'd won for teaching music. There were magazine images from the Army-McCarthy hearings in 1954, me with our new car in 1960, a clipping of homosexual pickets in front of the White House in 1965, the Stonewall riots in 1969, Polaroid color photos of all four of us watching Gay Pride celebrations in the 1970s. The world continued to change around us in unexpected ways.

Sometimes I study our old scrapbooks and puzzle to see those black and white photos of us. We thought we would always be as young as we were before Chinese Checkers, when Jimmy and I lived our happy life with Gwen and Charlie in the Sunny Grove neighborhood, amid a world of jazz speakeasies and silent movies. Before Chinese Checkers we lived in a world when men wore pocket watches, and time was something we occasionally took out of our waistcoat pockets. Now time is ever present on wristwatches. It was a world when pink was considered the "stronger, more decided color" for little boys, and blue—the more "delicate" and "dainty" color—was for little girls. Now, it's the other way around. A world where Charlie Chaplin and Buster Keaton were the great masters of silent comedy. Now, there is just talk. It was a time when Valentino could get away with kissing his buddy as he died on screen. Now the only one who can get away with kissing another man is a wise-cracking Bugs Bunny.

It was a time when the less said about homosexuality, the better, and that silence provided some measure of protection. Later, as homosexuality became common knowledge, its increasing awareness by the general public gave rise to greater scrutiny, greater male anxiety, greater hostility, and legal penalties, requiring an even greater need for discretion and secrecy. Back then we spoke of fairies and pogues and trade, punks and jockers, lambs and wolves. In recent years all we hear is gay and straight.

After 1930, when the economy seemed that it would never recover and the Depression began to demoralize the whole nation, Gwen's father died and her mother became ill. Following many trips to visit the farm, Gwen decided to move there to attend to her mother and keep the farm running. She argued that living out there she and Charlie would still be near enough that we could all visit, and they began making plans for the move. Because times were so hard, no one paid much attention when our wives moved away. Jimmy and I kept up the pretense of living separately for a time, but when he moved in to share expenses at our house, it didn't seem so unusual—everybody's life was in a state of upheaval because of the bleak economic conditions. We rented out the Beasley house and shared the small income with Gwen and Charlie. That helped all of us through the hard times. In turn, our wives brought us fresh produce, and what we didn't use we gave to friends or sold.

During one of their visits, while we were playing the new Chinese Checkers game, I said that I'd received a letter from my German friends Detlef and Heinz, whom I'd met during the American occupation of Koblenz. I had written them about the Depression and mentioned our new board game. Their reply referred to a similar game named "Stern-Halma" that had been sold in Germany for many years. They translated it as "Star Halma." Their letter also reported disturbing news about the political situation as the Nazi's consolidated their hold on power.

In the midst of my remarks, Charlie looked up from studying the playing pieces and said, "It's a Star of David."

Puzzled, we all looked at her.

"The game board," she explained. "It's the same as the Jewish Star of David."

After that letter, we never heard from Detlef and Heinz again.

Jerry the Fairy was arrested on sodomy charges in 1934, when he was entrapped by an undercover policeman in a movie theater restroom. He was convicted and sentenced to five years in prison. In 1935, responding to overcrowded prison conditions, Oregon's governor gave selected prisoners the chance for immediate parole if they volunteered to be sterilized. Jerry jumped at the chance. For the crime of committing unnatural acts, he agreed to submit to the unnatural act of state-sponsored castration. After parole, he came to see me from time to time for minor medical complaints. Then I didn't see him again until the late 1950s when he introduced himself to me as Germaine. She had undergone a sex-change operation to complete the work that the state had begun in transforming her body. With the help of reconstructive surgery and modern hormone supplements, she was leading a happier life as a woman. Germaine's new form also protected her from the anti-homosexual hysteria of the Cold War years when homosexuals were equated with "sex perverts" and Communists.

After the Second World War, Charlie wrote me a letter, about missing our old neighborhood.

"I even miss Minnie Mitchell, bless her soul," she wrote. "Minnie never did recover from losing Clark at Normandy in 1944. And when she lost her husband to a stroke, not much later, I can only guess how lonely she must have been. Remember that Jimmy was the one who made friends with her at long last. He did have a way with people. I used to enjoy playing Chinese Checkers with her in those days, when I would come in to visit while Gwen stayed out at the farm. The irony of it always amused me, playing with you and Jimmy, and Minnie as a fourth. I don't think she ever caught on. Have you ever thought that if it weren't for Minnie, none of us would have married? So in the end I guess we owe her a debt of gratitude. Minnie Mitchell was put on this earth for a purpose. And it is our responsibility to understand what we can learn from it. That's why you must write down your memoirs."

She continued to badger me to put my reminiscences to paper.

Gwen and Charlie settled into their new life on the farm, and Charlie found work with the phone company in Astoria. After Gwen's mother died, Gwen did occasional nursing work, but she devoted most of her time to keeping the farm going. They made new friends in the area, especially women friends, and they came to enjoy living in the country, away from the hustle and bustle of city life. Jimmy and I visited them from time to time, and they sometimes came into town to see us and go shopping, but we all knew that they would never move back to Portland. When people would ask about our wives, we would make excuses and say that they had to keep up the farm and Jimmy and I had to keep our jobs in the city. So Jimmy and I wound up living together and came to be known as the two husbands of Elgin Street. All the playing pieces had at last found their way home from there to here.

Those fresh-faced young men in the old photos never thought that they would grow old. But we aged, as everyone does. Like the bark of our ash tree in front of the porch, our faces grew furrowed with the worries and cares that shaped our lives. But we grew old together. And together, we became rich with memories. We shared our hopes and dreams, which faded with our youth, and as we matured, we found new and better dreams. But those, too, faded as we lost our health, our loved ones, and in the end the heartbeat that binds us to this ground.

In 1976 Gwen died of breast cancer after a long illness. I was devastated, but Charlie seemed to cope better than I did, even though I had Jimmy's support.

Jimmy died of coronary thrombosis in the autumn of 1980, leaving a great emptiness in my life that I am still coming to grips with. But I still feel his presence, and perhaps that is why I don't miss him more than I do. Sometimes, late at night, I imagine I can hear him playing the piano in the living room, and it's so vivid that I'm not sure if I'm actually hearing it or if it's a dream. But I know the piano is gone, and I know Jimmy is gone too.

After his memorial service, Charlie wrote me. "Oh, Carl, haven't we been lucky? To have loved Gwen and Jimmy, and to have led such full, rich lives. What more could we have asked for? All any of us can ask is to live our lives the best we can. And we *can* live good lives—leave behind memories that provide good examples."

So I have written his story—our story. Maybe it will keep his memory alive. Maybe somebody will find his life instructive. Maybe it will give someone courage.

— Carl Holman, 1981

AUTHOR'S NOTES
2018

Oregon's 1922 Compulsory Education Act, or the Oregon School Law, which was supported by the state and national Ku Klux Klan, tried to ban private Catholic schools by declaring it a crime if children between the ages of 8 and 16 did not enroll in public schools. The US District Court ruled that the law was unconstitutional. On appeal, the US Supreme Court upheld that ruling in its 1925 decision, *Pierce v. Society of Sisters*.

During the summer of 1925, the nation's attention was riveted on the Scopes "monkey" trial in Tennessee. Clarence Darrow and William Jennings Bryan argued the subject of evolution during the long hot days of July. Darrow's scientific witnesses were not permitted to testify before the jury, and in the end John Scopes was convicted of teaching evolution and fined 100 dollars. Later the Tennessee State Supreme Court upheld the law forbidding the teaching of any theory denying the divine creation of man.

In 1926, Rudolph Valentino died from complications following a perforated gastric ulcer. For years there were rumors about the film star's relations with other men, and speculation circulated that he never slept with his various wives, including his last, who was said to be a lesbian. Up to the very end, Valentino challenged the accusations that he was a "powder puff."

In the 1930s, an array of forces opposed to "sexual deviance" were busy in the United States. The Catholic Legion of Decency pressured Hollywood into a more stringent enforcement of the Motion Picture Production Code. Raids on establishments that catered to "deviants" increased, and police entrapment became more widespread.

During the Great Depression, the eugenics movement was reinvigorated partly by ideas from the German Nazi movement and partly by the dire economic conditions and the high cost of maintaining prisons and mental hospitals. A more aggressive state law was proposed for enhancing the 1923 Oregon statute mandating sterilization, by either tubal ligation or removal of the ovaries in women, and by vasectomy or castration in men. The legislation was enacted dropping the necessity for patient consent. Instead, it required the patient to initiate a suit to stop the sterilization order. Authorities believed that criminals and "deviants" were rendered harmless by the operation and could be released from incarceration, saving the government the expense of housing them. Over the years the majority of men sterilized in Oregon were castrated. Eugenics sterilization laws remained on the books in Oregon until 1983 and during that time some 2500 people were coerced into sterilization. In 2002 Oregon Governor John Kitzhaber issued a formal apology to those who had been sterilized.

After Sigmund Freud died in 1939, the American psychiatric establishment began to take an even more repressive stance with regard to homosexuality. On into the post-World War II years, this position became even more conservative, and in 1952 the American Psychiatric Association formally classified homosexuality as an illness. In 1973 that designation was finally removed from the official list of psychiatric disorders, even though many psychoanalysts continue to view homosexuality as a pathological adaptation.

Senator Joseph McCarthy's House Un-American Activities Committee began blacklisting members of the American entertainment industry in the 1940s, including the "Hollywood Ten." In the early 1950s they blacklisted Charlie Chaplin, one of the most popular film stars of the 1920s. When Chaplin traveled to England for the premier of his 1952 film *Limelight*, he was refused a re-entry permit and he chose to exile himself from the United States.

Under the direction of McCarthy, FBI Director J. Edgar Hoover, and others, the Lavender Scare of the 1950s purged hundreds of homosexual men and women from US government employment. Officials claimed that gays were a security risk and conflated homosexuality with Communism, thus ruining many lives and careers.

Sodomy laws remained on the books in Oregon from 1873 until 1972, nearly a hundred years. Although such laws were upheld by the US Supreme Court in the 1986 case of *Bowers v. Hardwick*, that decision was overturned in 2003 by a decision in *Lawrence v. Texas*, which found sodomy laws unconstitutional.

Although the US Supreme Court decisions in *Windsor v. United States* and *Obergefell v. Hodges* legalized same-sex marriage, these judgements could be overturned by a future, more conservative court. Should *Obergefell* be reversed, the laws in the 30 states with state constitutional provisions limiting marriage to a man and a woman could again become enforceable.

— Jeff Stookey, 2018

Esteemed Reader,

This is a self-published novel. You can help make it a success:

• Tell all your friends about this book.
• Post reviews on amazon.com and goodreads.com
• Sign up for my newsletter at medicinefortheblues.com
• Share about the book on social media networks and blogs.

Thank you for reading books.

Jeff Stookey

ACKNOWLEDGEMENTS

I must thank Merilee Karr, MD, for invaluable advice about medical details, for pointing me in the right direction in areas of medical history, and for directing me toward numerous resources. I thank her too for her encouragement and for implanting in my mind the dangerously liberating concept of writer's intuition.

Historians George Painter and Tom Cook, founding members of the Gay and Lesbian Archives of the Pacific Northwest, have both been extremely helpful. I am grateful for their generosity with their time, their resources, and their knowledge of Pacific Northwest gay history. The Archives are now housed at the Oregon Historical Society.

I want to acknowledge the memory of Jesse Bernstein (known as Stephen J. Bernstein in print). Even though he's been dead for all these years since his suicide, I have felt him watching over my shoulder as I wrote this, and I could never have done it without his example and his encouragement. I guess you won't mind, Jesse, that I used some of your ideas.

All my dear friends who read the first draft have my undying gratitude for saving me from numerous mistakes, and my writing group from The Attic contributed invaluable feedback. I want to thank my 2017-18 writing group for additional feedback, and Dick Porus for checking the accuracy and phrasing of medical details. I'm also grateful for proofreading provided by Mark Schultz at **wordrefiner.com**. This book would never have emerged into public form without the help and encouragement of my editor Jill Kelly. She reined me in and prodded me to judiciously prune countless twigs and branches.

And, it goes without saying (but those are exactly the things that must be said), that I am endlessly indebted to my partner, Ken Barker, for tolerating, and even encouraging, this peculiar obsession with writing words on paper. Thanks for your support in keeping me going and especially for helping me to keep from losing my nerve.

ABOUT THE AUTHOR:

Growing up in a small town in rural Washington State, Jeff Stookey enjoyed writing stories. He studied literature, history, and cinema at Occidental College and later got a BFA in Theater from Fort Wright College. In his 40s he retrained in the medical field and worked for many years with pathologists, trauma surgeons, and emergency room reports.

Jeff lives in Portland, Oregon, with his longtime partner, Ken, and their unruly garden. *Acquaintance*, Book 1 in this *Medicine for the Blues* trilogy, was his first novel.

Contact Jeff at *medicinefortheblues.com*.